Hoss's Limits

House of Lustz #2

Ciara St James

Copyright

ISBN:978-1-955751-73-5

Printed in the United States of America
Editing by Mary Kern @ Ms. K Edits
Book cover by Kiwi Kreations

Blurb:

Hoss's life is full of running his company by day and three nights a week working as a doorman and security for the House of Lustz. And when the mood strikes, he plays in the House. He fills his life by staying busy because his mind demands it, something not unusual for a Mensa-level genius. However, that's not enough for Hoss, especially since he has spotted the sassy, bratty Cady, best friend to his boss and friend Mikhail's fiancée Tajah.

Cady doesn't seem to want to cooperate and let Hoss determine if she might be more than a possible playmate. It takes a few encounters for him to determine the truth. Cady is perfect for him. She's the ultimate brat, and Hoss, well, his specialty is being a brat handler.

Cady's life has never been simple or easy, not even growing up. She throws her efforts into her clinic. Personal relationships never work out for her, so she's determined to avoid all men. The tall, dark, totally delicious Hoss is not in her plans, and she tries to keep it that way. After all, it would only end in disappointment and possibly heartache. She'll keep pushing her bratty behavior at him. It'll run him off, like every other man in her life except her brother, and even he has trouble understanding her.

Imagine Cady's shock when Hoss refuses to give

up and he informs her that the men in her past didn't know how to handle her, but he does. He not only wants the job of being her brat handler, but he also wants her as his, permanently, which includes marriage and children one day. She's in absolute shock.

Their path isn't without resistance, obstacles, misunderstandings, punishments, communication, and negotiation as he brings her into his life and world. Cady finds out that all she needs is the right man to love, protect, and cherish her. She doesn't need to change. She just needs to know when to let her brat out to play.

Welcome to the House of Lustz, where carnality, passion, and love unite. Enter at your own risk and prepare to be forever changed.

Warning

This book is intended for adult readers. It explores the world of kink, and some topics may not be to everyone's taste. Subjects considered taboo by some will be explored. It contains foul language and adult situations and may even include things such as stalking, assault, torture, kidnapping, and murder, which may trigger some readers. Sexual situations are graphic. If these themes aren't what you like to read or you find them upsetting, this book isn't for you. There is no cheating or cliffhangers, and it has a HEA.

Dedication

This book is dedicated to my wonderful friend, Brea, and her man, Mike. You know what you did that made this book possible. I can't thank you enough. Kisses, The Wife.

House of Lustz Characters:

Mikhail w/ Tajah
Hoss w/ Cady
Reuben w/ TBD
Carver w/ TBD

Reading Order:

Voodoo's Sorceress DFAW 17
Reaper's Banshee IPMC 1
Bear's Beloved HCAW 5
Outlaw's Jewel HVAW 6
Undertaker's Resurrection DP 1
Agony's Medicine Woman PSCMC 1
Ink's Whirlwind IP 2
Payne's Goddess HCAW 7
Maverick's Kitten HCAW 8
Tiger & Thorn's Tempest DFAW 18
Dare's Doll PSC 2
Maniac's Imp IP 3
Tank's Treasure HCAW 9
Blade's Boo DFAW 19
Law's Valkyrie DFAW 20
Gabriel's Retaliation DP 2
Knight's Bright Eyes PSC 3
Joker's Queen HCAW 10
Bandit & Coyote's Passion DFAW 21
Sniper's Dynamo & Gunner's Diamond DFAW 22
Slash's Dove HCAW 11
Lash's Hurricane IP 4
Spawn's She-Wolf IP 5
Griffin's Revelation DP 3
Twisted's Storm PSC 4
Diablo's Vengeance HOW 1
Player's Juno HCAW 12

For Ares Infidels MC:

Sin's Enticement AIMC 1
Executioner's Enthrallment AIMC 2
Pitbull's Enslavement AIMC 3
Omen's Entrapment AIMC 4

Cuffs' Enchainment AIMC 5
Rampage's Enchantment AIMC 6
Wrecker's Ensnarement AIMC 7
Trident's Enjoyment AIMC 8
Fang's Enlightenment AIMC 9
Talon's Enamorment AIMC 10
Ares Infidels in NY AIMC 11
Phantom's Emblazonment AIMC 12
Saint's Enrapturement AIMC 13
Phalanx & Bullet's Entwinement AIMC 14
Torpedo's Entrancement AIMC 15
Boomer's Embroilment AIMC 16
Daredevil's Engulfment AIMC 17
Vicious, Ashes & Dragon's Entrenchment AIMC 18
Ruin's Embattlement AIMC 19 (end)

For O'Sheerans Mafia:

Darragh's Dilemma
Cian's Complication
Aidan's Ardor
Aisling's Craving

House of Lustz:

Mikhail's Playhouse
Hoss's Limits

Please follow Ciara on Facebook. For information on new releases & to catch up with Ciara, go to www.ciara-st-james.com or www.facebook.com/ciara.stjames.1 or https://www.facebook.com/groups/342893626927134 (Ciara St James Angels) or https://www.facebook.com/groups/923322252903958 (House of Lustz by Ciara St

James) or https://www.facebook.com/ groups/14048941602108 51 (O'Sheeran Mafia by Ciara St James)

Hoss: Chapter 1

I scanned the two new faces strolling up to the entrance of the House of Lustz. By now, I pretty much knew who belonged here by sight, even if I might not know everyone's name. They were two men in their thirties, if I had to guess. They were grinning and laughing. There was nothing wrong with either of those things. We wanted people to feel joy and excitement here as long as it didn't go in the wrong direction. This meant I might as well start their membership off right, just to be sure.

I'd been leaning against the wall, but I stood tall now. I had a stool to sit on, but I rarely did that for long. A lot of the time, I paced. Sitting for long periods was a big no for me. I got enough of that in my everyday life. I made sure my arms were crossed as they approached. They raised their heads and glanced toward the door as they got closer. I must've been hidden in the shadows because they jerked and stumbled as if they hadn't seen me until then. Not to be a braggart, but it was rare for me not to be noticed.

As a six-foot-seven-inch Black man, people took notice of me. Add my other physical features to the package, and they often feared me. Sometimes, that fear came in handy, like it would if trouble started here. Other times, I detested it. Just because I was large and Black didn't mean I was automatically someone to fear. In my world, you had to do something to earn my beatdowns. Their walk slowed, and they stopped laughing and smiling. When they got close, I greeted them. I didn't smile since I had a point to get across, but I did speak to them nicely and without a scowl.

"Hello, gentlemen, welcome to the House of Lustz. I haven't seen you before. Let me guess. You're new patrons," I said.

"Y-yes, we are. We just got our official acceptances a few days ago," the taller one stuttered.

"That's nice. I know you've gone through online training and orientation, and the rules have been covered with you. However, I still like to cover a few things with anyone new entering. First, I'm Hoss. You'll see me typically here on Thursday, Friday, and Saturday nights. I'm the doorman and outer security. We should only see each other when you come and go unless you cause problems. Then you'll see me more. I recommend you don't do that. It won't make your night, trust me. Obey the rules, always have consent, and be respectful, and we'll get along fine. May I have your names?" I asked.

I preferred to know their club names. Most people here went by one to protect their identities, although some used their real first names. Last names were to be kept private. This was covered in orientation, and they were asked to decide on their name preference before coming here for the first time to play or observe.

"I'm Odin," the one who spoke to me said.

"I'm Atlas," his buddy said more hesitantly.

"Odin, Atlas, nice to meet you. If you have questions, please ask rather than assume. There are plenty of monitors, guides, managers, and Lustz disciples to answer them. Have a good evening." I reached over and opened the door for them. As they passed me, they gave me a side-eye glance.

Closing the door behind them, I got back to scanning the parking lot. I was more than the glorified door opener. I kept a watch for anything that may turn into a problem. We didn't want our patrons running into muggers or being waylaid by other patrons or strangers on our premises. Mikhail, the owner, would have heads if those things were occurring. He ran a classy establishment. Lustz wasn't some sleazy hangout where you had to worry about being drugged, raped, or murdered. Just because we catered to your sexual fantasies didn't mean we were into anything like that. A common misconception many people seemed to have.

Thinking of my boss and friend Mikhail led my mind to his fiancée, Tajah. I smiled. Tajah had that effect on people. She was a sweet, loving woman. When she joined the club, Mikhail had been gone on the first vacation I'd ever known him to take. I got to know her a tiny bit. She wasn't automatically scared of me and would stop and talk for a few minutes. When she explained she was there to do research for her romance series, I'd been intrigued and couldn't help but wonder what kind of material she'd get and how the patrons would react to her asking questions. Many loved to talk about the lifestyle, but would they be so inclined if it was going into books, especially romance novels?

What I didn't contemplate was what Mikhail would do when he returned. I should've. His response was to kick her out and revoke her membership. It was damn fortunate for him that he changed his mind. He would've lost out on the opportunity of a lifetime if he hadn't. He would've never landed his woman. As different as they were, they complemented each other perfectly. He was beyond blessed to have found her—a woman who understood his desires and was willing to actively fulfill them. Tajah was discovering what called to her, and he was equally able to do the same for her when it came to fulfilling her desires.

It was hard to find in our world, even though many would assume it wasn't. While we lived this lifestyle, everyone was different. We may have labels for our fetishes, kinks, proclivities, or whatever people choose to call them, but not a single one of us, even if we wore the same label, was precisely the same. Take me, for example. Yeah, I worked here, but in my free time, I also played. I was a patron. I had several interests, but my main one was as a brat handler. It should be easy for me to find a brat to handle and fulfill both our needs. Well, it wasn't. Some of my needs were satisfied, for sure, but not all.

I had a crazy successful company, all the money I could ever need, fancy cars, a gorgeous home—the works. I should need nothing, but I did. I didn't have a special someone to share it with. I was thirty-nine years old, and I was still single. Sure, I had sex, and I had women lined up to play with me in scenes, but it wasn't what I ultimately desired. I wanted what Mikhail had with Tajah—a true partner who loved him and who he loved in return.

Recently, I'd begun to hope that there might be someone who could fit the bill. I wasn't sure, of course, but I wanted to find out. She'd hooked my attention in a single tiny interaction. It lasted less than a minute, but it was enough. My second encounter had been slightly longer, but not much, and it had only ensnared me more. The urge to handle her grew. The funishments and punishments it brought to mind made me hard, and I fantasized about what we would do together. Her name was Cadence, or Cady, as she preferred to be called.

Except for how things had gone lately, it was doubtful I'd get an opportunity to find out. The night of Tajah and Mikhail's dinner party had been my second glimpse, and it was the night she'd stormed out. She'd been quiet and avoiding Tajah, who had been her best friend since grade school, since that party. I knew Tajah was worried about Cady. She talked to me about it. It wasn't like Cady to act this way with her. Even Cady's brother, Carver, another patron, was troubled by her behavior.

The impulse to find her, make her spill what was bothering her, and interact with her brat side was growing. Cady was a classic brat crying out for an experienced handler to take her in hand and not break her. She needed to soar and fully embrace who she was. Deep down, my gut told me that I was the man for her. But first, I had to get time to be near her, which was not an easy task. While I heard they were back to speaking to each other, Cady hadn't been here. Or if she had, not on the nights I worked. If something didn't change soon, I'd have to take steps to set the stage. Six damn weeks was more than long enough to live with this unanswered question. Was Cady the woman for me? Only being together would answer it. Well, I wasn't solving that dilemma tonight or in the next two. It would have to wait until I was off from this job.

☙ ☙ ☙

Walking into work on Monday at SacketEdge Technologies, I prepared for another busy week. It was never slow here, which was a good thing in my book. It meant my company was giving people what they wanted and needed when it came to computer software. I'd started the company at the raw age of twenty. I'd just graduated from college with my master's in programming and a few other minors, and I wasn't open to working for others. I'd seen enough in a few years of interning and working small jobs to know they wouldn't let my stuff stay as I created them, or they'd steal my ideas and get rich off my work. To prevent this, I formed my own company in my childhood bedroom.

It wasn't long before I moved out and was doing it from my apartment. The rest was history. I worked hard. I was determined to produce application software that was of high caliber and would keep customers happy. As time passed, I was able to expand into several different software platforms and areas. I began to hire staff to help me with the projects. They were carefully handpicked individuals who saw things the way I did and produced the highest quality in their work. If you don't have integrity, don't attempt to work for me.

We produced software for gaming, antivirus software, database management, graphics, and security, to name a few. As it stood, I could retire, and the company would continue without me. I picked my key people meticulously. However, I didn't just lie back and enjoy my money because I'd be bored to death in a week and probably homicidal in two. If my brain wasn't working on something the majority of the time, it would cause issues for me. It didn't have to be work, but it had to be something I was interested in. When

I wasn't mentally occupied, I needed to be physically stimulated. For me, that was satisfied with working out, doing extreme sports, and having sex.

Yet, lately, the sex part was lacking. I wasn't finding anyone who made me yearn to have sex with them. Even my play at Lustz had drastically decreased. I had plenty of offers, but they felt flat. In the past, the brats there had been fun to play with. Lately, they didn't stir my interest. Maybe I was getting old. I immediately discarded that possibility. I was still interested in brat handling and sex. My erections and excitement when I thought of playing with Cady proved that. The people I had available to play with were the problem. There I went, thinking about her again. *Hoss, you've got to put Cady out of your mind. You have work to do,* I sternly lectured my inner self.

"Good morning, Mr. Sacket. I hope you had a good weekend." Alicia Ann greeted me with a smile and a cup of coffee the way I liked. She was my righthand woman. To call her a secretary was to discount everything Alicia Ann did. She kept me on task. She'd been with me for the last five years. Without her, there would be no way I could work the nights I did at Lustz.

The only thing we disagreed about regularly was her insistence on calling me Mr. Sacket rather than Hoss. Most of my employees called me that, but she refused. In Alicia Ann's mind, it was disrespectful. I'd tease her every so often, asking if we knew each other well enough to have her call me that. Her answer was always no, to ask her again in five years.

"Good morning, Alicia Ann. Thank you." I indicated the coffee I took from her. "My weekend was good. What about yours? Did you do anything fun?"

"Mine was good as well. I went shopping and read a book I've wanted to read for a while."

"Alicia Ann, we've got to get you out to have more fun. Although, if you like to read, I have an author friend. Are you into romances? I warn you, they're steamy," I told her as I raised my brows and grinned.

"I do enjoy romances. As for whether they're the steamy kind, that's for me to know. I have friends who devour them, though. If you give me the author's name, I'll pass it along," she said without missing a beat.

"One day, I'm going to figure you out. I know you secretly want that name for yourself," I teased.

"Wouldn't you love to know?" was her comeback. She smiled. She came across as stiff and uptight to most people, but I knew underneath, she wasn't. She was highly professional. I tried not to tease her too much, but we both enjoyed it.

"I'll email it to you with her link. Okay, I guess I need to get to work. The day is full."

"Your first appointment will be here at ten," she called after me. I'd be lost if it weren't for her keeping my calendar. I greeted others I passed on my way to my office. When I arrived, I sat down to get to it.

The day flew by. I went from one meeting or project to the next. In between, I had conversations with various team members. Some were about work, but others were more personal. I liked knowing about my staff. Lunch was spent at a luncheon with a potential new client. The afternoon was more work, but the kind I truly enjoyed.

I might not get to create programs nearly as much as I used to, but I refused to give it up entirely. I had to have it. It was my creative side coming out. The afternoon was gone before I knew it. I surfaced when I heard people saying goodbye to each other. Standing, I stretched, then went out to say good evening to them.

I encouraged my people to have a work and life balance. When we had deadlines, that was one thing, but they needed to unplug the rest of the time. Too bad I wasn't as disciplined. I blamed it on being quickly bored and not having anyone to share my downtime with. I had friends, but that wasn't the same. None of them were available all the time. When I wasn't able to occupy my mind or body in other ways, work was always there to fill the gap.

Despite this, I knew that if I found someone special, that would change. No way would I add a woman to my life, one I hoped would be permanent, and then ignore her. Assuming we had kids, which I also wanted, they'd take more time. I might have enough money to hire a nanny, but I had no desire to have others raise my children. It would be their mom and me doing it.

After seeing my crew out the door, I returned to my office. I could go back to work or head home. My groove was interrupted, so I chose to shut down and go. If I had the urge to work later, everything would be accessible via my laptop, and I'd do it from home. Outside, in the parking garage, I climbed into my Bugatti Veyron. I had a thing for sports cars and the money to indulge. I didn't get crazy. It wasn't like I had dozens of them, but I did have a few. This one was my favorite.

Driving home, I enjoyed the fall air. October in Tennessee was still warm, and the trees were changing. I drove to my place in Belle Meade. It was a wealthy area of Nashville, consisting of grand houses and estates. It was originally the location of a plantation that later was converted into an elite residential neighborhood. I bought here due to the feeling of the area, its history, the streets lined with trees, and the architecture that called to me, not the exclusivity of it.

While the median price of homes was two million or more, I got mine cheaper. When it came on the market, it was neglected, and it showed. I saw the potential once it was restored to its former glory, so I snatched the property up. Even with the money I put into it, the estate was worth more than it cost me to purchase and restore it. I enjoyed walks through the fifty-five-acre botanical park and Percy Warner Park, which has its horse and hiking paths close by.

I parked in my garage and then went inside. I was hungry, and it was time to decide what to make for dinner. Generally, I ate healthy-ish. I cheated and had things that weren't good for you, but overall, I tried to stick to the healthier options. I knew there were some skinless, boneless chicken breasts in the fridge. I could make a couple of those, along with a side of steamed vegetables and brown rice. I upped the taste factor of the food I made, not with butter and oil, but with herbs and spices.

First, I needed to get out of my suit and into comfy clothes—jeans and a henley. With that done, I headed to the kitchen. It didn't take me long to fix my meal. After I was done eating and cleared away my mess, I put on a movie. I was hoping it would keep my attention long enough I would be able not to work. If it didn't and I restarted, I'd be up all night. I made it through, barely, but I knew I'd never be able to watch another. I was about to say the hell with it and get my laptop when my cell phone rang.

I had it tucked into the back pocket of my jeans. Fishing it out, I glanced down to see who was calling. Depending on who it was, I would decide whether to answer or let it go to voicemail. If it were my brother, then it would go to voicemail. If it were one of my friends, then I'd answer. The name *Mikhail* on the screen had me answering it. I was smiling when I did.

"Hey, Mikhail, you miss me already? It's not Thursday, but do you need me to come in?" I asked, trying not to sound too hopeful. Someone might've called off.

"Hoss, I don't love you that much. And I'm not calling to ask you to work or for a friendly chat. I wanted to know if you'd meet Tajah and me somewhere. If you're otherwise occupied, I understand. No pressure." His tone was slightly off, and I could hear the tension in it.

"I can tell there's something wrong. What is it? What do you need?" I immediately asked.

"You said you wanted a chance to get to know Cady. Well, here's your chance. She called Tajah and said she had an issue at her veterinarian clinic. It seems it was broken into after she left. Carver is out of town on business. Taj said she sounded upset. We're headed over, and I thought this would be a good way to get your foot in the door."

I'd told him what I thought when it came to Cady. I hadn't been as blunt or vocal with Tajah, although I hadn't hidden my interest. No way would I pass up this chance. Who knew when or if I'd get another?

"Hell, yeah, I'll go. Give me the address, and I'll

meet you there."

"Great. I'll text it to you. We're about to leave. I think it's somewhere between you and us. See you there."

"Will do."

Before he even hung up, I was headed for my boots. It took a minute to get those on and then out to my car. I entered the address he sent into my phone, and then I was off. It was after nine, so traffic wasn't an issue. During the day and at peak rush hours, it could've doubled my drive time. Mikhail was right. The address was between Belle Meade and The Gulch, where they lived on the third floor of Lustz.

They'd planned to move out to a house on his property in Culleoka, but a crazy Lustz employee put that on hold when she burned his house down. Ultimately, they took it as a positive since it would allow them to build a home that would suit them both. He had an architect drawing up the plans, and as soon as they approved the plan, they would have it built. I liked the wide-open spaces out there, but I wasn't sure if I'd want to give up my house. It would be a hard choice. Mikhail had been telling me there was a large property next to his. He said we could be neighbors. I informed him that was enough reason right there not to buy—him as a neighbor. Tajah had laughed herself silly when I told him that.

Finally, I pulled into a deserted parking lot. The closest building, the one that was the clinic, according to my directions, had lights on. If that weren't enough to tell me this was the place, the police car parked outside would. I didn't waste time getting my ass to the door. I yanked it open and walked in. I was met by a female police officer. She came walking toward me with her hand on the butt of her gun and a wary look.

"Hold it right there!" she demanded.

I stopped and raised my hands. "I'm expected. I presume Mr. Ivanova and his fiancée are here. I'm a friend. He called me."

"Who're you?"

"I told you, a friend of Mr. Ivanova."

"I want your name."

Usually, I would more than comply with a police officer's request, but I was anxious to see Cady and talk to them.

Instead of playing twenty questions with her, I called out, "Mikhail, mind coming out here and verifying I'm supposed to be here before this officer shoots me?"

The murmur of voices grew louder, and within moments, he, Tajah, a male officer, and Cady were in the lobby area. I saw shock on Cady's face and amusement on Mikhail and Tajah's. I grinned at them.

"Officer, he's fine. I asked him to come. I had no idea how extensive the damage was or what might need to be done. As you can see, he's got the muscles to help," Mikhail indicated with a chin thrust toward me. It was true, but it wasn't as if he was a five-foot weakling. He was six feet four and weighed not much less than me.

"Yeah, 'cause you can see, he's a weak pansy. The ladies need my muscles," I quipped back.

He scoffed at me. "Like hell. I've changed my mind. Shoot him," he told the female officer.

She was swinging her head back and forth like she was watching a Ping-Pong game. Tajah was trying to smother her giggles, but wasn't doing a very good job.

Cady was staring at me. The other officer was the one to say something.

"He can't be in here or touch anything. We've got to take prints. In fact, you all need to go outside."

"I can't. Those dogs in the back are upset. They hear us out here. I need to calm them down. They had surgery today and shouldn't be getting overly excited," Cady said.

"You've already dusted for prints. Cady didn't call us until you'd been here a while. What else do you have to do?" Tajah asked.

"Forensically, there could be other clues," the man added rather huffily.

"I would believe that if your CSI techs hadn't already been here and left. It's too late to gather more evidence. I have to get this place in order for us to open tomorrow. There's a full day of patients on the books," Cady told him. She had a slight bite to her voice. It wasn't her being a brat for the sake of being one. She was genuinely annoyed, and I couldn't blame her. Plus, she had made an excellent point.

"Officers, unless you bring your team back now and have more questions for her, we're getting to work. This place won't clean itself. When I came in, she was standing here staring off into the distance," I said as I pointed to the female officer. Her face flushed pink at me calling her out, but it was true.

The male's mouth tightened, but he must've known he was beaten. "On second thought, we're done here. There are so many fingerprints everywhere, it'll be impossible for us to determine who was in here illegally," he said snidely.

"Not on the lock, there aren't. I can understand

the door handle and front counter having a bunch, but not there. Only a few of us have keys to lock that. If it had been one of the employees with a key, they would've had the code to disarm the alarm. The alarm going off triggered you and me to be called," Cady reminded them.

Their radios crackled to life, and a female voice came across, rattling off codes and an address. This energized them.

"Ma'am, we'll let you know if we find anything."

Again, it was the male talking. If she hadn't asked for my name, I would've wondered if the female cop had gone mute. Right before exiting, he handed Cady a business card. Cady stomped over and flipped the lock when the door shut behind them.

When she turned back around, she looked at me with narrowed eyes. "What are you doing here?"

"Mikhail called and told me you had a break-in, and they were coming here."

"I got that, but why are *you* here?"

"I came to see if you were alright and if you needed my help," I told her, giving her my best smile.

"Well, lucky for me, I don't have an elephant in the back room. If I ever get one and the poor animal can't move, I'll give you a call," she snarked back.

I loved just being near her, but her brat showing herself lit a spark inside me, and my handler-self perked up.

"Feeling like some handling, Tiny?" I shot back.

"Handling? What the hell does that mean?"

"It means a brat like you needs a brat handler. And I happen to be an expert."

"I'm not a brat, and I don't play like the three

of you, so don't involve me in your games. I have no patience for the regular ones men play. Listen, thanks for coming, but I can take care of things. A little readying up the place, and we should be good to go for tomorrow. Why don't you guys leave? I'll call you tomorrow, Taj."

"Readying up?" I asked. It wasn't a term I was familiar with.

"Sorry, that's something they always said in my family. It means to get things ready, to clean up."

"There's no way we're leaving you here alone. It's dark, this place was broken into, and the animals need tending along with the cleanup. Neither Mikhail nor I can leave you. So, no more arguing. Us guys will do the readying up, and you ladies go calm the dogs," I suggested.

"This is my office. I say who stays or goes," she snapped.

"And I have size on my side. So unless you can pick my ass up and carry me outside, you're stuck with me, Tiny."

"Stop calling me that!" she hissed as she stomped her foot.

"I'll think about it if you do what I say," I smirked.

The growling sound she made deep in her throat had my cock stiffening even more. Without another word, she turned her back on me and stomped down the hallway. I assumed it led to the exam rooms and where the dogs were. Tajah smiled at me, kissed Mikhail quickly, and then went after her friend. Mikhail was grinning.

"You like to live dangerously, don't you? Cady is a brat, but something tells me she'll take a chunk out of you if you push her too far. Remember what Carver said. She's tiny but evil. He's afraid of her, I think." He chuckled.

I laughed. "And that is why I'll keep doing it. You know I like to live dangerously. Skydiving, parachuting, rock climbing, and the other things I do should've told you that. Was anything stolen?"

We began at the front counter. Drawers were open, and papers and other items were strewn everywhere, even on the floor. I saw chairs had been moved out of place and furniture overturned. It made me wonder what the rest of the office looked like.

"She said it didn't look like it."

"Do you have any idea why they broke in? Was it for money? Although, I wouldn't think much money would be kept here."

"They do keep some, but it's locked in a safe. It's not one you can pick up and steal, either. It's in her office and is built into the wall. That's always possible, but it would take time to break into it. They had to move fast with the alarm going off. Cady thinks they were looking for drugs. There are sedatives and painkillers they use on animals, as well as antibiotics. All of those are in demand, especially the first two."

"I can see those two, but why antibiotics?"

"Animal and human antibiotics are the same in most cases. They're packaged and sold as one or the other, but there's no difference. I didn't know that until she told us. This isn't a horrible area of town, but the crime rate has been rising. It was only a matter of time until this happened."

"If it's getting worse, they'll likely try again. An alarm isn't enough to keep determined burglars out of homes and other businesses. Why would it deter them from a clinic? And if the crime rate is worse, there's only so many cops to work. They can't be everywhere. She needs to move her clinic to somewhere safer," I said.

"Tajah mentioned it, and from what I got, it wasn't the first time she had. Cady replied that it wasn't so simple to up and move. I bet anything, it's a cost factor. She's the only vet here. She rents the place, not owns it, but even rent isn't cheap. When you add in paying staff, insurance, equipment, plus everything else, it's expensive. I'd offer to help her, but she'll say no." Mikhail sighed.

"Once she's with me, she won't get to say no. I'll do it and fight her afterward. Her safety and that of others means more," I muttered darkly. I thought I said it softly enough, but I didn't. Mikhail burst out laughing.

"Oh Christ, I can't wait to see the fireworks. Please, make sure I'm around when you do it."

I gave him a smirk. He could laugh, but I was serious. Tonight only confirmed that Cady was definitely for me. Now, all I had to do was bring her around to my way of thinking. The visions of how that would happen made me hard. Yep, handler versus brat. Let the fun begin.

Cady: Chapter 2

I had a pounding head. I worked late to get the clinic in shape to open today. Admittedly, I could've been here even longer if it weren't for Tajah, Mikhail, and Hoss. They helped me straighten things, even though I told them not to stay. Secretly, I was glad they had. However, it didn't do much for my sleep because I went home and tossed and turned most of the night. You would think it was due to worry in my mind over the break-in and what if it happened again? And you'd be correct, but only a portion was about the break-in. The rest was him, the man who set my teeth on edge and made me want to snap and snarl at him. At the same time, I would love to climb that man and have crazy sex.

Christ, crazy sex! Where the hell did that come from? I needed mental help. Who in their right mind wanted to have sex with a man who made them so frustrated? One minute, I wanted to be naked and naughty with him. The next, I wanted to choke him. I kept reminding myself that even if I got past my immense frustration with Hoss, it wouldn't matter. Sex always ended up being a letdown, and guys always walked. Or, in my case, they did.

Tajah hadn't had much luck in the love department until she met Mikhail. He came out of nowhere and swept her off her feet. I never imagined in a hundred years that she'd join a sex club and end up being a part of the life and engaged to the owner. It appeared she'd found her someone. I prayed it would last.

I let my cynicism show when they invited several of us to dinner almost two months ago. It was my first real exposure to Mikhail, and I lost it. I told her in front of him and others, including Hoss, that it wouldn't last and that he'd cheat on her before leaving. It was beyond shitty for a best friend to do that, I know, but it just came out. I let my personal feelings be reflected in their relationship.

Since that night, we have been slowly mending the riff I caused. She kept asking why I reacted that way, and I kept evading answering her. It hurt too much to explain, even to her. However, I'd watched the two of them since then, and I was ninety-nine percent sure I would have to eat my words. From everything I saw, Mikhail adored Tajah, and she had blossomed with him. I'd never seen her this happy.

"Cady, your next patient is here." Dottie's voice broke through my walk among my memories. I pulled myself together to answer her. I gave her a fake smile. Hopefully, she wouldn't know it was fake. She was my assistant, but she'd only known me for a short while.

"That would be Butch, right?"

"Yes, it's his annual physical and shots. His mom is very anxious for him." She grinned. The reason was we all knew Mrs. Gains, Butch's mom, was always anxious. She loved that dog and he was spoiled rotten. I already knew what I'd find, but I went anyway. I left my office.

"They're in room two," Dottie said helpfully.

"Thank you," I told her as I quickly scanned his chart to refresh my memory. When I had everything I needed, I pasted on my smile and entered the room.

Mrs. G was sitting on a chair, holding Butch. I almost laughed at the sight. I was impressed. She was a petite woman, built like me, with a massive bulldog on her. He practically obscured her. The impressive part was the fact she'd been able to lift him. She was seventy and not used to lifting heavy things all day like I was.

"Oh, Dr. Anderson, I'm so glad you're here. There's something wrong with Butch. He doesn't want to go for walks anymore. He sleeps all day and night. I don't know what's wrong with him. You have to fix him," she said frantically.

I'd given up on her calling me Cady. Leaving that alone, I got to work. "Mrs. Gains, I'm sure it's nothing too serious. Let me take Butch and put him on the table, then I can examine him," I said kindly.

I hefted Butch up. Let me tell you, it was no small feat. He weighed a ton. Putting him down on my exam table, he sank into a lump and closed his eyes. As I performed my examination, he snored the ceiling down and never opened his eyes. I held in my chuckle. He was so funny and cute in a bulldog way. Mrs. Gains sat there wringing her hands the whole time. When I was done, I told her what I found.

"Mrs. Gains, the only thing I can find with Butch is he's overeating. He's put on three pounds. That's too much. He was already overweight. The reason he's tired and won't walk is he's too heavy. You must cut back his food and treats as much as it pains you. And making him walk will help him shed the extra weight. When that happens, he'll become more energetic."

She'd been told repeatedly that he was obese, but she just kept feeding him. She gave me a pained look as she defended him with her usual excuse for his obesity.

"I can't do that! He's always starving, and he comes to me begging for food. I can't say no, and he's so sad when I do. I don't want him to be hungry."

"He won't starve, and I doubt he'll feel hungry. Most dogs have no off switch when it comes to food. They'll eat regardless if they're hungry. Butch is doing that. I promise you, cutting his food back won't make him starve. It will extend his life. His heart and lungs sound good, but that can change. I'll have the tech take some blood. He needs a couple of shots today. I'll also have them give you a diet sheet for him. I want you to have Butch for as many years as possible," I gently prompted her.

She gave a huge sigh, but she didn't argue. Maybe this would be the time she'd follow the diet sheet. Every other time she received it, nothing was done other than we wasted paper. I gave Butch a good head rub and scratch, which he enjoyed. His snoring eased, and a content sigh came out. My tech came in and took over so I could move to the next patient.

Thankfully, my day was busy, and time passed quickly. I had little time to dwell on the robbery attempt or Hoss. I enjoyed my interactions with all my patients. Animals were so much more straightforward than humans. Give them love and attention, attend to their basic needs, and they give you love and affection back.

However, the day did eventually end, and when it did, my mind went to the break-in, which amped up my anxiety. Would the thieves try again tonight? If they did, how would I recover? I lucked out last night, and they didn't have long to look. Why they didn't grab equipment, I didn't know. They could readily sell it. A lot of it wasn't cheap. The answer was they weren't here for those things. No, they wanted the drugs. I had pain meds, sedatives, and antibiotics, both in pill and injectable forms. All three were in demand and could be sold for much more than they cost. The only reason they didn't get them was I was a paranoid person and insisted, before leaving every night, that all such medications were brought to my office and put in a hidden panel in the wall. Sometimes, my quirks paid off.

The few employees who were allowed to lock up, such as Dottie, were the only ones who knew the vault's location, as I called it. They were given strict instructions not to talk about it to anyone, not even other staff. The reason for all of this secrecy was I'd seen what happened when drugs were stolen.

While interning as a vet, I worked with an older gentleman. He'd been a veterinarian for forty years. His knowledge was endless. He loved to teach, and I was given an amazing education. I was forever in his debt. The only thing he didn't do was secure his medications enough. I'd questioned him when I started. I asked him why they were only locked in a glass case. Anyone could break in to get the drugs if they wanted them. The lock was a tiny, flimsy one, too.

Dr. Hamilton waved off my concern, stating he hadn't had any issues in all the years he'd practiced. The clinic had locked outer doors and an alarm system. He assured me they were safe. It was as if fate decided to prove him wrong after I asked. Two months later, the clinic was broken into after hours. The men who did it were after the drugs.

Unfortunately, they had no clue the clinic wasn't empty. Dr. Hamilton had stayed late to work on something. The robbers surprised him. Instead of tying up the old man and grabbing the stuff, they shot him and left him to bleed out on his office floor. Everyone was devastated. Police were frantically looking for the men. The security cameras captured video of them, though they wore masks. The police weren't confident they'd catch them.

I didn't know what made me do it, but I asked to watch the video. I was determined those bastards wouldn't get away with what they did. I thought there might be a clue in the video to tell us who they were. I knew there was probably no hope in hell of there being one, but I asked anyway. I was shocked and so were the police when I found something. It was a tiny slipup, but in the end, it was enough to identify one of the two murderers and lead the cops to the second one. It came down to a tattoo.

One of the men's sleeves inched up when he removed the medications from the case, and I saw his wrist. It had a distinct tattoo. It was some blue devil's face with horns. I recognized it. A man had come in with his dog a couple of weeks before the incident. He said he was there because his dog wasn't eating. When we finished our examination, nothing was found wrong with his dog. I remembered talking to him and asking where he got his ink. He told me somewhere in Ohio. When I saw the tat again in the video, I told the police I had the man's name and address.

They were stunned that I remembered the tattoo and his name. I went into the office files to get his address for them. I explained that I had a thing for recalling things I read, and names always seemed to stick with me. It was enough for them to track him down, even though the address was fake. The dummy used his real name. Eventually, they found him, and pressure was applied to make a deal. If he gave them his accomplice, they'd reduce his sentence.

That had pissed me off. I knew it was essential to get them both off the streets, but to make a deal so a murderer wouldn't spend his entire life in prison? It grated on me, but I had no say. In the end, both men were found, convicted, and sentenced—the one who didn't make the deal got life without the possibility of parole. The dealmaker got twenty years and the possibility of parole. That was seven years ago. My secret prayer was they'd both die in there. Because of that horrible incident, I was extra careful in my clinic. I vowed it would never happen to me.

But here I sat, with dread building, as I worried it was happening and there wasn't anything I could do about it. What if they kept coming back to search? Or what if they returned and decided to steal the equipment to make a buck?

Other than my brother and Tajah, I only cared about my clinic. Well, I take that back. I was inching toward caring for Mikhail. He made it hard not to with the way he doted on my best friend. As for my clinic, it was my baby. A lot of hard work, long hours, sacrifices, and tears had gone into this. My cell rang, catching me off guard. I jumped. It was lying on my desk. I picked it up and read *Tajah's* name on the screen. Smiling, I answered it.

"Let me guess. You're running away from Mikhail because he's smothered you with too much love and attention, and you want to hide out at my place. What a bitch."

Her laugh was a long one. I leaned back and waited. Finally, she settled. "No, I'm not running from Mikhail. My bed is more than great right where it is. Why did you call me a bitch, though?"

"Because you have him entranced, where every woman would die to have a man or a woman. We all hate you because you have what we want. Watch out. Someone might kill you to get him."

"They already tried that, remember?" was her snappy comeback.

"Fuck, I guess so. Shit, it seems like forever since that crazy bitch went after the two of you. Have you heard anything about her, by chance?"

"Laura is still in the mental hospital, and from what Mikhail has told me, she won't ever be let out. She tried to strangle an orderly and knife a doctor to get free. Hopefully, she's the last obsessed person we have to deal with. Unless you want to attempt to take him." There was amusement in her voice. She knew I would do no such thing.

"Taj, there's no way I'd go for your man. He's great and all, but not my type."

"Hmm, yeah, you're right. He's not your type. Now, if he were like Hoss, you'd be all over him," she slyly added.

I wasn't about to get into Hoss with her. He mixed me up too much to try to sort him out. "In your dreams. Hoss is a chauvinist who thinks that because he's a man and the size of a mountain, he can boss people around, especially women. Well, I have news for him—not this woman. I need that like I need another hole in my head."

"Hoss is nothing like that, Cady. He's a great guy and smart. You shouldn't dismiss him. He's not a chauvinist." There was no teasing in her voice.

"Taj, whether he's one or not, it has nothing to do with me. I'm not looking to hook up with someone. I told you. I'm better off alone. I need to concentrate on building my business."

"What about a family? You've always wanted a husband and kids."

"I did, but it may not be for me. Not everyone settles down and has kids. If I don't, I'll just live vicariously through you. Yours will become mine. I'll be the cool, fun, and understanding aunt who sides with the kids and makes you and Mikhail insane." I said it jokingly, but inside, my heart hurt. I wanted a family as much as I did my clinic, maybe more.

"Cady, you know that's not true, not for you. Please, don't give up hope. There's someone perfect for you out there, and I'm positive you'll find him. But only if you don't close yourself off from the prospect of it. I know you've been hurt more than once. Forget those fuckers. Keep your heart open. You have so much love to give," she said softly. There was no teasing in her voice. Tears smarted my eyes. We had to get off this subject before I burst into tears.

"Alright, alright, I won't close myself off. Hey, I hate to rush, but I'm finishing up work. Was there a reason you called other than you wanted to hear my voice? If you're not looking for a place to stay, I don't know if I can help you." I made it sound like I was kidding again. I didn't want to get into the deep emotional shit.

"I called to see if you were doing okay. It's after

five. You shouldn't still be at the clinic. Please tell me you're not there alone."

"Tajah, I'm fine. I have everything locked, the alarm is set, and I have all the lights on. Only an idiot would try to break in here with all that. Whoever it was, they've moved on. I had a busy day and needed to catch up on my notes and do a couple of things."

"You can write your notes at home on your laptop. I know it ties into your system. And anything else can be done before you open. You have staff to do those things. I don't think you should be there alone anymore." Her worry was coming through the phone.

"Taj, stop it. I'm fine. And I don't want you calling Carver or telling that man of yours to check on me. I'm a big girl. I can handle myself. I love you and thank you for worrying about me, but I'm good. Now, I've gotta go. Love and kisses," I told her hastily.

She sighed before answering back. "Love and kisses. Be safe. I can't lose you."

"You won't. Go sex up that man of yours or something. Remember, you're getting sex for the both of us." That made her laugh before we said goodbye and hung up.

It took me almost half an hour after talking to Tajah to get my mind back in the game to chart. While I waited to get there mentally, I puttered around the clinic, cleaned things up, and ensured all the examination rooms were stocked for the next day's work. I'd been seated at my computer for maybe twenty minutes when there was a loud pounding at the front door—not a knock, but an actual pounding. My heart jumped, and I gasped, fright filling me until my brain kicked in. *A robber wouldn't knock first, Cady. Think.*

Maybe someone saw the lights and stopped to ask for directions or something. It had happened in the past, and once, a woman who ran from her boyfriend. She was trying to hide from him and asked me to let her do it in the clinic. You better believe I did.

With those in mind, I got up and went to the front. I couldn't see outside. Our door was solid, and the windows that faced the front of the building had the shades drawn. The thought of someone outside in the dark watching me freaked me out. Closing the blinds was a must when I was here alone. I stood on the other side of the door and waited. I jumped like an idiot when the pounding happened again. Only this time, it was followed by a voice. A deep, masculine voice that I recognized.

"Cady, I know you're in there. Open the damn door. I need to know you're safe," he hollered.

His bossy tone put up my back, and I didn't think, so I reacted. I unlocked and then yanked the door open. Hoss stood there towering over me, but I didn't care. I blocked the doorway, although it was ridiculous. My tiny body would be nothing for him to walk through. However, I still did it. I scowled as I looked up a long way at him. He was frowning as he met my gaze. I didn't give him a chance to say anything. I went on the attack.

"Who do you think you are? Coming to my work, making a racket, and yelling for me to open up. I have news for you. You're not my goddamn boss!" I snarled.

"You wanna do this out where anyone can hear us, or can I come in and we'll fight in private?" he asked calmly. I would've sworn the way his mouth was twisted that he was trying not to laugh. But what was there to laugh about?

"No, you need to leave. Then there's no need for you to come in or for us to stand out here. You've seen me. I'm great. Tell Tajah I'm beating her ass the next time I see her for calling you." The sneaky shit went to him. Next time, I'd have to tell her not to tell Hoss. Wait a minute. There wouldn't be a next time.

Arguing with myself and having conversations in my head was a habit from childhood. One I tried to work on but to no avail. It caused me to wait too long. As I went to tell him to leave a second time, Hoss took it upon himself to take the decision out of my hands. He stepped closer, reached out, and lifted me off my feet. He walked me inside, then kicked back his foot to snag and close the door.

This set me off. I wiggled hard, hoping he'd let go. Nope. So, I kicked out. I caught him in the shin, right below his knee. He grunted, but the ass didn't drop me. He kept walking and carrying me along.

"Hoss, put me down! I swear to God, if you don't, I'm going to hurt you," I hissed.

"You're cute, like a hissing, spitting kitten. You know, the kind that you just want to pet even if they're acting like a rascal. You know, if they'd just let you pet them, they'd calm down." The son of a bitch had the audacity to grin.

"Try to pet me and see what happens. I'll scratch your eyes out and bite your hand off," I growled.

"Don't make promises you won't keep. If you promise, I expect you to carry through. You can try to bite and scratch me if you want. I'll love correcting your behavior." He winked at me.

I didn't know what to say to this. Any other guy who I let loose on usually yelled back and then would storm out. After a few times of that, they'd get the message and stop. It worked well when the guy was someone who merely irritated you. It sucked when the guy was someone you were in a relationship with. Hence, this was why I was single and doomed to remain that way. It took a moment for it to register after my feet were placed back on the floor that he'd toted me all the way to my office.

"I need you to behave and stay here. I'll be back. I just need to lock the door," he advised me. He didn't wait to hear my answer before turning and walking out.

In a blink, I hurried to my desk. I'd grab my purse and phone, then slip out the back door through the kennel area. There were no animals to worry about giving away my presence tonight. I made it halfway to my office door before he filled it. He crossed his arms over his chest and gave me a stern look.

I was momentarily distracted from fleeing by how that pose struck me. It made his already massive upper body and arms seem to double. The bulging muscles made me want to moan and touch him. I was snapped out of my daze by his words.

"And just what do you think you're doing?"

"What does it look like, big man? Don't you know what a woman leaving looks like? You should. I bet enough have left you. Only they were probably way less dressed. That must be why you don't recognize it," I snarked back.

His left eyebrow hiked up. Instead of getting angry, he calmly asked, "Would you like to try to answer me again?"

His calmness and the way he subtly demanded me to have enough guts to stick to my remark or back down and change it made a tiny thrill race through me. I didn't know why, but I knew I wasn't backing down.

"Nope. I thought I was speaking English, but let me slow it down for you. I leave. Woman go. Not you." I said it slowly.

It was a mix of someone talking to someone dumber than a rock and someone who thinks talking slowly and using few words with someone whose primary language wasn't English. I thought it was ignorant and insulting when everyday people did it, but it was fun to use it against him this way. I knew he was far from stupid. Tajah told me he was brilliant. I braced for him to explode and make threats or storm out. Instead, he raised his brow higher. There was something sexy about it.

"Keep it up and see what happens, Tiny." His commanding tone, with that hint of risk and pledge mixed, made me shiver inside. I had to fight not to let him see it. God, what was wrong with me? *Shut up, get him out of here, and then go home!* I lectured myself.

"I thought I told you to stop calling me Tiny, Supersize."

He smirked. "Supersized is right. Everything I have is. Glad you noticed."

A heat flash made me feel like I was sweating. There was no mistaking what he meant. I wasn't able to stop myself from glancing down at his crotch. As I did, he chuckled, and I gasped. He was sporting an enormous bulge, Like if his cock was even close to that big, it was a monster. I tried to swallow, but my mouth was dry. The thought of him having a jumbo cock filled me with trepidation and exhilaration. I scrambled to regain my senses and to respond to his comment.

"Just what I thought. You're so insecure that you have to stuff socks in your pants. How sad."

"Imp, I don't need to boost my assets falsely. I can show you if you want." He reached down and put his hand on the belt of his slacks. He was dressed in what had to have been a complete suit earlier in the day, but his jacket was gone, and so was his tie. The top two buttons were undone, and the sleeves were rolled up his forearms.

I threw up my hand. "Stop! Enough. What are you doing here, Hoss? Tajah sent you, didn't she? I don't need someone babysitting me or breathing down my neck. I've worked here plenty of nights until very late and been fine. Go home. She shouldn't have made you do this." Things were becoming dangerous—it was time to get back on track.

"I came to check that you were safe. Tajah didn't send me. Mikhail asked if I was close and, if so, if I'd do it. I was, so I did. And you being here in the past wasn't smart, but it's twice as risky when this place was broken into last night. Damn it, Cady, whoever did it, could decide to come back tonight! Do you think the fact you're here will stop them? They could break in and beat, rape, kidnap, or kill you! Do you understand that? No money or stuff is worth your safety or life." There was no playfulness in his tone anymore. It was hard and insistent. He wasn't happy.

"I'm more familiar with what could happen than you are. However, this is my livelihood. I can't avoid it as soon as it gets dark. I have to stay over sometimes. When animals are here overnight, I must check on them to ensure they're doing alright. If I have an extremely sick one, I stay to watch over them. I'm here all the time alone. Whoever broke in would be absolute imbeciles to do it again, especially the night after they did it the first time. I'll call Tajah and Mikhail and tell them not to ask you to do this again. Thank you for being such a good friend to them. Now, you need to go so I can finish up."

"What did you mean when you said you're more familiar with what could happen than I am? Has something like this happened to you here before? Taj didn't mention it."

"Nothing happened here. Tajah is my best friend, but we don't live in each other's pockets. The longer you stay here yapping, the longer I'll have to stay after you leave. I have to get my documentation done on all my patients from today. Tomorrow is another full day."

Thank God he had let his hand drop away from his belt, but he moved closer. I had to force myself not to step back. He stopped when he was only a couple of feet away. He was studying me intently. I put on my best bland look. The silence stretched. I was about to break it when he did.

"One day, I promise you, you'll trust me, and I'll know all your secrets. Until next time, Cady. Don't stay too late. Be alert when you go to your car."

I was at a loss for words about the secrets and trust part, so I ignored them. "I'll be careful. Good night, Hoss."

We were moving swiftly from my office to the front door as I answered him. When we got to it, he unlocked it and opened it. He stepped outside and then swung around to face me. "Good night, darlin'."

And just like that, he strolled off. I watched as he got into a gorgeous sports car. It was so him. I had no idea how he fit in it, but he did. I admired the car. When he started the engine, I waved, shut the door, and locked it. My desire to stay and work was gone, but I had to remain for a little bit. If I didn't, I would feel like Hoss had won, and that wasn't happening. Moving back to my office, I made myself sit at my desk and work. I'd worry about Hoss and chew Tajah out later.

Hoss: Chapter 3

Last night at Lustz was quiet. I wondered if it would be the same tonight. Not that I was looking for trouble, but sometimes it would be nice to have a smidge so I wouldn't get bored. With my crazy work schedule, between SacketEdge and Lustz, I got one day a week off—Sunday.

When I wanted more time off, I took it. It was a perk of being the boss, and I worked hard the rest of the time to make up for it. Most thought that my working at Lustz Thursday through Saturday meant I was in the office at SacketEdge Monday through Wednesday. They were wrong. I was there Monday through Thursday. When I got off work on Thursday, I changed my clothes, grabbed dinner, and headed to Lustz. Those nights, I didn't start to work until eight o'clock. On Friday and Saturday, I was there by six o'clock. The club was open until three a.m. We could stay open longer, but serving alcohol had to be stopped at that time. However, alcohol consumption was prohibited if the patron wanted to do more than socialize on the first floor. We used a special marking system to track if someone consumed alcohol rather than a non-alcoholic drink. The earliest we opened was at five p.m.

In the off-hours, Mikhail, Reuben, and other staff worked on the books, ordering, cleaning, stocking, and many other things. It was never totally closed. If there was a need, during the day on Friday, I took meetings at SacketEdge, but only if I had to. I'd heard competitors grumbling about how I was never in the office a few times. They said they had no idea how anything got done. It must be because I found ways to steal other people's work. It was sour grapes. They damn well knew how I got shit done. I worked far more than they did, and I had the best when it came to those I hired. They didn't see the hours I worked from home while they were at parties, dinners, or during the work week on the golf course with their cronies. Golf bored me to tears. I'd rather jump out of a plane or something like that. Watching paint dry was more exciting to me than golf. Just the word made me gag.

I was on the verge of losing my patience, which was why I was anxious to have something or someone to focus on. And the reason was all Cady's fault. It had been three days since I went to the clinic after hours and tried to get her to leave. Most people would assume her stubbornness about not leaving and her sassy talk to me were the cause of my impatience. They'd be wrong. Her brattiness didn't make me feel that way. It stimulated me. It made me want to hear more and be able to calm it without breaking her of her sassiness.

As a brat handler, I didn't want to make her into a meek, mild, and submissive Stepford wife. I'd be bored to tears in a day. I loved her fire. I needed that just as she needed to express it. I knew why she did it. She felt out of control and insecure. I needed to understand why so I could help her get some control and feel more secure.

I'd been tempted to ask Tajah if something traumatic in Cady's past might've caused her to be so prickly and unwilling to rely on others, but I didn't. The reason was that I wanted to discover all there was to know about her for myself. It was like Christmas. Most people tore off the wrapping in a flurry to get to the gift inside. I'd always been more of a guy who meticulously removed it. To me, it made the discovery of what was there better. More satisfying.

However, in her case, I was finding the desire to open the door and see how she responded sexually was gnawing at me. Tuesday night, when I told her I'd undo my pants so she could see what I was packing, her eyes and that look of awe and trepidation had almost made me beg her to get naked with me. I had images flashing in my head all night after I left. Pictures of me with a nude Cady spread out on her desk, submitting to me. I'd ended up jerking off twice that night and every night since.

I'd looked at my calendar earlier today and realized it had been twelve weeks since I first saw her. Waiting to have sex with a woman for three months was unheard of with me. Not to say I pressured them into it. Hell no, but usually for me, since I joined Lustz especially, it wasn't hard to find women willing and eager to play. Sometimes, it was only play, but often, sex might be involved. I played with a few repeat brats, but I'd never had one long-term who was exclusive to me, nor was I exclusive with them. It wasn't due to me not being willing. It was purely because none of them had interested me enough to contemplate that. Several had asked, and some pleaded with me, but I couldn't.

I hadn't gotten to play in-depth with Cady, but the small amount I'd seen made me crave more. My gut told me that she would be the one to change my mind about the long term. Cady was the woman I was positive

I could play with for a lifetime. Never had a woman occupied my mind or made me ache for her the way she did. And if this were the result after four meetings, two of which lasted barely minutes, I'd be an idiot to walk away without doing my damndest to see if she could feel the same way about me.

"Earth to Hoss, earth to Hoss." Mikhail's voice penetrated my meandering mind. I blinked and focused on him. I'd gotten here early. The patrons hadn't started to arrive yet, though it shouldn't be long until they did. I straightened from where I'd been leaning against the side of the building.

"Hey, sorry about that. What's up?"

"Are you okay? You were really out of it, and that's not like you," Mikhail said, his expression worried.

"I'm fine. No worries. It won't happen again. Promise."

"Talk to me, Hoss. Something is on your mind. I can see it. This is your friend Mikhail talking, not your boss. If you need time off or to talk, I'm here."

Glancing around to ensure no patrons or other workers were nearby, I lowered my voice. "I don't need time off. That's not it. What I need is for there to be reasons for me to be near Cady. I don't see her unless I'm here when she is, which hasn't happened in two months. The two nights at the clinic were a fluke—or they better be. She doesn't want anyone babysitting her. If I go straight to her and say I want to spend time with her and ask her out, she'll say no. What the hell is a guy to do with that?"

He stared at me for a good minute without saying anything. I don't know if he thought I'd back down or give him another reaction. I stared back at him steadily.

Suddenly, a slow grin spread.

"Son of a bitch, I don't believe it! You undoubtedly have it bad for her. You said you were intrigued by her, but it's more than that. Let me ask you something. When she kicked you out Tuesday night and the past two evenings when she stayed over at work, did you do as she said and go home? Or did you park where she wouldn't see you and keep watch until she left?" He smirked. If it had been anyone else, I would've lied.

"I stayed where she was unlikely to see me, but I could still see the clinic. The stubborn woman is staying just to be bullheaded. It's like she wants those bastards to come back. How the hell did you know I did?"

"She is stubborn. That's a fact. Ask Tajah and Carver, and they'll tell you. As for how did I know? Well, see, I knew she'd run me off. Even after your Tuesday visit, Tajah was still worried, so I asked my cousin if I could have one of his guys, if he had any available, watch the clinic for a week or two. Luckily, he did, and his men can be discreet when they have to. His guy spotted you and recognized you. He was one of the ones who accompanied Matvey and Victoria to our house for dinner the night Cady stormed out. Matvey called to ask if you should be run off or not."

I groaned. I was outed by a damn Bratva soldier. "A Bratva soldier spotted me. Great, should I expect to be snuffed out?"

"Nah, I told him you weren't out to harm her. Matvey laughed when I told him she was driving you mad. I saw it the other night when we were at the clinic. I'm not going to lie. It's going to be hard to tame her." Mikhail warned me as if I didn't recognize what a handful she was.

"I don't want to tame her. I want to reduce her need to exhibit her stress and insecurity through her sassiness but remain a brat. I don't want it to go away for good. I adore her just the way she is. It's a rush when she spars with me and gives me her attitude."

"Tajah can sometimes be a brat, and my primal brain is more turned on by it. But I don't have the full tamer or handler mentality. Taj is perfect because she falls into my primal world effortlessly. It was as if she'd always been waiting for it, even though she had no idea she was. That's when you know a woman is made for you."

"Mikhail, you have no idea how I pray Cady is the same way, only leaning toward being my brat. If she does, I'll make it so she never wants to leave. I may have to regulate her, but I want her to feel safe being herself. I can give her the world if she gives me that gift."

I'd never spoken to anyone this way before. It was slightly weird to feel it, but if I was to do it, Mikhail was the one to tell. He would keep it confidential. The grin he gave me told me he might not tell anyone, but he would tease me about it.

"Go ahead, say it," I told him.

"No, I won't say a word, not yet. I want to see how this all plays out. I'll wish you good luck, and if I can do anything, short of it being something that will piss off my woman, all you have to do is ask."

"I will. Thanks. Well, I guess I should get back to work. Here comes our first patrons, and the boss doesn't like us to sit around doing nothing," I joked. Two men and a woman were coming across the parking lot. I recognized them. Mikhail punched me lightly in the arm.

"That's right, and don't forget it. No, seriously, if you want to talk, I'm here. And so is Reuben."

"I know, and I thank you. I have a feeling I might end up taking you up on the offer, maybe more than once." I stated ruefully. He grinned, let out a chuckle, then walked inside.

That trio was the start of the steady stream of patrons coming and going. The night remained just enough to occupy my mind, mostly. At three in the morning, I did a final check-in before leaving. I was startled to see that Mikhail was still downstairs. Since he found Tajah, he wasn't in the club as much, and certainly not this late unless there was a need. He practically lived there in the past, even though he had staff more than capable of managing and monitoring the club. It was good to see him letting go some. I walked over to him. He was talking to Reuben.

When they saw me approaching, they gave me chin lifts. "Is this a private conversation, or can anyone be nosy?" I asked.

"No, it's not private. We were talking shit about you," Reuben said.

"Oh, so the same thing you do all the time," I quipped.

"Yeah, now that you mention it," Mikhail said.

"Where's HR when you need them?" I asked as I pretended to scan the room.

"Pansy," Reuben muttered under his breath.

I elbowed him, which shifted him to the right. "Boss, he's touching me," Reuben pretended to whine. Mikhail chuckled and rolled his eyes.

"I swear it's like babysitting a bunch of kids. To answer your question, it's not a private conversation.

We were just downloading on how the night went. I assume nothing out of the ordinary happened outside since we didn't hear from you. I had a couple of patrons approach me about sponsoring someone. I told them to get whoever wanted to join to fill out the application, and we'd follow our process. We're always willing to take at least a look at anyone who applies, although having a current or former patron in good standing vouching for you helps," Mikhail reminded us.

"True. I'm going to head home if there's nothing else you need from me," I told them.

"Go. We're good. See you tomorrow night. Oh, before I forget. Tajah wants to have a small get-together at the apartment, and she wants you two to come. There will be fewer people than there were last time. She said she wasn't sure exactly when, but it would be a Sunday. I know that's your one day off, Hoss, but she would rather do it when we can all enjoy ourselves and not have to run off to work unless we do like we did last time and get others to cover your shifts," Mikhail informed us.

I never minded spending time with friends, and I considered Mikhail and Reuben friends, and Tajah had also been added to that list. But there was one other I wanted to be there even more. "Am I to assume another specific guest will be included?" I asked Mikhail.

He smirked while Reuben gave me a questioning look. "Yes," was all Mikhail said.

"Well, I was planning to say yes anyway, but this makes me even more eager. Regardless of which day you want to do it, I'll be there," I informed him.

"I wouldn't miss it, but I want to know who Hoss is all happy will be there. Or should I guess? Could it be a petite firebrand?" Reuben asked, sort of smiling.

"And if it is?" I shot back. If he were about to say he was interested in Cady too, I'd have to do something terrible, like torture him until he saw the light and would run every time he saw her.

"Damn, if looks could kill, man, I'd be dead. You have nothing to worry about, Hoss. I'm not interested in Cady. She's an attractive, desirable woman without a doubt, but her tongue and attitude would push my buttons if I had to put up with her all the time," Reuben said. Knowing his primary and secondary kinks and how he liked his life, I could understand it.

"Good to hear. Yeah, she'd put you through hell if she were yours. However, for a man like me, that tongue and attitude are perfect," I told him, smirking.

"More power to you, man. Alright, tell Taj to make it happen and just tell us when and what time. Oh, and if she needs us to bring anything," Reuben stated.

"Excellent. I'll let her know. I should have an answer for when next week. Good night, and drive safe," Mikhail told both of us.

A quick goodbye and man hug, and we went our separate ways. As I drove back to my place, I wondered how Cady was doing and if Taj would have trouble getting her to attend. Something in my gut told me my brat would resist, but I had news. She'd come even if I had to bribe or kidnap her and bring her ass there. I wanted more time with her. This was the only way I could think of to get it.

⚓ ⚓ ⚓

I got my wish to see Cady, but not how I imagined I would. It was the following night at Lustz. I was at the door working. It was crazy busy, with people constantly coming and going. Despite the number of people, no one had misbehaved outside. As for inside, if they had, no one asked me to help. There was inside security, and they knew their jobs. However, occasionally, I was asked to assist, especially if it was an altercation with several people involved or someone extra out of control.

I was outside minding my business when a guy came to the door. He tried to walk right past me. "Hold it. I'm sorry, but I don't know you. May I have your name? Are you a new patron? Or a guest?" I asked as I held my hand out to block him.

I was able to look up the names and photos of all patrons on a small tablet I had. If someone was bringing a guest or meeting them here, they were required to have Reuben or an associate approve the guest, and their name and photo had to be given to the staff. It was then added to our system. It ensured no one was sneaking in who shouldn't be here. People tried it all the time. They were curious about what went on inside. Lookie-loos were not wanted.

"I'm a guest," he said, trying to walk past me again. I put myself between him and the door. He scowled up at me.

"I need your name. And who is your sponsor?"

"Listen, I just need to get in to see my girl," he said snappishly.

"And I can't let anyone inside the club who isn't a patron or guest. And if your girl invited you, no problem. All I need is to check for your name." I reiterated. He didn't appear to be mentally slow. He was trying to avoid answering, which meant he wasn't on the list.

I could see the frustration growing on his face.

Through what I thought were clenched teeth, he said, "My name is Flint Reid."

I quickly opened the tab I kept pulled up at all times. It saved time by not having to reopen it repeatedly. Scanning the entries, which were in alphabetical order, I didn't find a Flint Reid. I even went to the Rs to be sure someone hadn't gotten the names reversed. Zilch.

"Sir, I'm sorry, but your name isn't on the list. I can't let you inside."

"She must've forgotten to put me on it! She's absent-minded like that. I'll tell you what. Just let me pop inside, and I'll find her and be back in five minutes. She can tell you." He made his voice sound reasonable and tried to give me a friendly grin.

There was no way he'd find her in five minutes in there, and I wasn't letting him search shit. I laid my tablet on my stool. "That's not happening. I can see if the patron you say invited you is here and if she can come out to speak to you, but if you're not on the list, then you've most likely not been cleared by management to be here. In that case, you can speak to her but not enter. That's the best I can do."

I had kept my voice calm and edged with friendliness. I hadn't crossed my arms or done anything to appear menacing. However, his following words began to change that.

"My fucking girlfriend is in there, and I want her now! And don't lie and say she's not because I saw her car. She and I need to talk. She has no business being in a place like this!" he shouted.

Unfortunately, from time to time, we did get upset significant others who found out their partner was enjoying the play at Lustz and not including them. The non-patron was often excluded due to unwillingness to explore with the patron, and the member needed his or her needs met. Most of the time, sex wasn't even involved, just consensual play. So, having a boyfriend going off wasn't new, and I barely felt any of my cool evaporating.

"Mr. Reid, I'm sorry if your girlfriend is in there and you weren't invited, but it doesn't matter. You aren't entering. If you tell me her name, I'll have someone see if they can find her and ask her to come out to speak to you," I offered a second time.

There was no way he'd be able physically to take me on and get past me. The guy was maybe five feet nine inches at the most and alright in the build department, but stacked against my six-foot-seven-inch bulky frame, he was a pipsqueak. I crossed my arms.

"Then fucking call her! Her name is Cady Anderson. I know she's in there. I want her out here now!" he shouted.

The dude was unraveling, but what made me lose my shit was him saying he was Cady's boyfriend. According to what I knew, she wasn't seeing anyone. When did it change? What did she see in this fucker? More questions crowded into my brain, but I let them go. I had one thing to do—send this guy on his way.

"Sir, I know Cady, but she's not here."

"Like hell, she's not! I saw her come here. She's in there. Either you let me see her, or I'm calling the cops and telling them you're holding a woman against her will."

We tried to avoid contact with the police. Most had preconceived ideas about Lustz and the people here.

Knowing Mikhail would be unhappy if the cops were on our doorstep, I took out my phone. There was one way to handle this. I'd call Tajah to see if Cady was here. There was a slight chance she'd come in before I got to work at six. If not, Taj could at least tell me when Cady had started seeing this joker. My gut churned with bile at the thought she was no longer unattached. Not that it would deter me from making a move. It just complicated things if she had feelings for him, although I couldn't see how it was possible. Nothing about him seemed to be Cady's kind of man.

Finding Taj's number, I pushed the button. It rang three times before Tajah answered. She sounded a tad hesitant as she did. "Hi, Hoss, uhm, is everything okay? Aren't you working at the front door? Do you need Mikhail? If so, he's downstairs."

"Honey, I'm sorry to bother you. I wasn't calling for Mikhail. It's you I need. I have a couple of questions. We have a person at the door demanding to be let in to see Cady. Is she there with you?" I paused to give her time to answer.

"She's not here, Hoss. Who in the world would be at the door insisting on seeing her?" I heard her puzzlement.

"He claims that he saw her car come here and that she's his girlfriend."

"His girlfriend! Cady isn't dating anyone. What's his name?" she asked suspiciously.

"He said his name is Flint Reid."

"Flint Reid! You tell that no-good son of a bitch to stay away from Cady. She's through with him, and no matter how many times he tries to convince her to get back together with him, it isn't happening. If he persists in refusing to leave, kick his ass and make him. In fact, on second thought, make sure he stays right there. I have a few things to say to that bastard. Be right there."

Before I was able to say anything, she hung up. I had no idea if she was coming alone or grabbing Mikhail. It might take a while for them to get here, so I lied as I put my phone away. I didn't feel an ounce of remorse for it.

"She's on her way. She said to stay here. It's crowded inside, and the place is big. It might take a few minutes, but she'll be here," I informed him.

"Good. I'm not having her do this shit. Why would she come to a place like this? It doesn't make any sense. She can't get anything here that I can't give her. Who were you talking to? It sounded like they were with her." He squinted his eyes at me.

"Just someone who would know if she was here or not."

As we waited, he paced. I studied him. It was a relief that Cady wasn't dating him. However, knowing she had, I wondered what the attraction was. How long had they been broken up? I'd known her for three months and never heard mention of a man. Had he been trying to get her back this whole time? Why did they break up in the first place? I was slowly driving myself a little crazy, wondering so many things. Luckily, we weren't alone for long.

A patron I knew well approached the door. I greeted him and opened the door as he went to enter, ensuring Flint couldn't slip inside. As the door closed, he questioned me.

"Why didn't you make him stop and check his name?"

"Because I know him. He's allowed in the club."

"So you stand here all night opening doors and checking people's names. God, how boring. But I guess for a big guy like you, there aren't a whole lot of jobs you can get other than bouncer duty," he said snidely.

I fought not to grin. He had no clue. To him, I was a big dumb muscle head. A lot of people made that mistake. In business, when people made the same presumption, it always came back to bite them in the ass. I didn't bother to correct this idiot's assumption.

Six minutes and fifteen seconds later, yes, I timed it, the door opened and out walked Tajah. Mikhail was with her. No surprise. She wore a ferocious scowl on her usually smiling face. Her eyes landed on Reid immediately, and they narrowed even more. I swore for a moment that I heard her growl. Mikhail was close but not saying anything. Tajah stamped closer to the unwanted guest.

"What the hell are you doing here, Flint?"

"Tajah, I'm here because Cady is. I need to talk to her. Why did she send you out? And what's with bringing another bouncer? Are you that afraid to face me?" He smirked.

Mikhail stiffened. Before he said a word, Tajah was on the attack.

"The day I'm scared of a piece of shit like you will be the day I stop writing. I came to tell you to your stupid face that Cady isn't here, But if she was, there's no way she'd talk to you. And she, for damn sure, has no interest in dating you. Why don't you give up? Find a woman who likes your bullshit. Cady doesn't. It's time for you to move on. She has."

"What does that mean? Is she seeing someone?

Who?" His smugness evaporated, and his agitation climbed.

"As if I'd tell you that. Have some self-respect and leave. She's not going to be yours. You had your chance, and you blew it. No second chances. You know she doesn't do those."

In his distress over Cady, he took a couple of steps toward Tajah. Immediately, before I could do it, Mikhail placed himself between them. His scowl was dark and filled with wrathful promise.

"You take one more step toward her, and I'll break your fucking legs. Stay the hell back. She told you Cady isn't here, and even if she were, she wouldn't want to see or talk to you. Leave right now."

"I'm not taking orders from a goddamn bouncer or whatever you two are supposed to be," Reid snapped.

"Well, it's lucky then we're more than that. I'm Mikhail Ivanova. I own the House of Lustz, and you're trespassing. Leave. Don't come back. You're never welcome."

"What the hell does this have to do with you?"

"Tajah is my fiancée. Cady is her best friend— end of story. And the big guy here, who I must say is showing tremendous restraint by not ripping your head and all four limbs off your body, is Hoss. I'd worry more about him if I were you." Mikhail smirked.

"And why is that? Just because he's the size of a small building?" Reid sneered. I had to give it to him. He didn't back off even when obviously unequipped to handle someone.

"No, because he's Cady's new man," Mikhail lied.

His self-satisfied grin made me want to roll my eyes, but I didn't. I let the lie go and then rolled with it myself. I crowded Reid. The glare I gave him should've scorched the fucker. He finally took a few hasty steps back. He was showing unease.

"Let me add to what has been said. Cady is mine. I take care of what's mine. If I find out you're trying to see her again, call her, leave a message, hell, even think about it, I'll find you. And when I do, before I tear off all your appendages, I'll make you hurt in the worst way. She's in the past. Keep it that way," I growled out as menacingly as I could.

At last, he was getting the hint. His face paled, and sweat had broken out on his brow. He swallowed noticeably. His mouth was opening. I waited to hear what he'd say next, but we were interrupted in a way I wasn't expecting.

Cady: Chapter 4

I was bored. There was no other term for it. It was Saturday night, and I was sitting at home, staring at the television. I tried to watch a movie. Nope. Next, I tried to read a book in my TBR, to-be-read, list. It was huge. I kept adding to it but not reading them fast enough. After an hour of trying to get into the book and failing, I gave up. I glanced at the clock. It was only ten o'clock at night. I knew one place I could go despite the late hour. Well, there were two, but I wasn't in the mood to hang out at the clinic tonight.

With her writing career, Tajah had kept weird hours for the past couple of years. You never knew when she was awake or asleep. A lot of the time, she worked in the middle of the night. Since she met Mikhail, it had gotten worse. While he did work during the day, he often oversaw his club at night—just not as late as he used to. I knew they'd still be awake. Deciding to see if I could hang with them, I texted.

Me: I'm bored. Can I come to hang out with you guys? Or are you and Mikhail in the middle of kinky time? ;)

I waited a smidge impatiently for her to respond. If she didn't within ten minutes, I knew to stay clear. Four minutes later, she did.

Taj: We'd love to see you. Kinky time was earlier, so I can last until after you leave, LOL. Come on over to the dark side.

Tajah kept telling me I needed to spend time at Lustz and explore. A part of me was curious, but I wasn't sure if I could handle what it might reveal, so I stayed away. I teased her that I wasn't kinky like her as my excuse, which she knew was a damn lie. I'd always been more into trying new things than her until Mikhail entered the picture.

Me: Brag much? I hope your crotch is sore, you rip. I'm coming. Poor Mikhail needs a break from your nymphomaniac ass.

Taj: Jealous much? Look who is calling someone a rip, ho. SYS, LYL.

Me: LYL x2

With her approval, I grabbed my purse, jacket, and car keys and left the house. The temperature had cooled off. It was late October, so it was bound to happen sooner or later. I shivered even though I had on my jacket. My car windows were fogged up when I got in. As I started it, I prayed it would warm up fast. I wished I had a garage to keep my car out of the weather. It froze in the winter and roasted in the summer. Unfortunately, that was the norm when you lived in an apartment like I did.

I would love a bigger place with a yard and a garage, but with the clinic, I couldn't afford it. One day, I'd be able to, I kept telling myself. And when I did, I'd have animals. There would be no landlord who said no pets are allowed. A policy like that for a veterinarian was like a knife in my heart. But beggars can't be choosers. Carver said I could live with him. His complex allowed them, but there was no way I would live with my brother. I loved him, but we barely survived growing up together in the same house. It was better to love him from afar. However, I did have home envy. His lawyer's salary paid well, and he didn't have the overhead costs I did from running the clinic.

At this time of night, the drive was quick and painless. Pulling into the parking lot of Lustz, which was filled, I was about to head for the private parking garage. That's where Mikhail, Tajah, their guests, and some key people parked. I would've done it, except I happened to glance toward the club's front door. I wasn't able to stop myself. It was Saturday night. I knew who would be on duty.

As I scanned for him, I was shocked to see not only Hoss but also Tajah and Mikhail standing out in front. However, what totally stunned me before morphing into pissed off was the fourth person standing there. Even in the dim light, I recognized his face. It was Flint. What the hell was he doing at the House of Lustz? And why was Tajah talking to him?

I stopped my car right where I was, which blocked in two other vehicles, but I didn't give a damn. I'd move it once I took care of the trash. Hopping out of it, I stormed toward the door and the quartet. They didn't see me until I was almost upon them.

Hoss's gaze met mine. I knew he was surprised to see me, but he hid it well. There was barely a flicker of his eyes. Flint was half-turned away from me. Mikhail was standing between him and Tajah, who was peeking around him. She wasn't happy.

"Would someone like to tell me what in the fuck is going on here? Why are you outside with this weasel?" I loudly demanded as I got closer.

Taj's gaze snapped up to meet mine. Mikhail gave

me an amused look. Hoss was partially scowling, but I got the feeling he wasn't upset with me. Flint whipped around to face me. The sight of him made me want to scream. What the fuck was he doing in town and here, of all places?

"There you are, babe. I've been trying to get inside this place to see you, but they said you weren't here. It sure looks like they lied. I've missed you." Flint smiled as he approached me.

He didn't make it more than a foot before Hoss placed his hulking self between us. While I appreciated he did it, I didn't need him or anyone else protecting me. I was a big girl. I could do it myself. I moved up until I was beside Hoss, and I could see the others again. I would've moved past Hoss, but his arm snaked out and hooked my hip. He pulled me so that I was brought flush against his side.

"Go with it," he whispered super softly out of the side of his mouth. Flint was distracted by Tajah pushing past him to stand by me on the other side. He didn't hear Hoss. I was lost. Go with what? Well, I found out moments later.

"No one lied. She just arrived. Cady is coming to see her man. She likes to do that sometimes, don't you, Cady Cat," Hoss said as he smiled down at me and squeezed.

The utter look of besottedness he was portraying momentarily left me thunderstruck and silent. I would've fallen at his feet if I didn't know it was an act for Flint's benefit. Damn, Hoss was good. He should've been an actor. Hoss almost had me convinced. They must've made up some lie to tell Flint. That was what Hoss meant by "go with it." Not wanting to ruin it, in case this whopper of a tale worked on the moron, I smiled back and tried to make my expression appear as adoring as Hoss's.

"I sure do, Sugar Bear. You know I can't stand to be away from you for too long. I get so lonely when you're gone." I didn't make my voice overly saccharine sweet, but I positively sounded way sweeter than I ever had with Flint the Loser. God, the day he left was still a great day for me. Why he didn't stay gone, I had no clue. Why come around after this long?

"You can't be with him!" Flint thundered.

"And why not?" I asked.

"Because we're together, Cady." He said it like he believed it and was incredulous I didn't.

"Flint, I have no clue what you've been smoking, shooting, or snorting, but whatever it is, stop. It's eating away your brain, and you don't have much to spare. You need enough to be able to breathe and keep your heart going at the same time. You kill a couple more cells, and that's not possible. Since you forgot, let me remind you. There is no us. There hasn't been for a long time," I snarked.

We watched as he went from confused to upset. "Don't give me that mouthy shit of yours. I'm not in the mood for it. As for us, we took a break like you asked for. It's been long enough. It's time to get back to what we were. Let's get out of here and head to your place where we can talk and be alone."

He reached his hand toward me. Before it even got halfway, Hoss had it trapped in his massive mitt of a hand. His giant paw engulfed Flint's and made his look like a toddler's. God, everything about the man was enormous, but it didn't make me fear him. I found him fascinating, which was something I had to battle.

"You don't touch her. Ever. I believe the lady has spoken, and she said there's no you and her. I understand losing someone as wonderful as Cady is hard, but you did. And I was the guy gifted with her heart. She's mine. Like I told you right before she came, I protect and keep what's mine. Now, I believe it's time for you to leave. Oh, and Reid, stay away from her. This is your only warning." The way Hoss glared at him, there was no way to miss the threat. It made me shiver, and he wasn't directing his basilisk stare my way.

I observed Flint drop his hand, step back, and then move away. As he did, he met my glare. "Cady, we need to talk. Call me. The phone number is the same."

Hoss growled and took a step toward him. Not wanting Hoss to end up in jail if he harmed the little shit, I grabbed his arm and clung to it for dear life. He barely slowed down. I was moving along with him. It was like I was a gnat on his sleeve. Flint took off running for his car. Finally, my pleading made Hoss halt. He squinted down at me. His anger eased, and a peek of humor broke through.

"Tiny, are you trying to stop me from killing that little irksome bug? Let me squish him under my shoe, and then we won't be bothered anymore."

I had to fight not to laugh at his description of my ex. "Hoss, if you touch him, he'll go to the cops. If you squish him, someone will find out and go to the cops. See the theme here? Maim and kill equals cops. Cops equal a locked-up Hoss. Hoss in a cage is bad," I said, being a smartass. I knew he wasn't dumb, but I bet many people thought he was, based on his size, so I played into it again.

"Oh, I get it, but I'm smarter than to get caught, Tiny. Unlike your ex, I have more than two brain cells. You sure upgraded when you got rid of him and got me," he smirked as he finished.

"Upgraded my ass. I now have three times as much male aggravation to deal with. It's a good thing I'm now a lesbian."

"Cady Cat, I can understand how Reid could drive a woman to change teams, but I can promise you, I can bring you solidly to at least a bisexual team. One time in my bed, and you'll never want to leave," Hoss assured me as he slowly ran his eyes up my body. I swore there was heat there.

Images of the things I wanted him to do to me in his bed had me hot all over. I felt tingles in my pussy and streaks of fire around my nipples. Christ, I had to escape before I did something beyond stupid. Like throwing myself in his arms and begging him to fuck me ten ways to Sunday. I wanted to know if that bulge in his pants the last time we saw each other was augmented or all him. I was pretty sure it was him. And if it was, God help me. I'd want to lick it like a lollipop or maybe an ice cream cone. *Cady, stop! You're drooling, and there are witnesses!*

It was challenging to pull my attention away from Hoss and focus on Tajah and Mikhail, who wore deeply amused looks. I thought I should get at least a medal or a gold star when I did. Kindergarten was so much more straightforward than being an adult.

"Would you care to tell me what I just walked in on?" I asked Taj. It was purely a diversion tool to give me time to sort my thoughts.

"Let's go upstairs where it's warm. I'm cold.

Misha, can someone come out and relieve Hoss? He should be there. It involves him more than us," she asked her man sweetly.

"Yeah, let's get you inside. Give me a second to call Reuben. He'll either do it himself or send one of the other security guys out."

"There's no need to pull Hoss away from his work or anyone else. You can fill me in, Tajah," I protested.

It did no good. Mikhail was on his phone within seconds, and I heard him say Reuben's name. I wondered if we could go inside before Reuben or someone else arrived. Maybe I'd get all the info from my best friend before Hoss was relieved and could join us. Then I'd make my escape. Coming here was a mistake. I knew Hoss worked tonight. What was I thinking?

Taj was telling me to let Mikhail handle it. I got so caught up in arguing with her that I was startled that only a minute passed after he hung up before the door opened, and out came Reuben and another guy. Frantic for an excuse to escape, I found one. "Wait, I'm blocking two cars. Let me go move my car."

I tried to turn to the parking lot, but Hoss held me hooked to his side. He shook his head. "Give me your keys," he ordered.

"I'm not giving you my keys!"

"I'm not trying to steal your wheels, Cady. Reub will put it in the private garage. I promise he won't put a scratch on it," Hoss swore.

"I can do it," I argued. I hoped he wouldn't hear the desperation in my voice.

"No, because I can see you tearing out of here and going home. I'm not stupid. Hand them over."

"Make me," I challenged.

It just came out, but the way heat flared in Hoss's eyes, I knew I'd done something wrong. I waited to see if he'd storm off or yell at me. He did neither. Instead, he leaned down to whisper in my ear.

"I can make you. Don't forget who's in charge, Tiny. Do you need your Sugar Bear to spank you or pet you?"

I was left speechless. A part of me wanted to smart off again, but another wanted to curl up and let him do either or both things. The warmth inside of me was rising and spreading. I had to get away from him. He was lethal. When I didn't say anything, Hoss smirked and dropped a kiss on the tip of my nose, chuckled, and said, "That's what I thought. Give me the keys, Cady Cat."

The next thing I knew, like a mindless zombie, I reached into my jacket pocket, took out my keys, and gave them to Hoss. He handed them off to Reuben, who I saw was grinning. I gave him the middle finger, but it only made the asshole laugh. Men. As soon as Reuben had my keys, we were on the move. Hoss guided me along. I tried to move away from him, but he held me clamped to his side. It wasn't until we got to the elevator that I was able to speak again.

"Can't find someone who'll let you paw them, so you think you can do it to me? Let go," I ordered, even though it was the last thing I wanted.

The infuriating man just raised an eyebrow and then turned to say something to Mikhail. I clenched my fist and jabbed him in the ribs with it. The bastard didn't even flinch or look back at me. I did it again, and he absentmindedly reached over with the hand not holding me to him and patted me on the top of the head!

What the fuck was I? A two-year-old or a dog?

My anger pushed aside my arousal, and I reacted without thinking. I lifted my hand and zeroed in on his nipple under his shirt. I had no idea how I found it so unerringly, but I did. I pinched down and then twisted. I heard Tajah gasp. Mikhail stopped talking. As for Hoss, he drew in a sharp breath. At the same time, the elevator door opened to the third floor.

"You go ahead. We'll be there in a minute," Hoss said calmly.

I saw Tajah's uneasy look as they got out. The door slid shut, and then Hoss pushed a button. The elevator stayed in place, but the door remained closed. I was trapped, and I had no idea what he'd do to me. I braced myself. I'd been slapped around by men before. I survived those times. I'd survive this one.

He swung me so my back was to the wall, and he towered over me. His arms trapped me in place. "Acting like a brat and having a tantrum isn't pretty, Cady. If you want my attention, all you have to do is ask. There's no need to misbehave. Good girls get good things. Bad girls get punished. I think you need to learn that."

I was scared, but I'd never let him see it. I thrust out my chin. "I don't throw tantrums. Maybe if you listened to me or picked up on cues, I wouldn't have resorted to twisting your nipple. But go ahead, do it," I challenged.

"Do what exactly?"

"You said I needed to be punished. Do it. Get it over with. Hit me. Throw me around by my hair. Slap me," I egged him on. I had no idea why, but my mouth was out of control. It often was when I was faced with a situation like this. The wise thing to do would be to stay quiet, but it was impossible.

His breath hissed out of him, and then he lowered his head until he stared intently into my eyes. I saw anger in his. I braced myself. If I survived whatever he dished out, I'd make sure never to be where he could touch me again. I had to have lost my mind to do this to a man like him. He could kill me with one blow from his fist if he put his power behind it. My knees were weak, and my mouth was dry. I locked my legs to keep them from shaking visibly.

"Who the fuck has done those things to you? I want names," he snarled.

I gulped. I tried to look away, but he grasped my chin to hold my head there. His touch was gentle, totally at odds with the fury on his face. I didn't say anything.

"Cadence, I asked you a question. I expect an answer. Who has done those things to you? And why?"

"You know why. I just did it. I'm mouthy. I smart off, and I push too much. Guys get tired of that. And when I don't behave, they get upset. I'm too much for them to tolerate. As for whom, I'd rather not say." My voice was too wispy for my liking. Where was the smart-mouthed ballsy bitch who stood up no matter what? Even if she knew it would end up with her getting beaten or worse.

He closed his eyes and took several deep breaths before he opened them again. "I want you to listen to me very carefully. No one has the right to abuse you, Cady. Some punishments and funishments are corrective but mutually acceptable. If they're not, then they should never occur. Slapping you, throwing you by your hair, or hitting you is a hard fucking no. I would never do that to you. Would I find ways to tame down some of your tendencies to be bratty sometimes? Absolutely, but you'd never be afraid or harmed. Those guys who've told you that you're too much, you should've told them if you're too much to go find less. They weren't the men for you. They don't know how to handle you, Tiny."

His voice was soft and soothing. I felt entranced by it. I found myself whispering back to him. I no longer feared he was about to get physical with me in an ugly or painful way. "And how should they have handled me?"

"Give you the sweet with the corrective. My Tiny Brat needs to be petted, celebrated, and given rules. To know she's safe."

I snorted. "Yeah, like a man could stand to stick around and put up with my moods and temper long-term. No man wants or needs that."

"Your brattiness doesn't turn me off. It doesn't scare me. It doesn't intimidate me. And it sure as fuck doesn't make me want to run," he countered instantly.

"Then what does it do?"

"It makes me want to get scratched by you, Cady Cat, but only long enough for me to make you purr and let me play with you. Oh, and this."

And bam, as those last words registered, he sealed his mouth to mine, and I knew what people meant when they said the earth stood still for the first time in my life. His lips were pressed firmly to mine, but not too hard. My lips weren't painfully ground against my teeth. He kissed me, altering the pressure a couple of times before his tongue joined the party. He didn't try to force it between my lips like most guys did. He teased my lips, tickling them with the tip. I willingly opened my mouth so I could feel him do the same thing inside. Plus, my tongue wanted to play. When mine touched his, he groaned softly and pressed his mouth a tiny bit harder to mine. A small battle, a wrestling contest, broke out. It was a tongue wrestling match. Our tongues twined together and tasted the other's dark, moist home. It was hands down the sexiest kiss I'd ever had. Period. It was the best kiss of my life.

I didn't know what to do. I was drowning, and I didn't want to save myself. There was no way he was real. Men didn't put up with women like me. I'd found that out more than once or twice. Men didn't stick around for me. I tried to change, but I couldn't. This thought had me pulling away from him, though I hated ending our kiss. I stared up at him.

"Hoss, we're not doing this. Whatever game you're playing, I'm not. Don't kiss me again," I warned him.

He slowly straightened. Poor man, his back had to be broken from bending that low. His expression was dead serious when he answered. "Cady, I'm not playing a fucking game. I see I have a lot of work to do to undo the damage your previous lovers have done. Believe me when I say I can do it, and I will. I'll let you think about that, and we'll discuss it again soon. However, now, we need to rejoin our friends and get you up to speed on what that jackass was doing here. I need details."

He leaned over and pushed the button without waiting for me to respond. The elevator door slid open, and I was guided out into the hallway, then toward Tajah and Mikhail's home. I was too stunned to do anything other than follow.

Hoss: Chapter 5

Four damn days and I was losing my mind. I couldn't wait any longer. The discussion on Saturday night in Mikhail and Tajah's apartment hadn't gone how I had hoped. Sure, we filled Cady in on what happened before she got there. She let it be known loudly and clearly that there was no understanding between her and Reid. She wanted nothing to do with him, which made me extremely happy.

What was less satisfying was that she wouldn't tell us, or more like me, what he did to her when they were together. The way she avoided the questions and her taunt in the elevator told me he was likely one of more than a few who had gotten physical with her. I wasn't talking about the mutually agreed-upon physical punishments and funishments I would do. Those men tried to outright beat the brattiness out of her. The thought of it made me see red every time.

Not everyone was equipped to deal with a brat like her. I got that. However, doing those things to try and stop it was ridiculous. I would never want to change her that much. If I did, it would eliminate a part of her that attracted me. Most people would say I was crazy to want her. If so, then I was crazy. In my book, it was stimulating and would keep things from becoming stale and boring. Again, my need to be stimulated most of the time was the likely culprit. Whatever the cause,

I'd embraced that need years ago. I was who I was. I had to allow the woman I was with to be who she was.

And there was zero doubt that Cady was the woman for me. The kiss we shared in the elevator had blown my mind. It took all my strength not to strip her bare and take her there. Only my desire to show her care and, for our first or hundredth time, not to be rushed had stopped me. She broke our kiss, but I was the one to let it remain broken.

By the time we finished talking at the apartment, I had to get back to work. Cady insisted she was tired and wanted to go home. Tajah tried to convince her to stay the night, but she refused. While they were talking, Mikhail told me to follow her home. He would have me replaced at the front door for the rest of the night. He knew me well. The idea of her driving alone at night didn't sit well with me. To do it without her knowing, I said goodbye and left before she did. Ten minutes later, when she pulled out of the private garage, I was waiting on the street to follow. I hung back, but I ensured she safely made it into her place. I scanned the neighborhood, just in case dickhead Flint Reid was lurking there. I had news for him. He didn't want me to be his enemy.

My gut told me Reid wouldn't stay away from Cady. Since I wasn't able to be with her twenty-four seven, first thing the next day, I made a call to the guy who oversaw security for my business and home. I trusted no one to look out for her other than him and his people if I couldn't. Iker Sullivan and I met by accident several years ago. We'd instantly hit it off, and after checking into and getting to know him, I hired his company to provide all my security. He did a variety of different kinds, including personal bodyguards. I typically didn't need that. I was more than capable of taking care of myself. But I was glad he did so that he could put people on Cady.

Mikhail chuckled when I told him there was no need for Bratva soldiers to keep an eye on her anymore. Iker's people would do that. I wasn't forgetting about the break-in at the clinic. I thanked him for doing it, but it was my job. Of course, he had a few things to say about that, busting my chops for wanting Cady. He did the protective thing and threatened me if I hurt her. I assured him it wasn't happening.

Iker was in my office now, sitting across from me. We were in the comfy visiting chairs, as I called them. He was giving me a personal update on Cady. Although, I knew his real reason was to tease me about her. It wasn't as if he didn't send me an update daily.

"Hoss, I get it. I saw her picture. Damn, she's a fox. I wouldn't mind following her everywhere, and my guys sure don't either."

"Iker, I swear to God. If you or one of your whorehounds try to make a move on Cady, I'll rip your heads off, shit down your necks, and shove your heads up your asses," I menaced.

His laughter was loud. A growl slipped out of me. Before I was able to stand up, he held up his hands in surrender.

"I'm just fucking with you. Christ, remind me not to do that with a territorial man. I swear. No one is after your woman. But to be clear, she is hot as hell, and if you weren't staking a claim, I know others who would. My people said she's feisty. The way she went after the delivery guy for throwing her package on the porch was a sight to see, they said. She had him running for his truck. She said if she caught him doing it again, she'd shove the box up his ass."

I grinned. Yeah, that sounded like my Cady Cat. I might not know her exceptionally well yet, but I knew that was totally her. "She is feisty, and I found that men in her past haven't appreciated her. They've been physically abusive to her." My grin was gone, recalling that.

He frowned. "And the one you told me about, Reid, was he one of those?"

"She wouldn't say, but I think so. I tried to get her to tell me names, but she clammed up on me. I'll get it out of her someday. When I do, those bastards better watch out."

"You know how I feel about abusing people, in particular women and kids. If you need or want some help, call me," Iker requested.

"I'll keep it in mind. Mikhail is right there with you. His woman and mine are best friends. He tried to get some details from Tajah about the men in Cady's past, but she's close-lipped. Either it's girl code, or Cady never told her about the abusive shit. Was there anything suspicious at the clinic last night?"

"Nope. She did stay until about nine-thirty. Your girl kept the lights all on. When she left, it was straight home. My guy walked the perimeter after she was inside and settled to be sure all the windows and doors were secured. I know you don't want her to know about us, but wouldn't it be better? I'd hate for her to spot one of them and call the cops."

"If I tell her, she'll argue, try to run them off, and probably for sure call the cops. Mikhail had Bratva guys watching until you took over."

"Christ, only you would have Bratva *boyeviks* watching over your lady." He snorted.

I'd been around Mikhail enough to know that *boyeviks* was the term for gunmen, warriors, or fighters. In the Russian Mafia, they were soldiers.

"Believe me, I never thought about it. Mikhail isn't officially a part of it, but his family does come through if he needs it."

"Oh, I'm not knocking it. Only a fool would go up against any of those guys. Was there anything you wanted me to do differently with Cady's protection detail? If so, hit me with it."

"As a matter of fact, there is. I only want ugly, married men who're impotent watching her. I'd say women are fine, too, as long as they're not lesbians. I don't need more people panting after her," I joked, though if you listened to my tone and looked at my face, it would appear as if I was totally serious.

Iker burst out, guffawing. He slapped his thigh. "Good luck with that, buddy. It's not fucking happening. It'll do you good if you have to worry. It'll make you bring your A+ game with her. From the sound of it, you'll need it. Leave it up to you to find someone perfect for your desires."

He was familiar with my lifestyle when it came to personal matters. I didn't hide my membership to Lustz or what my kinks were from those I considered friends. He was one of them. He wasn't vanilla either, although I hadn't gotten him to come to check out the House of Lustz so far. He was intrigued, though, so I knew one day he would.

"So, have you had any success in nailing her

down? I have to admit. I've never seen you so into a woman. This is a lot to go through for someone you want to have for a bit. I know you said she's not just a plaything. However, the others you've gone after to be more than a plaything you've never done this for in the past. Is it because she's the only one to resist?"

His assumption took me aback, but then it dawned on me. I never went into full detail about what I wanted with Cady. I told him I wanted her and that she was in danger, but that was all.

"Iker, Cady isn't anything temporary. She's it. I'm ninety-five percent certain she's the woman for me. Yes, she's resisting, but if what I suspect is true about the men in her past, then it's no wonder. She doesn't trust. Hell, she even lashed out at Tajah a few months back when she got with Mikhail, telling her he'd hurt her. Cady Anderson is going to be my wife."

His mouth fell open, and he stared at me in shock. He was silent for at least a minute before saying anything. "Fuck, why the hell didn't you tell me that!? I got you want her, and you're worried. But to know you already think you'll marry her shines a different light. I wouldn't have teased you like I did. I'm lucky to be alive."

"I thought I did, but I realized I didn't. The only thing I can see ruining that is if she absolutely hates my lifestyle."

"How likely do you think that will be?"

"Not very. I tested it out the other night, and she responded beautifully. She'll have to get used to me, we'll set up the parameters of our relationship, and she'll have to discover I won't deviate from what I promise. Once she does that, I can make her fall in love with me."

"You seem so doubtless. How?"

"Because I refuse to let anything else happen. Short of Cady hating me, I can give her her heart's desire, not just in monetary ways. I'll give her love, security, peace of mind, and more. She'll be the prima donna of my world."

"Beware what you wish for. A prima donna can be very demanding," he warned.

"They can, and she'll learn how far she can push me on that front just as I'll discover where the line is with her."

"Well, I wish you luck. Keep me informed. Now, I've got to meet her. Tie her down soon so I can. And if she's all that and has a single friend, tell her to introduce me," Iker said with a wink.

After a few minutes more of idle chitchat, he informed me he had to get back to work. I did, too. Walking him out the door, I mulled over what he said and asked about Cady. I wanted to speed up the process. It was time to stop sitting back and waiting. I was about to begin the courtship of my Cady Cat.

♣ ♣ ♣

My chance came the next night. Mikhail had a Halloween party at Lustz every year. People found it fun to dress up even more than usual. Costumes weren't unusual to see at Lustz throughout the year, but this night, more people participated. The whole night wasn't spent down in the club. For those Mikhail invited, they'd join him upstairs for a private party. I'd held out hope that Tajah would get Cady to attend. I knew Reuben, me, and a few others would be there.

Carver and Tajah's mom, Tamara, and her boyfriend, Gideon, were attending this year. I wasn't sure who else. It was my night off, so I wouldn't miss it no matter what.

I got the call I'd been praying for from Mikhail around three that afternoon. "Hey, what's up?" I asked when I answered my phone.

"I thought you might want to know that Cady will be here in an hour. She's helping Tajah get things set up for the party. She's attending. Taj made her promise. Everyone else isn't due until seven, but if you want to come over early, feel free." I heard the teasing in his tone.

"Have I told you lately what a fantastic boss and awesome friend you are?"

He laughed. "No, but you can start bowing and kissing my ass daily to make sure I don't forget it."

"Hold on, ass-kissing is Tajah's job. I'm not into that kind of kink," I jested back.

We baited each other back and forth a few more times before I got earnest. "I'll be over. I just need to grab my stuff, and I'll be there. Do you need me to bring anything?"

"Not that I know of. Tajah insisted she has it all under control."

"Then see you within the hour. Thanks."

"You're welcome. Later."

Mikhail used to hire someone to decorate and prepare food for his parties. That was a thing of the past. Tajah loved to do it and had a knack for decorating and cooking. I knew if it was a huge party, he'd put his foot down and make her accept help, but they hadn't run into that situation so far.

I'd brought my costume to work, intending to change before heading there. Since I was going early, I'd wait and change at the apartment later. Before leaving, I checked in with Alicia Ann in case something needed my attention. It didn't, thankfully. I wished her and others I ran into a good night and to stay safe. Some had small kids and would be taking them out. Others had parties of their own to attend.

Most people would think I'd hate to give up Lustz and Mikhail's parties to take kids trick-or-treating, but they'd be wrong. I looked forward to doing it with my children one day. It would be fun to pass out candy and help them figure out their costumes and all those great things.

The whole way there, I tried to picture what Cady's costume would be. I asked Mikhail before we hung up, but he said he had no clue. I parked in the private garage and rode the elevator up to their apartment. I'd texted Mikhail when I got there to see where he was. He said to go straight up. As I walked to the door, I noticed my insides were quivering with anticipation. I was dying to see Cady and spend time with her. I only hoped she wouldn't try to ignore me.

I knocked on the door and waited for someone to answer. About thirty seconds later, it swung open. My heart jumped. It was Cady. She gave me a hesitant smile, stepped back, and waved for me to enter.

"Hello, Tiny," I casually said as I passed her. The urge to reach out and touch her was almost overwhelming. I knew that by calling her Tiny, she'd have something to say, so I counted on it. She didn't disappoint. Her slight smile changed to a frown.

"Why do you keep calling me that? It's annoying.

Not everyone can be a damn giant."

"I'm not a giant, darlin'. I just ate all my veggies like a good boy growing up."

She snorted. "You haven't been a good boy a day in your life, Hoss."

I leaned closer. "I can show you how good I can be, Cady. I promise it'll change your world."

There was the ever-slightest hesitancy before she rolled her eyes and smarted off. "Don't bother to make promises you can't keep. Men always say that, and they always disappoint me. I won't hold my breath."

She shut the door and walked toward the kitchen. I followed her, my bag thrown over my shoulder. With her back to me, she missed me checking her out. Cady was super petite compared to most people but minuscule next to me. I typically went for taller and larger-built women, but there was something about her I wasn't able to resist.

She was maybe five feet two or three inches tall. I'd describe her as a pocket Venus. Despite her lack of height, she was generously curved in all the right places. Cady reminded me of the old movies with Elizabeth Taylor in them when she was young. Her hair wasn't black but rather a chestnut brown. The kind that had a deep reddish color to it and it was thick. My hands itched to sink into it and hang on. I'd only seen it in a braid, but it was to her waist. Her face was a classic oval. Her skin was a warm ivory color. Her skin and hair set off her medium steel-gray eyes. The swell of her hips, an ass you could fill your hands with, and tits that I had no doubt would overflow my huge hands was irresistible.

I was snapped out of my contemplation when she abruptly swung around to face me. I hoped my expression was guiltless. "Why're you here so early? The party isn't for several hours."

"I asked him to come and hang out with me. We're at you ladies' disposal if you need extra hands," Mikhail chimed in from the other hallway.

"Oh, well, it's your place, but I don't think we'll need help. Taj and I have it under control. Who all is coming to this thing, anyway?"

"Close friends and a few family members. Not a huge crowd. Most are the ones who come every year," he added.

"I just don't see you having a Halloween party, Mikhail. Dressing up in costumes and stuff seems, I don't know, childish."

"Dressing up can be fun. You should try it more often," Tajah said as she entered the kitchen. She came to me and wrapped her arms around me. We'd become close. I squeezed her close and dropped a kiss on her forehead.

"What did I tell you about kissing my woman?" Mikhail asked in his growly tone.

"Hey, there was no lip contact, and my hands aren't on her ass," I reminded him.

Mikhail was possessive of Tajah, and I couldn't blame him. However, he knew I meant nothing by it. He just liked to whip up an argument with me.

"Good thing, or you'd be dead," he reminded me.

"Oh, stop it. You know Hoss doesn't see me that way," Taj objected.

"He'd be the first guy who didn't think all women were fair game," Cady muttered.

I wasn't about to let that remark go unnoticed. "Cady Cat, you need to realize that not all men are bastards. If your experiences have been with guys like that Flint Reid, I can see how you would get the wrong idea. I guarantee you that when men like Mikhail and I find the woman of our dreams, we have no need or desire to look at or touch other women. We're faithful."

"So where is this paragon you're in love with? Is she coming tonight?" she snarked.

"As a matter of fact, she'll be here."

My answer shook her. I saw uncertainty spark in her gaze, and then it was gone. I would wait to clue her into the fact that she was that woman. "Whatever. Taj, we have more stuff to get done if we're going to have time to get dressed ourselves. Let's finish this up."

As they went to the fridge, Mikhail waved me to follow him. We ended up in his home office. Once the door was shut, he started to chuckle.

"When are you planning to let Cady know she's the one you want? I don't think she liked your admission out there about your woman being here tonight. I almost laughed." He went to the cabinet where he kept a bottle of Scotch and glasses. He took them out and poured us each a finger of liquor. Taking mine, I raised it.

"Here's to winning the woman of my dreams."

He added to the toast. "And doing it without her killing you." We both laughed before swallowing it down. I was ready for the chase and then the capture.

ஃ ஃ ஃ

Mikhail and I did help with a few things, mostly reaching items too high for them to manage. He made Tajah promise not to climb on chairs or anything to get stuff. He was worried she'd fall and hurt herself. I was of the same mind when it came to Cady. So when

I walked in and caught her standing on the counter to reach a bowl high in the upper cabinet, I expressed my displeasure. Tajah wasn't in there.

I walked up behind her. She didn't see or hear me coming. I grasped her hips, causing her to gasp and jerk. Her head spun to the side, and her mouth opened when she spotted me. She didn't say anything. I picked her up and sat her on the floor. I didn't let go of her.

"I catch you doing that shit again, and I'll warm that ass in a way you won't like, Tiny," I vowed. The sight of her up there had scared me. All I could picture was her falling and cracking her head open.

"Hoss, you're not my boss, and I'll do what I want."

"Then I don't want to hear a bitch out of you when you get spanked. You've been warned. I don't get it. Mikhail told Tajah not to be climbing. Why would you think it's okay for you to do it?"

"Because I don't belong to him. Taj might go along with his demands, but I don't have to."

"You do mine. No climbing. Ask."

"If you say so," was her bratty reply.

I didn't bother to argue. I wanted Cady to defy me. She'd find out I didn't say what I didn't mean. I lifted the bowl down and left her to do whatever she was doing. That was an hour ago. Cady and Taj had gone to get ready in the master bedroom not long after that. I used one of the guest bedrooms, and Mikhail occupied a third. Being men, we didn't take long to get dressed. Women loved to primp, although neither needed to do anything to enhance their beauty or sex appeal.

I was in the living room, and Mikhail was coming down the hallway when the doorbell rang. I was closer, so I moseyed over to answer it. It was a few minutes before seven. I tried to shut the door when I saw who it was. Reuben stuck his foot inside to block it. Behind him was Carver.

"If you make me get scuff marks on the door, Tajah will kick your ass," Reub warned me. Sighing as if it hurt to do it, I eased it open.

"Fine. I don't want Tajah upset. But I need to speak to her and Mikhail about their taste in friends," I joked.

As he walked in, he punched me in the gut and then kept walking. Carver gave me a hesitant smile. I knew him from playing doorman, but he was quiet and didn't say much. This was only the second time I'd be near him in a social setting.

"Ah, good. Someone is here. Welcome," Mikhail greeted them. Before closing the door, I saw more people coming up the hallway from the elevator. I wondered who put them on the elevator since you couldn't come up without a keycard unless Mikhail or Tajah had given them one. It was Tamara and Gideon.

"Hello, Hoss. It's good to see you again," Tamara said sweetly as they reached me.

I shook hands with Gideon and smiled at her. "It's good to see the both of you again, too."

Seeing no one else, I closed the door. Mikhail was playing host, getting drinks for everyone, while I was checking out how everyone was dressed. According to Mikhail, the plan was to have drinks and dinner, and then we'd go check out the club and see what it was like.

I was examining the costumes the others had on. Mikhail was dressed as a werewolf but not in a whole-body fur costume—no way he'd want anyone to mistake him for a furry. Mikhail was a primal, not into the furry kink, although some patrons were. He had a hood with ears, claw gloves, and tight pants. His chest was left bare, which I figured Tajah requested. Gideon was dressed like a man from the Roaring Twenties, and Tamara was a Flapper. Reuben was dressed as a pirate. In our cases, the costumes tended to lean more toward the sexier side. They would be nothing compared to some of the ones in the club.

Carver's outfit was what I recognized as steampunk, with tight brown leather pants and a belt slung across his chest. He wore a shirt, but it was unbuttoned and tucked into his pants. I was impatiently waiting to see what Cady had on. Where were they? Mikhail got a call before I could ask him if we should check on them. I heard him saying to send them up, so there had to be more guests. I tried to listen to the others' remarks about their costumes as he went to the door to wait.

"Hoss, I love your costume. You look like you're ready to tame something," Tamara said with a chuckle.

"Oh, I wouldn't say tame—more like handle someone. Thank you. You and Gideon look great in yours."

Voices drew our attention to the front door. Matvey, Mikhail's cousin, the Bratva *pahkan*, boss, and his wife, Victoria, walked in. Mikhail chuckled at his second cousin's outfit. He was dressed as a knight, and Victoria as a lady of that period. I went to greet them.

"Damn, if only I had the body to dress like you guys. Damn, that's it, Vick, we're leaving," Matvey groused good-naturedly.

She was smiling at us. "If you try to leave and not

let me innocently drool and see what Misha's club is like, I'll cut you, Mat. I've been dying to see it for so long." Matvey rolled his eyes as he smiled at her.

"Sorry, we're late. We had a costume snafu, but we're here now," Tajah called out behind us.

I turned, and when I caught sight of Cady, my breath stalled, and my heart skipped a beat. Christ, this had to be fate for her to be dressed the way she was. Standing there in a skintight black leather jumpsuit, with ears on her head and stiletto boots on her feet with cleavage to lead a man to sin, was my very own catwoman. Her hair was down in a thick wave to her ass. Her eyes were made up dramatically, and her lips were a shiny red. I dropped my hands so my erection, which was quickly growing, wouldn't be noticed.

Cady: Chapter 6

I procrastinated as long as possible, berating myself for choosing the costume I did. I knew when Hoss saw it, he'd think I wore it because of him. And he wouldn't be wrong, not that I wanted him to know it. Or maybe I did. God, the man had me all mixed up. I wasn't sure if I was coming or going.

Earlier, when he plucked me off the counter and threatened to spank me if I did it again, I'd flushed hot all over. It took restraint not to climb up again to see if he'd carry out his threat. The thought of his hands on my ass made me tremble. I'd been a mess getting ready still thinking about it. I didn't know how to take him.

Several minutes were bought when the zipper on Tajah's outfit got stuck, and I had to work it back on the track. She was dressed as a hot Red Riding Hood. I knew Mikhail was going as a werewolf. It played perfectly into their primal hunter and prey personalities. Taking in those around the room, I couldn't look away from Hoss. Oh my God, I needed a bath in ice water to cool me off.

Hoss's dark espresso skin gleamed, including his flawlessly bare head. The man had to wax it off or remove it with a laser because there was no stubble. A thin, faint goatee of dark hair outlined his mouth. His chiseled face was topped by the darkest brown, almost black eyes. He wore tall black boots that hit below his knees. Tucked into them were tight black leather pants belted around his waist with a whip curled up and secured at his side. He had a red sleeveless ringmaster jacket with a black lapel and gold buttons on his upper half. It was unbuttoned. Underneath was nothing but his bare skin. I salivated at the sight of his skin bulging with muscles. He had mostly black-and-gray tats on his arms and chest, with some having a silvery metallic shine. In his hand was a black top hat. I fought not to let out a purr and rub up against him like a cat in heat.

"Go lick him," Tajah whispered. I wanted to smack her. She'd been questioning me the whole time we got ready about Hoss and what I thought of him —asking if he would be someone I'd consider dating. I kept telling her no, but she knew me better than anyone. She knew I was lying out of my ass.

If there were a way to guarantee I wouldn't be hurt and left like a nuisance or worse, I'd be tempted. However, my experiences taught me that I wasn't what men wanted. They might have thought so in the beginning, but as time passed, they came to hate me and want to change me. I was never good enough the way I was.

"Shh," I hissed at her.

The voices of everyone else washed over me. I vaguely responded to greetings, but I was mesmerized when Hoss came stalking toward me. There was no other word for it. He stalked. My body was on fire and vibrating inside. Shit, I should've never come here. There was no way I'd survive this—not with Hoss here. I should've run for cover, but I remained there frozen. When he reached me, I looked up his towering frame. When our eyes met, I swore his eyes were blazing with fire. His pink tongue slipped out to moisten his lips. I held in my groan by the skin of my teeth. He ran his gaze up and down my body.

"Cady Cat, you look beyond incredible. Christ, that outfit is you." His voice was deep and growly.

"Thank you. You don't look bad yourself. Where is she?"

"Who?"

"You said the woman you want would be here tonight. Where is she?" I was desperately grasping at any line to save myself. Reminding myself he had someone would do the trick.

His puzzlement changed to mirth. "Oh, you'll see. Later. Let's join the others."

The next fifteen minutes were a blur. I spoke to Tamara, who was like a mom to me. From her, I was passed to the next person. The last one I came up to was my brother, who was frowning.

"Hi, big brother. You're looking good. I love your costume. Are you alright? What's up with that frown? Tonight is supposed to be fun."

"Please tell me you're here for the private party, and then you're headed home."

I blinked in confusion. Carver sounded upset. "I was planning to stay the whole time. Tajah has been asking me for weeks, and I promised I'd join them tonight. Why?"

"Because you shouldn't be there. This isn't the place for you."

"Carver, what's the big deal? Are you afraid I'll see what you like? What difference does it make? You're an adult. Tajah has seen you. It's not any different. Surely, you know I won't judge you."

"I'm not afraid of you judging me."

"Okay, then what?"

He didn't get a chance to reply. He was called over to Gideon. I'd like to say that was the end of it, but it wasn't. While we enjoyed each other's company and had a drink before we went to sit down to dinner, the conversation flowed, and the rest acted relaxed, except for Carver. Hoss wasn't tense, but he was acting very alert for some reason. I guessed it was the anticipation of seeing his woman later.

The thought of her made my appetite flee. There was no way I wanted to see the perfect specimen it would take to capture a man like him. I bet she was a damn supermodel. The fact he flirted with me when he had someone angered me. As time came nearer to head downstairs, I considered how to make an excuse and leave, or I was until Carver set my back up.

We were all gathering to go down as a group. It was still relatively early, but we were assured plenty of people would be there. I'd gone to check my hair and makeup with the other three women. I was pretending I was all excited to go, but I was frantically trying to think of an excuse not to. As we neared the men, Carver snagged my arm and pulled me to the side. He was scowling harder than earlier.

"Carver, what in the world is wrong with you?"

"You can't go down there!"

"I told you. I don't care what you do sexually. As long as I don't have to watch you do it in front of me, we're fine." I scoffed. I tried to pull my arm loose, but he hung onto it. He shook it lightly.

"I don't give a fuck about that! I'm not having my sister dressed like this being ogled and hit on by the guys and some women down there. No way. If you want to go, then change into regular clothes. And stick next to me. No wandering off on your own," he ordered.

Any thought of ducking out flew out the window. My hackles went up. I was pissed.

"I don't know what bug crawled up your ass, but you'd better get it out right this second, or I'll dig it out with my boot. How dare you? I'm a grown-ass woman. I can go wherever I want and do whatever I want. Who cares if someone finds me attractive? It's not like I'm going to fuck them there under your nose," I said in outrage.

"Goddamn it, hush. You better not dare cause a scene. I'm trying to look out for you, Cady. Starting something with someone here will only end in disaster. It always does. You can't be in a relationship. Don't raise expectations only to let the guy down. I don't want you to get hurt again. I heard Flint is back. Don't you remember how that ended?"

Tears pricked my eyes. To have my brother throw back in my face how I always ended up hurt and was never able to keep a guy stung. It stung worse than if he'd punched me. My barriers were rising, and I was about to blast him, but I was stopped short by the arrival of Hoss. He came to stand next to me. I was afraid to meet his eyes in case he overheard what Carver said.

His hand cupped my chin, and he lifted it so I had no choice but to meet his gaze. "Why don't you go make sure Tajah is ready to go, Cady Cat? I need to speak to your brother for a minute before we head downstairs."

Glancing at Carver, I noted his warning look. That decided it. I smiled at Hoss. "I think I will. Take your time."

As I walked off, I heard Carver hiss my name, but I ignored him. I had no idea what Hoss wanted to speak to him about, and I didn't care—as long as I was free to move away from my infuriating brother before I punched him in the face. Who was he to talk? He wasn't in a committed relationship. His had all ended for one reason or another. He was no one to throw aspersions on mine. He might've had a few last longer, but so what? He acted as if I was the poster child for fucked-up relationships. He had no room to talk. Both of us had shit that shaped us into the people we were. If he kept it up, I'd have to remind him. As I arrived beside Tajah, she gave me a sympathetic look and wound her arm around mine. I felt a slight, comforting squeeze as she whispered to me.

"Forget Carver. You know how he is, Cady. I want you to enjoy tonight. I'm excited and scared to show you Lustz."

"I'm trying. He's such a pain sometimes. You know what? We're going to forget him. Let's go. Show me this den of sin your man has enticed you into." I grinned.

She giggled. "Damn, I need my notebook. I like that. Den of Sin. Hmm."

Her eyes got this far away, unfocused look. I knew what it meant. She had a story or scene idea. Before she could wander off and begin writing, I tugged on her arm and yelled.

"Danger! Danger! Hurry! Taj is getting a scene in her head. She's gonna write," I cried out frantically as I pulled on her arm.

Her mom, Carver, Mikhail, and I knew what that meant, even if the others didn't. Carver was busy, though, in an intense argument with Hoss, so he didn't comment. Tamara and Mikhail reacted.

"Go, go!" Tamara said as she got behind Taj, lightly pushed on her back, and aimed for the door. Mikhail swooped in and wrapped her in his arms.

"You're coming with us, Sweetest Dove. I promise you can write tomorrow."

Tajah was laughing as she protested. "Stop it! I'm not that bad. What will Reub, Hoss, Matvey, and Victoria think? They'll believe I'm crazy."

"*Dorogoy*, sweetheart, what makes you *bezumnyy*, crazy, isn't your desire to write. It's attaching yourself to my cousin. I knew you were mad when he was able to capture a woman like you. You're like my Victoria. I have no idea how I was ever so fortunate to find a mad woman to love me." He gave his wife a tender look. She raised on her tiptoes while he lowered his head. They kissed. Seeing them so in love after many years of marriage was beautiful and depressing. What would it be like to have that?

There was lots of clamorous laughing and commenting as we moved out of the apartment and down the hallway to the elevator. I anxiously waited for it to arrive, and then, as we got inside it. I was waiting for Carver and Hoss to appear. The doors were sliding shut when a large hand blocked them. I stared up at Hoss as he got in. My brother wasn't with him. Shit. I went to get out, but Hoss prevented me by grasping my arm.

He leaned down to quietly whisper in my ear, "He's fine. He'll be down in a few minutes. I swear. I didn't touch him. I just told him a few truths. You need to relax and have fun tonight, Tiny. Please, truly see what Lustz is like. Ask questions. We'll take you through the whole tour. I want you to understand what it is and what it means."

There was a begging quality to his tone. It puzzled me. "Why are you so anxious for me to understand the club?"

"Tour first, then I'll explain later. Just keep an open mind."

I don't know what made me do it, but rather than argue with him, I merely nodded and said, "I'll be open."

"Thank you, Cady."

Our arrival on the first floor prevented me from saying more. It was time. We exited, and to my surprise, we were taken to the front of the building. We started where Hoss usually stood. The tour began. We started with the spiel about the doorman's role by Hoss, to my surprise, and moved inside to the person who greeted patrons and ensured they had the correct beads on their wrists. Tajah had explained the color system to me before. But it was still fascinating to see and hear more. Those of us who didn't have one—meaning me, Tamara, Gideon, Matvey, and Victoria, were issued a bracelet. They had a white bead and an orange one. We were told to put them on our right wrists.

The woman behind the desk explained the code. By having both those on the right, we were saying we were observers only with the white and unwilling to play now with the orange. Those beads had other meanings if worn on the left wrist. It seemed once you were a patron, most wore two bracelets. At least Mikhail, Carver, and Hoss did. I snuck a peek at the ones on Hoss's wrists. I wanted to grill him about their meanings, but I didn't. I'd ask Tajah to go through the color system later. I found I was dying to know what kinks he had. His confession out front that he was more than an employee had stunned me. I don't know why it surprised me he was.

From there, we were taken through the first floor. This floor was a vast, elegant bar with a large dance floor. There was music playing and people dancing. Patrons and guests could hang out and talk, dance, and drink here. It was explained they didn't necessarily play or observe every time a patron came. Many felt it was a comfortable place to socialize and to meet like-minded individuals to have conversations.

We were about fifteen minutes into the tour when Carver joined us. He didn't say a word. His face didn't appear angry. It was more contemplative. I wanted to ask if he was alright, but he avoided me, so I stayed away.

After we were shown the first floor and its various amenities, Mikhail explained, "If you want to observe others at play or if you desire to participate in scenes, you have to move to the second floor, although only those who haven't had alcohol can play."

We took the stairs to the second level. The place was crowded. The patrons had embraced the costume idea. However, in their cases, many were very skimpy outfits. Unlike many women, my skintight getup covered most of my skin. We were getting more than a fair share of glances. Many were curious, some interested, and others appeared upset. I ignored the men ogling us. I didn't care what they did as long as they left me alone. What did bother me was how some women were staring at the men.

Their eyes ate them up. I saw coveting glances

thrown at all the men. Matvey was the oldest in his sixties but still a fit and magnetic man. Carver was my brother, but I wasn't blind to his good looks. He'd had girls and then women chasing him for as long as I could recall. Mikhail, while not my type, was sexy and good-looking, the same with Reuben. That didn't bother me. What did was the looks I saw thrown at Hoss. When I caught women and even a few men greedily soaking in the sight of him, I wanted to hiss at them and scratch their eyes out. Christ, I must be off my rocker. Why would it matter? He wasn't mine. I kept lecturing myself, but it wasn't helping.

Going to the second floor compounded the problem. Here, active sexual acts were happening. There were stages in the open, where select patrons and workers would perform scenes, and others would be free to watch. In addition, we were told and shown a few of the rooms, which were theme-based on various kinks and fantasies. The theme was noted on the door. There were windows into the rooms for those who were comfortable having voyeurs watch them. If you weren't, those could be covered with a privacy screen.

The press of bodies up here was denser. As we navigated around and through throngs of people, I was guided. Hoss stayed glued to my side. His hand would rest on my back and gently steer me. If someone weren't paying attention and were about to bump into me, he'd prevent it. Sometimes, this consisted of him stepping between me and them. Other times, he'd bark out a command to watch out. It was amusing to watch them take in the giant he was and scurry out of the way, apologizing. After he had done it a fifth time, I had to say something. I knew Mikhail was doing it for Tajah.

Matvey and Gideon were shielding Victoria and Tamara as they should. They were their women. I could take care of myself.

"Hoss, you don't need to keep growling at people. I can get out of the way or tell them to move their asses myself."

His mouth twitched as if he was trying not to smile. "Cady Cat, there's no way I'm letting someone step on you or bump into you. You could get hurt. A tiny thing like you needs to be protected."

I bristled at his assertion that I'd get hurt because I was little. My height, or lack thereof, had been the bane of my existence. As a kid, I was always the smallest, the one to be picked on. Bullies loved people like me. I learned fast how to stand up for myself. It was true that Carver would do it, but he couldn't always be with me. He was five years older. If he was nearby, he always stepped in. And God knows, we had no help from home to protect us.

I didn't hit my top height of five feet two until I was thirteen. Suffice it to say, I had a lot of practice. Even as an adult, some people saw my petite stature as something to remark on or that I wasn't someone they had to contend with. They soon learned the error of their ways.

"I don't need or want anyone to protect me. I can take care of myself. Don't let my size fool you. I'm neither a child nor weak," I snapped.

The others had pulled ahead of us. Reuben pointed to one of the raised stages where two women were dancing. Hoss gripped my arm and tugged me into a dark corner—his firm grip wasn't painful. I wasn't sure why I didn't put up a fight. There was no one nearby. He swung me so I had my back to the wall, and he blocked the rest of the room. That move should've put me in defensive mode, but for some reason, it didn't. I had no fear that he was about to do something horrible to me. He lowered his head closer to mine.

"I need you to listen closely to me, Cady. Being protective of you isn't due to me believing you're a child or weak. I fucking know you're neither. I'd do the same if you were over six feet tall. And I know you are more than capable of taking care of yourself. It's purely due to my principles or whatever you want to call them. You never need to safeguard yourself when I'm with you. That's my job. People are rude, and they need to learn some manners. I won't have you hurt, not even a broken nail."

His declaration left me dumbstruck for several moments. I had no rebuttal for it. I tried not to let the warmth it caused inside me show. Other than Tajah, Tamara, Tajah's father when he was alive, and Carver, I'd never had anyone give a damn about me. I didn't know what to say or do. Why him? Was it part of his doorman slash security personality or something else?

"I can see those wheels in your head turning, Tiny. What are you thinking? It's not like you not to have a comeback." he sounded somewhat amused.

"Why are you doing this, Hoss? You don't know me. If Mikhail arranged for you to do this, I'll tell him it's unnecessary. Just because I'm Tajah's best friend doesn't mean he needs to assign someone to babysit me."

A frown peeked out. "Mikhail didn't ask or order me to do anything. It's my choice. And no matter how much you bitch or tell me to stop, I won't. In general, women and children should always be protected, but some are steps above the general protection level. You fall into that category."

"What the hell does that mean?"

"Let's get through tonight. Enjoy the experience, and afterward, you and I will sit down this coming week, and I'll explain. Will you do that?"

"Why wait?"

"Because I said we need to. This night is important to Mikhail. I won't ruin or interrupt it."

His steely gaze told me he wouldn't back down on this. As much as I wanted to push him to tell me now, he did have a point. This was Mikhail and Tajah's night. As her bestie, I couldn't mess it up for them. Sighing, I rolled my eyes so he knew I was doing it under duress.

"Fine, but if by this time next week, I'm still in the dark or I don't like your explanation, all bets are off. I'll kick your ass myself to make you stop."

He threw his head back and laughed. I couldn't help but admire his masculine beauty again as he did. "I might just wait so I can get that ass kickin'."

"Don't say you weren't warned, big guy."

"I won't. Alright, wanna rejoin the others? You're missing the fun."

I nodded and let him lead me back to the others.

"Everything okay?" Mikhail asked.

"Everything is great," I said. I caught Carver studying us. Was it because of whatever Hoss said to him earlier, or was he still upset with me? I should've asked Hoss to tell me what he said to my brother. Oh well, I'd find out one way or another.

"We're good," Hoss added.

As time passed, we not only got an education on the club, but we met a ton of people. When Mikhail was in the house, patrons and staff loved to stop and talk to him. He was gracious and made lots of introductions. It slowed down our tour somewhat, but I found those interruptions informative. Overall, I was enjoying myself. I tried not to show it too much. No one needed to know the things I was seeing were intriguing. Sure, there were things I would never attempt in a million years. However, there were several I was captivated by.

I was entranced by a scene on one of the stages—so much so that I forgot the others were nearby. A man was disciplining a woman. He hadn't started that way. At first, they were talking. It soon turned into her back-talking him. The way she acted reminded me of myself. He worked at correcting her verbally. When it didn't work, it went from there.

It was clear that there were rules, and she knew them but broke them. When she refused to follow them or to modify her behavior, he eventually resorted to punishment. If he'd slapped her, hit her with his fists, flung her around by her hair, berated her, or called her foul names, I wouldn't have stayed. I knew what that was like and didn't know why anyone would want to be treated like that.

I jumped when warm breath blew across the back of my neck, and heat hit me. "Do you know what his kink is? What hers is?" Hoss asked softly.

I shook my head. "No."

"Has Tajah told you about her research, or have you read about brat tamers, handlers, and their brats?"

Thinking about it, I vaguely recalled Taj mentioning them but couldn't remember what was said about them. "The terms sound familiar, but I don't recall what they mean."

"Pay close attention, and I'll explain."

How could I say no?

Hoss: Chapter 7

Being this close to Cady was making me feverish. I wanted to remove her from the club and carry her off somewhere. That somewhere was my place so that I could have her all to myself. The number of men undressing her and admiring her with their leering eyes was making me want to tear off heads. I knew she'd attract attention. Even in a pair of ratty sweats, she'd do it. Dressed like she was, it was a wonder there hadn't been a fight. She pushed back on me protecting her. Well, I had news for her. I'd always do it.

As the night passed, I kept a close eye on her. At times, I'd catch Carver watching us. Whenever I did, he was quick to look away. I knew he was disturbed by our talk upstairs earlier. I wanted Cady's brother to like me because if I got my way, she'd be in my life for the rest of our lives. However, if he thought he was going to make her feel bad about herself by saying and doing shit that put her down, I had news for him. It wasn't fucking happening.

When I saw them arguing in the apartment, I got as close as possible. Hearing him tell her to leave and that he didn't want her downstairs upset me. Seeing the pain on her face when he threw her past failed relationships in her face made me furious. I knew I had to put a stop to it. Recalling our conversation after she walked off made me want to growl.

I made sure she was out of range before I rounded on him. I let him see my displeasure. He took a step back. "What the fuck was that about?" I snapped.

"Nothing you need to worry about."

"Like hell, it's not. Let me tell you this. If you get a wild hair to do something like that again, you'll know why you shouldn't. I won't have anyone making her feel bad about herself. Your sister isn't to blame for the men who she dated in her past being assholes and bastards. It's plain that they had no idea what she needed or how to handle her. That was their failings, not hers."

"And you think you can handle her?" he hit back.

"I know I can."

"She's not a plaything in the club or outside, Hoss. Don't fuck with my sister."

"What Cady and I do is between us. I can promise that I won't hurt her. Ever. End of discussion. Why don't you stay here and either cool off and join us when you've straightened your ass up or leave. Excuse me. I have a beautiful woman to escort." I stomped off, leaving him there. I didn't give a shit if he stayed or not. I had to race to catch up to them at the elevator.

Of course, that conversation flew out of my head when I noticed her being enthralled with a tamer scene we'd stopped to watch. I did it on purpose. One of the other guys who was into taming and handling was up there with his regular brat. They weren't an actual couple outside of the club. They came together to play, but each had a different partner at home. Individuals outside our lifestyle might find this incomprehensible, but for many, it worked—as long as there was honesty and open communication along every step.

It was a reality that some people's long-term

partners weren't into aspects of their partner's lives, so they got that fulfilled here. I started explaining to Cady the roles the couple in front of us was playing and the importance of communication. If she were to be mine, she would have to know this and more. I prayed that she'd be receptive and willing to work with me. If she weren't, no matter how insanely attracted to her I was, we'd never work. I didn't want to have play partners and Cady. I wanted her to be the complete package. The same way I wanted me to be all she needed and wanted. The thought of the former being the case made me sick.

"The woman, Justine, is a brat, and the man, Sam, is a brat tamer. However, there's another possible role in a dynamic like theirs. It's called a brat handler."

"A brat? What does that mean? And how is a tamer different from a handler?"

My heart thumped harder at her questions. There was a note of interest in her voice. "Well, a brat is someone, male or female, who expresses sassy behavior to get reactions. There's a variety of reasons a brat wants and needs that, which will take time to explore. The brat tamer is someone who engages with the brat. Usually, brats are masochists who get pleasure from being put in his or her place by their tamer or handler." I paused. She was hanging onto my every word as she watched them.

"A tamer or handler is a giant brat who takes the responsible, authoritative role. He or she is the dominant in the relationship. The brat is the submissive. A brat isn't a stereotypical sub like many people imagine. They don't bow down to or obey everything their dominant says. A brat is a mouthy and misbehaving person who wants to be punished.

Brats crave it, and they love to find loopholes in rules and break them on purpose, but never only for their gratification. Their Dominant's pleasure has to be achieved by the brat breaking the rules. If it doesn't, neither get what they crave and need. It's a game where brats defy authority in order to receive punishment from their tamer or handler.

"A handler, who you'll sometimes hear referred to as a wrangler, too, enhances the brat's tendencies. They don't want to change, destroy, or mold away their brat's sass. A handler or tamer is usually a sadist, which makes sense when most brats are masochists. We enjoy punishing our subs, but only for minor offenses. We're there to teach submissives when engaging in brat behaviors is okay. When the sub doesn't follow the rules, the Dom will dish out punishments to achieve that obeying. The woman we're watching is a true brat. She'll obey at times and only break the minor rules that in no way disrespect or dishonor her Dom. She knows when it's okay to engage in bratting and when it's not."

I paused again. I noted the color in her cheeks was high, and she was breathing faster. If I wasn't mistaken, my Cady was turned on by what she saw. Christ, how could she not be? I was too, but not from the couple. It was all due to Cady. I itched to have her up there on that stage, giving me her attitude and allowing me to punish her, but only in the agreed-upon ways.

"W-what do brats do to break the rules?" she asked breathlessly.

"It differs by brat and even by the handler-brat relationship, but some common things are eye-rolling and saying no, but in a playful way. She might call him names, but only jokingly. A brat may turn down a command, ignore their tamer or handler, speak when they're supposed to be quiet, or have a temper tantrum. It's all based on what they negotiated prior to engaging in the bratting. They communicate before they get to this point. What will be considered bratting, what are the punishments, safe words, promise to submit to the established punishment, and so on? There are punishments for bratting, which aren't the same as punishments for disobedience."

Cady shuddered, but not in revulsion or disgust when Sam spanked Justine with a short crop. He made sure when it landed on her ass, it left a red mark. Justine cried out, but instead of stopping, she looked back at her Dom and rolled her eyes again. He landed another swat. The others had wandered off, watching other shows and even talking to patrons not otherwise engaged. It was the two of us left there. My cock grew in my pants as I pictured me and Cady were up there.

Assuming she'd consent to it, I wondered what punishments—or, in our case, funishments—we'd agree to for her rule-breaking. I had so many ideas, but they'd never happen unless we were both on board with them. I didn't want to break or tame my Cady. I longed to make her feel secure, happy, and satisfied. If I could do that, I'd receive the same in return.

I was about to ask her if she had more questions, but we were interrupted in one of the worst ways imaginable. As soon as I heard my name purred out, I cringed inside. There was no hope of pretending I hadn't heard or that Cady didn't. It was done loudly, and the voice carried. My only hope was to divert as fast as possible. Cady was turning around to look behind us. I reluctantly did the same. As I did, hands landed on my arm and wrapped around it as far as they could. Smiling up at me with a come-hither smile was Fleur. I made sure not to groan and kept my facial expression bland.

"Thank God you're here! I've been dying to have someone worthy to play with, Hoss. You have no idea how hard it is to get someone who matches me. It seems like it's been forever since I've seen you not working. We have to enjoy the fun. We never get time together anymore. Come, let's find a room or stage. I don't care," she said excitedly as she insistently tugged on my arm.

I had no idea what her problem was. She knew not to touch unless invited, plus she and I hadn't played in ages. About nine months ago, I'd made the colossal mistake of engaging her for a scene. I'd been desperate for a new partner and thought to try out some of the brats who didn't have a permanent tamer or handler. It only took a few times for me to know she wasn't the one for me. There were various reasons why, but one was she desired a tamer, not a handler—a sadistic monster, to be exact. The other was she didn't adhere to any of the rules. I got zero pleasure from our few encounters.

I'd tried to be nice when I informed her I didn't want to play anymore, but she either was as dense as a tree or refused to listen. Avoiding her was another reason I hadn't been inside playing much. I thought I'd be safe tonight because more than a few people told me she wouldn't be here. She was supposed to be out of town. Either she lied, or her plans changed. The first thing I did was shake my arm. She clung to it, so I used my free hand to pry her claws off me. As I did, I reprimanded her.

"Fleur, you weren't invited to touch me, and I'm not going to join you. You know the rules. Find someone else," I ordered.

She looked at me, startled for a second or two, then smirked. "No. I won't."

Son of a bitch, she thought I was playing. "I'm not kidding. This isn't a scene. Stop it. You know better."

"I don't know why you're pretending, but I know what you want. It's been so long, Hoss. I need you," she moaned and gripped herself between her legs. I curled my lip in disgust. What the hell? We'd never had sex, only bratting, not that she hadn't tried. But the ways she was acting, you'd believe we had.

"Is there a problem here?" Mikhail asked as he came to stand next to me.

"Yes," I said.

"No," Fleur said at the same time.

"What's the problem, Hoss?" Mikhail ignored her.

"She came up and grabbed my arm and was insistent that I do a scene with her. I told her no and told her to find someone else. I wasn't kidding, but she wasn't listening. I don't need this shit, Mikhail." I growled the last low under my breath.

He knew why. I could only imagine what Cady was assuming. I didn't dare glance at her until I got rid of pain-in-the-ass Fleur. I dreaded what I'd see. I wasn't ashamed of my past, but I didn't want this when I was still trying to win her.

"Fleur, you know the rules," Mikhail told her sternly. You could hear the reproach in his voice.

She wasn't smiling coyly anymore. "Master M, I'm sorry. I thought we were doing a scene. If I hadn't, I would've never touched or disobeyed Hoss. Please, it won't happen again. I got excited since we haven't been together for so long."

I'd heard enough. The bitch was lying, but I would leave her for Mikhail or Reuben to deal with. They had the say on who stayed or went. I had to talk to my woman and explain what this was all about. As I shifted back to face Cady, I was hit with a new problem. Cady had vanished. Tajah was standing to the side with Victoria. Matvey was next to them. They were watching the drama. Frantically, I glanced around.

The place was so crowded that it was hard to see, but I had the advantage of height. But Cady was so short that she was lost in a sea of taller bodies. Panic began to fill me, and I rushed over to Tajah.

"Where did she go?"

She gave me a sad smile. "She took off. As soon as you started talking to that woman, she said she had to go. I tried to get her to stay, but she said she was tired."

"Jesus Christ!" I snarled.

"She told me you'd wasted enough time on her tonight. Now that your woman was here, she was going home," Tamara said as she walked up. Gideon was with her.

"What?" I exclaimed.

"I caught her leaving and asked why she was cutting the night short. That's what she said. I tried to get her to come back, but she wouldn't." Tamara looked unhappy.

"I've got to go," I shouted to whoever needed to hear me, and then I took off. I pushed my way, not very gently, through the masses when people didn't get out of my way. Most, if they saw me coming, cleared a path. My expression warned them not to fuck with me or try to talk to me. I kept scanning the area on the off chance she hadn't made it out of the building. Nothing.

I came to a halt when I reached the parking lot. Goddamn it. She wouldn't have come this way. She parked in the private garage. I'd forgotten in my panic. I took off running across the main lot to the private entrance. I ignored the doorman working tonight when he shouted and asked if I needed help. I waved off his offer but didn't speak. Going this way was faster than returning inside and riding the elevator. My heart sank more when I got there and found her car was missing. Thankfully, I had my car keys in my pocket. I fished them out and jumped into my car. Firing up the engine, I tore out of there. It was all I could do not to drive like a lunatic. As I sped out of the parking lot, I called Mikhail on my phone. He answered after the third ring.

"Did you catch her?"

"Hell, no. She's gone. I'm headed to her place. Make sure to tell Fleur I better not see her anytime soon, or I may forget I don't hit women."

"Drive carefully. It won't do you any good to kill yourself. When you get to her place, make sure to explain what you want to her. Enough sitting back and waiting. If she's who you want, then tell her. If she resists, then work to show her why she needs to say yes —unless you've changed your mind."

A growl came tumbling out of me. "Like fuck I've changed my mind. She's the only woman I want. I was getting somewhere before Fleur fucked it to hell and back. Mikhail, I'm not telling you how to run your club, but I'm warning you, if Fleur stays as a patron, she'd better never come near me or Cady again."

"Hoss, calm down. She won't. I've suspended her for the time being and told her I had to consider if it was permanent. I wanted to give us time to think. I swear, if we do let her back, which I'm not inclined to do, she'll be made to understand. I keep thinking of Dominus and the second chance I gave him. I regret I did. I don't want to make the same mistake with her. Besides, if she stays, my woman may hurt her. If I hadn't stopped her, Tajah was about to hit her in the face." There was a touch of amusement in his tone when he said the last part.

My lips twitched at the thought of Taj doing it. She was calmer than my woman. "Good idea. Listen, I need to concentrate on the road. I'll call you later. Sorry for ruining the party."

"You didn't ruin it. Go take care of Cady."

"I will. Thanks," I grunted out before hanging up.

My mind raced with thoughts of how much rebuilding I'd have to do with Cady. I felt her walls slipping tonight. She was less bratty, asked questions about our lifestyle, and gave every appearance of not being turned off by the things she saw and learned. That last scene with Sam and Justine had been resonating with her. I was so close to broaching the subject of my preferences and my desire to be with her when Fleur shattered it.

By the time I reached Cady's place, my hands were sweating, and my heart wouldn't stop racing. I saw her car outside. The unit that was hers was dark. Surely, she hadn't had time to get here and go to bed. Well, if she had, I was about to wake her up. This wasn't something that could wait. I parked next to her car, stormed out of mine, and flew toward her front door.

As I neared it, I saw there was a light, a very faint one, coming through the blinds. Immediately upon noting that, I heard shouting. I sped up and hit the door with my open palm. It wasn't locked, and if it was latched, my charge was too much. Her door flew open. I didn't slow down. I was ready to defend my woman and kill whoever was in there with her. I heard anger and a touch of fear in her voice.

In the faint light, I noted I was in her living room. Standing in the middle of it was Cady, facing off with Reid. My first question was, where the hell was her security? They should've prevented this or at least intervened. I shoved those questions aside as I barreled up to them. They were arguing so loudly they somehow hadn't heard me. She was glaring up at him with her fists on her hips. He was towering over her, scowling and trying to be intimidating. I had news for him. That shit stopped now.

I made a growling sound, which finally snapped their attention to me. Cady's eyes widened, and her mouth dropped open. Reid kept his scowl, but I saw him take a step back before he caught himself. Good. He'd better be afraid of me. I could tear him apart with my bare hands. I not only had size and strength on my side, but I'd learned several martial arts over the years, and I was skilled.

When I got to them, I swept her with one arm slightly behind me, but I allowed her to stay to the side so she could see. I knew she would hate not being visible. I could protect her no matter if she was behind me or not, so I gave this to her. If he had a gun out, then no, I would've used my body as a shield. I was watching to be sure he didn't pull one. If he did, he'd find I was armed, too.

"What the hell is he doing here? And why would you let him in your apartment, Cady?" I snarled. She knew better.

I heard a frustrated huff, and then she answered, "What the fuck are you doing here? And as for letting this moron in, I'll have you know, I didn't. I'm not stupid. He was waiting inside. Somehow, he got in. If you don't mind, why don't you leave so I can take care of this imbecile? I don't know why you're here anyway. You have better people, I mean, things to be doing." Underneath her anger and sensor, I detected what I thought was hurt when she mentioned doing things. Her use of the word people was intentional—a little dig.

"I'm here because my woman left the club without telling me. Surely, you knew I wouldn't settle for that. We have stuff to talk about, but that can wait until I get rid of the riffraff here."

"Get the hell out! This is between me and Cady. I don't give a damn who you are. You have no right to interfere. We don't need an audience. And as for calling me riffraff, fuck off," Reid snapped.

I guess between last time and this one, he'd grown some balls. As I studied him closer, I amended that. He hadn't grown a pair. He was high. His pupils were dilated and bloodshot. He was fidgeting, and his eyes kept darting. I'd seen enough addicts during my life to know what one looked like. All I had to do was remember my brother, Max. My irritation increased, and so did my caution. An addict was unpredictable. I took two steps to the left, partially covering Cady.

"You need to leave before I have to make you. Believe me. Leaving of your own free will is better for you," I warned him.

He gave me a humorless laugh. "I'm not going anywhere. It's time me and my girl settled shit. I know she hooked up with you to make me jealous and to pay me back for something. However, it's done. Get lost. She's not warming your bed any longer."

My temper rose when he mentioned her no longer warming my bed. While I wanted her there, the idea of her and him in bed together pissed me off. Over my dead body, would she go back to a man like him. Even if she wanted nothing to do with me, she deserved so much more than a schmuck like him.

"Cady isn't a piece of meat to be passed around. She's a strong, passionate, intelligent woman, which explains why she got rid of you in the first place. I don't believe for a second she wants you back. If she does, why did you have to resort to breaking into her apartment?"

He snorted. "You haven't shown him that mouth of yours, I see. Wait until you get a load of it. You'll know why I took a break, but I'm back. Cady won't find anyone better at putting up with her when she gets out of control than me. Who cares if we take a break once in a while? At least she won't be alone."

There was so much insult in his speech the urge to punch him grew. Did he even hear what he was saying about the woman he supposedly wanted to get back with? Who in their right mind would do it? I glanced at Cady but made sure to keep the asshole in my peripheral vision. She was glowering at him. If looks could kill, he'd be dead.

"Tiny, is what he said true? You want him here and back in your life?" I asked, praying she'd say no, but there was still a slim fear she'd say she wanted the shithead. If she did, I didn't know what I'd do. The way she was tying me in knots, I might beg, which I'd never done in my life.

She gave me an incredulous look before

answering me. She moved forward and out to the side. "I don't want this cockhead near me, let alone in my life. We broke up a year ago, and I said good riddance. I haven't seen or heard from him in six months or more. He moved as far as I knew. I have no idea why he's suddenly appearing and talking like we took an agreed-upon break. From the looks of him, he's high. It must be the drugs eating his brain up, although he didn't have a lot to begin with," she remarked acidly.

I wanted to laugh. Her indignation was cute, and I loved to see her fired up. I gave her a wink and smiled. Her lips twitched, but she held in her smile. I looked back at him. He was standing there, swaying on his feet. He stared at her stupidly as if what she said went over his head, which it might've. He blinked, and then his face darkened.

"I've had enough of your fucking mouth and games, bitch. I—" I didn't let him finish. Calling her a bitch pushed my last button. Growling, I lunged at him. He squawked and tried to backpedal, but he tripped over his own feet.

Before he could hit the floor, I had him by the neck. I picked him up and headed for the door. He gagged and fought for air. I shook him a couple of times just for fun. I let him know what would happen to him if he came near her again. I was giving him another chance, although I had no idea why, maybe because his drugged state reminded me of my brother.

"Listen close, you little pissant motherfucker. If you come near Cady, her business, her home, hell, even stay in Nashville, it'll be tragic for your health. If I catch you calling, texting, writing, or even thinking about her, I'll beat you to within an inch of your life. And I can promise you, when I do, you won't heal quickly. It'll be filled with pain, and no one will ever find your body if you keep it up. If you think I'm lying, I dare you to try me."

Outside, I dropped him. He stumbled and then fell on his ass on her sidewalk. He continued to gasp and gag for air as he rubbed his throat. I could've crushed his windpipe with one hard flexing of my hand. It was tempting. Cady had followed us. She came to my side and wrapped her arms around mine.

"T-tell me you don't want this big, dumb Black bastard," Reid the Wretch croaked out.

"Don't you dare call him that! His skin color means nothing to me, you bigoted asshole," she said indignantly.

"Cady, it's alright. I've been called worse. You have two minutes to get your ass in whatever vehicle you came in and leave. Don't return," I ordered him.

He rose unsteadily to his feet. He swayed as he faced me, though he kept several feet of space between us. "You won't stay. No one can handle her mouth. I'll see you when he's done with you," he told her with a sneer. Turning his back on us, he slowly staggered away. I took a step to go after him for telling her he'd see her, but my Cady stopped me. She tugged hard on my arm and held tight.

"Hoss, no, forget him. He's talking out of his ass. He's just butt sore. Let him go."

I halted but kept my eyes on him. He got in a car parked down the street a few hundred feet away. As high as he was, he shouldn't have been driving. He squealed his tires as he took off. As his taillights faded in the distance, I glanced around at her neighbors. There wasn't a single light on. It was impossible that no one was home in some of them or that they heard nothing. What the hell was wrong with them!?

"Cady, it's cold out here. Inside," I directed.

I didn't wait for her reply. I eased her around and began walking toward her door. She either came with me, or I'd carry her. She walked and waited until we were indoors, and the door was closed. It must've been unlatched when I hit it with my hand because the lock nor the frame was busted. I had no trouble locking it. Once it was, I faced her. And she let loose on me.

Cady: Chapter 8

This whole night had my head spinning from spending hours with Hoss to coming home and finding Flint in my home. I should have quit while I was ahead. That would mean thanking Hoss and sending him on his way. Did I do that? No, I had to yell at him. I wasn't angry with him over Flint. I was upset over seeing his woman and knowing a man like him was out of reach of me. I'd let myself dream a little as he stuck close to me all night. And I recalled the kiss in the elevator. Even though all women knew a guy kissing you didn't mean much. To cover my disappointment and hurt, I attacked.

"What're you doing here? You need to leave. I've had all of the male species I can stand for a night. Go," I tried to pass him to get to the door. He prevented me by grabbing my upper arms and drawing me close. I struggled to get loose, but there was no way I could without going crazy. I resorted to threats.

"I swear to God, if you don't let go of me, I'm going to kick you in the balls. I'm not in the mood to be manhandled, yelled at, or abused. You need to get back to your woman. You know, the one who's dying to play with you." I hissed the last bit.

Did he let me go? Or say anything? No, though he did react. I gasped as I was jerked against his chest, and his mouth took mine. He wrapped me up so tight I couldn't get away. I still tried, but as his kiss sank in, I went weak, and like an idiot, I gave in to it. It was too perfect to resist. As I kissed him back, I promised myself this would be the last time. After all, he had someone in his life. Poor thing had no idea he flirted and did lord knows what with others. Another reason I didn't want a man in my life. They lied and cheated.

A moan of desire was torn from me when his hands cupped my ass cheeks and squeezed them. I squirmed because his fingers were so close to my pussy. The pussy that was wet and throbbing to be touched. It was hard not to shift, so his fingers touched me where I needed them. I had no doubt if he did, I'd come. I was that turned on.

Part of it was due to how he'd acted at Lustz and the scenes we'd seen. A tinier part was due to how he'd handled Flint, and now he added the kiss to it. How could a woman resist? The next thing I knew, I was hoisted upward by his hands under my ass and wrapping partway around my thighs. The air tried to cool my skin, but I was on fire, so it didn't help much. Vaguely, it registered that we were moving, but since his lips never left mine and that talented tongue of his was still playing with my tongue, I didn't pay attention.

My back met softness as he straddled me. I hazily noted I was lying on my couch. I had my hands hooked behind his neck, holding him to me as our teeth, lips, and tongues devoured each other and teased. I whimpered when his hand slid up from my ass and ended up cupping my breasts. I still had my leather catsuit on, but it felt wonderful. My nipples in my suit were rock-hard pebbles. They must've been noticeable because he unerringly found them through the thin layer of leather and plucked them. I cried out, but his mouth captured it.

He strummed his thumb back and forth over it, causing zings of electricity to flash through my tits and radiate down to between my legs. I whimpered as I tried to press my legs together to get relief, but he had one of his knees between mine, which prevented it. Suddenly, he shifted, his knee pressed against my core, and he gently thrust it back and forth. I tore my mouth away from his and screamed as I came. I'd never come that hard before from barely a touch.

My head was thrown back, eyes closed as I shook. I had no idea how long it took before I began to come down, but when it happened, reality started to set in. Along with it came rational thought and guilt. I'd just let him get me off and touch me, and he had a woman. He was a cheating bastard, and I'd let him taint me as the other woman. Shame and guilt flooded me. He was hovering above me, smiling down with a satisfied smirk. Anger hit me.

The way he was situated placed not only one of his legs between mine but one of mine between his. Without a second thought, I raised my knee and kneed his family jewels. He grunted in shock and pain. As he was twisting away from me, I rolled and got out from underneath him. I didn't waste time. Backing up, I ordered him.

"Get the hell out. I won't be a plaything or whatever this is. You have a woman. You told me you did, plus I saw her. Why don't you try being faithful? Oh, wait, I forgot. You're a man. That's genetically impossible. Well, screw you, Hoss. I'm not ever knowingly hurting another woman the way I've been hurt. Stay away from me. You can find the door."

I didn't stick around to hear what he'd say. I knew it would be excuses and empty promises. I darted to the door. I was over this shit. It seemed I needed to find a place where no one could find me tonight. I snatched my purse off the entry table along with my car keys. When I came in, I'd put them there before Flint revealed his presence.

"Cady, wait," he gasped hoarsely.

Ignoring him, I went out the door, slamming it behind me. I fled to my car and cursed when my shaking hand made it hard to get it started. As soon as it was, I put it in reverse and got out of there. Tears kept trying to obscure my vision, but I angrily wiped them away.

As I drove, I tried to decide where to go. Going to Tajah and Mikhail's was out. They were friends with Hoss, and I didn't want to place them in this mess. Carver was a no-go. After the way he acted earlier, he'd be telling me *I told you* so and lord it over me. There was no need to give him more ammunition to use against me. I didn't have other friends to go to their place and crash. There was always the clinic, but if Hoss or Flint wanted to find me, they'd look there. That left me only one option. I'd have to stay at a hotel. Nashville was full of them. It shouldn't be hard to find one. I simply had to avoid ones close to my home, work, and the club.

Scanning the darkness surrounding me, I got my bearings and headed further up the interstate. I'd go toward Victory Park and find a hotel in the Capitol area. I had to fight not to think of Hoss, the kiss, or my orgasm. If I didn't, I'd be sick. At the moment, I wasn't sure who I was more disgusted with—him or me. I'd acted like an amoral slut. Why didn't I resist? Kick him out? Why?

&& && &&

The morning didn't bring me any revelations. I'd barely slept. I couldn't stop thinking about what happened. I had to turn off my phone right after I got to the hotel and into my room. It rang, and the screen flashed up, showing Hoss's name. Tajah had given me his number after the break-in in case I ever needed help and they weren't available. I hit *ignore,* then shut it off. I wasn't in the mood to speak to him or listen to calls and texts all night.

It was barely seven in the morning. I groaned as I dragged my aching, stiff body out of the bed. I stumbled to the bathroom. I'd shower and then get a coffee. I'd have to go straight to the clinic to be there on time, but that wasn't a problem. I kept extra clothes and other supplies there. I did that for those times I had to stay the night with a sick animal. It wasn't always possible to run home and get cleaned up.

Looking into the mirror while the water in the shower heated, I cringed. I looked like hell. My hair was a tangled mess, and I had dark circles underneath my mascara-smeared eyes because of my lack of sleep and makeup remover. I looked like a raccoon who'd gone on an all-night bender. Thankfully, I had a small makeup kit in my purse. I was sure I had concealer in it. I slept in my underwear after getting out of the catsuit. I hated the thought of wearing it again, but I had no choice. Maybe if I hurried, I'd get to the office before anyone else, and no one would see me in it.

Jumping into the shower, I took a speedy one, not the leisurely one I wanted. I was in and out, ready to go within twenty minutes. Five of those minutes were due to me wiggling myself back into the leather suit—not an easy feat. Baby powder was my friend, and I had none. As I exited the hotel, I saw the looks I was getting. I didn't pay them any mind. I didn't know them, and they didn't know me. I let them think I had a wild night.

Traffic was already heavy, so it took me longer to get to the clinic than usual. Even so, I was relieved to see I arrived before any of the staff. Parking in the back, where there were a couple of spots, I hurried to unlock the back door. I'd go in through the kennel. There were no barks or meows greeting me when I got inside. We had no overnight patients.

Locking the door and rearming the alarm, I headed up the hallway to my office. I'd grab my clothes, get changed, and fix my hair. My makeup was enough to cover the circles, and I'd put on some lip and cheek color so I wasn't so dead-looking. We didn't open until nine, and the first staff usually didn't arrive until eight-thirty. I had plenty of time to get myself in order, and none of them would be the wiser.

If only things worked out the way we wanted. Unfortunately, it didn't work for me. Oh, I got changed, no problem, and I even tamed my hair enough to put it up in a bun and not have it look like a bird's nest. What didn't work out was me flying under the radar. I should've known when I turned off my phone and didn't tell anyone where I was going that someone would show up at my work. Usually, I would've, but my mind was a churning mess. That was my excuse, and I was sticking to it. I got clued into that when I heard pounding on the front door. I almost didn't answer, but then I scolded myself. I was no coward. Whoever it was, I'd handle them.

I marched to the main door, turned off the alarm, unlocked it, then yanked it open. My scowl was firmly in place when I did. I assumed it was Hoss or Flint. I was wrong. There stood Mikhail and Tajah. Before I could say a word, they swept inside, and the door was slammed shut. Tajah threw her arms around and hugged me tightly.

"Where have you been? We've been going crazy with worry! You run off from the club, and then later, we get a call from Hoss. He said Flint broke into your place, then the two of you had a misunderstanding, and you left. He had no idea where you were. He tried calling you, but his calls went right to voicemail. I've been trying for hours and the same thing. Cady, how could you do that to us?" she cried as she gave me a shake. Mikhail was behind her, watching me with a frown on his face. I disentangled myself from her arms. She appeared taken aback.

"Tajah, I love you, and you're my best friend, but I'm not talking about last night or what happened. I'm an adult. If I want to spend the night away from my apartment, I can. It's not that unusual, is it? For adults to stay in other places."

She blinked and looked surprised. "You spent time with a man? Who? You didn't tell me you were seeing anyone."

I hadn't meant to give that impression, but now that it was out there, why not go with it? It wouldn't hurt anyone, and in fact, it would give me a degree of protection. Maybe Hoss would stay away if they thought I was with someone.

"I didn't want to jinx it, so I stayed quiet. We've been seeing each other for a while." The lie just tumbled from my lips so easily.

Mikhail's brow went up, but he didn't say anything. Tajah's face was filled with surprise and a smidge of hurt. "Cady, I know how badly relationships seem to go for you, but I'm your best friend. You could've told me. I understand waiting on others, but I wouldn't have said anything. Now that I know, can I ask his name? How did you meet? When might I get to meet him?"

Crap, there she went. I either had to make up more lies or come clean. I was opening my mouth to do the latter when there was knocking at the door.

"What the hell is this, Grand Central Station? I've got work to do. The clinic will open shortly. I don't have time to chat right now. I'll call you later," I told them as I went to the door.

They were lagging behind me. Mikhail was whispering something in her ear. I opened the door to find Hoss standing there. He was furious. Panic hit me. I wasn't ready to see or speak to him. I tried to slam and lock the door on him, but he was too fast and strong. He caught it with one hand and held the door open.

"Tiny, you and I have to talk," he stated loudly.

"We don't have to do shit. My name is Cady, or, better yet, Dr. Anderson. I want all of you to leave. This is my place of business. I have employees and patients coming soon. I have preparations to make."

"I'm not fucking going anywhere until we straighten this shit out," Hoss growled.

"Man, we need to talk first," Mikhail said from behind me.

"Cady, please, we need to talk this out," Tajah pleaded. I knew she was confused and hurt that I hid something from her, but it wasn't real, and I wasn't about to come clean with her before these two. They were all talking loudly and over top of each other. After a minute, I couldn't take any more.

"STOP!" I shouted as loud as I could. They did, much to my surprise. I hurried to continue while I could. "I need you all to leave. My staff will be here any second. Tajah, we'll talk later. Hoss, we have nothing to say. Mikhail, please take her home."

Tajah looked hurt, but she moved closer to Mikhail. Her man wrapped his arm around her shoulders and hugged her close. He kissed her temple and whispered in her ear again. Glancing away from them since their closeness made me feel hollow and sick, I found Hoss was studying me. I waited for him to refuse. I swear if he did, I'd do more than knee him in the balls again.

I was startled when Hoss spoke first, and he didn't argue. "Mikhail, Tajah, let's go. Cady is right. This is her work. This isn't the place or time. It can wait." He was calm as he spoke, shocking me. I saw no anger or other emotions on his face. Mikhail gave him a contemplative look, while Taj wore a shocked one.

"Of course, you're right. Forgive us for barging in on you like this, Cady. We were just worried when no one knew where you were and if you were alright. Now that we know you are, we'll go. See you later," Mikhail said pleasantly.

For once, Tajah and I didn't hug before leaving each other. She gave me a sad look. I hated it. Mikhail nodded. As they went out the door, I steeled myself for Hoss's next words. Maybe he only wanted them out of the way.

HOSS'S LIMITS

Imagine my shock when he wordlessly turned and walked out. I stood there frozen for a long time. What got me moving was the door opening sometime later, and Dottie walked in. She jumped when she saw me standing there. Her hand came up to clutch her chest.

"Oh my God, you scared me, Cady. Is something wrong? The blinds are still shut. For a second, I thought we'd closed for the day."

"Nothing is wrong, Dottie. I was daydreaming and lost track of time. Here, let's get them open and ready before anyone else thinks we're closed today," I offered with a slight smile and a fake chuckle. She grinned, so I must've been convincing.

After Dottie arrived, the others did, and before long, patients began coming. I had a relatively full day, so I had little time to think. I went from patient to patient. Some were there for general check-ups and shots. Others for specific problems. In a few cases, X-rays and other tests were needed, which led to my unbooked time becoming booked. I barely had time to scarf down half of a sandwich Dottie got me for lunch.

This continued right up until closing time at five. In fact, we ran over, and the last patient didn't leave until five-forty-five. As soon as they were gone, I shooed Dottie and the others out. They'd done enough. I got protests and offers to stay, but I refused. I did say if anyone wanted to come in early, they could. I was so blessed when all of them said they would. They ordered me not to restock or clean anything. They'd do it in the morning. I had the best people.

After they left, I closed the blinds, locked up, and set the alarm, but I didn't leave. I had charting to

133

do, plus I wasn't in the mood to do it at home. The reason was as the day passed, I kept replaying the scene with Hoss, Mikhail, and Tajah this morning and how they'd all easily left. I should be relieved, but it had the opposite effect on me. My tension was growing the longer I thought about it. There was no way any of them were okay with it. Why back down so quickly?

This unease made me reluctant to go home. Maybe I'd stay at a hotel again. I had more clothes here. I'd take them and my other stuff with me, so this time, I'd be able to properly get ready before work. The thought of going home and being confronted by Flint or Hoss didn't appeal to me. In Flint's case, I never wanted to see him, period. With Hoss, it wasn't a matter of not wanting to see him. I couldn't. What if I broke again? It wasn't fair to the poor woman he was involved with. He might be fine being a cheating dog, but I wouldn't be a relationship wrecker.

It was dark outside. It always was this time of year. Sitting at my desk, I forced myself to do my charting. I kept having to shake myself to resume when I'd space out. So it took longer than it should. It was after nine, and I was down to the last two. I was yawning and hungry. Last night's crappy sleep and the hasty half of my lunch had caught up to me.

I flexed my back to relieve the cramp. I was bending back to my keyboard when I heard a crashing sound that sounded like glass breaking. The alarm didn't go off. Why? I know I set it. I stood to go see what the cause was. Had something fallen in one of the rooms? As I took a step, I heard footsteps. That's when I realized I hadn't turned on all the lights. Since the break-in, I had the lights blazing as a warning whenever

I stayed over. My conversations with Hoss, Mikhail, and Tajah distracted me when I locked up, and I didn't turn them on. The only light was the one on my desk. It didn't shed much light.

Hastily, I reached over, snapped it off, and closed my laptop. It wasn't pitch black in here. Enough ambient light was filtered between the cracks in the blinds to let me see, barely. The footsteps were coming from the back of the clinic through the kennels. Again, we had no overnight guests, so no one to alert me.

Grabbing my purse, I crawled under my desk. It was an executive type, so I was hidden where the chair would usually rest. I dragged the chair as close to me as possible. If I were lucky, whoever it was wouldn't find me. As I waited for those steps to reach me, I tried not to shake. I was scared. Whoever it was had no alarm chasing them off this time. The alarm company wouldn't get an alert, which meant no help was coming to rescue me.

The steps kept going past my office, but I knew they'd come in here when they didn't find what they were looking for. Based on the sounds that started moments later, they were searching the examination rooms. Biting my lip, I fumbled for my phone in my purse. I found it, and with shaking hands, I called 911. It rang a couple of times before it was answered.

"Hello, this is 911. John speaking. What is your emergency?" a brisk man's voice asked when the call connected.

"This is Dr. Cadence Anderson. I'm at my veterinarian clinic, and someone just broke in. I'm hiding, and I have no idea how many there are. Please, send someone. This is the second break-in in less than two weeks," I whispered as softly as possible.

"Ma'am. Stay calm. I need your address. It shows you're calling from a cell phone," he said calmly. I was glad one of us was. I hurried to rattle off my address. When I was done, he was quick to reassure me.

"Dr. Anderson, I've dispatched the police to your location. Until they get there, stay on the line with me. Is there anything else you can tell me? Do you hear voices? What are they saying? How many of them are there?"

His composed voice helped to settle my nerves. I strained to hear, but there were more crashing sounds, muttering, and swearing. Then, I clearly heard a conversation.

"Jesus Christ, where the fuck is it? He said she has them," a man's voice suddenly shouted.

"I don't know! Keep looking," a second voice shouted back. Those were the only ones I heard.

"I hear two men. They're looking for something. I'm pretty sure they want drugs," I told John.

"Good. Do you recognize either voice? Are there accents?"

"The only accents are the typical slightly Southern ones you hear around Nashville. I don't recognize either voice."

An extra loud crashing sound made me jump, hit my head on the underside of my desk, and hiss in pain.

"What's wrong?" John asked.

"Nothing. A loud noise made me jump, and I hit my head," I admitted to him ruefully.

He chuckled softly before saying, "Then don't do that."

His humor made me snicker. "I'll try to remember

that. How long until the cops get here?"

There was a long pause. "They're approximately six minutes out. Just stay calm. Where exactly are you in the clinic? I need to inform the officers."

"I'm in the next to the last office on the left as you come in the front door. I'm in the knee well of the desk."

"Good. Stay there. If the robbers come into the room, just keep the line open and don't say anything. You're doing great, Dr. Anderson."

"I think under the circumstances, you can call me Cady."

"Cady, it is. Thank you. And you can call me John or Johnny. How long have you been a vet?"

He asked two questions before I heard the stomping of feet coming toward my office. "They're headed my way. I can't talk," I whispered.

I lay the phone down and reached into my purse again. This time, I took out my gun. If it came down to it, I'd shoot them. I wasn't keen to kill someone, but if it was them or me, I wanted myself to prevail. I gripped the handle tightly. I jumped when the door was flung open and hit the wall. I flinched.

"It has to be in here. This is her office. Tear this apart," Mr. Gruff said.

"We looked in all the cabinets and drawers last time. There's nothing here," the other thief whined.

"Just do it. Do you want to go back and tell him we failed again?" the first guy asked.

"No."

"Good. You start with the desk. I'm checking this cabinet."

I scrunched myself back in the corner as far as I could. I wish I could shrink. If he moved the chair and bent down, he'd see me. I pointed my gun toward the chair. Where were the police?

My desk shook as a drawer was yanked open. Paper rustled and then fell to the floor. Another one was opened. My anger was growing to overshadow my fear. The mess they were making would require us to close the clinic for the day. More income lost. Suddenly, the chair was rolling away. I saw legs. Oh shit! My hands shook. My finger was almost on the trigger when I heard the sweetest sound ever.

There was a loud thumping sound, then a voice yelled, "This is the police."

The legs in front of me disappeared. "Fuck, I thought the alarm was disabled," the whiner said. I heard the panic in his voice.

"It is. There must be a secondary one or something. Let's go," Number one ordered, and then I heard thundering footsteps as they ran out. There was shouting for them to halt. Arguing and lots of noise followed the running. I stayed in my spot, but I picked up my phone.

"John, are you still there?"

"I am. You did so good, Cady. Stay in there until the cops come for you. If you have a weapon, declare it and come out without it."

"I have a gun, but I won't have it out for them. Thank you so much."

"I'm happy to do it. You can hang up now. I'm glad you're safe."

"All due to you. Thank you."

He made a happy humming sound before he hung up. I didn't waste time stowing my phone and gun back in my purse, then I waited. My legs were cramping, but I was afraid to extend them or get out of my hidey-hole. As I waited for the all-clear, I couldn't help but think about how mixed up and crazy the past twenty-four hours had been. My life was spiraling out of control. I had to do something to stop it.

Hoss: Chapter 9

I was pacing my living room, trying to decide what the best course of action was. I'd been thinking about it all day. My worry and anger over last night had abated a bit, but I was still upset. Cady still had no idea who Fleur was. Her words and the knee to the balls at her place told me she thought I was involved with Fleur and cheating on her by getting cozy with Cady. That knee had ended the second sexiest kiss of my life. I never wanted it to end.

When she ran out last night, I was in no shape to run after her. It took several minutes for me to be able to stand. Even then, it was painful, and I walked funny. Not knowing what else to do, I locked up her apartment. I then called Mikhail and told him what happened. He was sympathetic and promised to get Tajah to contact her since she wasn't answering my calls or texts. I tried more than once, and they went straight to voicemail. I doubted Cady would go to their place. And after the way Carver acted, I doubted she'd seek him out.

When she didn't answer any of us, I grew more worried. I called Iker. I needed him to tell me where she went. And I wanted to know how the fuck Flint got into her place, and her bodyguard didn't know it. Recalling that phone call still pissed me off.

"Hey, Hoss, I thought you had a party tonight. Are you having too much fun?" he asked as he answered. It was

eleven at night.

"I was having fun until shit went sideways, and Cady left. Imagine my surprise when I got to her place, and I found her with an unwanted intruder. One who had broken in somehow and was waiting for her. I want to know how that happened when she was to be watched. It was Reid, goddamn it! The main one I wanted her protected from. If I hadn't come, God knows what he could've done to her!" I was shouting by the end. If Iker had been in front of me, I might've choked him.

I heard him say, "Fuck. Let me find out." There was a long pause. I was about to ask if he had forgotten me when he began talking.

"Hoss, I swear to you. I put a man on her. He was supposed to be outside her home and clinic. I just sent a text to him. I'm waiting for him to respond. Is she alright? Reid didn't hurt her, did he?" There was concern in his tone.

"No, he didn't, but after I got rid of him, she took off. She's not answering her phone, no matter who calls. If your man isn't following her, then I need you to get someone to track her phone. She's out there upset and alone."

"What happened to make her run?"

"That's between us. All I need is for you to find her. She'd better not have a scratch on her when we find her, or I'll be taking it out on your man's ass tenfold, and you and I will be having a talk you won't appreciate," I promised him.

"I get it, and I don't blame you. Let me get someone on it. I have her number from what you gave me on her before. They can do a trace rather quickly."

There were more rustling sounds and silence. Several minutes passed before he came back on the line. As soon as I heard his first words, I knew it wasn't good.

"Goddamn it, I'm sorry, Hoss. Poe was assigned to

her. He was watching her until she ended up at the House of Lustz. He knew she would be surrounded by friends, and you had security. The party was to last until after midnight, so he thought it was safe to duck out and be back before midnight to follow her when she left."

"He didn't think to ask anyone?" I snapped.

He sighed. "No, he didn't. He's new but still a competent guard. I'll speak to him right away, and I can assure you it will never happen again. It was an unfortunate misunderstanding. The good thing is she wasn't harmed. You got there in time."

"Yeah, that's good, but I can't have this happen. I don't want Poe watching her again. Assign one of your oldest and most competent people."

"Hoss, you know I'll do everything I can, but I don't have anyone else available until after tomorrow. They're all out on assignments. Poe won't mess up again."

"No, I don't want him there. I'll do it myself until you can get me someone else. I don't have time to talk about this anymore right now. I'll come by and see you in the next day or two."

"Okay. Oh, and as for her phone, she has it off. There's no way we can trace it. I'm sorry."

That led to more cursing and then to me hanging up angrier. I didn't sleep all night. This morning, I headed over to the clinic. I knew she'd never stay away from her furry patients. I wasn't too surprised to find Mikhail and Tajah there, even though I didn't bother to tell them that I was planning to catch her there this morning.

I'd been relieved to find her unharmed, though she appeared tired. Her refusal to talk to us and insistence we go had made me want to pick her up and haul her out over my shoulder, but somehow, I held myself back. I knew once I got started, it would last a long time, and I didn't want any interruptions. I was planning not only to clear up the misconceptions about Fleur and my character but also to let Cady know what I wanted with her. I kept praying it wouldn't blow up in my face.

I wasn't able to concentrate on work, so I had Alica Ann reschedule my meetings. I went home and tried to do work from there after taking a quick nap, but it didn't happen. I spent my time pacing and rehearsing what I planned to say. During the day, I did get a call from Mikhail. He told me how upset Tajah was. She was eager to go see Cady as soon as the clinic closed.

"Mikhail, I know they're best friends and Taj is upset and worried. I get it. But please, I beg you. Convince her to stay away and let me talk to Cady first. I have to do this before I explode. I need her to know who Fleur is and what I want. This uncertainty is killing me."

He sighed. "Hoss, I get it. Believe me, I do. I still remember what I had to do to win Tajah's heart. I'm in a hard spot between my woman and my friend. I'll ask her to hang back, but I might not be able to talk her out of it. If she insists, I'll take her."

"All I'm asking is to plead my case. I understand if she still wants to go. This talk I plan to have with Cady will be a long one."

"Just remember, wear a cup," he snickered. I knew he was trying to lighten my mood. It worked.

A faint smile spread as I gruffly told him, "Go fuck yourself. Later," then hung up. I heard him chuckling as I did.

That call was several hours ago now. Checking the

clock, I saw it was six. She had to be done by now and headed home. I'd go there first, and if she weren't there, I'd hit the clinic. God help us both if she was at neither place. I couldn't go another night without clearing this up.

Due to the time of day, I expected to hit traffic, which I did. By the time I got to her place, it was seven. Disappointment filled me when I didn't see her car. But to be sure, I went to her door and knocked over and over. If she had been there, she would've come out yelling for me to stop. The next logical place was her clinic after eliminating her apartment. I got back in my car and headed that way. That was when fate decided to fuck with me. Traffic was still relatively thick, but nothing I wasn't used to.

I was navigating through the throngs of cars and watching out for idiots. Only I didn't have enough eyes to watch all the idiots given a driver's license. Horns honking was my first clue. Then, there was a screech of metal on metal and a loud bang. It happened so fast. There was nothing to be done. Two cars had hit head-on. I stomped on the brake, like so many others. Both cars were right in front of me in the intersection.

Jumping out after putting mine in *Park*, I raced over to see if anyone was injured and needed help. In one car was a dazed businessman based on his suit. In the other vehicle was a mom with two small kids. The kids were screaming and crying in fright. Mom appeared dazed and had a bleeding cut on her forehead. The businessman was getting out of his car under his own steam, so I focused on the mom and kids.

"Ma'am, you need to sit still. Your head is bleeding. The paramedics are coming," I told her.

I hoped someone had called. With all the lookie-loos, surely someone did. Her window was down, so she was able to hear me. I had to jerk a few times to get the passenger door on the driver's side open. Sticking my head inside, I smiled at the two children. One was a toddler, a girl maybe two or three years old. The other was a boy. I'd gauge him to be five. Both were crying and calling for their mom. She was trying to talk to them and comfort them from the front seat. Their eyes grew round when they saw me. I knew my size alone made me scary, then add the bald head, tats, and the fact I was Black, and it was worse. I hated it, but it was reality.

"Hi guys, my name is Hoss. I'm here to help. Can you stop crying so I can ask you some questions? Your mommy is worried about you, so I have to make sure you're alright for her."

It took a couple of minutes of cajoling before they settled so I could ask them my questions. I wasn't about to just take them out. If they had a spinal injury, it might make it worse. Emergency trauma care was one of those things I took a course in years ago. I'd done it because I was interested, and it relieved my boredom. Plus, with all the extreme sports I did, it was wise to know.

As I went through a variety of questions, which I asked all three, I began to be hopeful there were no serious injuries. By the time I'd determined they could get out, I was interrupted by paramedics and firemen. Someone tapped me on the back. I eased back out of the car and stood. When I did, I saw the paramedic who had been the one to tap my back. He backed up and had to look up a long way to meet my gaze.

"Glad to see you guys. I think they're safe to move.

Mom has a laceration to her upper left forehead. It was bleeding pretty hard, but it has slowed down. I had her apply pressure. The kids were securely fastened in their car seats and are more shaken up than anything."

"Are you a doctor or something?" he asked.

"No, but I've been trained in emergency care."

"Well, thank you for your report, but we have to do our own assessment. Would you mind moving back?" he asked nicely.

I moved further away. The next thing I was asked was a bunch of questions by firemen and then the police. Mostly, it was about what I saw and what I'd done to treat the family. When it was all said and done, it tied me up for two hours. By the time I left the scene, it was almost nine-thirty. Shit, Cady probably already left the clinic, but I was close, so I decided to check anyway. I couldn't wait to get one of Iker's best on her security detail. I hadn't turned out to be any better than Poe, although I might not tell Iker that.

Coming around the turn on the street where her clinic was and seeing the parking lot filled with police cars with flashing lights made my heart fall to my toes. Christ, what happened? Was she alright? I got as close as I could before I parked, got out, and then took off running for the front door.

Some cop tried to step out and block me, but I dodged him and kept going. I heard shouts to stop, but I wasn't worried about me. I had to be sure Cady wasn't harmed. Three cops were standing, blocking the entrance. "Cady, where are you?" I shouted. If she didn't answer, I'd be barreling through their asses, cops or not.

When she didn't answer right away, I took a few steps closer. They were watching me warily, and their hands were on their tasers. I was about to risk being shocked when I heard her voice.

"Hoss, what are you doing here? Hey, you, move it so I can get out. That man isn't a patient person," she said snappishly.

They parted, and she came walking out. I didn't wait for her to make it to me. I rushed forward and scooped her up in my arms. She gasped. Before she found her voice and reprimanded me, I kissed her. It was one way for me to reassure myself she was here and unharmed.

I swallowed her gasp and then felt her melt into me as it went from me kissing her to us kissing each other. Her arms came up around my neck. I lifted her off the ground so I didn't have to stoop so far. I wasn't sure how long the kiss lasted before we were interrupted by someone clearing his throat and speaking.

"Sir, we need to finish our work, and we need Dr. Anderson for that. Could you tell me who you are?"

Reluctantly, I pulled away from her. Her face was flushed, and she had a dreamy look about her. I wanted her to stay that way. An older officer was standing there. He was trying not to smile, I think. I slowly lowered her back to her feet, but I didn't let go of her completely. I kept an arm circling her waist.

"My name is Magnus Sacket, but most people call me Hoss. What happened here? Cady, are you alright?"

She gave me a sheepish look, but no answer. I glanced at the officer. He asked another question.

"Mr. Sacket, I'm Officer Callahan. I understand this is the second time this has happened in less than two weeks. Why are you here at this time of night? And what exactly is your relationship with Dr. Anderson?"

The suspicion was there. Did I have something to do with this?

"I'm—" I started but was interrupted by Cady.

"Wait a damn minute. You're not accusing Hoss of having something to do with this, are you? If you are, you're way off base. He has nothing to do with the break-in. I heard the voices of the two men who broke in. They sound nothing like Hoss, I can assure you."

Callahan cleared his throat nervously. "Dr. Anderson, we have to investigate everyone you have contact with. Mr. Sacket shows up in the middle of the night when the clinic is closed. Why? I'm sorry if it upsets you, but this is my job."

"And we get that, but I'm not the one breaking into her clinic, nor have I hired anyone to do it. I presume that would be your next question. As for why I'm here, I came to find Cady when she wasn't home. We have things to discuss. Unfortunately, I got here later than I wanted due to a car accident."

Her breath hitched, and she glanced up. I saw concern. "Are you alright? Shouldn't you be at the hospital getting checked out?"

"Tiny, I wasn't the one in the wreck, thank God. I witnessed it and then rendered aid until the firemen and paramedics got there. Afterward, I had to answer a lot of questions. If that hadn't happened, I would've been here almost three hours ago. I would've prevented this burglary or at least caught them in the act. I'm worried about you. Did they hurt you? What did they say they wanted? You said you heard their voices. That means you were here."

There were no visible injuries, and she seemed to be moving fine, but I couldn't be sure short of stripping her bare and examining every inch of her. And as much as I wanted that, this wasn't the time or place. She was shaking her head before I was done firing off my questions. She tried to move away from my arm, but I kept a hold of her.

"I'm unharmed. Yes, I was here, and when I heard glass crashing, I knew someone was coming in uninvited. I hid under my desk and called 911. Thankfully, the two men who entered started in the examination rooms first. They were only in my office a few minutes before the police arrived."

"You could've been killed! After the last break-in, why do you insist on staying late? It's not safe. Whoever these men are, they don't seem to want to quit. Did you catch them?" I asked Callahan.

He shook his head. "No, we didn't. They got out the back. We pursued, but they lost us in the dark. There were so many places to hide around here that they probably ducked in somewhere or had a car waiting. "

"What is she supposed to do? Wait for them to come back a third time and maybe get herself killed! You said they came into your office, and that was where you were hiding. Did you see them? Can you identify them? What did they do when they saw you? Why did you have to call 911? The alarm company should've dispatched them." I was ramping up on the agitation scale, and I knew it, but my worry over her was increasing with every word. Her hand squeezed my upper arm.

"Hoss, calm down. It's not their fault. The alarm didn't go off, and before you ask, yes, it was on. They somehow bypassed it. They didn't see me, which means I didn't see them. I can't identify them. I may recognize their voices again, but that is a huge maybe. I was hidden under my desk. They barely got started ransacking my office when the police showed up, and they took off. As for why I stay after dark, you know why. My work isn't nine-to-five. It was crazy today and I had charting to do on my patients. I chose to do it here."

"Do you still think they're after drugs?" I asked.

"I do. It's the only thing I can think of. Twice, they walked right past expensive equipment that would fetch them money if they stole it. There's nothing else of importance in there," she insisted.

"Yes, there is," I grunted.

"What?" she asked, puzzled.

"You. You're more important than the drugs, equipment, and anything else you have in there. What happens if they come again and they find you? They'll force you to give them what they want. When they've gotten what they want, what's stopping them from harming or killing you?"

She didn't answer me immediately. I was waiting. Eventually, she sighed. "There's nothing to stop them from doing any of those things. However, this is my work, my livelihood. What would you have me do?"

I knew what I wanted, but this wasn't the place or time to tell her. Instead, I turned to Callahan. "Is there more you have to do here? Or can she lock up and go home? It's late, and she has a full day tomorrow."

"Our CSIs are dusting for prints, but there are so many it's hard to know. We've got elimination prints from the first time, so it should help speed it along. Other than that, there's not much for us to go on. I suggest you have the alarm company check into how the system was bypassed. If they did it once, they can do it again. Give us a half hour, and then we'll be out of your hair. Dr. Anderson, may I ask you a few more questions?" he asked politely.

I would've preferred to stay with her, but I had work to do. "Tiny, go with him. I'll catch up. I have to make a call."

She seemed reluctant to go with him, but she did. As soon as she was out of earshot, I called. It took only two rings for it to be answered. "What's up?" Mikhail asked. I knew they weren't in bed this early, or if they were, it wasn't to sleep.

"Hope I'm not interrupting anything."

He chuckled. "Not yet, but if you called in a half hour, probably. Did you speak to Cady? How did it go? It wasn't easy keeping Tajah here."

"I haven't spoken to Cady, or at least not about that, but I am with her at the moment. I'm at the clinic. I went to find her after work, but she wasn't home. I got caught up in an accident on my way to the clinic. It wasn't me who had the accident. By the time I got here, the place had cop cars out front. Whoever broke in before did it again. Only this time, Cady was inside." I paused to inhale deeply to push down my rage at the idea of one of them touching her.

"Son of a bitch! What the hell? How? Is she alright?"

"She's shaken but physically fine. They bypassed the alarm somehow, Mikhail. She hid under her desk and had to wait for 911 to get the cops there. The burglars were in her personal office when the police arrived. She could've been found at any moment. I want to know how they got in. That biker you talk about all the time, the one who does your background stuff..."

What's his name?"

"You're talking about Outlaw. What do you need him to do?"

"I want him to figure out how these fuckers got past that system. Something is fishy here, and I want to know what. She's not safe here, and at home, we have old Flint Reid sniffing around."

"I'll get Outlaw on it right away. In the meantime, take her home and get her to pack a bag. She can stay here with us."

"I'm taking her home, and she'll pack a bag, but she's not staying with you and Tajah. Her sweet ass is coming to my house," I growled.

He laughed. "I kind of thought you'd say that, but I had to offer. Does she need anything? Tajah and I can come down there if you think she needs Taj."

"I'll let you know. Right now, I'd say no. If it changes, I'll buzz you. Thanks, and tell Outlaw that money isn't an object. I'll pay him whatever he wants."

"Hoss, that's not how he works. He'll never charge for protecting your woman. At most, he may ask a favor, and it's nothing you're unwilling to pay. The Archangel's Warriors are good guys. You've met Payne. The rest are like him, in a way. I think it's time we get off here. I'll call, and you take care of Cady. Talk tomorrow."

"We will, and thanks, Mikhail. I owe you."

"You don't owe me shit. Don't insult me by saying it again. Night," he said gruffly before hanging up.

I knew Mikhail hated for anyone to think or feel that they owed him. I knew he did, but I still meant it. Making Cady safe was all that mattered to me, and I was willing to pay or owe whatever I had to make it a reality. Before heading in to find Cady, I made one more call. He answered, sounding half asleep.

"Yo, what's up?" Iker asked. I heard him yawn.

"Will you have someone tomorrow for Cady?"

"I will. He can be at her house before she leaves for work. You don't want him hanging around during work hours, do you? Because the man will need to sleep sometime."

"I need someone to follow her to work and then home and to watch at night. However, she won't be at her place in the morning. She'll be at mine."

"Hey, damn, you moved fast. Congrats."

"It's not that. We're working through stuff, but her clinic was hit again tonight, and she was there. It was a miracle she wasn't found and hurt. I'm taking her to my place where I know she's safe and I can keep an eye on her. I'll bring her to work, and your man can start there."

"Are you fucking kidding me? They did it again. What the hell are they up to?" he muttered.

"Who knows? I was supposed to be here, but there was an accident, and I got caught up in it. They bypassed the alarm somehow, Iker."

"Shit. Do you want me to see if my guys can figure out how? It shouldn't be that easy. My guy snooped at hers, and it isn't one that you snip a wire outside and it's done. They'd have to do it from inside the building or remotely, and those systems aren't open for just anyone to mess with. You have to know what you're doing."

"Thanks, but I've got someone checking into it. He's a computer whiz. All I need is to be sure she has someone watching when she's not at work during regular hours."

"You know, if you get her to stay with you every

night, that'll help," he said slyly.

"I'm working on it, but I'm not assuming anything with Cady Cat. She's not one to bow down."

"And if she were, you wouldn't be interested."

"Damn right. Okay, send over the details on whoever the new guy is so I know him. If he has issues, tell him to talk to me. Thanks, Iker. I'll let you get back to sleep, old man."

"Old man, my ass. I was up for thirty-six hours, that's why I'm in bed. Fuck off," he grumbled good-naturedly.

I wound up our call by laughing before hanging up. With those out of the way, it was time to get Cady and get her packed and to my house. I wondered how much of a fight I was in for. My skin tingled, and my heart raced a bit in anticipation. Pocketing my phone, I went into the clinic. The police and their team seemed to be wrapping up. They were milling around rather aimlessly, in my opinion. I found Cady in her office talking to Callahan. When I entered, they both glanced over at me.

"Are you about done? I see people just moseying around out there. If there's nothing else, we have a long night ahead of us," I told him.

"No, we're finished. Dr. Anderson, you have my card. Call me if you have questions or if you think of anything." Callahan stood and held out his hand. She shook it and smiled.

I didn't like it. He was touching her, and the way he smiled back told me all I needed to know. Officer Callahan found Cady attractive, and he was interested. Another man I'd have to scare off. I might have to stop working so I could stay on top of running off unwanted suitors. However, if I got my way, it would soon be my job. Cady Anderson was meant for one man—me. If she gave me an in, there was no way I'd let anyone take her from me. I was a vicious fighter.

Lucky for Callahan, he walked off, or I would've been baring teeth at him. My patience was almost gone. I had to get Cady to safety and then have this beyond-important conversation with her. I held out my hand to her. She slowly took it. I walked her out to the lobby. The cops and their people were filing out the door. Callahan was bringing up the rear.

"Hoss, my car is parked in the back. I'll go out that way," she said softly.

"Hang on, and I'll walk you out to it. I want to lock up the front."

"You don't have to hang around. I'm headed home as soon as I lock this up," was her next remark.

I gave her a quelling look, which she heeded. Callahan gave her one last look and smiled. I slammed the door on him and threw the lock. Swiftly turning, I led her through the building. "Is there anything you need to grab before we go?" I asked.

"No, I've got my purse."

We reached the back. Next to the rear door, there was broken glass from something. It wasn't from a window. There were none of them near the back door.

"I need to clean that up," she muttered.

"Cady Cat, it's late. You're tired. The office is a mess. You'll have to close it tomorrow anyway to get it cleaned up, so this can wait until then. What you need now is to de-stress. Come on. Leave it," I ordered, but I did it in a less demanding way.

She sighed. "You're right. I can't face this tonight.

Thank you for stopping. I have no idea why you did, but I do feel better not walking out into the dark parking lot alone." She paused and glanced at the alarm system's control panel. "Well, this is kind of useless to set. They got by it. Hell, I don't even know if it's working."

"Why don't you try? It can't hurt. Maybe whatever they did was a one-time thing, and the system will be fine. We'll get people working on it to fix it, too."

I didn't tell her it was already in motion. I stepped outside while she punched in her code. There was no beep to signal it was armed. I heard her utter "Fuck," and then she was closing and locking the door. As soon as she was done, I escorted her to her car. At the car, I took her keys and unlocked it with her key fob. She faced me. She gave me an uncertain look.

"Thank you. I can take it from here. You need to get home. You have work in the morning, just as I do."

"I'll follow you home."

"Hoss, there's no need to do that. The robbers are after the clinic. I seriously doubt they know where my home is," she protested.

"Maybe they don't, but Reid does, and don't forget, he got in last night."

There was a flare of emotion in her eyes before she hid it when I mentioned last night. "I can handle Flint Reid if he's stupid enough to come back. I'll be fine," she declared.

"I'm not taking any chances. Now, we can stand out here in the cold and argue all night, or you can get your sweet ass in that car, and we can get to your place. When we get there, you're to pack a bag. You can't stay there, not tonight. You're being taken to stay where it's safe."

"Let me guess, Tajah and Mikhail said to bring me to their place," she grumbled as she rolled her eyes.

Since it wasn't a lie, I agreed. "They did. Let's go, Tiny. It's late." I opened the door. She got inside while grumbling.

"You've got to stop calling me names. Don't think just because I'm going along with this, that you or anyone else can boss me around. If you do, it's your own fault when you get an attitude adjustment."

I chuckled. "Warning received. And we'll talk later about your names and other things. Don't race off. I have to get to my car out front. Drive safe. I'll be right behind you." I resisted kissing her before I shut her door. As she started her car, I jogged to get to mine. She did stop and wait for me, a miracle.

Being as late as it was, there was little traffic. We made it to her apartment in record time. The whole area was dark. I didn't waste time getting out and helping her out of her car and then to the door. When she went to put the key into the lock, I took it from her.

"Hey, what's—" she said, but I cut her off.

"I go first. I need to clear it. You stay here until I say it's safe to enter."

"I swear, if you give me one more order, I'm kicking your ass," she hissed.

She gave me a frustrated look. However, the more telling part was that she stayed still when I opened the door. Switching on lights as I went, I swiftly searched her place. It wasn't huge, so it didn't take long. When I came back to the door, she was standing there tapping her foot. I grinned at her as I swung her door wide open.

"It's clear. Go get your things. I'll make sure everything is secure."

She harrumphed as she passed me, but I was glad to see her head to her bedroom. While waiting for her to pack, I tried every window to be sure they were securely latched. Of course, someone could always break them to get in. There were none broken. So, how did Reid get in? She had no alarm system here, which I would be fixing ASAP. Did he still have a key? Wanting to know, in case that meant re-keying her door, I hurried to her room. The door was open, and she was putting things in a small suitcase.

"Cady, I've got to ask. Is it possible Reid still has a key to your apartment? Is that how he got in last night? I don't see any windows unlocked or with marks from being forced open."

She stopped and faced me, frowning. "No, it's not possible he has a key. I never gave him one. I don't know how he got in. The door was locked when I got here. I used my key. Maybe a window was unlocked, and after he came in, he locked it."

"Do you usually leave them unlocked?" If she said yes, I'd spank her ass. In my opinion, she was too lackadaisical about her safety.

"Typically, no, I'm very cautious and check that I don't leave windows or doors unlocked, but it's always possible."

"Finish up. I'll check to see if the lock shows marks that he picked it."

"You can tell that?" she sounded incredulous.

"Yes, you can if you know what to look for."

"And you do?"

I smiled at her as I winked. "There's a lot you don't know about me yet, Tiny. You'll have to be patient. I promise you'll know everything soon." As I walked out, she snorted. I held in my laughter.

My examination of the lock did show scratches, so I thought it was most likely how he got in. Her door needed a better locking system and an alarm. I'd call Iker in the morning to get one of his people on it right away. I was about to go look for her when she joined me. I took her suitcase. The next part would be tricky. I knew if I outright told her she was coming to my place, she'd refuse, and we'd fight about it. To avoid it, I needed to get her in my car.

"Ready?" I asked.

"I am. Let's go. It's late, and I don't want Tajah and Mikhail waiting up all night."

When I held out my hand, she handed me her keys. She was learning. I locked the apartment door and slipped the keys in my pocket. Taking her hand in my free one, I directed her to the parking lot. I bypassed her car and stopped next to mine.

"Hoss, this is your car."

"I know it is. It's best to leave yours here. Anyone coming by, such as Reid, will think you're home. If those men at the clinic do know where you live, they might think twice before stopping if they believe you're home." I was rambling and had no idea if what I said made sense, but if it got her in my car, then I was almost home-free.

Her brow wrinkled, and she didn't appear convinced, but with a nudge from me, she gave in. She must either be more tired than I thought, or the strain was getting to her. I put her case in the backseat and then helped her into hers. When I got in the driver's side, I caught her rubbing her hands on the leather. She smiled as I started it.

"Your car is beautiful."

"Thank you, it's one of my favorites."

"I can see why. I'm not a car person, but even this one makes me drool. So, you're a man who loves speed, obviously. What else?"

"Cady, there's so much more to me. It would take a lifetime to learn it all, just as I imagine it is with you. I can tell you I love to be busy and challenged, and I'm an adrenaline junkie, as some would call it."

"The busyness and challenges doesn't surprise me. I'm curious about what you call adrenaline junkie activities." Inquisitiveness was apparent in her voice and on her face.

"Skydiving, slacklining, parasailing, rock climbing, and helo-skiing to name a few."

"What the heck is slacklining, and is helo-skiing what it sounds like?" she asked unbelievingly.

"You take a chopper up to mountain peaks that are unreachable any other way, and then you ski the mountain. That's helo-skiing. You get to see things few others ever do. Slacklining is when a rope is stretched between two objects. The rope isn't tied between two trees or posts and only a few feet off the ground. In my case, it's things like a deep lake or a hundred-foot canyon that's underneath me."

"God, are you crazy!? What if you fall? Or get caught on a mountain in a spot where no one can find you or an avalanche gets you?" she shrieked.

"The risk of those happening is part of the thrill. I'm very cautious. I do my best not to have those things occur. As for the slacklining, I do have a safety belt around my waist to catch me in case I do fall. It's a rush. Haven't you ever done things purely for the rush of it?"

If she said no, that might be an impediment to us as well. While I didn't need someone to do everything with me, if she was too afraid to do anything, it would lessen our connection.

"Sure, I have, just not those. I've done bungee jumping, riding in jet boats and skiing behind one, roller coasters, gliding, surfing, and riding snowmobiles. I've never heard of those two things you mentioned."

Hearing that she had an adventurous side, after all, relieved me. I was more than okay doing those activities with her. Maybe over time, she'd be open to more extreme ones. "If you were ever offered the chance to do others, would you?"

She thought about it for a minute before she answered, "I would say probably, but it would depend on what. Slacklining would be a no for me. Mountain skiing, maybe. Do you only love the thrill, or do you have a secret death wish?"

"Babe, I have no death wish, I assure you. It's all for the thrill and to keep myself occupied. If I get bored, it causes me issues. My brain and body have to stay busy."

As we drove, we kept talking about activities we liked and those we had no use for. It was enlightening, and it was just the type of stuff I wanted to know about her and have her know about me. That was what learning about someone was all about. We were so caught up in the conversation that I got her into the Belle Meade area before she noticed we weren't in The Gulch. She straightened and glanced into the darkness around us. With fewer houses and bigger properties, it wasn't as lit up as other areas of Nashville. She glanced over at me with an adorable frown.

"Hoss, where are we? This isn't the way to Mikhail and Tajah's place."

"I know that. This is Belle Meade. Haven't you been here before?"

We were almost to the long driveway leading to my house. Nearing it, I pressed the remote button to open the gate and allow us access.

"I've driven through it. Why are we here?"

"We're at my house," I said as I pulled through the gate and then pushed the button again to close it behind the car. She gaped at me as I drove up the long, slightly windy driveway. The house was set back far enough that it wasn't visible from the road. I was prepared for her to fight me, but I had news. She'd lose.

Cady: Chapter 10

My exhaustion and hunger, combined with the latest drama, was what had me going along with Hoss when he more or less ordered me to go home, pack, and let him take me to Taj and Mikhail's place to stay the night. If I'd been at my best, I would've pushed back on him. Add to it the way he and I chatted on the way there. It had distracted me. I liked getting to know some things about him, although I shouldn't. All those things combined were why I hadn't been paying attention to his driving or where we were until we were practically entering a gated estate.

As we made our way up the winding driveway after he told me it was his house, I was at a loss for words. Even in the dark, I could see enough to know that it was expansive and gorgeous. The lawn was maintained. Flowerbeds and trees were strategically and artistically arranged. Even though they were mostly dead since it was winter, I knew in the spring and summer, they'd be a riot of colors. One would never get tired of exploring or seeing them.

Belle Meade was the most expensive part of Nashville, or at least one of the top three. There was lots of old money here. Discovering that Hoss, the doorman slash outer security for the House of Lustz, lived here raised more questions about him. The primary reason is why would he work at Lustz if he could afford to live here? However, that question and others would have to wait. At the moment, I only had one.

"Hoss, why are we at your house? We're supposed to be at Mikhail and Tajah's. They're expecting us. Do you need to get something?" Maybe that was why. Yeah, that made sense, though what would he need this late that couldn't wait for him to get home after he dropped me off?

As we topped the rise, I could see what was hidden from the street. It was a house—no, make that a mini-mansion. The exterior was lit up, with lights shining on the landscape. I gasped as I took it in. The house was covered in stone. I had no idea what kind, only that it appeared to be a dark, almost chocolate color, and the stone was stacked. Looking at it reminded me of a castle. There were pointed, peaked roofs, stone edifices, double ornate doors, and more. A large courtyard was in front of the entry. As the car drove down into the courtyard, I glanced at him. He hadn't said a word since I asked why we were there and if he needed to pick something up. He brought the car to a stop outside a garage built into one side of the house. He shut off the engine, undid his seatbelt, and then twisted himself so he was able to see me.

"I'll explain, but we need to do it inside where we can be comfortable."

"I don't need to go inside. Just grab what you need, and then we can go." Even as I said it, I knew he had no intention of getting anything or of leaving here.

His head shook as he undid my seatbelt and then got out. He closed his door and made his way to mine. It was opened, and he reached for my hand. When I refused to give it to him, he sighed.

"Cady, it's late. We're tired. Please, don't fight me on this. Come inside. Let me explain."

"Why can't you explain out here? Or better yet, take me to Tajah and explain another time?"

"First, because this has gone on long enough. Second, I expect her and Mikhail are already in bed. If they're not asleep, they're definitely otherwise occupied." His lips twisted into a smirk.

"I don't know what you mean by this has gone on long enough. As for Mikhail and Tajah being asleep, that's fine. I can go to a hotel. Or I'll call someone else and stay with them."

Before I could say more, I was literally picked up and taken from his car. I wiggled and tried to get loose, but he was too strong for me. I pounded on his rock-hard chest with a fist as I shouted at him.

"Put me down! I insist you take me home or to a hotel this instant. I'm not playing with you. I'll scream," I threatened.

"Scream all you want. There's no one to hear you. As for taking you home or to a hotel, that's not happening. I'm not playing either. You and I need to settle a few things and clear up some misconceptions. While we do, we'll be comfortable, and you'll be safe."

I let out a frustrated scream and hit him harder. The ass just laughed and kept going. I hoped he'd have to set me down to unlock and open the door. When he did, I'd run for it. The fence around the property shouldn't be that hard to climb. I'd hiked my ass over taller things. Sure, they were when I was younger, but I could do it. As I prepared to run for it, the bastard ruined my plan. He was able to hold me with one arm while pressing his thumb to a screen next to his front door. A green light flashed, and then he opened the door. I was whisked inside. Before I knew it, the door was closed and locked.

I tried not to get distracted by the inside and its beauty. I was in the mood to fight, not admire the architecture and decor. He didn't put me down. I wiggled again.

"Put me down," I demanded.

I gasped in shock as he smacked my ass. "Settle down, Cady Cat. I'll put you down when I'm ready and not a second sooner. I know you think you can run, but you can't. We're going to relax and have an adult conversation."

His audacity left me speechless. Then, my inner mouth kicked in. "If you say so."

He gave me an amused look, which I wasn't expecting. I'd have to turn up the irritation factor. I knew, given time, I'd anger him enough to be glad to get rid of me.

We entered a vast living room. I expected him to sit me down and take a seat. Wrong. My breath caught when he sank down on the couch with me still in his arms. This ended with me sitting on his lap. It was too reminiscent of last night and us on my couch. We knew what happened then. I tried to pry his hand from my middle, but he was too strong for me. I glared up at him.

"Hoss, I'm warning you. Let me up. If you want to talk, this isn't the way to go about it. Honestly, I have no idea why you and I need to talk about anything. Thank you for stopping in tonight, although I don't know why you did. I'm perfectly capable of taking care of myself."

"First, let's get clear on something. I don't want you to call me Hoss like everyone else does. It's a nickname."

As he paused, I jumped in. "What do you prefer that I call you? Dickhead? Asshole? Pain-in-my-ass?"

"If you choose to call me those, be aware that I'll have to discipline you for it. However, I can be a pain in your ass if you want. Just know my version will be far more enjoyable than the kind you meant." He winked.

I flushed hot all over. I knew exactly what he meant. He was referring to him putting things in my ass, and from the heated way he was staring at me, his cock would be one of them. I wanted to moan. I enjoyed anal sex, but my experiences had varied from enjoyable to painful. In his case, I imagined he was proportionate. The thought of his massive cock entering my ass both scared and thrilled me.

He groaned. "Fuck, you can't look like that, Cady. It just makes me want to say the hell with talking. Be good. At least for a while."

Before lust overtook my whole brain, I shook off the haze and scowled at him. He wasn't going to find me an easy target again. I wasn't falling under his spell like I did last night. I had to keep my wits and remember, he was a player and cheater. He freely admitted last night he had a woman, and then I saw her. I had no idea what game he thought he was playing. Or did he think I was a woman who wouldn't care? That being a side piece was good enough for me. The thought of any of those being the case had my anger rising.

"Go to hell, Hoss. You have nothing I want to hear or nothing I want. Play your games with someone else. I'm not interested." I jabbed my elbow into his ribs. I hoped it would make him let go of me. Instead, it made him wrap his arms tighter around me. I could still breathe, but I wasn't able to get free. However, I wiggled my hardest to try.

As I did, I became aware of a hardness growing under my ass. I gulped. I tried more frantically. I had to get away. I whimpered when teeth bit down on my earlobe, making a slight pain go through it, then a warm, wet tongue sucked on it as if to soothe the pain. His growly voice made me shiver.

"Cady, you keep wiggling that delicious ass all over my cock, and I'm going to strip you bare, feast on you, drive you wild, then I'll sink my cock inside that pussy and fuck you until we both come and can't move. Is that what you want, Tiny?" he rasped.

"No. I want you to stop playing this game or whatever with me. Your woman can't approve of this behavior. Does she know you cheat on her? Why can't you be faithful? Why bring me or other women into your love life? Oh, wait, I forgot. You're a man. Men are genetically hardwired not to be monogamous," I said acidly. I'd heard that excuse more than a few times.

His face tightened. I held myself ready for him to give lame excuses, lie out of his ass, or get angry—typical man reactions.

"First, let me tell you that I'm not playing a game with you. Second, I'm not cheating on my woman. Third, I can more than be faithful to a woman. Monogamy isn't a dirty word to me."

I hissed at him. I mean, I literally hissed like a cat. His response pissed me off to no end. "You're lying right now! Last night, you had your tongue in my mouth and your hand on my body. If I hadn't stopped you, are you telling me you would've stopped? And how can you say that wasn't cheating? Does only penetration count? I hate to tell you, but most women consider what we did as cheating. Therefore, you can't be monogamous."

"I did have my tongue in your mouth and my hands on your ass and tits. And no, I wouldn't have stopped. But it wasn't cheating. It—"

I cut him off. His denial was making me sick. "How the fuck is it not cheating!? God, men make me sick. No wonder I'm over the whole bunch of you. I swear, I think being a lesbian is where it's at," I snarled. I sank my short nails into his arm, attempting to get him to let go so I could get up. I was out of here, even if I had to climb the fence and walk my ass all night to get home.

He let out what sounded like a frustrated growl. Suddenly, I was airborne. I squawked in surprise. Before I could gather my wits, I was on my back on the couch, and he was hovering over me. Lashing out with my knee, I went for his balls. Pain shot through my leg when I made contact with hard plastic or something where his balls should've been.

"Ow, what the hell?" I cried out.

"Did you honestly think I'd be that dumb again? I knew you'd likely get combative, and I wanted to be sure we didn't have a repeat of last night. It's called an athletic cup. Now, before you do something to hurt yourself more, let me finish what I was saying. It wasn't cheating. The woman you saw at Lustz isn't in a relationship with me, Cady."

"She knew you, Hoss. She sure seemed to know you sexually and what you like. Or is it that you play with so many of the women there they all know? How can you keep them all straight? For a man, the club is an all-you-can-eat or, in this case, all-you-can-fuck smorgasbord. I don't know how Tajah can stand for Mikhail to be around all the women he's been with. She's convinced he won't stray, but give it time."

"Christ, babe, I get it. I do. Men have always disappointed and hurt you. I'm sorry. I am, but it doesn't make every man a liar or cheater. I can guarantee you Mikhail will never betray Tajah. He'd cut off his own arm first. As for Fleur, yes, I know her. We scened together a couple of times months ago. I was looking for a partner and thought I'd try her. I ended up not liking it and told her never again. When she came up to me at the party, she was delusional and causing trouble. I got rid of her and went to find you. That's when I discovered you'd left and came after you. I have never had sex with Fleur. Are there women at the club I have had it with? Yes, a few, but a lot less than you think. I've played with more than I've ever had sex with."

"Played with? What difference does it make? Playing is sexual and intimate."

"It can be, but in my case, they are different and separate. There are only a few women I have done both with."

I let what he said sink in, but I knew that even if what he said was true, it had nothing to do with me. "Say what you just said is true. Why should I care? It has nothing to do with me. I'm not in your club. I'm not looking to play with someone or to have a fuck buddy. So there's no reason for you to continue whatever this is," I pointed my finger back and forth between us. I had to find a way to get him to let me go. If not, I'd crack, and my mouth would be on his, and I'd be begging him to touch and fuck me.

His head lowered until his forehead practically rested on mine. I was almost cross-eyed. His gaze burned into me. "There is every goddamn reason for this. I told you my woman would be at the party last night. That wasn't a lie. She was. The only problem is she has no idea I want her to be mine. That I crave her like a fucking drug. Just the sight of her, hearing her name, and catching a whiff of her scent is enough to drive me wild.

"I want to spend every minute I can with her. I want to know her better than anyone. I want her to give me all her worries and troubles. I need her to want and crave me the same way. I'm hanging on by a thread due to my overwhelming need to claim what's mine."

I was stunned at his admission and then angry. I shoved at his chest, but he didn't move. "If you have someone like that, then why are you doing this!? Playing head games with me isn't what you should be doing," I shouted at him.

"You're so damn dense," he muttered. I growled at him which made him smile. His head had raised away from mine a tiny bit. "Cady, you're the woman. I want you. I've been waiting for you to get to know me, but it hasn't happened. I can't wait any longer. That's why I kissed you. If you hadn't run out of Lustz or run off after our kiss at your place last night, you would know this. Woman, you've got a running problem I'll have to cure you of, but I'll enjoy doing it." He winked.

"You, I, uhm, did you...," I rambled.

I was in shock, and a part of me was in denial. There was no way a man like Hoss would be interested in me. Even if he were, it wouldn't last. I grasped at that. "Hoss, let me save us both time and heartache. You may feel that right now, but give it a few weeks or months, and you won't. I'm not long-term girlfriend material."

He scowled. "And what makes you say that?

Cocksuckers like Flint Reid and your past boyfriends? The men who have slapped you, flung you around by your hair, and more? Those sons of a bitches? Because I can tell you right now, I won't do that to you. And I have no doubt you're long-term girlfriend material, but that's not what I'm after."

"Then what? Do you want a play partner?" He was confusing me more.

"No, I want you as my woman in every way for the rest of my life. I want you the way Mikhail has Tajah —as my play partner, lover, and, eventually, wife. And if you're willing, as the mother of my children. The last isn't a hard must if you don't want kids. What I'm not willing to do is play with someone else."

"What if I don't like what you do when it comes to playing?"

My heart was galloping half out of my chest. I was finding it hard to think. Excitement was bubbling up inside of me, but along with it was trepidation. I knew even if he said he wanted me, he'd grow tired of me and my attitude. All men did.

"You'll enjoy it. I saw the way you watched and reacted to Sam and Justine at the club when she was letting her brat out, and he responded. The only differences between them and us are they're only scene partners, not lovers, and he's a brat tamer while I'm a brat handler. I know you think your brattiness will anger me or eventually turn me off, but it won't. I happen to love your sassiness, and I want you to give that side free rein. I'll show you when it's acceptable to let that all show and when it's not. The problem with the guys you knew in the past is they had no idea how to handle you. You needed me."

My body was screaming at my mind to believe what he was saying. If it were up to my body, we'd already be naked, and I'd have him inside of me, which was crazy. I didn't respond to men this way. I'd never been insane to have sex with a man. Sure, I'd had interest, but it was nothing like the intensity of my attraction to Hoss.

"Hoss—" he put a finger to my lips to stop me.

"Back to what I started to say. I don't want you to call me Hoss. It's fine that others do. I've had that nickname for a long time. But with you, I need to hear something else."

"What? Sir? Master?" I taunted without thinking.

He smirked. "Maybe when we play, but outside of that, I want you to call me Magnus. It's my name, after all, Magnus Sacket."

I'd heard him tell the cops that, and I secretly thought it was an awesome name. To be asked, no told, to use it was surreal. I knew from Tajah that few people called Mikhail by his actual name, and even fewer used Misha as she did. I wasn't sure what to say.

"I know I'm dropping a shit ton on you all at once, but you're elusive, Cady. It's been a fight to get to know you. You avoid me. I've got to know. Is it because you don't like me? My instincts say it's not, but am I wrong?"

His slight uncertainty was endearing—as if any woman in her right mind wouldn't want Hoss—I mean Magnus. However, this uncertainty might be my chance to avoid an imploding relationship. I was over those. I should tell him I didn't like him and take the out. I didn't need or want more heartache. And something told me that he would hurt more than all the others combined when he left me.

"Hoss... Magnus, you haven't thought this through. Even if I liked you, this wouldn't work. The best thing for both of us is to forget we ever had this conversation." I tried to move into a better position, but he still had me trapped underneath him, although he wasn't lying on top of me. If he were, I wouldn't be able to breathe.

His eyes seemed to grow darker, which shouldn't be possible. They were almost black as it was. The light was shining off his bald head. I yearned to run my hands all over it. I'd never been with a bald man. I would've said I didn't find one sexy, but Hoss made me change my mind. I'd been dreaming, when I was alone in my bed, of having him naked and exploring all the muscles I knew were underneath his clothing, as well as running my hands over that smooth head. I'd use my hands and mouth on every inch of him. Thinking those thoughts made my nipples tighten more, and the slickness between my legs from feeling his erection minutes ago increased. Unconsciously, I squeezed my legs together. Of course, he noticed, and a sexy smirk appeared.

"Babe, are you wet for me? I bet if I put my hands on those bare tits of yours, your nipples are hard pearls, aren't they? I saw your intention on your face. You're going to tell me you don't like or want me, but that's a goddamn lie. Your body doesn't lie. Tell me why. Tell me why you're so afraid. If you do, I'll help you with that ache."

He brushed a feather-light finger over my nipples. Even though they were covered in my shirt and bra, it was enough to make me whimper in want. "Tell me," he whispered before he placed a barely there kiss on my mouth and then moved away.

I was weakening. I wanted him to touch me. To do whatever he wanted to me. My resistance was eroding. I tried to fight to hold onto it. "Hoss, stop. This isn't what either of us should do." My voice didn't sound convincing. It was hesitant, weak. *Damn it! Try harder,* I scolded myself.

He raised his head. He'd been kissing along my neck. "Cady Cat, it's abso-fucking-lutely what we should do. What we have to do. Tell me why you fear it. I think I know, but I have to be sure."

"Tell me what you believe."

He shook his head. "Nope. You first."

The brat inside of me was pushing for me to smart off, but I didn't. Instead, I confessed. After I was done explaining, surely he'd see the light and back off. If he didn't, I was afraid tonight would be the night I threw myself at him and begged him to fuck me.

"The reason is simple. After putting up with me and my attitude, smart mouth, and obstinate behaviors for a few weeks or even months, you'll grow to hate them. And when that happens, you'll hate me. That's when things get ugly—verbally and physically. We'll part ways, not as friends, and heartache can result. No matter what, our friends, Taj and Mikhail, are together. We'd be exposed to each other after breaking up. I've done this dance, Magnus. It never works out. I'm not long-term material. I told you that. Hell, let me give you the names and numbers of my exes. They'll tell you. No man can put up with me. I'm abrasive and unlovable." I made sure to include some of the words used by my prior boyfriends. It still hurt to know I was seen that way, but after so many declaring it, I had to admit it was true. And changing my attitude was something I'd never been able to do.

"And I can't change. I've tried," I added. I was fighting to keep tears out of my eyes.

He closed his eyes and groaned. I wasn't sure what his expression meant. When he opened them moments later, I swear there was a fire in the depths. I gulped.

"Let's sit up. This requires all our attention, and having you under me this way is far too distracting," he said before he was up and tugging me into a sitting position.

As I got into it, he sat back down next to me. He had us touching knees as he angled himself to be able to see me. I mirrored his angle. He took both of my hands in his. His thumbs began to rub back and forth over the back of my hands in a soothing way. Who knew hands that huge could be so gentle?

"Cady, baby, I need you to hear me out. Please don't interrupt. You'll have a chance to speak after I'm done, I promise. Will you do that for me?"

I found myself nodding yes. He gave me a pleased smile.

"Your attitude and mouth, as you call it, are classic brat behaviors. As I said, I'm a brat handler. Being able to handle someone who is a brat feeds a need inside of me. I like to be responsible and to be in control. However, unlike those men you've been with in the past, I don't want to stamp out your brattiness. They were idiots and had no right to engage in a relationship with you. They needed to nurture your brat in the right way, not destroy it.

"I know you're just beginning to learn about the fetish lifestyle and, in particular, bratting and handling.

I'm not a tamer. They like to try to get rid of the behaviors. What I want and need is to teach you when it's okay to engage in your bratty side and when not to. There are rules to it. Some are universal, but many are individual to the brat and his or her handler. They're agreed upon in advance, just as any punishments are. Remember, I told you that.

"You're a submissive but a unique kind. You push and try to top your partner from the bottom, as we say. This means you require a strong Dom who has a high threshold of patience and wants the attention and responsibility of you. You demand a lot from your partner. Those others couldn't cope with those demands. And let me say, talking about your past lovers fucking pisses me off. I will take you up on your offer of names and numbers, but at a later date and for a very different reason. However, they're important because they set up this erroneous idea in your head that you're undesirable and need to change.

"I don't want you to change other than to learn when and where to be a brat. And I'll more than enjoy teaching you those boundaries. There isn't a single inch of you that's undesirable, Cady. You're challenging in the perfect way for a man like me. If you put yourself in my hands, I promise you I'll worship the ground you walk on and give you everything you want and need. You're insecure, and that's what has led you to be a brat. Let me be your safety."

When he paused, I felt dazed and overwhelmed. No one had ever spoken to me that way. It was hard to absorb. Was he right? Had those men in my past not been right for me, and that was why we failed? It wasn't because I was unlovable, unruly, infuriating. His assurance that I didn't need to change completely was a shock. To hear him say he'd worship the ground I walked on and give me everything was every woman's dream for a partner to do. Was it possible? When he stopped, he patiently waited while I grappled with everything and was able to find my voice.

"Say I believe what you just said. And it's true, my knowledge of the kink lifestyle is in its infancy. You said I'm insecure. Why am I? Why did I turn into a brat? And you mentioned punishment. What did you mean? What punishments do you dish out? Knowing the right time and place to be a brat. What does that mean?" So many questions were filling my brain as hope began to peek out from my soul.

"There could be a variety of reasons you're insecure that led to your brattiness. We'd have to explore, but it likely started when you were a kid. If your life wasn't one that made you feel safe and able to express yourself honestly, that is a likely cause, or at least partially." He paused after dropping that nugget on me.

Knowing my past, I snorted. "That explains a lot."

"And soon, I want you to share what it was like for you. If I know how it began, I can decide how to fulfill what you're lacking. But that's for later. As for punishments, there are actually two categories. Punishments are for disobedience, and funishments are for minor infractions to the rules. Before you ask which is which, you and I would talk through them, and they'd be agreed upon by both of us. I'll never do something to you that you don't consent to, Cady.

"I'm a sadist, but I do not get off on subjecting my sub to horrendous pain or from her fear.

Communication is vital in our type of relationship. Just as it is for Mikhail and Tajah, they've had lengthy conversations and set the rules together. We'll do the same. What you need to know is my punishments will never cause you irreparable harm, scarring, or pain. Doing so would lose me what I want most—you. I never want that. I need to take care of you.

"The right time and place will also be negotiated. I'll never leave it ambiguous. Clear boundaries will be established. You'll know which circumstances will lead to a funishment for misbehaving versus punishment for disobedience. Remember, I want you to continue those behaviors only in the right way. They feed something inside of me."

I mulled over what he said. It was still confusing, but it did raise another question. "If being insecure in my childhood led to me being a brat, what made you a handler? Do you know?"

He gave me a tiny smile. "Actually, I do know. It was my younger brother. Let's just say he pushed, and my parents let him push them and have complete control even when it led to him and others being hurt and more. They always had an excuse, and he constantly misbehaved at the wrong times. More than a few times, I tried to get them to intercede or to let me, but it was always no. They enabled him to his detriment. I crave control, Cady.

"So you see, our childhoods create our adult selves in many ways. There's more I can tell you about that, but we can save that for later. Do you have any more questions? It's late, and I'd like to know before we retire if I have to continue to fight for you, or will you make me deliriously happy and say yes to a relationship with me?"

I sat there going over everything he said. I was scared and worried, but the desire to find someone who could handle me and make me feel loved and wanted was overwhelming. I'd told myself for a while that there was no one out there for me. I'd end up alone. Hearing him say it didn't have to be that way was a dream come true. Then, add in the physical attraction I felt for him and it was impossible to say no. *Please, don't let this be a disaster, and I get my heart torn out,* I prayed seconds before I answered him.

"Magnus, I hope like hell you mean what you say. Because if you end up hurting me, I'll tear out your heart," I threatened.

He grinned. "I'd expect nothing less. Now, kiss me, and then we have to get to bed. We have a long day tomorrow and lots of work."

I didn't wait for him to tell me twice. I grasped his face and lowered it to mine. I latched onto his mouth and engaged my lips, tongue, and teeth to make it the best kiss of his life. His groans told me it was working. The way he responded had me moaning and ready to have him strip me bare and take me by the time it ended, which was his doing. I was panting, and so was he.

"Fuck, babe, I hate to do this. Don't hate me. But as much as I want to take you to bed right now, I can't. Morning will be here too soon, and the clinic needs to be taken care of. I don't want anything to dictate how long I keep you in my bed once I get you there. However, I'm a masochist, too, I guess, because the thought of sleeping with you and not touching you is torture. Will you sleep in my bed tonight but hold off on our lovemaking until tomorrow night after work?"

I was stunned he'd ask it, and I wanted to say no, but he did have a point. "But you work tomorrow night at Lustz."

"I can have someone else cover for me. In fact, I'll have them cover the whole weekend. I don't want any interruptions. Is that a yes?"

"It's a yes, but I can't promise not to attack you if you get handsy in your sleep," I warned him.

He laughed. "Baby, if I get handsy, you're free to attack, and the same goes for me if you do."

"Deal."

And that was how, less than thirty minutes later, I was showered and sliding into a massive bed with Magnus Sacket. I was nervous, but he didn't allow me to wallow in it. He tugged me to him and wrapped me in his arms. It seemed he liked to cuddle. I thought for sure I'd have trouble sleeping, but I didn't. Instead, within minutes, I was drifting off, ensconced in a warm cocoon.

Cady: Chapter 11

After the best night of sleep of possibly my life, I was further stunned when I got up. Hoss had risen before I did. I found him in the kitchen finishing making breakfast. He informed me that he would be coming to the clinic to help with the cleanup, that he'd arranged for someone to check out the alarm, and that Tajah and Mikhail would join us.

My arguments that it wasn't necessary to pull them or him away from their work were ignored. After consuming breakfast, which was delicious, by the way, better than I could do it, he bundled me into his car, and off we went. I tried to take in more of his house and estate in the daylight, but we didn't have time. He saw me craning my neck. Hoss assured me I'd get to see it plenty.

When I drove to my apartment last night to get clothes, I'd placed a call to Dottie. I told her what happened and that we needed to reschedule the patients for today, even though it was the last thing I wanted. I also asked her to let the other staff know it would be a day of cleaning and readying up the clinic rather than seeing furry faces. She promised she'd handle it. When we arrived at the clinic, I saw a couple of cars there. One belonged to Mikhail, and the other was Dottie's. We were early, so I knew the rest of my staff would be there soon.

As Hoss shut off the car, this time a different sports car—I had no idea how many he had—he made a growling sound when I pulled the lever to open the door. I glanced at him to see why. "Stay. I'll get it. You need to get used to your man opening doors, helping you in and out of places, and pulling out chairs."

I was about to mouth off, but his expression told me this was one of the rules I had to follow, so I subsided and let him get out and come to me. He treated me as if I was precious as he assisted me out and then held my hand as we walked to the door. Dottie had a key, so I knew they were inside. Opening the door for us, Hoss made me go ahead of him. As we entered the lobby, I called out.

"Hello, where is everyone?"

I heard the murmur of voices, then the sound of feet. Within seconds, all three were standing before us. Dottie cast a questioning look at Hoss. He was still holding my hand. Mikhail appeared satisfied, and Taj was grinning. I knew she'd find a way to get me alone today and pump me for information. I wasn't sure how much I wanted to tell her. We were still too new, and I was afraid to talk about it in case I jinxed it.

"Good morning, Cady. I hope it's alright that I let these two in. I know Tajah, but I'm not familiar with him. She said he's her fiancé," Dottie explained.

"He is, and it's fine that you did. Everyone else should be here soon. Was anyone unable to come?"

"No, I got a hold of them all. They're just as upset as I am that this happened again. I wish the police would catch whoever keeps doing this. Please tell me that you won't be staying after hours anymore. What if they come back? They could've hurt or killed you, Cady,"

Dottie said as if I didn't know it. I knew it was out of concern for my safety. Before I was able to answer her, Hoss did.

He held out his hand to her. "Hello. Let me introduce myself. I'm Hoss. Nice to meet you. And to answer your question, no, she won't be here alone after hours. Last night was close enough of a call. As for catching the culprits, if the cops can't, I have people who will. She'll be safe."

She shook his hand as she studied him. Dottie was an excellent judge of character. After they dropped hands, she glanced at me and then back to him. "It's nice to meet you, too. I'm Dottie. I'm Cady's assistant. I'm glad someone else sees it the same way I do. Although I have to ask, who are you? And how do you plan to make sure she isn't alone? She's stubborn as a mule."

"Dottie!" I gasped playfully as if shocked she'd say that. However, I wasn't because I couldn't deny what she said about my stubbornness.

Hoss chuckled. "Dottie, I know she is. It's part of her charm—most of the time. As for how I can make sure, I'll just say I have my ways. Now, your question about who I am... simple. I'm Cady's man. You'll be seeing a lot of me."

His easy proclamation and the way he smiled at me after he said it made me want to melt. I heard Dottie gasp, and Taj's smile grew. Mikhail raised his brow at me and winked.

"It's about time she got a man worthy of her. And you'd better be worthy. If you jerk her around or break her heart, I'll jerk a knot in your tail and castrate you. I know how to do it. I've had years of experience with neutering," Dottie warned him. Or more like she threatened.

"Ma'am, I would never do that to Cady, but if I did and survived her revenge, you're more than welcome to knot my tail and castrate me. I'd deserve it," was his reply.

Dottie smiled and nodded. "I like him, Cady. And he's sexy as hell and a delight to look at. Yum, where can I find one like him?" she asked.

Dottie was in her late forties and divorced. She had her two kids young, so they were grown, and she was alone. She was open to finding a man but had rotten luck. Something we had in common.

Tajah and I both laughed as the guys remained quiet. "Dottie, we'll talk later. Not sure we can get you one exactly like Hoss, but there is a chance we can find someone interesting for you," Tajah told her.

"Honey, I'll take one of him or your man, so just tell me where to go."

"Ladies, you're going to make us blush. I hate to interrupt the talk of hunting grounds, but first, we have a mess to clean up. Where do you want us to start?" Mikhail asked.

I wanted to giggle at his use of the term hunting grounds. As a primal, that sure described him based on what Tajah had told me. I saw them exchange heated looks. Damn, we'd better get to work before they throw down or wander off to get wild.

"The rest of the staff should be here any minute. Why don't we wait for them, then we can divide and conquer the rooms. Most of the work will be picking up and returning the papers and items to the correct places."

I didn't get to say more because the door opened,

and in came my other three workers. They were startled to see Hoss, Mikhail, and Tajah, although it was more the two men. They knew Taj. Wanting to get the show on the road, I quickly made introductions.

"Everyone, these are my other staff members. This is Joey, Darlena, and Vera. Guys, you know Tajah, so no need to introduce her. The man next to her is her fiancé, Mikhail. And this is Hoss." I paused to take a breath before telling them he was mine. Dottie beat me to it.

"He's Cady's boyfriend," she said in delight.

I received many astonished looks. I knew the questions would abound when he was no longer here. I wanted to groan. Hoss and Mikhail acknowledged them, and then we got to work. I insisted I take my office.

I wasn't into cleaning even an hour before Hoss wandered in. He shut the door. I raised my brow. He gave me a sexy smirk and then stalked to the bookcase where I was putting things away. I held up my hands.

"Hold it right there. This isn't the time or place for hanky-panky."

He laughed. "Hanky-panky? You sound like an eighty-year-old. I'm not here for that. But if I were, it would be called flaming hot sex. I just need a kiss, then I have something to tell you."

I let him encircle me with his arms and bring me close to his body. I looked up at him. "I'll get you for the eighty-year-old remark, but that can wait. Kiss me and then talk," I demanded.

His mouth molded to mine, and he took over my mind. By the time he broke it, I was ready to say the hell with the office and if anyone was there. My desk would make a great bed. He must've read my mind because he chuckled.

"Babe, I'm not fucking you on your desk. Not that it isn't hot and won't happen one day, but not for our first time. I came in to tell you someone is here who needs to talk to you about your alarm system."

"Who? I didn't call the alarm company to send someone out?"

"It's not someone from the alarm company. It's the guy I use for security and such at my company and home. He's here to go over what you have and to recommend something better."

"Your company? What company? Magnus, I have no clue what you're talking about. I know you work for Mikhail, but you have another job? Is that how you can afford a home in Belle Meade? After seeing it, I thought you inherited your wealth."

There was so much for us to learn about each other. I guess discovering what he did for a living to afford the lifestyle I'd just gotten a glimpse of was a good place to start.

"I was planning to tell you about it, but we've been busy. Yes, I work for Mikhail, but I own a company called SacketEdge Technologies. We're mainly computer application developers."

"Then why are you working at Lustz? If you have a computer company, it has to be making money. You couldn't afford your house and cars on what you make working from Mikhail three days a week."

"You're right. I work at Lustz to decompress. Tiny, I'll explain more later when we're at home, but for now, will you please come talk to Iker? He's been nice enough to make time for us," he coaxed.

Not wanting to be a bitch, especially after his guy made time at the last minute, I nodded. Hoss gave me a peck on the mouth and then led me out of my office and to the lobby. I examined Hoss's guy. He was in his late forties if I had to guess. He had dark hair silvering at the temples. He was tanned, fit, and attractive. Even though he was at least fifteen years older than me, I would've given him a second glance. Or I would've before meeting Hoss. With him around, I might notice a man was attractive, but that was it.

Besides, Iker was eyeing Dottie, and she was pretending not to notice. I think his interest was elsewhere. It was unusual for her to act this way. I knew he would catch her attention, so why she was ignoring him made no sense. She was typically a person who went for what she wanted. Even though she was his age, she looked younger and took care of herself. She didn't lack men focused on her. They just never seemed to be the right kind. After her husband, she wasn't one to put herself in a situation that would land her with another one like him. He'd been abusive.

"Iker, this is Cady Anderson, my woman. Cady, this is Iker Sullivan. He owns a security company. I asked him to come take a look at your setup to see if there's more we can do," Hoss supplied.

I held out my hand, and Iker took it. "It's beyond a pleasure to meet you, Cady. Hoss has told me about you, but he didn't nearly describe your beauty enough. Your pictures don't do you justice, and those were beautiful. You're way too good for him," he teased.

"That's funny, I'd say it's the opposite. Hoss is too damn good for me. I'll have to spend my time beating the women off with a stick. So tiring. I might have to reconsider my decision based on that. Hmm," I said with a straight face.

Iker laughed loudly while Hoss gave me a stern look. It made me wonder what he'd do to punish me for it. My nipples tingled at the thought, and my pussy pulsed. He leaned down and whispered in my ear.

"Keep it up, and you'll see what happens, Tiny." He made a growling sound, then nipped my lobe before straightening up to address Iker.

"Dream on, buddy. She's mine, and your suave shit isn't stealing her away," he warned.

"That's alright. I see something scrumptious. I was only warning Cady, not offering myself up." As Iker said scrumptious, he glanced back at Dottie. She was looking his way. I saw her face go red. Without another word, she scurried off. His gaze followed her until she was out of sight. Once she was, he glanced back at me.

"Sorry. Where were we? Oh yeah, I'm here to check out your alarm system and other security measures. I understand the burglars have broken in twice, and the last time, the alarm didn't go off."

"That's right. I have no clue how it was possible. They wouldn't know the code to enter, and when they came in, it didn't go off like it should until someone entered the disarm code within the prescribed time, which means it wasn't on. But I know I armed it when I locked up for the night."

"We'll figure it out, Tiny. Let Iker do his thing, and I have someone else checking into how they bypassed it," Hoss assured me. I wanted to ask him who was doing the latter, but I decided to wait.

"Feel free to wander, Iker. There's a panel here and at the backdoor. They came in the back last night while

I was in my office. Do you want me to show you the panels?"

"No, you go do whatever you were doing. Hoss can show me. If I have any questions, I'll come find you. How does that sound?"

"It sounds great. Thank you."

Before I went back to my office, Hoss gave me another kiss. The man sure liked the PDA. I floated there. As time passed and rooms were straightened up, I was given reports. My staff knew the clinic as well as I did. They'd know if anything was disturbed or taken. Zilch. This convinced me even more that the burglars were after the drugs. Making sure my office door was closed and locked, I went to the panel in the wall.

When I rented this space, unbeknownst to the landlord, I made some modifications to this room. When I was done, it looked no different from the rest. However, if you knew where to look, you'd find the hidden storage behind a section of one wall. It was where I kept the more serious and dangerous medications—sedatives, pain meds, and antibiotics. There was an area where a small refrigerator was for those requiring to be refrigerated. The wiring had been a little outside my wheelhouse, so Carver had helped me with it. I trusted my brother not to tell anyone.

Since I was the only vet, there was no need for anyone else to handle them. Before the clinic opened each day, I'd take a look at my cases and see if I needed to remove any. If an unexpected case came up, then I'd get what I needed without drawing attention to where I fetched the meds from. Although the staff knew it was from my office.

Staring at the meds, I wondered if I should find a

different place to store them. Taking them home with me every night would be a pain, but if thieves kept trying to break in to steal them, I couldn't have that. If they started to bust into the walls, they'd find my hiding place. A sharp knock at the door made me jump.

"Who is it?" I called out.

"It's me. Are you alright? Why's the door locked, Cady Cat?" Hoss asked, his voice concerned.

Closing the wall, I went to the door, unlocked it, and then opened it. I stepped back to allow him inside. I shut and locked it behind him. He was checking out the office, which I'd straightened up. He switched his gaze to me.

"Babe, what's going on in here? Why do you need the door fastened?"

"What if I told you it was none of your business?" I asked.

"I'd say if it concerned your safety or well-being, then I'd have to disagree." He crossed his arms and waited for me to answer.

"If you must know, I was debating something."

"What?"

"Are you always so nosy?"

"Yep, when it comes to you, I am. Get used to it, Tiny."

"Err, has anyone ever told you that you're vexing?"

"Nope." He grinned.

"Liar. I bet you've heard it all your life and from hundreds of people."

"Has anyone told you that you're a brat and need to be spanked often?"

"Nope," I said just as tongue-in-cheek as he

answered me. We both laughed.

I gestured to the wall as I walked toward it. He followed me. I opened it, earning me a surprised look. "This is what I believe the burglars are searching for. They want the medications I have. I told you that. This is why they can't find them and keep coming back. I was debating whether I should start taking them home with me at night."

His head was shaking adamantly. "No, you don't want to do that. Cady, if they break in again, which is very unlikely after Iker and my other friend are done, there's no damn way they'd find the meds unless they knew where to look. This is cleverly hidden. If you take them home, you'd have to carry them out in a case of some kind. What's to say they won't be watching you and get suspicious seeing you suddenly carrying something you never did before? I'm not trying to scare you, only to make you cautious. You can't take them home. It puts a target on you there."

"Well, I can't keep letting them break into my business! The next time, they may steal equipment, break things, or tear up the place worse. If they break into the walls, they'll find them. I can't afford to replace stuff, Magnus. The upgrade to the security system will come out of my pocket. My landlord won't pay for it, and it won't be cheap."

"Have you considered moving locations?" he asked softly.

"Of course I have, and not just due to this, but I can't. The rent here is as high as I can afford. A better location costs more. I've only been on my own for a few years. I'm growing, but not enough to afford anything like that."

"What about taking on a partner or another vet so more business could be done?"

"I don't want another vet as a partner. Working with me would be alright, but the increase in cost would negate much of the increase in income."

"And what about a silent partner who doesn't want to make the decisions or anything, just to be a part of it?"

"Those are few and far between. I wouldn't know where to find one of those."

"He's standing right here. I can help you with all this and move the location to a safer area where there would be more traffic."

His bold offer left me standing there blinking with my mouth hanging open. I was hallucinating. Hoss hadn't offered to help with my clinic. Had he? I shook myself.

"Sorry, I just had a hallucination. What did you say?"

He chuckled. "It wasn't a hallucination. I asked, what if I became your silent investor? You'd have the final say in everything. All I would ask is that you let me help you find a new place and that the security there be up to my standards. This isn't the nice area it once was, Cady. The crime rate, in general, is rising. Mikhail and I talked about it. I don't want you somewhere you're not safe walking outside, especially if it happens to be dark."

"Hoss," I paused and changed my wording when his eyebrow went up. "Magnus, I can't let you do that."

"Why not?"

"For one, it's too much. Two, we've only just agreed to try dating, and that's a huge risk to take on someone. What happens if we break up? You and

I would be stuck together in a financial relationship. Then, there's no guarantee, if I let you do it, that I'd make enough to pay you back on your investment. More patients don't automatically equal more money, or not in proportion, since supplies and other costs will increase. Plus, a better location and security system costs more. I thank you for the offer, but I can't."

"Yes, you can, but I see this will require us to talk long and hard about it, which you don't need today. So, instead, I wanted to let you know that Iker is finished and has an idea for the security system upgrade. Can you talk to him, or are you in the middle of something?"

"Of course, I can talk to him." I closed up the wall, and we went to find Iker.

I wanted to giggle when we found him. He was in our small employee breakroom. He was trying to talk to Dottie, but from the looks of it, he wasn't having much success. She was red-faced and trying to get out of the room. When we entered, she swept past him to make her escape. Before she got far, I caught her.

"Dottie, is everything cleaned up?"

"It is. With so many hands, the work went quickly."

"Good. Then, tell everyone else to go home. There's nothing more for them to do. We'll open on Monday at the usual time. I'll see them then. And that goes for you, too."

"I can stay and tidy up more to prep for next week."

"No, you can't. I'll need you all well-rested. Go."

She looked at me disgruntled before muttering, "Fine. See you then. Call if you need me."

"I need your number to do that," Iker interjected

as he gave her a sexy smirk.

She gave him a bewildered look before she turned on her heels and marched out.

"Damn, she's a hard one. Next time, she'll cave. I see he found you, Cady. Okay, let's sit, if you will, and go over what I found and suggest," Iker said after casting one more look after Dottie.

We sat at one of the two tables we had there. "Cady, your system is old, and honestly, I don't know how it's kept anyone out as long as it has. Hoss says you rent. Your landlord obviously hasn't put any money into the security since he probably built or bought this place. I know Hoss had a friend checking into how it was bypassed. Do you want to tell her what he said?" He directed this to Hoss.

"You heard from him? When?" I asked.

"About twenty minutes ago. Plus, Iker and Outlaw agreed that this system is archaic in terms of effectiveness. Outlaw said a twelve-year-old with decent computer skills could hack it. He messed with it and was in and out in mere minutes. He had suggestions on systems to replace it with. I have a list. Iker read over it, and he not only agrees but also stocks some of the ones suggested, so there would be no need to wait for it to be ordered. It could be installed by tomorrow."

"Additional security measures you should consider are having the doors fitted with steel and windows that either have security shutters that can be closed or decorative security bars. There are some really nice ones that look more like decoration than a prison," Iker added.

His suggestions were valid, and I wasn't opposed to them, but all I could see were dollar signs. There was no way I could afford them, and that was assuming my landlord would allow it. I knew he wouldn't pay for them, not even half. I held up my hand to stop him.

"Hang on. Listen, I appreciate you doing this and coming up with options. However, there's no way my landlord will pay for the doors, security shutters, or bars, no matter how stylish they may be. Even a new security system will be a no. I might be able to swing the new system on my own, depending on how much it costs to upgrade. The rest, I can't. Why don't you work up a quote so I can see if it's feasible to do that much?" I asked.

He glanced at Hoss. They seemed to exchange some kind of nonverbal communication, and then Iker addressed me again, smiling as he did.

"I'll tell you what. I'll give you the full quote with breakdowns for each thing—the doors, the security shutters, the security bars, and the upgraded alarm system. I noted there are no cameras as part of this system, either inside or outside. I'll include the cost of those. That way, you have it and can make an informed decision. Hoss is right. I have the system and cameras in stock, so those can go up right away. If you want security shutters, those have to be ordered, but the reinforced steel doors and security bars are other items in stock. I'll have it written up and over to you by tomorrow."

"I don't want you to go to a lot of trouble. The alarm and the cameras are enough." I tried to manage his expectations.

"It's not. I'll have them done, just in case. Hoss is not only a good customer, but he's a friend. It's the least I can do for his lady." Iker winked.

I couldn't help but smile, but it wasn't due to his wink. It was the reaction it got from Hoss. He let out a low growl.

"Iker, you know I can have you gone in a blink. If you want a chance to try your luck at getting Dottie to talk to you, let alone possibly go out with you, you'd better keep on my good side."

"But Hoss, you don't have one of those," was Iker's snappy comeback.

I was giggling at their antics when Tajah came rushing into the room. Her half-pissed-off and half-panicky expression had me sobering.

"What's wrong?" I asked at the same time Hoss did.

"We have an unwanted visitor in the lobby. I came to get you so you wouldn't stumble across him without warning. Mikhail is telling him to leave. I've got to go before my man kills him." she hastily spat out, then she turned and rushed back out.

I didn't wait to see if Hoss or Iker was coming. I jumped to my feet and hurried after her. I heard Hoss swear and then the thunder of feet. As I got near the lobby, I knew who she meant. I heard his voice. Hoss's hand on my shoulder brought me to a halt. I glanced back at him.

"Cady, stay here and let me handle him. He was told, and he didn't listen."

"I can fight my own battles, Magnus."

"I know you can, but why do it when you have me? Just hang back and see what he says and does."

I wanted to argue, but the way the muscle was ticking in his jaw, I knew that he wouldn't be able to let me face the bastard on my own. I sighed.

"I'll try, but I can't promise. I've been fighting my own battles most of my life, Magnus."

"I get it. Just try for me."

"Okay," I said, and then I let him go ahead of me. As we entered, my pain-in-the-ass ex launched his verbal attack.

"Cady, what the hell is the meaning of this? I came here to talk to you, and these two are here, and now I find this guy is, too. Who's this other one? What's going on? I let this crap slide the other night, but we need to talk. Let's go into your office. I tried to see you last night, but you weren't home even though your car was there."

I narrowed my eyes on Flint. What was his malfunction?

"You need to turn your ass around and leave. You were told to stay away from Cady. She's no longer your concern. That means don't go to her home, her work, or anywhere else seeking her. She doesn't have anything to say to you. And the reason she wasn't home last night is she was at my house, in my bed. Does that paint you a picture?" Hoss asked with a smirk. He reached back, captured my hand, and drew me forward to stand next to him, and then his arm came around to cuddle me to him.

The feel of him, the warmth, and his scent enveloped me, making my pulse speed up. I wanted to be finished with this day so we could go back to his house and get naked. I saw Flint clench his fists. Surely, he wouldn't be stupid enough to take a swing at Hoss. Not only did Hoss tower over him by almost a foot, but he was way more muscular. I knew that look, though. It was the one Flint got before he lost his temper and went off. When he did that, he would say and do anything. It was his temper and the fact he'd gotten physical with me that was the primary reason I broke up with him.

I must've tensed or something because Hoss lowered his head. "He won't lay a finger on you, Tiny. If he tries, I'll tear his fucking head off and shove it up his ass. His days of laying hands on you are done. He has a reckoning coming, just not right this second."

The low rumble in his voice told me he was barely holding himself back. Somehow, he knew that Flint had caused me not only psychological but bodily harm. And from what little I'd discovered from being around Hoss and his remarks, he wasn't a man to tolerate anyone being mentally or physically abusive to someone, especially a woman or a child.

"I know," I whispered to him.

He gave me a brief kiss, then straightened back up and glared at Flint, who was staring holes through us. He wasn't happy, and I didn't give a damn. The days of me caring what he wanted or liked were long over.

"I don't believe I stuttered or said it in non-English. Or do I need to translate for you?" The next thing I knew, Hoss was repeating what he already said to Flint in Spanish. When he was done, he did it in French, then German, and finally in Gaelic, if I was right. I knew Spanish and French enough to get by. The other two, I recognized the sound, if not the words.

"Did one of those work? Or do I need to do more?" Hoss smarted off.

I wanted to ask how many languages he spoke, but this wasn't the time or place.

"I can translate it into Russian if you want," Mikhail offered with a grin.

I don't know what made me do it, but before

I thought, I said what I was thinking. "Don't confuse him. He's lucky if he can speak and understand English. He sure as hell isn't smart enough to know more than one language—unless it's dog. He's one, so he should understand it. Woof."

Iker snorted and chuckled. Tajah burst out laughing while Mikhail and Hoss cracked up. The fury that came over Flint's face was a flash, and then he lunged at me. I let out a startled yelp as I cringed away from him. It was a reflex. I recalled how his hands could hurt. Like lightning, Hoss had me shoved behind him, blocking access to me. When I peeked around his massive frame, he had his hand around Flint's throat. He shook him like a rag doll.

"I warned you what would happen if you came near her. You didn't listen. Well, you will this time. This is your last warning, and to be sure it sinks in, I'm going to beat it into that hard head of yours. Mikhail, will you stay here and keep an eye on Tiny while I deal with this inconvenience?"

Mikhail was standing closer, with Tajah behind him. Iker had moved to stand off to the side of me. All three of them weren't looking happy.

"I can, although I'd love to watch you teach him a more than deserved lesson. After what Tajah told me he did to Cady, I want a piece of him, too."

Oh God, what had she told him? She looked over at me and shrugged.

"What did she say he did to Cady?" Hoss demanded.

"Magnus, it's not something we need to talk about right now. As much as I'd love for him to be educated, I'm afraid a douche like him will run to the cops, and you'll be the one to get in trouble. He's not worth it, Sugar Bear." As I called him that name for the second time, I ran my hand up his chest.

"Cady Cat, I can guarantee you, if he goes to the cops, it'll be as if he never existed," Hoss promised.

"He's right, Cady. Hey, I have a thought. Why don't we have Matvey's guys come get him? They can take him somewhere and keep him company until we're done here. Then, after we get the women home, we can both have fun," Mikhail suggested.

"Hell yeah, I like that idea. Go ahead and call him. I can promise you if this one is stupid enough to go to the cops with your cousin involved, he'll sign his death warrant for sure," Hoss said, sounding pleased.

As they talked back and forth, Flint was gasping for air and trying to pry Hoss's fingers from his throat to no avail. Hoss was letting him have just enough air to remain conscious, but that was it. His face was turning colors.

"I'd like to watch," Iker threw out.

"If you're determined to do this, why do we ladies have to go home and wait for you? Why can't we watch the entertainment?" I asked.

"Are you sure you want to go?" Mikhail asked.

Before either Tajah or I could answer, the door opened, and one of my regular clients walked in. She stumbled to a stop when she saw all of us standing there. While she was scanning us, Hoss hastily let go of Flint. Like a weasel, he took off running out the door. He almost ran her over in his haste. I knew the guys wanted to go after him, but they remained there, smiling.

As I dealt with her and her drop-in, which was to see if we had time to do the annual checkup on her dog, I explained that we were closed but had an opening the next day. The others separated and left me with her, except Hoss. He remained on alert, staring into the parking lot. Wow, would this day ever end so he and I could be alone? That was all I kept thinking.

Hoss: Chapter 12

I thought the day would never be over with. In between helping to clean up the clinic, I called Reuben to see if he could find someone to take my place tonight and tomorrow night at Lustz. He said he'd do his best and get back to me. When he asked why, I told him I needed alone time with Cady. He chuckled and said he'd make it happen.

My talk with Cady about being her partner in the clinic hadn't gone as I hoped, but I'd work on her. She was independent, and I knew that. It would take time for her to learn to lean on me.

Our discussion with Iker on his recommendations for her security would've gone better if I was already her partner. I could just tell him to do everything, and I'd foot the bill. However, I knew that wouldn't happen. I had no idea what her financial situation was, but the way she watched her costs, I was sure she wouldn't be able to afford to do the new alarm and cameras without wiping out her savings or having to put it on charge cards if she had available limits. It angered me that her landlord hadn't put anything into the building since it was built, which, based on its looks, was thirty years ago.

But the icing on the cake was when Tajah came to say Cady had a visitor, and we walked out to discover Flint Reid standing there. I wanted to punch him the second I saw him. For him to demand he and Cady go talk in private had pushed me closer to the end of my restraint. But when he lunged at her after she made her smart and funny remark, I'd had enough. Mikhail, alluding to Reid doing awful things to her, hadn't helped. I was seconds from having Mikhail get Matvey to send over some of his men when that customer interrupted, and to prevent her from running out and calling the cops, I let the little bastard go. He ran like a rat. That was alright. I'd get my hands on him again.

When the customer left, there was only about half an hour more work to do, and then we were able to lock up and go. Iker promised he'd give the quote to us sometime tomorrow. Tajah and Mikhail asked us to go to dinner, but we said no. While we enjoyed our time with them, tonight was about us. I knew we'd have to eat, but I preferred to do it where it was just the two of us, and we could relax. I was ready to claim my woman.

I'd been dreaming of touching, tasting, and sinking my cock into her for months. If there was one more delay, or if anything or anyone fucked it up, I'd go on a killing spree. I had to have her. Once I did, there would be no going back. She would be mine forever. She could think we might break up, but I knew better.

I talked her into coming back to my house, but she insisted she had to stop at her place and grab a few things she'd forgotten to pack. I had no trouble doing it. Before we got there, we talked about dinner and settled on bringing in Chinese food. While she packed, I placed our order with a restaurant I loved. She had never eaten there. They would deliver it after we got home. Before we left her apartment, she insisted on taking her car with her so she had a way to get home.

I had news—she wasn't going home tonight, and if I had my way, she'd stay for the foreseeable future. After having her, there was no way I'd be able to sleep alone. If she insisted on going back to her place, I'd stay the night with her there. Only seeing each other once or a few times a week wouldn't work for me. My craving was all-encompassing and growing by the hour.

After she had what she needed, I made her drive so I could follow her. During the drive, I got a text from Reub.

Reuben: Nights covered. Enjoy yourself.

I could picture the smirk he probably wore. I sent a quick one back.

Me: TY. And enjoy is such a tame word. I'm about to be in heaven. Lucky me.

I didn't have long to wait for his reply. I laughed when I read it.

Reuben: Bastard. Good luck. She's more than a handful.

How right he was, and I loved it. Anticipation and desire were warring inside of me. I hoped I'd be able to make it through dinner before jumping her. I couldn't recall ever feeling this way about another woman. None had caused me to be distracted, unable to work, or invaded my dreams except Cady. That there was enough to tell me she was the woman for me, and not temporarily.

I knew it would take convincing with her past. When Mikhail indicated that Tajah had told him things about how Flint treated Cady and that he wanted a piece of him, it confirmed what I had already suspected. Flint had laid hands on her. Before this was through, he'd pay for that as well.

When we got close to my property, I hit the button to open the gate so she didn't have to stop. Seeing her driving onto my property gave me a warm sensation like she was home. At the house, I opened the garage and parked my car inside. She left hers outside. I'd have to make room. I had another garage not far from the house. I'd shift one of mine there so she'd be able to park inside.

I was pleased when she stayed in her car and waited for me to open her door. I had to hold on to her hand as I took her inside through the garage access. I needed the contact. I saw her trying to look around. We had a little time until the food came. They'd call up to the house from the gate when they arrived. Last night, she hadn't seen much of the house. I'd rectify it tonight. I wanted her to be able to make herself at home, which meant being able to navigate it.

"Cady, we still have time until the food comes. Why don't I show you around? That way, you know what is where."

"I'd love it, but I don't think just by showing me around, I'll be able to navigate it. Magnus, this place is massive! Does your tour come with a map?"

I was carrying her bag with the extra items she picked up at her apartment. We'd start in my room and go from there. I laughed at her question.

"I hadn't thought of that. I'll get right on it. Come on, we'll put this away and then go from there." I held up her bag.

"Lead away. If I get lost, I hope there's a way to call for help," she continued to tease.

Several minutes later, the tour was well underway, and she kept me laughing with her remarks.

They weren't all jokes. Many of them were about the beauty of the house and how much she liked it. I took notice of what she said. This would be our house if things went my way, and I was determined it would. When she moved in, she'd have a relatively free hand at redecorating anything she disliked. The house boasted not only a kitchen, dining room, office, and two living spaces but seven bedrooms and eight bathrooms, a laundry, mudroom, pantry, and morning room. Outside were terraces, a veranda, and a deck. It was close to eight thousand square feet between the two floors. When we returned to the kitchen, she was shaking her head.

"What's wrong?" I asked.

"I—" she was cut off by the buzzing of the front gate. I went to the entry where there was a monitor screen. I saw it was my usual delivery guy, so I buzzed him in. He knew the routine and how to get to the house. As we waited for him, I indicated for her to continue.

"I was about to say this house is incredible, and you need a map so as not to get lost. It's so amazing, but why in the world did you buy such a large house? A small army could live here, and it's only you."

I chuckled. "I admit it is too big for me or even for a small family. You're right. However, in my defense, when it came on the market, it was too good of an investment to pass up. Plus, I loved the architecture and property. I knew I might end up living my life alone in it, but I didn't care. I wanted it so I bought it. You should've seen how rundown it was. The previous owners neglected it, and it showed. This allowed me to snap it up cheaper than anything else around here. Even with the money I put into it, it's worth more than it cost all combined. Lucky for me, I now won't be the only one to enjoy it."

Her mouth dropped open. I grinned. A loud knock at the door signaled he was there. I left her in the kitchen to think over what I had just said. At the door, the delivery guy and I greeted each other, and I gave him a generous tip. He thanked me and said he'd see me next time. Closing the door, I went back to rejoin Cady. She was in the same spot I left her. She appeared somewhat dazed. Sitting down the bag of food on the island, I got out plates and utensils. She came to help me open the boxes and place spoons in them. This simple domesticated thing made me happy.

As we arranged our feast, I added to my previous remark. "To be clear about my prior remark, us entering into this means I see it going the distance, Cady. There is no doing it halfway. We're all in. There will be bumps, difficulties, and disagreements. However, we'll work through those. I love this house, but if you absolutely hate it, we'll find another we both like. Mikhail has been trying to get me to buy property in Culleoka, where he's rebuilding. I like it there, so it's an option. It would put us close to Tajah, and I know that might be a factor in favor of doing that."

As I spoke, we filled our plates—well, I did. She put small amounts on hers. I'd have to see if she ate it all or not. I knew someone my size took a ton more food to fuel me than her, but I still wanted to be sure she ate. Not wanting to move into another area, I pulled out a stool at the island for her. After she sat down, I did.

She took a bite and chewed. I noted she was thinking. I wondered what she'd have to say. Finally, she spoke. "Magnus, this is a lot to take in. You've just shown me a house most people only dream of seeing, let alone living in. Then you say you don't want to live in it alone, but if I hate it, you'll get another. Oh, and it sounds as if you won't let this fail between us. Am I right? And this house is still way too much for the two of us. How can I clean it?"

"You won't clean it. I have a cleaning person. And yes, failure isn't an option. I told you already. I want you as mine in every way—lover, play partner, wife, and, if you're willing, the mother of my children. If we have those, some of this space will get used. And I'm willing to move if that's what you desire."

"H-Magnus, you can't turn your life upside down for someone. And what if, no matter how much we try, we can't make it work? I told you. I'm not an easy person to be around."

I lay down my chopsticks. "How long have you and Tajah been friends?"

"Since grade school. Why?" she asked in puzzlement.

"She's someone who stuck around despite your personality. Your brother is still in your life, although he was being an asshole the night of the costume party. Are there others like them? What about family outside of Carver?"

"True, Tajah and I have been there for each other no matter what, even when her marriage imploded. As for Carver, he's been a defender on and off throughout my life. Other friends are more like acquaintances or work friends. And we don't have family."

Her tone told me there was a story there. I'd have to explore it with her at a later date. For now, all I wanted was to get her to see that she hadn't run off everyone in her life, and she wouldn't do it with me.

"Then I'll be joining a very elite group. As for family, do you want kids?"

She coughed and had to clear her throat. I resumed eating. "I'd like to have children. I always wanted a few, but lately, I figured I'd have to be content to be an aunt to Tajah's kids or, if he ever settles down, to Carver's. I'm not sure what kind of mother I'd make, though."

I heard a throb of an ache in her voice. She was trying to be casual about it, but I knew she wanted to be a mom. "Babe, you will make an excellent mom. I want them, too. The exact count we can negotiate later. I think that's enough talk about those things for now. Let's finish off our food, then I have plans for us."

Her face flushed, and her breathing picked up. I wanted to follow with my tongue where her tongue licked her bottom lip. My appetite disappeared, or at least the one for food. The one for Cady was ramping up fast. Dinner couldn't be over quickly enough.

⚘ ⚘ ⚘

Forty minutes later, I was pacing the master bedroom. After finishing our meal and putting away the leftovers, I'd told her to go to the master bathroom and take a bath or shower. I'd use one of the others. The only reason I didn't join her was I didn't trust myself not to jump her. A cold shower hadn't helped. I was hard and raring to go. I'd slipped on a pair of shorts. I didn't want to greet her fully nude. It might scare her off.

An occasional splash or humming sound came from the bathroom. She was in the tub. I lay on the bed and turned on the television. Maybe it would help to occupy my mind while I waited. Flipping through the vast selection of channels I had, nothing was jumping out at me. I was about to turn it off and toss the remote when I came across a financial report show. They were talking about tech companies. I stopped there. It was always good to know what the industry was doing and how SacketEdge stacked up to our competitors.

It didn't take up all my attention, but it was enough to divert me some. In fact, it was sufficient that I was caught off guard when she came walking into the bedroom. I was leaning back on the pillows. Seeing her made me sit up. Without conscious thought, I shut off the television and sat there, running my eyes up and down and all over Cady. She stood in the doorway between the bathroom and the bedroom. She wore a slightly uncertain look. Oh no, she wasn't to be left feeling uneasy or awkward.

I gestured with one hand as I demanded, "Come to me."

She hesitated only a moment before beginning a slow walk toward me. I was about to ask if she was torturing me on purpose or trying to kill me. As she trekked closer, I cataloged her. She was wearing a short, translucent nightie, babydoll, or whatever it was called. It was sheer and had a zig-zag lace strip which ran under her tits. Through it, I saw that she was wearing a pair of panties with the same lace along the top. It was dark green, which stood out against her hair and ivory skin.

"Turn around," I growled as I inched forward on the bed.

She stopped and slowly twirled. I had to fist the comforter to stay in place. The back had racer-back straps, and the panties were actually a thong. Seeing the lace disappear between her plump ass cheeks and the slit that went clear up the side to meet the band of lace on her thong made my cock jerk and leak in my shorts. As she faced me again, I let my leash slip a bit.

I'd wanted to take my time with her and drive her mad with lust before ultimately sinking my cock inside of her, but she was too much. I'd give her as long as I could. I rose and stalked over to her. She gave me a hesitant smile. I reached out and brought her closer.

"Cady, Jesus Christ, you're beyond exquisite. I can't believe you're mine. This outfit showcases your beauty. I want to apologize in advance before we go any further."

She frowned. "Apologize for what?"

"I intended to make this the longest and best night of your life. I was going to explore you from head to toe and take my time driving you out of your mind. I'm sorry that I won't be able to do it. But I'll do my best to give you as much as I can before."

"Before? Give me as much as you can. Magnus, you're not making sense."

"I know it. You've got me riding the edge of my control, Tiny. I won't be able to hold back from taking you for long. All I can say is I'll make sure you come, and I'll explore you thoroughly once my hunger is sated a little. Tell me if I do anything that you don't like and if there's something you want. It's your fault for being so fucking stunning and driving a man mad with desire."

I ended my speech with a low growl then I stooped enough to grab her ass in both hands and hoist her in the air. She squealed, and her arms went around my neck. As they did, I sealed my mouth to hers, and I kissed her ravenously. She kissed me back, and our teeth and tongues went aggressively after each other. Bringing her lower body to meet mine, I growled into her mouth as her pussy made contact with my throbbing cock. Her heat was noticeable through the fabric. I ground my cock into her pussy, causing her to whimper. My fingers dug into her ass cheeks.

I knew I shouldn't have done it, but I had to. The desire to thrust inside and fuck her against the wall was almost too much. However, our first time together wouldn't be plastered to the wall. She deserved more than that, although I wouldn't be opposed to doing it later, just like her desk was on the list. The places I already had that I wanted to take her were extensive. Suddenly, she tore her mouth from mine.

"What's wrong, baby? Too rough?" I asked hoarsely.

"No, never, but I need something," she said softly. She was rubbing herself against my erection. Her body was undulating on mine. God, she was a temptress.

"What?" I croaked.

"I need to see you, all of you, and then I want you to fuck me. Please, Magnus, I'm dying. I need you," she pleaded.

Her words blew my mind and almost broke my tenacious hold on myself.

"Fuck me," I muttered as I swung around and walked toward the bed.

The minx giggled as she informed me, "That's what I'm trying to do if you'd cooperate, Big Man. I've been dreaming of what your cock will look, taste, and feel like. I'm done waiting. Show me what you've got in these shorts. It feels big and rude. Let me see and taste it," she demanded.

Lightly bellowing, I gently threw her down on the bed. As she bounced, which made her glorious tits bounce, I shoved my shorts down and let them fall to the floor. I hadn't worried about underwear after my shower. I gripped my cock at the base and stroked my hand up and down it a few times. Precum had leaked out, and it helped my hand to glide. She raised up on her elbows, and her eyes were glued to my cock. I wanted to preen when I saw the wonder and awe there tinged with a smidge of fear. I was a big man, and my cock was proportionate.

As much as I wanted to ram it inside and fuck her senseless, I didn't want to scare or hurt her. Instead, I shook it at her and smirked. "Is this what you wanted to see, Cady Cat? Think you can handle it? Wanna touch it? Taste it? Then come get it," I taunted. I wanted to see a hint of her brat.

She rose to the mark. She sat up, gave me a challenging look, and then smarted off. "Is that all you got? Maybe I shouldn't waste my time with something so inadequate."

"I'll show you inadequate. You need glasses, babe. This cock is a monster. I bet you're too afraid to take it on," I taunted back.

Her response was everything I could want and more. She scooted to the edge of the mattress, and then she was on her knees in front of me. She smacked at my hand, so I slowly removed it. Her small, soft one replaced my big, rough one. Her touch was jolting. She stroked up and down my length, stopping to gather precum at the head and drag it back down. She hummed. Her grip was exactly how I liked it without any direction from me.

"Hmm, let me get closer," she whispered before she stretched her neck up and sucked the head into her tight, hot mouth. I groaned. She swirled her tongue around it a couple of times, then popped off.

She glanced up and let me see the heat in her eyes. "My first chocolate cock. Yum. It tastes so good."

"It's your only chocolate cock, or any cock for that matter. You'd better love it because it's all you're ever getting, Cady Cat. Hurry up and explore because I'm about to throw you flat on the bed and bury my face in that pussy. I know it's dripping wet. I need a taste. Soon." I warned her.

She winked at me before sucking my cock back in her mouth. She did it slowly and lashed me with her tongue. I was thick, and her mouth was stretched wide. Unable to resist seeing what she'd do, I slid my thumb in beside my cock and used my other hand to push her head further onto me. I would've stopped if she pulled back, but she didn't. She took me deeper. I removed my thumb, but she kept going. When she began to gag, I tried to withdraw, but she shook her head and forced herself to take me further.

A lot of women hadn't given me head out of fear of my cock. They sure as hell didn't try to deep-throat me, but Cady did. The more she gagged, the more she tried to take me even deeper. Her fingers were teasing my balls as she did it. Drool was escaping onto her chin, but it was one of the hottest sights I'd ever seen. My balls were trying to draw up, but I wouldn't come in her mouth, not this time. I reluctantly withdrew. She tried to follow and suck me again, but I stopped her. She pouted up at me. I wiped the drool from her chin.

Grasping her under her arms, I lifted her and laid

her back on the mattress. I made sure to put her in the middle. Getting on the bed with her, I positioned her so I was next to her. She was panting.

"I hope this isn't a favorite outfit," I told her.

"Why?"

"Because," I muttered, then I grabbed the top and ripped it. She gasped as I tore it down the middle. It fell open. Before getting distracted by her tits, I gripped the sides of her thong and tore it, too.

"Oh my God!" she cried.

"Not God, just Magnus. I'm gonna taste those tits, and I'll atone later for not giving them the loving they deserve this time, but I've got to get a taste of your pussy before I fill it with my cock."

Without further talk, I lowered my head and sucked a hard bead of a nipple into my mouth. I sucked and thrashed it with my tongue in between biting it as I tugged on the other with my fingers. She moaned and arched her back, driving her tit further into my mouth. I laved it and then switched to the other one. She was whimpering and wiggling on the bed. Her panting breaths were loud.

"Please, please, I need your mouth on my pussy, Magnus," she begged.

It was what I wanted, too, so I licked, nibbled, and kissed my way down her body. Moving between her spread legs, I let myself fully look at her snatch. It had a small strip of short red hair down the center. The rest of her mound and the surrounding area was hairless, and based on how smooth it was, she waxed or had it lasered off. I lay down on my stomach, which pushed my throbbing cock into the mattress. I groaned.

Lifting my thumbs to her, I gently spread her

labia. Delicate pink lips greeted me, and her scent filled my nose. I inhaled deeply, then lowered my head and took the first taste. I swiped my tongue from her hole to her clit. I moaned at her slightly salty mixed with sweetish flavor. Greedy for more, I lapped at her while tracing my fingers all over her folds and around her hole. She was moaning, and then her hand landed on my bald head, and she pressed me closer.

This sent me seeking to make her come. I licked, bit, sucked, and after a few of those, I inserted my finger into her cunt and started to thrust. She was soaked and tight as hell. I kept building the pleasure and tension in her. As I did, I worked a second finger inside her. Curling them, I scraped across her G-spot several times.

She screamed, and my mouth was flooded with her juices. She shook, but I didn't stop. I kept going and prolonged it as long as I could and then pushed her toward a second one. I did that so I had a chance to work a third finger into her. I stretched her by scissoring my fingers as wide as possible. She had the tightest pussy I'd ever felt. I didn't want to hurt her. It took only a few minutes to have her orgasm again. While she came down from that high, I lifted and wedged myself between her thighs. She was gasping and gave me a dazed smile.

"Are you on birth control?" I asked gutturally. I was dripping precum on her mound. I prayed she'd say yes, not that I gave a damn one way or the other.

"Y-yeah," she said brokenly.

Not waiting for more, I lifted her ass onto my thighs, lined my cock up with her hole, and slipped the head inside. I growled at the tightness of it. She whimpered. "Tell me if it's too much," I gritted out between clenched teeth.

She shook her head hard. "Don't stop. More."

I slipped further inside. I knew she wouldn't be able to take all of me. No woman ever had, but what she could, I knew, would be heaven. She whimpered and twisted but didn't tell me to quit. I worked myself in and out, sinking deeper. When I hit her cervix, I stopped. I took a moment to breathe, and then I pulled out and thrust. She screamed, but not in pain. Her nails raked my arms as she tried to move and take me deeper.

"Son of a bitch, look at that. Your pretty pink pussy is swallowing my black cock. It knows who it belongs to," I snarled.

The two of us, in such contrasting colors, was a further turn-on. Sure, I'd been with other white women, but they all paled in comparison to Cady. I was thrusting faster. Her sticky juices glistened on my rod. She raised up on her elbows to look down at where we were connected. She moaned.

"Stop, stop," she suddenly ordered.

It was the last thing I wanted to do, but I also didn't want to hurt her. Slowly, I halted and then withdrew. The next thing I knew, she was rolling over and coming up on her hands and knees. She wiggled her ass at me. "Take me this way. I want more of your cock. It'll go deeper like this."

That was what made my mind go off the rails. Snarling, I rose higher on my knees, lined up, and thrust into her. I did it harder than the first time. She cried out but pushed back to meet me, driving my cock deeper than it had ever gone with anyone. Motherfucker, she was like a glove and massaged me so goddamn good. I felt the cum boiling in my balls, and I knew I'd blow soon. As I pounded her cunt, she chanted.

"Fuck me, fuck me, yes, oh God, yes! Give me that ginormous black cock. Come in me, Magnus. Fill me up."

Growling, grunting, and I don't know what else, I caged her body with mine and thrust my cock in and out while tugging on her nipples and then pinching her clit. It sent her over the edge fast. As she bucked and came, I got in three more strokes, and then I froze and bellowed her name as I shot my load deep. I came and came, shooting my cum into her magnificent tightness. It was my first time going bare, and I knew I'd never have it any other way. As I finished emptying myself inside her, I slumped over her and placed a gentle kiss on the back of her neck.

"That was fucking incredible," I panted to her.

"I know," she whispered before slumping to the mattress. I followed her down. I wasn't ready to disconnect. I rolled us so I could spoon her and remain snuggly inside. Exhaustion hit me, and my eyes drooped. I'd wait a minute and then see how she felt and when we could do this again.

Hoss: Chapter 13

After having Cady for the first time last night, all I wanted to do was stay in bed with her for the next month and do nothing but make love and explore each other. After we recovered from that amazing first time, we cleaned up and then had a second round. That one, I was a little more in control, so I got to explore her lush body more and brought her to release three times before I finally sank my aching cock into her again. The sensation of going bare would never get old.

However, reality had to be a bitch and make it impossible to be alone for a month. Morning came way too soon, and we had to see about things. It being a Saturday, we should've been free to do as we pleased, but a call from Iker telling me he had the quote and wanted to go over it put a crimp in those plans. If I didn't want to get more security at the clinic, I would've told him to fuck off and it could wait until the following week. Since I couldn't, I grudgingly agreed that he could come to the house.

I grumbled and bitched about it, causing Cady to laugh and think it was hilarious. I'd have to make her pay for it. As if that wasn't enough, she ended up getting a call from Tajah, wanting to know if they could hang out. I sent Mikhail a text when I heard that.

Me: WTF? I need time with my woman. You must be falling down on the job if yours is looking to do girl time.

Mikhail: Fuck you. I'm giving it to her good all the time.

Me: Then why is she calling Cady?

Instead of another text, my phone rang. I grinned when I saw it was him calling.

"Hoss's How to Satisfy Your Woman Hotline," I said as I answered it.

"Fucker, I don't need a hotline, a tip line, or anything else. You sound pretty full of it. Does that mean Cady finally gave in and slept with your pathetic ass? No wonder she told Tajah she had nothing to do and was bored."

"Nothing to do, bored, no, needing to regain feeling in her legs, hell yeah."

"You wish."

"You don't have to wish when you're a sex god," I slammed back.

At the same time, I heard a snort of laughter from behind me and giggling on the other end of the phone. I glanced back to find Cady standing there with her hand over her mouth. Mirth danced in her eyes.

"You got something to say, Tiny?" I asked. I inched up an eyebrow as I asked. I knew she'd have something sassy to say.

"I thought referring to yourself as God last night was a mindless slip. I guess delusions are more like it."

That asshole Mikhail chuckled, and I heard Tajah giggle again.

"Woman, you know that being a brat will get you punished. Are you sure you want to go there? I know we haven't laid out the rules yet, but that's no excuse."

"Then you'd better hurry and lay out those supposed rules I'm not going to listen to, Sugar Bear because I feel that I won't be able to behave long or at all," she mouthed off.

"You tell him, Cady," Tajah shouted through the phone. I heard Mikhail tell her to behave.

"Sounds like we both need to have private time with our ladies. Tajah, I happen to have Iker stopping by to go over the clinic estimate. He'll be here at eleven. If you want to spend time with your girl, be here then. I make no promises how long I'll allow you to have her, though, so you've been warned. When I kick your ass out, you gotta go," I warned her.

"And if she doesn't go?" Cady asked insolently.

"Then she'll get to see this big black cock as I fuck you on the kitchen table," I fired back.

Cady's gasp, combined with her blush and the way she squeezed her legs together, told me rather than embarrassing or offending her, I'd turned her on. Hmm, was Cady Cat into having others watch her during sex? Something to explore.

"Oh, shit, Cady, see you at eleven. Bye," Tajah said. Mikhail was still laughing when they hung up.

Disconnecting, I curled my finger at Cady. She stood where she was. I did it again, except this time, I issued an order. "Tiny, bring that sexy ass over here."

She shook her head and stayed where she was. She was biting her bottom lip and watching me closely. I knew what she was doing. She was testing her boundaries with me. She was still unsure that I'd be able to take her resisting and being a brat with me. I didn't blame her. She'd never had total acceptance from anyone she'd been with. To a degree, I'd have to do the same thing with her. I'd have to work to discover what she could accept from me and how far I could push things with her. I was looking forward to it from both angles. Bring it on.

"Cady, the first thing you need to know is I love to play, and that's what we're doing right now. Later today, after everyone leaves, we need to sit down and talk."

"Talk about what?" The merest hesitancy was in her voice.

"We need to set the rules of when it's okay to be a brat and when it's not. And if there are any punishments for breaking the rules. If there are any absolutes that either of us cannot stand. Those sorts of things. Once we do that, then we'll be free to play, and neither of us will have a doubt if what we're doing is pleasing or angering the other. I can tell you're unsure. I don't want that."

She cautiously walked closer to me. I waited. Finally, she was standing in front of me. I tugged her down on my lap. I rubbed her back, hoping it would relax her. Tension melted away.

"Baby, I want to ask you something. It's important to me."

"Okay, what?"

"Yesterday, Mikhail mentioned he wanted to dish out part of the beating on Flint. He said it was because he knew what Reid used to do to you from Tajah. I'm the only one out of the four who doesn't know. I need you to tell me."

She stiffened, but I kept rubbing and held her close. Silence reigned for a good minute or more before she said anything.

"I don't want to tell you."

"Why? We need to be able to share everything."

"I know, and I'd like to, but it doesn't show me in a

very good light. I don't want you to change your opinion of me or be disappointed or disgusted by me."

"Cady, I don't know how to prove to you that nothing you say will do that. Whatever happened, share it with me. It obviously weighs on you. How about you tell me when the two of you broke up and how long were you together?"

I saw her debating before she gave in. "We dated for six or seven months. At first, he was super nice. If he hadn't been, I wouldn't have dated him. It wasn't until after we became intimate that things changed. I made the mistake of letting my real self out, and he didn't like it. I would anger him, and that led to arguments. We'd fight and stay mad at each other. I tried to hold back, but I couldn't." She stopped and glanced at her hands, which were in her lap and clenched together.

"He was unequipped to handle a brat. Got it. Go on. There has to be more."

"There is. He grew angrier and angrier with me. One day, he lost it, and he slapped me. I knew I pushed him too far, so I let it go. It wasn't like I hadn't pushed others to that point. I worked extra hard to curb my mouth. It didn't last. Things escalated until I knew that we were wrong for each other. That's when I broke up with him. That was about a year ago. He tried a few times over the first six months to get back together, but I told him no. The last I heard until he showed up at Lustz was he'd left town."

Outrage was growing at the thought of him abusing her. I needed to know what else he did besides slap her. "You said it escalated. What did he do?"

"Magnus," she pleaded.

"Tell me," I demanded.

"Fine. He slapped me, punched me, and a couple of times, grabbed my hair and dragged me."

"And he wasn't the first to do that you said. Did he force you to have sex?" I snarled.

"No, not ever that."

"Did anyone else?"

When she didn't immediately answer, I knew someone had. I let out a roar. She jumped. I hugged her to me. "Shh, it's alright. You're safe. I'm sorry I scared you. I'm just enraged at what not only he did but also others. Does Tajah know everything? Is that what she told Mikhail?"

"No, I never told her the worst. She knows I've been slapped, punched, and my hair pulled. Once, I was kicked out of a car and left to walk home alone in the dark. She's seen bruises. That's what Mikhail probably meant by he knew. I was always too ashamed to tell her."

I gathered her closer and rocked her. She rested her head on my chest. As some of the tension eased in her body, I talked to her.

"Cady, you need to know, no matter how far a brat has ever pushed me, not once have I slapped, punched, dragged her, and most certainly not forced her to have sex with me. It's not in me. Ultimately, I want to please, care, and protect you."

She said something, but my chest muffled it. I eased her back. "Say that again."

She wasn't looking up at me, so I tipped up her chin with a finger under it. So much uncertainty and fear was there. "What if the reason is none of them were as bad as me? I can be terribly bratty, Magnus."

"Tiny, the only way you'd make me angry, and it still wouldn't lead to any of those things, is if you refused to follow the rules all the time. There have to be times when you behave, and we don't have the back and forth."

"If you don't resort to those to correct me, then how will I know you're mad? Do you yell?"

"I rarely ever yell. Only if you were endangering yourself would I do that. I'll go silent on you. The punishments will become non-stop demands. I have a look that will tell you I'm not kidding."

"What kind of punishments will you use?"

"This involves a long discussion. Please put that on hold until after our unwanted guests come and go."

She giggled at me, calling them unwanted. We still had a little time until anyone was to arrive, so we spent it kissing and revving each other up without the ultimate ending of a release. It was torturous for me, but I noted it was worse for her. It gave me an idea of a punishment for her.

We both had to stop eventually and make ourselves presentable for our company. Cady fluttered around the kitchen, ensuring she had various things to drink. She probably would've baked if I hadn't picked up to-die-for cookies a couple of days ago. She insisted we had to have refreshments as she called them for guests. She was already making changes, and I didn't mind.

I was notified that a car was at the gate about five 'til eleven. Checking the security monitor, I saw it was Iker. I pressed a button so I could talk to him over the speaker. "Come on up."

He raised his hand to acknowledge me and waited as the gate opened. While he drove up the long driveway, I went to tell Cady he was there.

"Tiny, Iker is here. Stop fussing. He's never had

refreshments unless a beer or a whiskey counts. He won't know what to do. And I don't want to give him even more reason to try and steal you from me." I grumbled as I hugged her and gave her a small kiss.

When we parted, she lightly smacked my chest and smiled up at me. "Magnus, you have nothing to worry about. Iker isn't out to steal me. He just likes to push your buttons."

"Oh, you think? Well, you're wrong. If he could charm you away, he would. I should drop him as a friend now that I think about it."

I said the last part because I knew he was in the house and could hear me. He knew to walk in, and the door had his print in the system to allow it. I only had a few people I permitted that kind of access. He was one, along with Mikhail and Reuben. I'd have to add Cady and Tajah. Carver was yet to be determined. In Iker's case, since he put in my security system, the fucker probably had a backdoor to get in any way.

"You're stuck with me, so don't even think about it, asshole. See what I have to put up with, Cady. You should really rethink your choice," Iker said as he strolled into the kitchen wearing a huge grin. He winked at her and gave me the finger.

"That's it, he's banned. We need attack dogs, babe. Ones that will eat him upon sight," I joked.

She shook her head and rolled her eyes while he laughed. "Bastard, you'd come to me and ask where to get them, which means I know the dogs. They'd eat you, not me. Animals love me. It's that inner animal magnetism I have," he said boastfully.

"Damn it, he's right. Okay, not only oust him as a friend but also as my security consultant."

"Whoa, whoa, that's too much. I'll tame down my charisma, so it's less likely she'll leave you," was his concession.

I walked over to him. Cady was watching us with a degree of unease. Opening my arms, I gave him a man hug, but I made sure to pound the hell out of his back. He did the same to me. We were smiling when we parted, which made her smile.

"Hello again, Iker. Can I get you something to drink? Magnus has beer and alcohol, but I have iced tea, lemonade, water, coffee, or sodas," she offered.

He went to the island where she was standing. He acted like he was about to hug her, so I growled. He stopped and then held out his hand instead. "It's good to see you again. I'll hug you when he's not around. I'd love some lemonade and a few of those cookies. Did you make them?"

"Babe, he can get his drink and cookies. He knows where shit is."

"I don't mind."

"Hey, it's nice to have a proper hostess. If I'm lucky, you just throw a bag of pretzels at me and tell me to get my own drink and bring you one," Iker claimed. He wasn't too far off. With friends, I didn't stand on ceremony. They were to make themselves at home. They didn't need to ask if eating or drinking anything was alright.

"Magnus, no, you don't!" Cady exclaimed.

"He's a friend. He knows to make himself at home."

She was shaking her head. As she plated the cookies, another voice entered the conversation. Turning, I grinned. There stood Mikhail and Tajah.

"That's exactly what he does. If you want it, you'd better get it. Hoss isn't big on niceties in that way," Mikhail informed my woman.

Tajah came hurrying over to hug her girl. I waited for Mikhail to get to the island before standing up to greet him. We back-slapped each other, and then, without a word, he began to fix two glasses as he said hello to Cady. He knew the routine well. Cady tried to stop him, but he waved her away. Once we all had refreshments, it was time to get down to business.

"Cady Cat, why don't you and Taj relax and visit? She hasn't been here before. If she wants a tour, feel free to show her around."

"Can I? Oh God, Tajah, you have to see this place," she said excitedly. As she tugged on Tajah's arm, she leaned over and kissed me.

After she was done, she said, "We'll be in the smaller living room if you need us,"

"Have fun."

They happily left. I rounded on the other two as soon as they were out of sight. "I know you have the quote. Whatever it costs, no matter what she says, I want everything. She'll be as safe as I can make her at that place until I get her moved." I got amused looks from both of them. Might as well get the small stuff out of the way first.

"I figured as much," Iker said.

"I'm surprised Cady let you talk her into moving her clinic so easily. Tajah has been trying for ages to get her to do it," Mikhail stated.

"It's easy when I have no intention of leaving her there. We talked about it, and she gave me all the reasons she can't, which all boil down to money. I asked her to consider making me a silent partner and take on another vet. I saw she was intrigued by the idea, but we had to leave the conversation to be continued."

"Telling Cady what she's going to do isn't usually productive, from what I hear. She'll fight it," Mikhail warned.

"I know she will, and I'm prepared for it. Ultimately, I want her not to have to work so hard or worry constantly. It's only money, and I have plenty of it. "

"I get it. I do. I'd be the same way if it was Tajah. I'm finding being in a permanent relationship with a strong woman isn't always easy, but it is more than worth it. I'm fucking happy that you and Cady are making a go of it. She deserves a good man and happiness," Mikhail added.

"Speaking of a good man and happiness, mind telling me what Tajah told you about the men in Cady's past that have you wanting a piece of Flint Reid?" I threw in.

He grimaced. "I shouldn't have said anything, but he's garbage and deserves everything he gets. Have you asked Cady? It should come from her."

"I did ask her. I want to be sure she didn't downplay or leave anything out."

"Alright, Tajah said that the men Cady had been with before were unable to handle her feisty side. Her sassiness made them angry, and they'd fight. Lots of the time, the guys would get physical on top of being verbally abusive to her. The abuse took the form of slaps, hair-pulling, punches, and kicks. In Reid's case, he did all those as well as he choked her. According to Taj, the choking incident was the last straw, and Cady kicked him to the curb."

I was already pissed about the other things he did, but to know he choked her. No woman deserved that unless it was done consensually during sex. I clenched my fists. "Well, that's not the worst of it. She claims Reid didn't do it, but I asked if any of them ever forced her to have sex. She didn't answer me, which I took as yes. You know what that means," I stared hard at Mikhail and then Iker. Neither was taking what was said lightly. Both were upset. Their expressions said it all.

"You want Outlaw to find out where they are, and every one of them will be taught a lesson. Those who took it to the point of rape will get a more severe one," Mikhail stated.

"Damn right, they will. If I ask Cady for their names, she'll probably hold back. Can you get Tajah to tell you? At least enough so Outlaw has a way to track them?"

"I don't believe Tajah knows the raping part. However, if I tell her it's to avenge Cady, yeah, she'll do it. Taj detests those men and would love nothing more than to watch them suffer. She did say not all of Cady's exes became physical. Some just got tired of it and left. They would sometimes get verbal, but then so did Cady."

"I'm not as worried about those. None of them knew how to handle her or her need to be a brat. I do."

"That's for sure. I don't think I could do it," Iker confessed.

"Taj has a bit of brat in her, but not like Cady. I believe she's with the right man." Mikhail slapped my back.

I grinned. "She is."

"Alright, I'll get those names from Tajah and get Outlaw to work. You realize it might be a while, depending on what's happening with the club."

"I do. And as badly as I'd like to hunt them down and exact justice tomorrow, I can wait."

"Done," was all he added.

I turned to Iker. "Now, back to you."

"Should I assume you want me to install a top-of-the-line alarm system at her apartment, too?"

"No, that won't be necessary. She'll be staying here as much as I possibly can get her, and if she insists on staying there, I'll be with her. On the nights I work late at Lustz, she'll have one of your people watching her."

"She will. Okay, I think that takes care of that. I'll email you the quote. Do you want me to stick around and talk to Cady about what the charges will be, or are you planning to do that? Don't get me wrong, a good fireworks show is always fun, but I got the impression you want to be alone with her as soon as possible," Iker's grin was broad.

"He does. He barely allowed us to stop by so the women could see each other. He finally got some last night, and he's eager for more," Mikhail chimed in.

"We're not talking about my sex life with Cady. Do I ask you what you do with Tajah?" I fired back.

"No, but you can guess, and I can guess what you and Cady are or will be up to. So can Iker. And it's due to a healthy dose of self-preservation and the knowledge of how much I love being alone with Tajah that I swear we'll get out of here as soon as I can pry them apart," he promised.

"And that's what makes you such a wonderful

friend."

"Hey, I'm one too. I will say, watching the two of you and the way you're acting so besotted with your women is making me fucking jealous. I want one. You've got to find me a woman like yours," Iker partly pleaded.

"If you'd just come to Lustz, you might find one perfect for you. You keep going after the ones who have no hope of keeping up with you and your needs. We've told you that," I reminded him.

He sighed. "You have, and I have no good reason not to come. Okay, you've talked me into it. I'll do it if it ups my chances of finding Mrs. Right. I'm not out anything if it doesn't. Finding women I can play with to pass the time, if nothing else would be fun. I'll fill out the application and be in touch. Now, if you don't mind, I'll sneak out while the ladies are occupied. I don't want Cady to corner me on the cost. That's your can of worms. Good luck."

He came to his feet. Mikhail and I walked him to the door, giving him a hard time about being a coward. He didn't deny it, though he referred to it as being smart. After he left, we went to find our women.

Cady: Chapter 14

My visit with Tajah was great. I enjoyed the time not only with her but also with Mikhail and Hoss. It was intimate and relaxed. Or it was after I got over the fact Iker had left and was sending the quote to me through Hoss. When I asked him why, he said we'd talk about it. I knew that meant he thought he would pay for it. Well, I had news for Mr. Sacket. I wasn't a kept woman.

His cars and house told me that his company did exceptionally well. He was a rich man. I didn't want anyone, especially him, to think I was with him due to his wealth. I had never been, nor would I ever be, a gold-digger. Just the thought of it made me shudder.

Taj and Mikhail hung out with us for a couple of hours. Long enough to have lunch and catch up. Before the guys joined us, she wanted me to tell her if Hoss and I had slept together and, if we had, how it was. Just recalling that conversation made me smile. I was waiting for Hoss to finish a call he got from someone at his office so I could revisit that conversation.

"So, tell me. I see you and Hoss seem to be cozier. You stayed all night with him. Does that mean what I think it does?" Tajah asked coyly.

Wanting to mess with her, I shrugged and adopted a disinterested look. "We've talked some. He was worried about the Flint issue because he showed up at the clinic after being in my house and at Lustz. I didn't want to disturb you and Mikhail, so I took him up on his offer to stay here. I mean, you saw this place. He has a ton of bedrooms to spare, and none of them are less than comfortable."

She huffed. "I get that, but are you telling me you stayed in a guest bedroom and didn't jump that man's bones? Good God, he's scrumptious. You'd have to be crazy to say no to him. I mean, even if all it turns out to be is sex. Go for it. What do you have to lose? If you're worried he'll treat you like those other losers, I don't see it happening. He's not that kind of man, Cady."

"Taj, does Mikhail know you think Hoss is scrumptious?" I teased.

"I have eyes. And he knows I can appreciate an attractive, sexy man without wanting to sleep with him. Mikhail is perfect for me. Something in my gut tells me that Hoss is perfect for you if you only give him a chance. Don't let the past dictate your future. Not everyone is like your exes or parents, especially your dad." She gave me a sympathetic look when she said the last part. My stomach cramped, even thinking about Dad.

"I know that intellectually, but emotionally, it's hard, Taj. I see what you have with Mikhail. And I look at others I've known who've had successful relationships. I know it's possible. However, with my past, I don't want to get my hopes up. If I do, and it doesn't work out with Hoss, it'll hurt far worse than anything I went through in the past."

"Which should tell you that he's most likely the man for you. And I don't see him hurting you. It takes a strong man to let you be you and not be diminished or threatened by it. I believe Hoss is that guy."

I let my excitement peek out. She clapped her hands.

"*You did sleep with him! I knew it. Tell me. How was it?*"

"*It was the best sex of my life by far. He made me come so hard and long it was unbelievable.*"

"*Oh, that's great. I'm not asking for specifics, but I have to ask. Is all of him in proportion to the rest of him?*" *She wiggled her eyebrows.*

"*Oh, yes, he is. And that's all I'm saying.*"

"*Bitch,*" *she said with a mock frown. This set us off giggling. Once we got control, we moved on to other topics.*

"What're you smiling about, Tiny?" Hoss asked, causing me to jump. I hadn't heard him enter the room. He was stealthy for such a big guy.

"Just remembering something Tajah and I were talking about earlier. All done with your call? Do you need to go to work?" I was praying he wouldn't.

"No, I don't have to go to work. They can handle it. Just needed to check with me on a point or two. I have excellent people. I'd like to know what the two of you talked about to make you smile that way."

I fought not to blush, but I wasn't successful. He grinned, then sat down on the couch next to me. He ran his thumb over my cheek and then my mouth. "Cady Cat, were you talking about us? Did Tajah want to know whether we've had sex yet or not? What did you tell her?"

"It was, if you must know, and I told her yes. I didn't give any details away."

"But you told her I was a God in bed, I bet."

"No, I said you would be adequate with guidance and tutoring," I snarked.

Instead of getting upset, he threw back his head and laughed. When he finished, he added more. "I know that's not true. The way you couldn't move afterward and how you came told the truth. However, your brazen lie does bring up what we were discussing earlier. I think before we get further into this, we should set up some of our rules and establish punishments."

This made me sit up straight. Having never done anything like this, I was nervous. Taj had shared some with me about how she and Mikhail established theirs, and of course, I knew what she'd written in her first book, but that was it. And with Hoss being a brat handler and Mikhail a primal, they would differ, no doubt.

"Okay, what do I need to do?"

"Just be totally honest with what you want, don't want, hate, and are willing to consider. Once I know those about you and you know the same things about me, we can set the rules and write out the contract."

"It's written, as in we sign it?" I didn't recall Taj mentioning if they signed one or not.

"Yes, that way, there are no misunderstandings. Some people only have them verbally, but I don't. However, if we find that over time, we need to add or delete things, it can be modified. Let's start with sex itself. Are there things you've tried or not that are a definite no for you?"

I thought about my past experiences and what I knew. I wasn't the most experienced woman on the planet. I'd had boyfriends, but not dozens or more. I suspected Hoss had many lovers. It made me uneasy. What if I ended up not being enough?

"What just went through your mind?" he asked abruptly. While I was thinking, he'd picked up a notebook and pen lying on the table in front of us.

"I, just something I hadn't thought of. Okay,

things I hate. Hmm, I don't like to be hurt. What I mean is no cutting, shocking, burning. And no group sex. I don't want to be shared or to share you. And I've heard from Tajah about people who're into things like urine, feces, and such. No way. I'm fine if others like it, but it's not me, no matter how much you try to convince me." I grimaced despite not wanting to. I was trying not to offend in case he was into any of those.

"Babe, I'm not into urophilia, emetophilia, klismaphilia, coprophilia, or any of those. The first term is for those into golden showers, the second is vomit, the third is enemas, and the last is feces. I agree. If others like them, more power to them. Now, when you say shocking, what does that mean? Are you saying no to a violet wand or a much harder and more painful shock? Cutting I have no interest in. Burning, there's wax play, which does have a burning component, but you're not permanently scarred or injured by it."

"I could've survived not knowing the names of those things, but I guess I can say I'm more educated. I don't know what that wand does or feels like. Does it hurt a lot? I just said no shocking because I heard that some do shock their partners," I shared.

"There are two types of violet wands and many attachments that affect the shock. I won't get into those differences, just know what I'm talking about is a wand that takes the current in an outlet and turns it into a steady stream of zaps. The zaps energize your nerves and stimulate your skin. If you're into erotic and sensuous sensations or even intense ones, the wand can give you that. It can be combined with all kinds of other scenes."

He paused after explaining it. I admit, the idea of

sensuous or erotic called to me, but I wasn't sure how intense I'd be able to stand. "A wand I'd possibly put in the maybe category. I'd have to try it to know for sure," I told him. I watched him jot words down.

"Next, the burning. Wax play maybe, yes, or no?" he asked.

"Do you like it? Either to receive or to give?" I asked.

"This is about you. I don't want to influence your answers. When we're done with you, I'll tell you my limits. I've lived with mine for a long time. I'm comfortable with them and won't hold back telling the truth."

"Well, I've only ever played with it once. The guy used a candle, and when he poured the hot wax on me, it burned my skin, causing me to get a blister. I didn't like that at all."

"Do you know if he used a regular candle? There are ones that are made for play which aren't as hot. Those that are colored or scented or made of beeswax melt at a higher melting point, so they burn more. I'd stick to soy ones. They have a lower melting point. Also, the height at which you drop the wax affects how hot it is when it hits your skin. Some people like the more serious burn. In your case, I see you as more into the sensual, like the wand."

Again, an explanation changed me from no way to maybe. He took me through more likes and dislikes. When I was done, he hit me unexpectedly with his earlier question. "What went through your mind that made you concerned when we got started?"

He waited patiently for me to answer. I took my time and then decided to go for it. He wanted honesty, so I'd give it to him.

"You're a member of a sex club. You've been around countless women. I have no doubt you've played a lot and not just there. You're a very captivating man. You've undoubtedly had lots of lovers and partners. I've had boyfriends, but not on the scale you've been with women. And with them being part of the club scene, I know they've tried a lot more than me. They know what they like and don't like. What if you find me boring? Or you want to go back to that life or want things I won't do?"

He sighed and brought me closer. "Babe, I haven't been with hundreds of women. Let's be clear on it. And many of the ones at the club I did scenes with but didn't have sex with them. The two aren't mutually exclusive. As for being bored with you, I don't see that ever happening. We didn't do anything out of the ordinary last night, and you made me come harder than I ever have. I'd catalog it as the best sex of my life, and that was without any kink. As for wanting to go back to the club, I do enjoy it. But I'd only ever do it if you're with me. We can watch if that appeals to you, or if you want to be seen, we can do scenes and allow others to watch us. Or we can watch others and then go to a private room together—any of those work for me. You reacted the other day, and I wondered if you might have exhibitionist tendencies. Do you get turned on at the thought of someone watching you have sex?"

At the thought, a shiver went through me. "I've never tried it, but I admit, the idea of it makes me wonder. My body reacts by getting all tingly at the thought. Although if I ever tried it, I might freeze and hate it."

"And if you do, then we'd stop. I can tell you that I've never cared if someone sees me or my partner, and seeing others is hot. However, I'm not sure if it'll change with you. Watching is one thing, but touching you in any way is a hard no. I won't share you, and I don't want to be shared. Some of the things I like are impact play, anal play, and edging my partner. That's not all, but it's a good place to start."

"Do you enjoy receiving any of those?" I knew what they were from Taj.

"Edging, yes. Anal, I've never wanted to try. Impact play, maybe. It might be fun with you."

"And what if I said I want to perform anal on you?" I asked.

"Are you willing to let me do it to you?" was his comeback.

I hesitated, then answered him. "I've played with dildoes and stuff. I've had anal sex and enjoyed it in one case and hated it in another. Your size scares me. I don't know how it wouldn't hurt terribly. You're a big man, Magnus."

"It would hurt, but I'd do everything I could to prepare you to make it as comfortable as possible. Degrees of pain can enhance the experience. We'd take it slow. And to answer you, I'm willing to give it a chance if you're willing to let me try. Toys and my fingers are a given. My cock is negotiable."

"But you enjoy doing anal," I added.

"Honestly, I think I would, but I've never had a woman agree. My size is a factor."

As soon as he admitted that, I wanted to be the one woman who gave him something no one else ever had. I leaned closer to him. "Then let's put that in the definitely maybe category for both of us."

He inhaled sharply, and the heat that it brought to his gaze told me we'd better hurry up with this negotiation. His next words verified he was feeling the same.

"I think we have enough to start with. Now, to discuss funishments and punishments. The latter will only come into play if you misbehave in a situation that is a hard, no-play environment. For example, I'm pretty good with you being bratty, but I don't want it when we're around my work clients or employees. It could cause them to believe I'm not someone they can rely on. If we're in a dangerous situation, I don't want you to do it then. If I give you my signal, which will be a word, then there's a good reason I don't want you doing it right then, and I expect you not to. You can tease me and call me names if it's done playfully outside those instances. But if you disrespect me for real, then no. Another thing I won't allow is you to make disparaging remarks about yourself. Lying is a big no-no. That includes telling what you think are small lies, such as you're alright with a toy we use or you don't tell me something is too painful because you want to please me. Lying won't do it, and I will know, Cady. You'll establish a safe word to use. When you do, if you don't use it when you should have or if you use it to get out of being punished, that won't be tolerated."

"What is your word? And if I were to be a brat in those hard no situations, what are my punishments?"

"My word is pineapple. As for punishments, I'll add more as we go along, again after we agree, but based on what you've shared with me, I think I have a few. Orgasm denial is one. I'd get you to the edge, then back off and not let you come, and I'd do it for hours. You'll be begging and in tears when I'm done with you. Another would be sensory deprivation. You said you don't like to be unable to see and hear at the same time. I'd cover your eyes and ears, so you have neither sense."

I squirmed because he'd hit on ones I knew I wouldn't enjoy at all.

"You need to have a safe word, Cady. What will it be?"

"Since yours is a fruit, I'll stick to that theme, and it'll be Kiwi. I hate them."

He chuckled. "Kiwi it is. We've more to discuss, but I think we've made a good start. What would you say about leaving this for tomorrow and us doing something else?"

"What do you have in mind?" As if I had to ask. The bulge in his pants told me he was turned on.

"Stripping you bare, laying you out on the dining room table, eating your pussy until you come, then fucking you until we both explode. Then, after a rest, we'll do it again, but in a different place, and throw in some fun toys. I've been dreaming of you since the first time I saw you. I hoped I'd get the chance to have you. I've been collecting toys and other items for us. Wanna come see what I have?"

I hopped to my feet. "What are you waiting for? Show me what you've got. Or is that too much for you?" I taunted.

He rose to his feet and slapped his hand hard on my ass. It stung, but it sent a jolt through me, too. Spanking was on my yes list, but only to a point. I bet he'd add the harder spanking to my punishment list once he discovered my line. He took my hand and moved toward the dining room. I could hardly contain my growing excitement. I was ready. I'd gone long enough without him. I needed him desperately. All this talk about sex and boundaries had turned me on just as it had him.

When we entered the room, he let go of my hand. I wasn't sure why. He walked to the window and drew the drapes, blocking out all the light. Why was he concerned about that? No one could see us. Once he closed them, he went to the light switch and turned on the light. Over the table, the chandelier came on, and the way the crystals reflected bits of light all over the table and room was dazzling.

On my tour, I admired the dining room set. It was made of dark wood, and it was a statement piece. Most of the furniture and decor in this house was. He had good taste and the money to indulge it. The table was rectangular and long enough to seat a dozen, though there were extra chairs along the wall, making me think there was an extension that you could add. The room was large enough to expand it.

He turned to stare at me. He didn't approach, though. He crossed his arms. "Strip," he commanded. The authority in his tone made my body react, but the brat in me wasn't that easily subdued.

"Okay, and why should I?"

An eyebrow went up. "Because I told you to."

"Seems like a you problem, Supersized. I think I'll take a nap. I'm bored," I said, then I deliberately presented my back to him and took a couple of steps toward the door. I wanted to push him. I hadn't let my full brattiness out to play. This wouldn't be my best. But it would tell me if he could handle me like he said and what he'd do to punish me.

"Think before you walk out that door, Cady Cat. If you do, you reap the punishment for not doing as I told you," his voice sounded deeper when he spoke.

I paused, glanced over my shoulder, shrugged, and sassed more. "Yeah, sure thing, Hoss."

I knew calling him Hoss rather than Magnus would push him. I watched as his gaze caught fire. Suddenly, he was stalking toward me. I took off running. His footsteps pounded loudly behind me on the hardwood floor. I thought I had the advantage of a smaller size, making me swifter. I learned I was wrong. I didn't make it more than ten feet, if that, before I was grabbed and lifted in his arms. He held me tightly. I struggled to get away, but he didn't seem to notice. I was swung around, and we headed back into the dining room.

He paused to shut and lock the door, then took me to stand by the end of the table before putting me down. He gave me a quelling look. Surely, he knew it would take more than that to tame me temporarily. I'd never been able to engage in my brat self fully.

"Are you going to do as I say, Tiny?"

"No. What're you gonna do about it?" I taunted.

His smile was kind of chilling. The next thing I knew, I was picked up and placed on the table. He pushed me flat. I saw him reaching underneath it. I didn't struggle because I was too busy trying to see what he was doing. My mistake. When his hand came up, it was holding a black strap. My brain tried to decipher what it was, but by the time it registered, he already had a loop tight around my wrist. In a flash, he was reaching under the opposite side. I tried to sit up, but he pushed me back down, and just like that, my other wrist was bound.

"I warned you. Now, you're at my mercy. Although, I think I need to do a little more." He smirked.

I wiggled and tried to get free, but it was no use. He pushed me further up the table, and then he pulled out more restraints, and my ankles were bound. When he was done, I was tied spread eagle on the table. I'd be a liar if I said it wasn't turning me on, but I wasn't ready to tell him that. In our talk, I'd indicated I wasn't opposed to being restrained, only leery of it.

"Let me up," I demanded.

"Are you going to use your safe word? We've barely begun." He waited.

There was no way I'd safe word out and not for something turning me on like this was and this early in the game. I shouldn't have felt like I could trust him this early and this way, but I did. I shook my head.

"Words, Cady. I need you to say yes or no."

"No, no safe word."

"Good. Hmm, I like seeing you like this, all subdued and at my mercy, but this picture needs more."

"What? You need an instruction manual."

His smile was slightly intimidating. He walked over to the side buffet and opened one of the drawers. I hadn't peeked into it, so I had no clue what was in the drawers. I gasped when he came up out of it with a silver knife in his hand. Fear slithered up my spine. Was I about to find out he was into cutting and had lied?

He came back to me. When he saw my face, he gave me a tender smile. "Baby, you don't need to be scared. I'm not going to cut you, I promise. Just hold still so I don't accidentally do it."

Trusting him, when I wouldn't have trusted another man in a similar situation, I lay perfectly still. I watched as he lifted the bottom of my pant leg and sliced slowly up the entire length of my leg. It was a pair of yoga pants. It cut easily. He didn't stop until he cut through the waistband. He repeated the same thing on the other side. After he had them cut off, he jerked the ruined fabric out from underneath me and tossed it on the floor.

He studied me and shook his head. "Tsk, you've been running around without underwear on while we had other men in the house, Tiny. I don't think I like that. What if they saw the outline of your delectable pussy through the fabric? This is my cunt. I own it. I decide when and if it's visible to others."

I shivered because he ran a finger between my lips. I was wet. He lifted his coated finger and sucked it clean, and hummed in approval, but that was it. Leaving me there hornier than I was seconds ago, he moved up to my upper body.

He leaned over and thrust his tongue into my mouth. I tasted myself and eagerly tried to kiss him. He pulled away. "Taste that? It's mine. Only good girls get to share it and get a kiss. You've been bad. Where was I?"

I wiggled on the table. I was burning up from just that little bit. That's when I began to learn what it meant to be punished by my man. He proceeded to caress, nibble, and lick all over my lower body, but he stayed away from my pussy. On my upper half, which was still clothed, he kneaded my breasts and touched any exposed skin. I had no idea how long it went on, but it was close to an hour, by my calculations, or it felt that long. He now had me to the point I began to beg.

"Magnus, please, I need you. Let me loose. I want to touch you."

"No. I'm trying to figure out what to do. I need a manual, remember?" he mocked.

"No, you don't. I'm sorry. I should've never said that. You don't need any help to pleasure me."

"We'll see," was all he said.

I was almost a whimpering puddle. He picked up the knife again. He made precise cuts on my T-shirt and removed it. I did have a bra on. I was too self-conscious to go without one around people. My breasts were on the large size for my frame. Plus, if I had to run, the bouncing hurt, and I had to hold them down.

If I thought he'd cut my bra away, too, I was wrong. He teased all around my breasts, but that was it. Kisses would be given, but just fleeting ones. I'd had enough. I jerked hard on the straps, but they held.

"Let me up! I can't take any more of this," I whined.

"Oh, yes, you can. You're being punished. You don't get to decide when it's done. I do. I'm in charge. Maybe next time you'll listen."

I moaned and whimpered. I continued to plead when I couldn't hold it in. I was creating a puddle under my ass from where my cum was soaking me. I felt insane. When he cut free my bra, I sighed in relief, only to cry out more as he teased me mercilessly.

Finally, I gave up and lay there. I sobbed, and tears were running down my face as I begged one last time. "Stop. It hurts. I can't take it anymore. Just let me up. I want to go."

As soon as I said it, and I knew I sounded broken, he was at my ankles, releasing them and then my wrists. I was too weak to sit on my own when I was free. I tried to roll, but he stopped me. He pulled me to the end of the table and took a seat as he hugged me. I laid my head on his chest.

"Shh, you're alright. I've got you, baby. Let me take care of you," he said softly, rubbing my back soothingly.

He kissed all over my face and then planted a sweet one on my mouth. When he was done, he eased me back onto the table. I wanted to protest, thinking he was about to start the punishment again, but that went out of my head as soon as he widened my thighs and his mouth came down on my dripping pussy. I was so sensitive from all the play and orgasm denial that all it took was one swipe of his tongue, and I came. I screamed as I shook uncontrollably, and more cum squirted out of me. He made a hungry sound and lapped faster.

If I thought my coming would make him stop, I was wrong. He kept me on the edge so that I never wholly came down from my orgasm before I was climbing toward another. The man was diabolical. I was gasping as the third one ebbed. I was about to call time out when he stood and yanked off his shirt. His pants immediately followed it. I'd seen the bulge he sported the whole time he tortured me. It hadn't gone down. When his cock bobbed into view, I moaned. It pulsated with veins, and precum coated at least half of it.

He grasped my hips and rolled me. I weakly tried to help. Lying flat on my front hurt the girls, so I pushed my upper body up. He spread my ass cheeks, and then I felt the head of his cock probe my entrance a second before he pushed inside. It burned a bit, but I loved it. I cried out his name as he thrust until he was all the way in for me. I knew there was still part of him not in, but he filled me to capacity. He stopped.

"Hang on, Cady. You've got me on edge. Tell me if I get too rough," he said hoarsely.

That was all the warning I got, then he began to pound my pussy. It was glorious, and I moaned and cried out in ecstasy as he fucked me hard and fast. I swear, I felt those veins rubbing my insides. He would hit the head on my G-spot. It only took a couple of minutes for that to get me coming. I waited for him to flood me with his cum, but he didn't. He somehow held back and kept stroking in and out.

God, I didn't know if I could take any more. Then he lifted me to stand, and his hand came to my front to fondle my tits. I moaned louder. Then that hand slipped down to tease my clit. I lost it and came again. As I did, his other hand rose and gripped my throat. I could still breathe, but I had to work at it. As I struggled and realized his choking me this way actually made me come harder, he let out a roar and jerked over and over as he filled me with his cum while I was still squeezing down on him. When we both stopped coming, I would've fallen if it weren't for him holding me up.

He sank back in the chair, taking me with him. I sat on his lap with his cock still inside of me and our combined cum leaking out. I hoped we didn't ruin the leather seat. He was kissing my neck as he murmured to me.

"Cady, Jesus, that was so fucking hot. You have no idea how good that was for me. I hope you loved it as much as I did. I didn't go too far, did I? I was waiting for you to say Kiwi. Was the punishments okay?"

I weakly nodded my head. "During it, I thought about using my word, but even as insane as you made me, I couldn't. I have no words for what happened. You've ruined me for anyone else. I loved it," I confessed.

He growled in my ear, "Good. I want you always to want me. There will be no one else. I'll give you whatever you need and want. After last night and today, there's no way in the world I'll let you go. As long as we communicate honestly, we've got this.

"Mm," was all I could say. I was drifting off asleep.

He chuckled. "It's time for me to take care of you, Cady Cat."

He lifted me, so we disconnected, and I made a disapproving sound. Then he stood and swung me up in his arms. He strode out of the dining room toward the master bedroom. I snuggled into him.

Cady: Chapter 15

Our weekend passed too fast for my liking. We spent it holed up in his house, exploring our newfound relationship. Part of that consisted of completing our discussion about what we wanted and forming the contract, which we signed Sunday evening. The rest of the time, if we weren't asleep, was filled with getting to know more about each other in general and the hottest sex ever. Even when I ended up being punished, ultimately, it was worth it.

We had so much going on that I didn't think about the quote Iker was supposed to send me via Hoss. That was until after he dropped me off at the clinic. Yeah, he insisted on driving me there and back. He was determined I'd stay the night with him again. Since I wanted to be with him, I didn't object.

It wasn't until I was in the building after Hoss checked to be sure it was safe and everyone arrived to start our day that I recalled the quote. I wanted to call Hoss immediately and ask if he had it and, if so, to send it to me, but I was hesitant. He had meetings this morning, and I didn't want to interrupt. His work was important, just like mine, so I hung onto my patience.

Due to Friday's cancelations, I had a jam-packed day ahead. Not all those canceled were slated to be seen today, but several were. The rest were worked in for the remainder of the week.

I didn't get a chance to sit or catch my breath until lunchtime. I had twenty minutes, so I went to my office and sat down. I was hungry, but I needed the rest more. A tap on my office door had me opening my eyes. Dottie stood there, giving me a sympathetic smile. She walked in and held out her hand. In it was a bowl. The aroma coming off it was divine.

"I knew you wouldn't eat. Here's some stew I made. I brought plenty, so don't say no. You need to take better care of yourself, Cady. I don't think that man of yours would like it if he knew you're not eating."

I gave her a grateful look as I accepted it. I waved for her to have a seat, which she did. I took a bite and hummed in approval. It tasted as good as it smelled. Once I chewed and then swallowed, I commented on her remark.

"What Hoss doesn't know won't hurt me."

"It will if I narc you out. If it's the only way to force you to take care of yourself, I'll do it," she warned.

"Hey, you work for me, remember? What if I fire you for narcing me out?" I fake threatened.

She laughed. "Good luck finding someone to put up with this bunch who can also keep this place running smoothly."

She had a point. If she didn't do what she did, I'd lose my mind and kill people. I gave her the middle finger, which made her laugh harder. I wouldn't have done that to the others, but Dottie and I had a closer relationship.

I gobbled down the stew. Even when it burned my tongue, I kept going. She seemed content to sit there and watch me eat. When I was done, I sighed.

"That was wonderful, Dottie. Thank you. How's it

going out front? Anything I need to know or address?"

"Nope. Just getting people in and out as quickly as we can. It's been quiet otherwise. I didn't see your car this morning in the lot. Did your man bring you to work?"

"He did. He said it was silly to both drive when I was going back to his house tonight."

"Oh, so you're sleeping over. I hope you're doing more than just sleeping." She winked. I threw a crumpled piece of paper at her.

"Pervert, I'm not telling you!"

"You just did. The look on your face and that flush, yeah, he's giving you the anaconda."

This made me burst out laughing. She joined me. By the time I got myself under control, it was time to see the next patient. I shoved her playfully out of my office. Boy, she had no idea how true it was.

The afternoon was humming along. I was happy with how well it was going—that is, until Dottie came to find me. She seemed flustered.

"What's wrong?" I asked.

"That man is here again. He's asking for you and says he's here to work."

Immediately, I thought of Flint, but he'd have no reason to say he was here to work. "Which one? Not Flint."

She shook her head. "No, not that prick. I mean the one Hoss had come and check over the place. You know, Iker."

That explained why she was flustered. Something about him got to her. However, it didn't explain why he was here to work. A sneaking suspicion entered my head. Surely, Hoss hadn't told him to come install the new alarm system and cameras? I hadn't even seen what they would cost. I left the empty treatment room and followed her. She took me to my office. He was sitting there. When he saw me, he got to his feet. Dottie didn't hang around. I saw his eyes follow her.

"Hey, Cady. It's good to see you again. I'm here to start the new installation," he said cheerfully.

"No, you're not. I haven't seen your quote yet, so I didn't approve you to do it."

"Hoss didn't speak to you?"

"No, he didn't. When did he tell you to do this?"

"Uhm, I got an email this morning saying it was a go. I assumed you two had discussed it."

"No, we didn't. I'm sorry you wasted a trip for nothing, but until I go over the quote, there's no way I'm letting you install anything. And even if I say yes to some of it, I have to get with my landlord to ensure it's alright. I don't own this property, Iker. I can't make changes without his approval. Hoss shouldn't have told you to do it. I'm sorry, but you'll have to leave. I'll have a talk with Hoss so he doesn't get upset with you for not doing the job."

"Cady, I've known Hoss for a few years. He's a very decisive man. When he sees a need, he fixes it if he can. You're his lady. He sees that you're not safe here. If you believe he'll let you go without because of money, you don't know him yet. He won't."

"Well, that may be so, but Hoss isn't the boss of me. He doesn't run my life. We need to discuss this, not for him to make a unilateral decision about it and expect me to go along with it like an airheaded bimbo."

I was losing my cool and didn't think venting my anger with Hoss on Iker was fair. "Forgive me. I'll deal with this. You're free to go. Thank you for coming over. I've got to go. I have more patients to see before the end of the day."

I was able to hustle him to the front and out the door. Dottie was nowhere to be seen. I was seething but couldn't do anything about it right then. I hadn't lied. I had more animals to see. When I had spare moments for the remainder of the day, I thought of what I would say to Hoss about this whole thing. Undoubtedly, Iker would tell him I kicked him out, and Hoss would be ready to defend his choice.

When five o'clock arrived, I was glad to send the staff home. When Hoss dropped me off this morning, I told him not to come to pick me up until six, so I would have time to chart and restock the rooms for the next day. However, I was too upset to concentrate on anything, and I wasn't willing to sit around waiting on him either. I didn't have my car, so I did the next best thing and called for a ride.

I was in luck. There was one nearby, and I only had to wait ten minutes. Locking up the clinic sans worthless alarm, I got in the car and gave the driver my address. Maybe it would be better for me to stay at my place so I have time to calm down. I'd wait until I got there to text Hoss and let him know.

It was a quarter 'til six when I was dropped off. I wearily unlocked the door. It seemed like it had been weeks since I was here. The apartment was stuffy, so I opened a couple of windows to air it out. Going to the fridge, I checked to see if there was anything in it that I could eat for dinner. The few items in there were past their expiration date. I had items in the freezer and pantry, but the thought of thawing or going through a bunch of steps wasn't worth it. I gave up and went to my bedroom. Stripping off my clothes, I turned on the shower. Maybe a hot one would help me feel better. Right before I got in, I sent off a text to Hoss.

Me: Don't bother to pick me up. I'm staying at my place. I need to be alone. I'll let you know when we can talk.

As soon as I sent it, I turned off my phone. Childish, maybe, but I wasn't in the mood to fight with him. I wanted quiet. My head was pounding. I knew it was stress. Perhaps I'd take my medication tonight. I had some for migraines. It put me out when I did. A good night's sleep would do me good.

I stayed in the shower until the water turned cold. Stepping out, I briskly dried off and rubbed some lotion into my skin before walking to my bedroom. I didn't bother to put anything on. I face-planted on the bed and closed my eyes. The ceiling fan was on, circulating the cool air from the window I had open. It made a faint humming sound that acted as white noise. I found myself drifting off despite my headache.

I had no idea how long I drifted just under the surface before I was jarred alert by the loud pounding on my door and Hoss's voice calling out. "Cady, I know you're in there. Open the goddamn door," he shouted.

Anger flared inside me as I got off the bed and stomped to the door. I unlocked it and then flung it open to glare at him. His eyes flashed. The next thing I knew, I was being pushed backward, and he came charging into my apartment. He slammed the door behind him and flipped the lock.

"Just what in the hell do you think you're doing, Hoss? You have no right to barge into my home or to push me!" I snarled.

"I'll tell you what gives me the right. I find my woman has gone off in a tizzy and has shut her fucking phone off, so I can't talk to her. When I show up on her doorstep to figure out what the fuck is wrong, she answers the motherfucking door naked! Anyone could've seen you, Cady. And my damn name is Magnus," he snapped.

I'd forgotten I was naked, and I wouldn't usually have answered it without any clothes on, but since I did and I was still pissed at him, I went with it.

"So what? If I want to let the whole world see me naked, I will. I'm a free woman. I can do whatever I please. And what I please is for you to leave and let me sleep. I'm not in the mood for you or your shit, Hoss."

"Call me Hoss again and see what happens," he threatened.

"Go to hell. You know the way out, Hoss," I said before turning my back on him and walking off. I was headed back to bed. My head was worse. I was starting to get other symptoms, which told me I was in for a killer migraine. Spots and lights danced in my peripheral vision, and my stomach churned.

My only warning was a growl seconds before I was hoisted in the air. I was clutched in his steel-hard arms. I kicked back, but my foot landed harmlessly on his shin. It hurt my foot more than his leg. I wiggled as I demanded. "Put me down!"

"Not on your life. We're talking, and you can be a brat and throw a temper tantrum all you want. It won't do you any good," he said as he marched to my bedroom. He went to the bed and sank on the edge, placing me on his lap. I tried to elbow him, but again, I hurt myself more than I hurt him.

"You want to tell me what has your nose out of joint?"

"Don't pretend you don't know. You know exactly why I'm mad."

"Don't tell me this and running off from the clinic is all because I sent Iker to change out your security system."

"Damn right, it is. You had no right to do that. It's my business and my decision."

"Babe, no one said it wasn't your business. As for it being your decision, it would be, in most instances, but I knew you'd say no. You'd say it was too expensive. It's not optional, Cady. You need to be safe there."

"When will you get it through your head that I needed to determine whether I could swing it? And if I could, I still had to ask my landlord if he was okay with it." I wiggled so I was sitting sideways. It allowed me to see his face as we argued. I fought to ignore the erection that was growing under my ass.

"If your landlord said no, I'd handle him. As for the cost, I can afford it. When I become your silent partner, these would be things I'd do anyway."

"You aren't becoming my partner."

"Why the hell not?"

"Because!" I shouted.

"Because why?"

"Forget it. You can't understand, Hoss."

"I warned you," he uttered. Then, I was flipped and rolled so I was positioned face down across his lap. Before I could move, a hand came down hard on my bare ass. I cried out in shock and pain.

"Stop!"

He didn't listen. Instead, he spanked me three

more times. "That's one for each time you called me Hoss. Are you ready to behave and talk to me like an adult, or do I continue?" he asked.

Tears pricked my eyes. I fought to contain them. I refused to cry in front of him. The churning in my stomach increased, and I knew I was about to vomit.

"Let me up," I mumbled.

"Not until you agree to talk."

"No," I mumbled. Another smack landed on my stinging ass cheeks.

"Kiwi," I sobbed.

He instantly eased his hold on me. "Babe, I didn't think—" I rolled off his lap, stumbled to my feet, and then ran for the bathroom. I barely made it to the toilet before I was throwing up. As I heaved, I whimpered.

Hands pulled back my hair and held it out of my way. After bringing up what little was in my stomach and bile, I dry heaved a couple of times before I weakly hung over the toilet bowl. Hoss flushed it after moving my head to the side.

"Here, let's rinse your mouth," he said softly. He stood up and went to the sink. I stayed where I was. He was back in no time with a glass of water. When I took a drink, I found it had mouthwash in it. I eagerly swished and spit several times until the nasty taste was gone. He took the glass away.

"Do you think you're done?" he asked.

"I think so."

He slowly lifted me and then carried me to the bed. This time, he put me on the mattress. I curled up on my side. I felt the bed dip, and then he was behind me, spooning me. His hand came up to push my hair away from my face.

"I'm sorry, baby. I didn't mean to hurt you. And I sure as hell didn't mean to make you sick. I had no idea spanking you would do that. Say you forgive me." I heard the worry and pain in his voice. He truly thought my vomiting was his fault. There was no way I'd let him believe that, no matter how mad at him I was.

"You didn't make me sick. I just need to sleep. Go. We'll talk later about this."

"Cady, I'm not leaving you here alone, especially when you're mad at me and sick. We'll talk about what upset you later, but for now, I'm taking care of you. Do you know what caused you to throw up? Was it something you ate? Or are you coming down with the stomach flu?"

"If I'm coming down with the flu, you should leave so you don't get it."

"Not happening. Is that what it is?"

I sighed. "No, it's not that or something I ate. I'm having a migraine. When they get bad, I throw up. I'll take some of my medicine and go to sleep. It'll be fine by morning. There's no need for you to stay and watch me sleep."

He cuddled me closer. I admit, it felt good to be held. His lips landed on my temple, and he kissed me. "Tiny, I don't want to be away from you, period, let alone when you're not feeling well. If all you do is sleep, then so be it. I'll be here to keep an eye on you. What if you get worse and need medical attention?"

"If that happens, then I'll call an ambulance."

"Is that what you did in the past? Did none of your boyfriends bother to take care of you?"

"Magnus, I can't talk to you right now about this. I need to take my medicine," I let him hear the pleading in my voice. I didn't want to end up throwing up again.

"I'm sorry, you're right. Tell me where it is, and I'll get it for you."

"It's the only prescription bottle in the medicine cabinet in the bathroom."

He eased off the bed. I hated to lose his warmth. However, he was back in no time with a pill and a glass of water. I hurried to swallow it. Sitting up made my head hurt worse. He put the glass on my nightstand when I was done.

"Anything else you need?"

"If you'll make sure the blinds are fully closed on the window, that'll be good. Light makes it worse."

He did it while I lay down again. I heard him making rustling noises, and then he was back in bed. When he drew me to him, I gasped. His hot, naked skin was against mine. I tried to roll over, but he held me in place.

"Shh, go to sleep. Relax. I've got you." He kissed me before snuggling me to him.

I let his warmth and the comfort he was giving me lull me to sleep. I was out in no time.

☙ ☙ ☙

When I woke up, I knew hours had passed. The room was pitch dark, and there was no sunlight peeking out along the edge of my window blind. I was alone in the bed. I guess he must've left after all. Disappointment filled me, but I shook it off. It wasn't like I was used to a man helping me anyway, other than Carver.

I got up and went to the bathroom. I used the toilet, splashed cool water on my face, and brushed my teeth. Before I went out to the kitchen, I threw on

HOSS'S LIMITS

a nightgown. Opening my bedroom door, I saw light coming from the living room. I guess he left a lamp on for me. As I entered it, I was shocked to find Hoss sitting on the couch. He had the television on mute with the closed captions on.

He came up off the couch and hurried over when he saw me. I was slightly disappointed to see he was wearing his suit pants, although his naked chest wasn't anything to sneeze at. His arms came around me as he brought me close.

"Cady, you should've called out. I would've gotten you whatever you needed. How're you feeling?"

"I didn't know you were still here. And I feel better. The medicine worked."

"Where else would I be? I told you I won't leave you alone. Do you think you're up for some food?"

"It's not worth the hassle. I'll eat in the morning. Besides, everything in the fridge is old or expired."

"It's no hassle. You're hungry, so you eat. Sit and rest. I'll warm you up some dinner." He guided me to the couch and lowered me to it.

"Where did you get dinner?"

"I made it. I figured you'd be hungry once this passed, and I didn't want you to worry about fixing food. I came out here after you fell asleep so I wouldn't disturb you. I found the ingredients and threw together a casserole. I hope you like chicken, rice, and broccoli casserole. It's nothing fancy, but I think it's filling. Since you had all those ingredients and the others, I assumed you liked them."

He was taking out a large casserole dish and scooping food onto two plates as he talked. I was stunned. No guy had ever cooked for me and they sure

263

didn't wait on me. They expected me to do it for them. When I didn't answer, he stopped.

"Babe, do you want something else?"

"No, no, that's great. I was just shocked, that's all."

"Shocked at what?" He went back to preparing it.

"Well, that you stayed and then cooked. I've never had anyone do that. Now, you're waiting on me."

As the microwave heated the food, he leaned back against the counter with his arms crossed. He was scowling. "Do you mean to say no one has ever cared for you? I know Tajah has to have done it."

"Oh, yeah, she has. I meant a man."

"Not even Carver?"

"Carver has, but in a different way. I meant any other man. I don't know how to react."

"Fucking useless bastards," he muttered. The microwave beeped, which had him turning back to it. A minute later, while his food heated up, I was presented with a plate, fork, napkin, and a drink. He put it on the table in front of my couch. "Anything else you need?"

"No, this is perfect. Thank you."

"Go ahead and eat. Don't wait for me," he said.

"I'd like to wait."

It wasn't long before he joined me. I took my first bite. I moaned. It was delicious. "If you cook like this on top of everything else, tell me why you haven't been snapped up long ago?"

"Basically, because I hadn't found the woman right for me. Sure, there's been women who wanted me for my wealth, sex, and the kink, but they didn't want all of me."

"I wasn't referring to your money or possessions. I meant you're caring nature. I hope you don't think I'm with you due to your money. I'm not."

"You've made that very clear. In fact, it seems to be a sore point with you. One I'd like to understand. I get the feeling there's a story there. Just like there's a story behind why you're a brat."

I kept eating. He didn't push me to answer. When I was done, I put my plate down. I swung my legs up on the couch so I could face him. I knew what I was about to say wouldn't be easy for me. I hoped I'd be able to make him understand why I didn't want him paying for things like the alarm system.

"It is a sore point, as you call it. My reasons for being a brat are tied to it, now that I think about it. You know Carver is my brother, and he's my only sibling. Neither one of us had what you'd call a loving, happy childhood. In our house, there was constant yelling, anger, and accusations between our parents. And those spilled over onto us. We tried to stay under the radar, and when things got bad, we tried to stay out of the way, but it didn't usually help."

I paused to swallow. Recalling it made a knot develop in my throat. He inched closer and took my hand. "Go on. Tell me. You'll feel better once you do. And after you tell me your story, I'll tell you mine. More about why I'm a handler."

"Our parents never acted as if they liked each other, let alone loved one another. I found out as I got older that they married because Mom got pregnant with Carver. Why they had me, I don't know. Maybe another accident? Anyway, they'd fight all the time. Dad was never faithful to her, and she'd scream at him about it. He'd verbally attack her and say the only reason she got pregnant was to trap him because of his money."

Hoss groaned hearing this. I kept going. Now that I started, I couldn't stop. "Dad came from a well-off family and worked in his family's business. We had a lovely house, cars, you name it. I would've given it all up to have loving parents and peace. They would fight and throw things. Carver and I early on tried to get them to stop, but we'd then be in the line of fire. As we got older, the accusations about ruining their lives and only wanting his money were thrown at us."

"I was lucky that I befriended Tajah. She knew what my home life was like, and I spent as much time as possible at her house. Tamara was who I consider my real mom. She's the total opposite of mine. Tajah's dad was great, too. Carver would hang out at some of his friends' houses to get away. We hated it when we had to be home. It was demanded when Dad and Mom wanted to trot us out to pretend we were the happy, perfect family. See, they didn't want Dad's family to know it wasn't. They were very hardcore family-oriented and believed that once you married, you didn't get a divorce. Dad emphatically believed if they did divorce, he'd lose his inheritance and job. So instead, they lived in misery and made us miserable with them."

"When you say they took it out on you guys, was it only verbally, or did they hit you?" he asked.

"There were slaps, and sometimes we'd be locked in our rooms. It could've been worse. They could've neglected our needs, beat us, or worse, sexually assaulted us. But it still hurts, and I guess I developed my brattiness as a way to cope and get a rise out of them. When I turned eighteen, I moved out. Dad threatened to cut me off if I didn't go to college and get a degree he approved of. He thought being a vet was stupid. We'd never been allowed to have pets. He didn't like animals. Fortunately, I had a small inheritance from an aunt who died. I used it to pay for the bulk of my education, and I worked to earn the rest. I had to work in order to have a place to live. Carver had an inheritance from the same aunt and used it to pay for college and law school. I was so jealous that he got out five years ahead of me."

"Why didn't he take you with him?"

"He couldn't. He tried, but our parents wouldn't allow it. He offered to stay, but I told him no. I escaped most of the time to Tajah's, so it wasn't too terrible. By then, I knew how to handle it."

"And that's why you are so adamant about not allowing me to pay for anything."

"It is. I can make it on my own. I don't need to be bolstered or to take your money. It's not why I'm with you. I don't want you or anyone else ever to think I am."

He reached over and gently pulled me to him. He arranged me on his lap so we were staring into each other's eyes. "Cady, I'm happy you shared this with me. It helps me to understand you. But I want you to know that I have never and will never think you're with me due to what I can give you monetarily. I know you're not. As for others thinking that, if they do, then they don't know us and aren't our friends, so who gives a fuck what they think? As long as our friends and we know the truth, they can go to hell. Now, let me tell you about me and what drives me."

"Okay. please."

"I grew up with overall loving parents and a younger brother, Maxwell. He's two years younger than me. We weren't rich, but we were comfortable. Our parents didn't fight like yours or take out their anger on us. I had a pretty happy childhood until I was fifteen. That's when we discovered Max was getting high. He was smoking weed with his friends. Mom and Dad tried to say it was a phase and he'd get over it. Dad admitted he'd smoked some in his youth, and he turned out fine.

"I wasn't convinced because the crowd Max was hanging with was into a lot more than just weed, and he was a follower. He'd do whatever he thought would get them to like him. I tried to tell our folks that, but they waved it off. As the years passed, he got worse and into harder and harder drugs. I continued to argue with our parents. I wanted them to put him in rehab. They denied it was serious enough to warrant that. This was despite the fact he was now stealing from them to feed his habit.

"I guess for me, I went to the opposite end of the brat spectrum because I wanted responsibility and control and, in a way, the attention. They were always making over Max and claiming that he was misunderstood and it was hard for him to make friends because of x, y, and z. They made every excuse they could for him. I was more extroverted and independent. They enabled him by denying his problem and letting him steal from them. It got worse, and they began to give him their money, and there was no limit to what they'd do. It cost them their savings, most of their possessions, and their home years later. As for Max, he'd get upset when they didn't have the money and tell them if they loved him, they'd help more."

"Are they still doing it?" I asked.

"No, they died when I was twenty-five. There was a car accident. I helped them as much as I could but never by giving them money because I knew they'd hand it over to him. I went to college early and graduated at twenty. I started my business in my bedroom, and as soon as I could, I moved out. When they died, there was nothing to leave Max. He was on his own."

"Do you have contact with him?"

"Only when he comes around looking for a handout. I don't know why he does it. I never give him anything. I've offered to pay for his rehab numerous times, which he refuses. He says he doesn't have a problem. He tries to guilt me by saying family takes care of family. I anticipate every year, I'll get the call telling me he finally overdosed. So you see, my family shaped me. Despite not helping Max, I need to help those I consider family and love. When I offered to pay for the alarm system and other upgrades, it was due to my need to make you safe, Cady. I don't know what the hell I'd do if you were hurt or killed."

"This thing between us is moving fast. Your offer is wonderful, but I can't pay it back, or not anytime soon."

"It's fast in some people's books, but not mine. I don't expect repayment. I know I'm risking it all telling you this, but the truth is, I'm falling in love with you. If I weren't, we wouldn't have talked about a future and marriage. I'm in it for the long haul. With time, I pray you'll love me, too."

His declaration stole my breath and made my heart pound. I should tell him he was crazy, but if I did, then I'd have to admit I was as well. Taking a deep breath, I confessed. "Magnus, if I weren't feeling the same thing for you, then we wouldn't have talked about those things, nor would I have signed the contract with you. All I ask is that you be patient with me, and I'll do the same with you. Alright?"

He grinned, and then I was kissed as if his life depended on it. I gave myself up to it. We'd figure this out.

Hoss: Chapter 16

It had been over three weeks since Cady and I had our heart-to-heart about our childhoods and how they shaped us and our needs. After that night, I was able to talk her into allowing Iker to install the upgraded alarm system and cameras. She refused the steel doors or security shutters or bars. She and I both spoke to her landlord to get his permission. His only concern was what it would cost him. When he discovered nothing, he was fine with it. The slimy bastard made me want to punch him, but I calmed myself by telling myself she wouldn't be there long.

I was in the process of finding her a new location. Once I found it, I'd approach her about moving her clinic. I knew to let her settle on the upgrades first. The way I got her to agree was to say she could pay me back. I didn't want to, but I'd battle her later about the money. I would get her to the point where she'd accept things from me without feeling guilty or the need to repay me.

There had been no more attempts to break into the clinic. It might have been due to the new system, or maybe the men had given up. I'd heard other veterinarian clinics had been broken into around town, and their medications were stolen. It had to be the same guys. And her apartment hadn't had any more unwanted visits from Flint. It might have been due to the fact that she was rarely there, or when she was, I stayed with her. Regardless, it made me happy.

Iker's guys who watched over her when I wasn't around hadn't seen him. We assumed he either left town or was lying low. I wasn't ready to say he was gone for good, so I kept the guards watching her, not that she knew. I was biding my time. I'd eventually catch up to him, as well as her other exes who'd dared to be abusive to her. Tajah had provided the names to Mikhail, and he shared them with me. Outlaw was in the middle of stuff with his club and others, but he promised he'd find them. I told him there was no rush.

Besides Flint and her exes, everything else between Cady and me was going great. We were learning more about each other every day. She was relaxing, and I was able to integrate her more into my home and life and vice versa. I was eager to have her move in with me. I was waiting for the right time to ask her.

Tonight, we were taking a huge step for us. She'd come to me and asked if I would be willing to take her to Lustz. I told her, of course. That's when she added that she wanted us to go as a couple and observe and, if the mood struck, to play. She wasn't sure if she'd be able to do it in front of others or if we'd have to go into a private room, but she wanted to give it a try. Suffice it to say, I was all for it and assured her we'd only do what she was comfortable with. If we got there and she decided she only wanted to observe, we'd do that and then leave.

She did have one ask. She didn't want Tajah, Carver, or Mikhail there for the first time because she thought it might inhibit her. She and Carver had barely begun to speak again since the Halloween incident a month ago. She didn't want to rock the boat. I took on the task of asking him which night he wasn't planning to be there, and when he asked why, I told him. I saw he still wasn't thrilled with the idea. I laid it out for him.

"*Carver, I know you don't want Cady to be hurt. You think by going to Lustz, she's getting into something she shouldn't, but I can promise you she's not. I won't let it happen.*"

"*And what if her being with you is what hurts her? I love my sister, but there are things you don't know about her. And picking guys isn't her thing. She's left hurt every time.*"

"*I know about those guys and what they did to her more than you do. And I know about your parents and how you grew up. Cady's brat side is a direct result of that. I know how to give her what she needs, and I plan to give her everything she wants and needs. I'm not using her for a bit and then dumping her for another.*"

He appeared surprised I knew so much. "You can't know that you won't, good intentions or not."

"*I do because she's agreed not only to be my brat but mine. She's my girlfriend, and one day, she'll be my wife. You can either accept it or not.*"

My declaration further stunned him. He'd agreed in the end to wait and see. I left it at that after getting from him the nights he wouldn't be there. It wasn't hard. He didn't want to see her at play, he said. I suspected it was for way more than that reason.

Cady talked it over with Tajah and got her to agree that she and Mikhail would stay in their apartment tonight. Tajah was excited for her to give the club a try. I knew she and Mikhail were all for our relationship, so there were no issues with them. I asked Cady if Reuben would bother her. She said no.

She had a short day at the clinic, so we were able to leave work early. She was nervous, and I wanted to get her to relax, so I surprised her at the house. I'd arranged for two masseuses to come there to give us a couple's massage. I enjoyed a good massage and discovered she'd never had one. She was a little apprehensive, but with us both being together, she soon relaxed. When it was over and they left, she told me she had really enjoyed it.

Afterward, we had an early dinner, and then I left her to get ready. She'd asked the other day what she should wear. I told her whatever she felt most comfortable in. While I loved the catsuit she wore at Halloween, there was no need to wear it or anything extremely sexy or revealing unless she wanted to. I had no idea what she finally settled on. I knew she talked to Tajah about it.

It didn't take me long to get ready. When I was, I went to my office and called Mikhail. He answered quickly. "Are you on your way?" he asked.

"Not yet. Cady is still getting ready. Is everything set?"

"It is. All you have to do is signal Reuben or one of the Lustz Disciples if you have a problem. The room is reserved and ready for you. They've been briefed. Do you think she'll play, and if so, out in front of people?"

"I don't know, but either way, I'll be happy. I don't need to be seen to enjoy it. And I don't know if I'll be able to handle others seeing her. It was never an issue in the past, but my partners weren't Cady. I didn't want them to be mine forever, nor was I in love with them."

"Ohh, so you're tossing the L-word around already. That's serious. Have you told her? What does she say?"

"Aren't you nosy?" I teased.

"Hell yeah, I am. You're one of my closest friends, and she's my woman's best friend. Of course, I need to know."

I chuckled. "Fine, then to answer you, yes, she knows and feels the same way about me. We haven't outright said I love you yet, but we've admitted we're falling in love. Otherwise, I wouldn't want to move her into the house or look for a ring."

"Christ, you are a goner. I can't tell you how happy that makes me, Hoss. You deserve it. If you hurry the hell up and ask her, assuming she says yes, we can have a double wedding."

"No way. I can only imagine what would happen if we let those two plan a wedding."

"Hey, it's mainly Tamara doing it, and you know she'll want in on yours, so why not do it together? Just think about it, and after you ask her, we'll talk it over with the women."

It wasn't a bad idea. I wouldn't actually care. What mattered was if Cady wanted us to have ours separate. "We'll see. Now, if you've got it all ready, I'll talk to you later. Thanks, Mikhail."

"Any time. Have fun."

"Thanks, we will. Night."

I hung up. Since the office door was closed, I opened up my computer search and went surfing for more rings. I'd been looking at different ones for a week. I didn't know what I was looking for other than I'd know it when I saw it. There were a few that caught my eye, but they didn't scream Cady to me, so they were on a reserve list. It was a good half hour before I was interrupted by her knocking on the door. I logged off and then got up to answer it.

Opening it, I saw her standing there. She was dressed in heels and had a long coat belted around her waist. I wasn't able to see what she had on underneath other than to know her legs were bare. Her hair was twisted up on her head in a sophisticated knot. Wisps of hair were loose at her ears. She'd put on makeup and wore glittering hoop earrings.

She gave me a hesitant smile. "Are you ready?"

"I am. You look beautiful, Tiny. Do I get to see your outfit before we go?" I took her arm and secured it over my arm as I walked toward the garage. I was taking the Veyron tonight.

"No, it's a surprise. You look very handsome and edible, Magnus."

"Babe, thank you, but don't talk about eating me, or we won't leave the house," I warned her. She giggled.

I got her situated in the car, and then we were off. As we drove, she sat back, and we chatted about random things. Out of nowhere, she touched the tiger-eye beaded bracelet I had on my wrist. "I've been meaning to ask you if this has significance or if you just like it?"

"I do like it, but there is more to it than liking it. Tiger-eye is thought to bring clarity and help you see people's true colors. It signifies stability, protection, and empowerment. I don't know if it truly does those things, but it never hurts. I believe I'm a good judge of character, and I've worn this for a long time, so who knows?"

"Either way, it's lovely. I've been admiring it."

"Then we'll have to find you one, but it'll be one much more delicate and prettier than mine."

"You don't need to do that," she protested.

I gave her a speaking look. She subsided. "I know I don't have to. I want to. We're almost there. We'll park in the private garage and then take the elevator up. I thought we'd start on the first floor, have a drink, and then when you're ready, we'll go to the second. I spoke to Mikhail, and he said they're in for the evening."

"Good. That sounds like a plan. I wish I didn't need them and Carver not to be there, but I think I'll feel more at ease if they're not. If this becomes something I want to repeat, I won't expect them to stay away."

"Babe, if you do, then you do. They'll understand. It's not as if we're going to the club to play every night. I love my private time with you at home too much to do that. Besides, we have so many places yet to explore and have fun at the house." I winked at her, causing her to laugh. Lacking places to have sex wasn't in short supply in that house, and we hadn't even tried the grounds. It was wintertime, and that would have to wait until warm weather.

In no time, we were pulling into Lustz's parking lot. It was pretty full despite it being a Wednesday night. I rode to the private garage and found a spot. As we rode the elevator up, I could feel the tension growing in her. I broke it the only way I knew how. I tugged her against me, and then I claimed her mouth. I put all the passion and love I felt for her into it. I didn't let go until the elevator beeped to remind us to either get out or push the button. I escorted her out onto the first floor.

People were talking, laughing, having drinks, and dancing. There was noise all around us. I took us straight to the bar to get a drink. Jack was the bartender. He came to us right away.

"Hey, Hoss, it's been a while since you've been here other than to work. I see you've brought company. Hello, I'm Jack. What can I get you, pretty lady?" he asked with a smile. I knew he didn't mean anything by it. He had a natural flirty nature, and it came out with the ladies. It earned him the bigger tips, too. However, I wanted it to be known far and wide that Cady was more than a date or a play partner.

"Jack, this is Cady. She's my girlfriend and Tajah's best friend. Cady, what would you like to drink? They have just about anything."

"Shit, I had no idea you were dating someone. Or that she was Tajah's friend. It's doubly nice to meet you, Cady. If you like, I have a few suggestions?"

I listened to her answer, and he made his recommendation, which she took. I told him I'd have the same. As we waited for our drinks, we scanned the floor. Down here, no overt sexual acts were happening. You might catch people kissing and doing light petting, but that was it. If you wanted to do more, you went to the second floor.

Taking our drinks when he returned, I escorted her to where she could check her coat. When she removed it, I had to hold in my moan. She was wearing a form-fitting black dress. It had a square neckline that showed off the outline of her generous tits and gave a hint of her cleavage. The flowy long sleeves were made of see-through gauzy material and gathered at her wrists. It clung to her more bountiful curves and ended in the middle of her thighs. Her skin gleamed in the lights.

I leaned down and whispered. "Jesus Christ, do you want to give every guy in here a heart attack? That dress is fucking unbelievable on you, Tiny. Stick close so someone won't whisk you away."

She smiled. "I'm happy you like it, but I think I'll be fine.

"I more than like it. I love it. And you won't be fine. I'll have to use all my self-restraint not to strip that off you in the next five seconds. Christ," I muttered. She threw back her head and laughed.

From there, we slowly made a circuit of the floor as we drank our drinks. There were numerous people who recognized me. Most called out greetings. A few stopped me to talk. I made sure to introduce Cady every time as my girlfriend. One reason was that I was proud that she was mine and that I wanted them to know. The other was to prevent those who wanted to play from asking. Even though I wore a bracelet with a red-and-black striped bead on my right wrist now, which meant I was in a committed monogamous relationship, there were those who would try. Cady wore an identical one.

I noted some were more surprised than others. Some I knew were just adept at hiding it. In all my years working and coming here, I'd never brought a date or had a girlfriend. As expected, Cady got more than a few interested looks. When I saw them, I gave them a warning look. They heeded me. And it wasn't just men who gave them to her.

We spent about half an hour on the first floor before she told me she was ready to move upstairs. I didn't delay. When we got up there, it was to see it was less crowded than downstairs, but not a lot. The noise was much less. We didn't have the music to contend with, or at least not as loud. Taking our time, I led her from stage to stage. There were different scenes going

on at each one. There were those who were in some of
the themed rooms who had their windows open to be
observed. She showed interest in several. I found myself
turned on, but it wasn't due to the people performing
or having sex. It was by watching Cady. I knew from
the way she was breathing and her flushed face she
was turned on by what she was seeing. I filed that
information away for future reference.

Wouldn't you know it? We were in luck. We found
Sam and Justine doing a scene on one of the stages
like last time. Cady came to a halt. I stood behind
her and wrapped her in my arms. As we watched, my
woman began to squirm in my arms. Her breathing was
more labored, and I even noted her shudder when Sam
spanked Justine with a leather paddle for mouthing
off. I had only ever used my hand on her so far, but I
wondered if she'd enjoy the leather.

Those around us were into the scene or their own
thing. We watched them for a good fifteen minutes
before I decided to take a chance. I lowered my mouth
and kissed Cady's neck, then licked up to her ear. She
trembled and moaned.

"Look how well she takes his taming. I bet she's
wet, but I know you're even wetter, aren't you, Cady
Cat? Are your nipples hard and your pussy soaked,
imagining that's us up there? That all these people are
watching me discipline you. Only if it were us, you
wouldn't be in your underwear and bra. I'd have you
naked, and everyone would see how soaked you get. If
you were a good brat, I'd eat your pussy and let you
come all over my face."

I ground my erection into her back as I tweaked
her nipple through her dress. She trembled harder and

whimpered as she pressed herself back against me.

"That's it. Yeah, my baby is excited. Let me see if your honey is running down your thighs yet," I growled as I slipped my other hand down between her legs and then slid up under her dress. Her head fell back to rest on my chest, and her eyes were closed. She was panting. I knew that look.

"Almost. But God, I can feel the heat coming off your sweet cunt. I don't know how long I can stay in control, Tiny. I want to eat your pussy then fuck you until you scream. My cock is aching to be inside your tight snatch. To have you strangling it and pulling the cum out of me." I wasn't lying. My cock was throbbing, and precum was oozing from my slit. I pressed into her harder and circled my hips. We both groaned.

"Cady, I need to feel your tits. Can I lower the top of your dress?" I asked somewhat desperately.

Her eyes opened, and she hesitated. I was about to suggest we go to the private room I had reserved for us, but she shocked me when she said, "Yes, do it."

I brought the hand I had under her dress up to join the other, and then I slowly lowered the top of her dress. She pushed my hands away, and then, with a flick of her fingers, her bra opened. It was a front-closure one. Her tits spilled out. I caught them in my eager hands, and I got to work. I kneaded them and then tweaked her taut nipples over and over, causing her to moan and wiggle.

I noted that we were drawing attention. More and more eyes were watching us. I didn't call her attention to it because I didn't want to make her uncomfortable. Desire was on our audience's faces as they watched me pleasure her in the simplest way. If this were all she allowed, it would be enough. I was kissing her neck and sucking lightly on her skin. That lasted a minute or two before she stiffened, cried out faintly, then shook. She was having an orgasm from just me playing with her double-D tits. As she came, I knew I wouldn't be able to take any more. I was about to lower my zipper, hike her skirt up, and take her right here. We had to get to our room.

There were murmurs of approval from those near us. As she surfaced from her orgasm, she became aware of them. Before she could get upset or self-conscious, I turned her to face me. "Let's go. I have a room reserved just for us. I need you, Cady. I've got to be inside you before I die." I confessed.

She squeezed my cock, making me groan. "Then what are you waiting for, Magnus? Show me to our room and take me."

Letting out a loud growl, I gathered her close and began to wind our way through the people to our room. When we arrived, I whisked her inside, then slammed and locked the door. This one was themed with everything a brat tamer or handler would need to work with his or her brat. I wanted to try many of them with her, but not this first time. That would have to wait until I took the edge off.

I wore a white-linen button shirt paired with jeans. As soon as we were locked inside, I began to unbutton my shirt. She was watching me with desire and licking her lips. I wanted that mouth around my cock, but I wasn't sure I could hold back my load if I let her do it.

"Strip," I demanded.

"And what if I don't want to?" she taunted.

"You'd better, or I'll tan that ass until you can't sit, and then I'll strip you myself and fuck you until your right there, then I'll stop. When I finally blow, it'll be in my hand rather than inside of you."

I'd discovered she hated the thought of me not coming inside of her or on her. She gave me a frustrated look, but she began to remove her dress. While she did, I hurried to get naked. Once we both were, I stalked to her. She backed up to the bed that was in the center of the room. She turned and crawled onto it, then lay on her back, spreading her legs before cupping her tits and squeezing them. I was gripping the base of my cock to stop from coming at the sight.

"Hurry, Magnus, I need you, Give me that massive cock. Fuck me until I scream."

I was more than willing to oblige. I joined her on the bed. I hooked her legs over my forearms and pushed them toward her chest. Her pink lips spread, letting me see how wet and swollen she was. She grabbed the back of her thighs and held her legs up. I teased up and down her drenched slit, coating the head of my cock in her cum. She moaned and wiggled as she tried to impale herself on me.

"What's wrong? Are you needy, brat? You want your man's cock taming you and pounding that pussy?"

"Yes, God, yes, fuck me. Please," she whimpered.

"Since you asked so nicely, here it comes." I notched it at her hole, then slowly pressed inward. I refused to slam into her like a beast. She was too small, and I was too big for that. She whimpered and bucked, driving me deeper. When she took all she could, I took a couple of deep breaths and then pulled back to slide back into her. As I picked up speed with my strokes, she began chanting my name. She was scalding hot and so damn wet.

Suddenly, she said, "Stop."

I did. Had I hurt her? "Baby, did I hurt you?"

"No, I want something before we go further."

"Anything." I hoped I could give it to her before I lost all control.

"Open the screen, so if anyone wants to see us, they can."

I blinked, thinking I'd heard wrong. "Cady, did you say you want the screen open?" She nodded. "Are you sure? There's no need to do it for my sake. I'm more than fine with it being us in private."

"I know, but out there, when you had your hand under my dress and then on my naked tits, I liked it, And finding people watching us was a turn-on. I want to see if I like more."

I was still hesitant for her sake. "If you're sure, I'll do it, but we'll keep the remote here on the bed. If you want to close it at any time, we will. I don't want you to do this unless you're sure you want to."

"I'm sure I want to try."

I was able to reach the remote on the table next to the bed without pulling out. Giving her one more chance to say no, I hit it. The screen slowly began to rise. Wanting to distract her, I lowered my head and took her mouth. Our tongues twined together as we kissed each other hungrily. By the time we broke apart, the screen was open. She went to turn her head, but I held her in place.

"Don't. You watch me."

Slowly, I began thrusting again. As the desire ramped up, she started to whimper and beg. It was fucking exhilarating. I plucked her nipples, bit her skin, and teased her clit. I kept mixing it up and stimulating her in more than one place. She detonated about five minutes into it. As she clenched around my cock, I had to hold back. To buy time, I pulled out and flipped her onto her knees. She rose and presented her ass to me. A quick glance to the right showed me we had an audience. As I thrust back inside, I brought her attention to it.

"Look at all them watching us, Cady. Those men out there wish they were me. That it was their cocks buried in your snug cunt. That your honey was running down their cocks and soaking their balls like you're doing mine. Jesus, you just got wetter. You like that, don't you? The thought of them watching you and wanting you. Well, they can, but know they'll never have you. You're mine. I'm the only man who'll ever have his cock inside of you ever again." I stroked faster. My balls were gathering close. I knew I was nearing the end.

She panted loudly. "And those women are out there wishing that big monster of yours was in their pussies, but it's mine. If you dare to give it to someone else, I'll cut it off and then kill the bitch. You're mine, Magnus. Mine. Now, fuck me like you mean it and fill me up. Show them how hot we are together."

I grunted, then let loose as much as I dared. She kept thrusting back to meet my strokes. As my balls tightened, I pinched her clit, causing her to tip over the edge with me. As I hollered her name and she shouted mine, and our cum mingled, I hit the button to lower the blind. It was enough for one night. As soon as we rested, it would be more lovemaking, and I didn't want an audience.

"How was it?" I asked her as she slumped to the mattress a minute or two later.

"It was incredible, but then it always is with you."

"You're right. We are incredible together, and there's no one I want more than you, Cady Cat."

"Me either, Magnus."

Cady: Chapter 17

I couldn't believe what I'd done tonight. To have sex where others could see us was a new experience. When Magnus first began to touch me out on the floor, I'd been nervous and almost told him not to do it, but I was so needy from watching the various scenes, especially the one between Sam and Justine, that I pushed it away and let him. The fact he made me orgasm just by playing with my breasts surprised me and only pushed my desire higher. When he said we should go to a private room, I was all for it. I was desperate to have him inside of me.

As I undressed in the room, I saw the toys. Many of them intrigued me, and I wanted to know what it would be like to play with them. Those thoughts made me burn hotter. Hoss's dirty talk when we were in the moment made my pulse race. I loved hearing him say those things about me and knowing that I affected him so much.

The relief I felt when he sank into me was unbelievable. I wanted, no, I needed him to take me like a madman. It wasn't until he got started that I realized I wanted those people out there to be able to see us. To see the passion and even love between us. They needed to see that he was mine, I was his, and how much we loved each other. There was no denying I was in love with Hoss. That's when I did the deed and asked for the screen to be lowered. I saw his concern, but I was dying to try. I'd never know if I could do it or would like it unless I tried.

His distraction as it lowered was the right move, and I was too into what he was making me feel to care who was watching us. After having an orgasm that made me weak and almost pass out, I couldn't care less who had witnessed the scene. All I cared about was Hoss.

After he raised the screen, I was treated to the softer, caring side of him. He went into aftercare mode, as he called it. I was reaping the benefits of it right now, but I wanted him to feel cared for, too.

We were in the attached bathroom, which had every convenience. He ran a tub of hot water filled with aromatic bath salts, knowing I liked to soak in a tub rather than take a shower. Before it got too full, I turned off the water. He gave me a puzzled look.

"Is something wrong, babe?"

"No, but that's enough water for two. We don't want to flood the bathroom. Come soak with me, Magnus." I held out my hand.

He took it and brought me close. "Anything for you, Cady. Here, let me help you in first."

He held my hand to keep me from falling until I was safely seated, and then he got in behind me. His legs had to remain bent, even in this sizable tub, due to his height. It was snug, but I didn't mind.

"They need to make their tubs bigger for guys like you. This one isn't bad, but you have to keep your legs up," I complained as I rubbed my hands up and down his sparsely hair-covered legs.

"They'd have to get them custom-made. That's

what I did for the ones in the house."

"I figured as much. God, this heat feels good," I groaned.

"Are you sore? Did I get too carried away?"

I heard the concern in his voice. "Magnus, no, you didn't get too rough. You're a big guy, and it does burn when you stretch me. I might get a tiny bit sore, but it's nothing to worry about. I don't want you to change how you have sex with me. I'll let you know if it's too much. Stop worrying."

"I don't ever want it to become too painful. If it does, you have to tell me. And I don't have sex with you. I make love with you. No matter how wild and dirty we get, it's done with love, Cady."

I twisted so I was able to see his face. He had such a serious expression. I smiled at him as I tried to wipe away his frown with my fingers. "Magnus, listen to me. I know you do it with love. It's what makes it so special. I hope you can tell that I do the same. I adore us wild, but I love it equally as much slow and easy."

"Thank you, baby," he said before he kissed me. That kiss began to reawaken my desire. I found with him that I didn't stay sated for long. I'd never craved a man like I did him. He slowly drew away. I chased his mouth, but he chuckled.

"Let me wash you, then maybe I'll give you more," he taunted.

I admit. I whined a little, but he refused to give in. I had to relax and let him touch my entire body. He did it in a way guaranteed to light the fire inside me again. By the time he was done, I was close to attacking him. I decided to let my brat out. I pretended to yawn.

"That was nice," I said in a bored tone.

"Oh, really."

"Sure. You're excused. I think I'll soak alone and then take a nap. I feel bored," I added, making sure my disinterested tone was more evident. I knew this would trigger his handler side to come out.

"Are you sure you're up to what you're cruising for, Cady Cat?"

"If I thought you could bring it, I might be scared, but I'm not." I taunted.

"Keep it up and see what happens, brat."

"I'm weary of this."

I barely got that out before he was standing. I admit I was distracted by the water running off his dark skin. I wanted to lick him all over. His cock was hardening. I reached out to stroke it, but my hand was pushed away. He shook his head.

"Good girls get this, not brats."

"Maybe if you gave me that, I'd be a good girl."

"That's not the way it works. First, you be good, and then you get a treat. Wouldn't you like to have this cock in your mouth so you can suck it like a lollipop? You love giving me head. And you love it even more when I shoot my load down your throat. Do you want that?"

I fought to say no, but I couldn't. The thought of him in my mouth had it watering. I nodded.

"No, I need you to say it. Say you want it."

Begrudgingly, I said, "I want your cock."

"Where?"

I made a frustrated sound, which made him smirk. Bastard, he knew I was edging toward mindless lust. I remained mute. He shrugged and went to step out of the tub. I caught his leg.

"I want your cock in my mouth. I want you to fuck my face with it."

He let out a low growl, and then his hand was buried in my hair, bringing me face-to-face with his now fully erect cock. "Hold it."

I gripped the base and fondled his balls.

"Open and lick it once, then stop," he ordered.

He knew how hard it would be for me to get a taste of the precum already oozing from his slit and then stop. He was diabolical, but I still did it. I moaned as his flavor burst on my tongue. I craved his cum. Most women hated the taste, but I loved his. There was a slightly fruity flavor to it. It was probably due to all the fruit he ate. The man had it more than once a day.

I sat there impatient, waiting for him to let me do it again. As time stretched out, I thought, fuck it, and I did it again. I was yanked off him by my hair. It stung a bit, but it wasn't terrible. Even like this, he was careful.

"I didn't say you could have another taste. You need to learn to listen. For that, no more." He let go of my hair and, this time, got out of the tub before I could stop him. A sense of panic erupted inside of me. If he denied me, I'd go crazy.

"Please, come back. I'll behave," I pleaded.

"No, I'm going to lie down. Maybe I'll take a nap." He finished drying off and then walked out of the bathroom.

That was all it took. In a flash, I was on my feet, trying to get out. In my haste, I almost fell. There was a thumping sound and a loud splash as I caught myself.

"Cady, are you alright? Answer me," he called from the other room. He was worried. I knew not to pretend with this. It would break one of our rules. Never downplay or lie about being hurt.

"I'm fine. I almost fell, but I'm good."

"Do you need me to help you out?"

"No, I got it. You need to change your mind and let me have my treat," I called back as I got out and started to dry off.

He chuckled. "I don't think so."

I hurried through it and was out in the main room in no time. He was stretched out on the bed. The man had his cock in his hand, slowly stroking up and down. The precum had increased. I licked my lips. I had to have it. I stood at the bathroom door.

"What do I need to say or do to get another taste? And what will it take to let me suck you off?"

"Let me think. Hmm. Why don't you come over here and lie down with me? We'll cuddle. I need that."

He was torturing me, but I did it. I slid onto the bed, and he dragged me against him, spooning me from behind, which allowed him to bury his cock between my ass cheeks. He thrust a time or two as if finding a comfortable place, and then he went still.

"That's it. Let me get the lights. It's too bright in here to sleep," he muttered, and the next thing I knew, the lights went out.

I lay there, working to forget he was naked and hard. It was impossible, especially when he began to caress me slowly. My body lit up more. I moaned softly, though I tried to hold it in.

"Is something wrong?"

"You know there is. If you want us to sleep, you can't touch me."

"But it comforts me."

I didn't bother to respond. He kept it up, just

barely grazing my key spots. I had no idea how long he did it until I decided I'd had enough. If he wanted to deny me, I'd take care of myself. I rolled onto my back and put distance between us. As I did, I spread my legs and slid a finger along my wet slit, then sank it into my hole. I moaned.

"Cady, what're you doing?"

"Nothing. Go to sleep."

I rubbed up and down, and when I came to my clit, I rubbed in circles. It wasn't going to take much to get me off. I sped up. Suddenly, I was blinded by the light coming on. A growl came from him.

"Did I say you could touch yourself?"

"No, but since you can't get the job done, I decided to do it myself. Or maybe I should see if someone out there is willing to help me," I taunted. As soon as I said it, I knew I'd fucked up.

He snarled, and then he was over the top of me, staring down at me. There was a wildness to his look. He tore my hand away from my pussy. He brought it up to his mouth and sucked it clean. When he was done, he pinned both of my wrists to the bed with one hand.

"You never threaten to let someone else touch you, Cady. I'm a possessive man. You're mine. If anyone touches you, they die. I see you want to push me into getting you off. Okay, let's see if you like what you get."

The look in his eyes told me I was in for payback.

"No, no, I was just teasing, Magnus. Don't," I begged.

"Too late."

He began to run his hands all over my body. He grazed those trigger spots, but that was it. I thought that was bad enough, but then he got out of bed and

CIARA ST JAMES

went to a small fridge I hadn't noticed. He opened it, scanned it, and then took something out. When he came back, he had it hidden by his leg.

"I want you on your stomach and spread your legs," he demanded.

I was wary of what he had, but I did it. When I was in position, he lifted my bottom and placed a pillow underneath me, raising my ass in the air. Then he got on the bed. I tried to look over my shoulder, but he barked at me. "Eyes forward. If you want to come at all tonight, you'll do as you're told."

I did it, but reluctantly. I felt something cold and wet circle my asshole. I tensed for a moment, then relaxed. We'd been playing with him, placing his fingers in my ass and even some toys. I enjoyed it once you got past the initial burn. After several circles, he then slowly pressed the object inside. It felt like a wet and cold dildo. Maybe the cold was supposed to make me not like it. Well, I had news for him. It would do just fine to make me get off. Hoss began slowly thrusting it in and out. I relaxed into it. He paused at one point and pressed my ass cheeks together and held them for several moments, then let go. He went back to thrusting. As my excitement grew, I began to burn. At first, I didn't pay any attention to it, but it kept increasing. I wiggled. He slapped my cheek. The burning increased.

"Stay still."

"Magnus, something's wrong. It's burning."

"It's supposed to. You've been bad. I can't let you get off without you being punished, can I?"

"Punished? How?" I asked. The burn was becoming worse.

"Remember I told you about figging. Well, I

thought this was a good time to try it."

I gasped. He'd told me about the practice of inserting fresh ginger root into the anus. It caused a deep burning sensation. In the past, it had been used to torture prisoners and others. Another slap landed, making me clench. It increased the fire. I tried not to clench my muscles, but he made it impossible. In between spanking me, he was rubbing my clit, causing my pussy to pulsate, and that affected my ass. I was sobbing for him to stop.

"Bite the fucking pillow. You can take it. Show me how you can take my punishment. If you do, I'll give you what you want."

Despite the pain of the burning, I was turned on more than ever. It was like the ginger was painful yet pleasurable, too. I wanted to scream my safe word, yet another part of me wanted to ride it out and see what happened. I was shaking and sobbing into the pillow still when the burn and the stimulation peaked. As it did, I screamed and almost came off the bed with how hard I was shaking. I came and came. I was gasping for air throughout. I vaguely felt him remove the ginger. Then I gasped more as his cock slid into my pussy. I was still orgasming, which made him moan.

"Fuck, you're milking my cock. Yes, that's it. God, you did so good, baby. And you're gonna come again," he muttered.

I became a ball of sensation as he pounded into me. I was climbing in no time.

"Goddamn, that was so hot to watch. All I kept thinking about was it was my cock in your ass. I hope one day you'll say yes. I'd love to know what it feels like. The burn of the root and my cock together. I bet our orgasms would be explosive."

The thought made me wilder. I pushed back to meet his next thrust. "You get me off in the next two minutes, and I promise to let you have this ass. Just work me up to it, and we'll do it," I promised.

"Fuckkk," he moaned, and then he was really going for it. It didn't take him two minutes to have me gushing and squeezing the hell out of his cock as we both came and roared out our pleasure. I hoped everyone heard us, was the last thought I had before I closed my eyes. I vaguely felt him pull out and then carry me to the bathroom to clean up. I kept my eyes closed, even when he put me in the tub. I was boneless and so tired but in a wonderful way. I was never so happy to be a brat as I was with him.

⅗ ⅗ ⅗

I was at Hoss's house. It was nine o'clock at night. He was at work at Lustz. I hated the nights he worked there. The bed felt so empty. I knew he did it for stress relief from his regular job and the demands of his company, so I never told him that I detested when he left me. I suggested that I stay at my place those nights, but he wanted me to stay here. He claimed he needed to come home and crawl into bed with me, even if we only got to sleep together a few hours before I had to get up and go to the clinic on Friday mornings. His Friday and Saturday nights were better since we had no reason to be up early and could sleep in and play when we felt the mood strike.

I read a book for a while, but it didn't keep my attention. I didn't want to intrude on Mikhail and Tajah's time together, so it left me with loose ends. My work charting was caught up, and so was any of the business side of things, such as supply ordering and paying the bills. Thank God Dottie helped me do the supplies.

Dropping into a chair in the living room, I turned on the television to see if, by some miracle, there was something on it worth watching. I wasn't holding out hope. As I surfed, my mind drifted to last night and what Hoss and I did at Lustz. I was still astonished that I actually had sex where other people could see me. While it made me somewhat nervous, I enjoyed being watched. I felt sexy and empowered. It was proven. I was an exhibitionist, and I'd even say a voyeur.

A loud buzzing caused me to jump in fright. It took a second for it to click that it was coming from one of the speakers throughout the house. Due to its size, Hoss had a few of them scattered around. It allowed you not only to activate the alarm but to see who was ringing in from the gate. Going over to the panel, I saw the screen was showing a man there. He was in a car and appeared upset. I had no idea who he was. I decided to ignore him. No way was I letting a stranger onto the property when Hoss wasn't home. He pressed it again, but this time, he spoke through the speaker.

"Come on, open the fucking gate. I don't want to sit out here all fucking night. Open up, Hoss," he shouted.

His pissy attitude sparked my temper. I pressed the button on my end to talk back.

"Hoss isn't here, and I'm not opening the gate. You can come back when he's home."

His scowl deepened. "I don't take orders from my brother's fuck toys. Open the gate. I'm tired, and I need a place to crash. He won't be happy if he finds out you didn't let his brother in."

"First of all, how do I know you're his brother? Secondly, if he wanted you to have the ability to crash here, you'd have the code to open the gate and wouldn't need to buzz in. And from what I know, Hoss doesn't give a damn what you do."

"Listen, bitch, open the gate or else," he shouted.

"Or else what, bitch?" I smarted off.

"You're fucking with the wrong person! Open the hell up! Is Hoss having his tarts speak for him?"

"I'm not a tart. I'm his girlfriend, and yes, I speak for him when I know what he'd say or want. And he doesn't want you on his property or in his house. Go away. If you want to speak to him, go see him at work."

"Work! He's not there this late, dumb bitch. He must be out screwing another woman while your dumbass is at home thinking he's at work," he said with a smirk. He had no idea Hoss worked at Lustz, and I wasn't about to tell him where he was.

"Max, leave, or I'll call the cops, and they'll make you leave."

"No one tells me what to do, especially not some split tail," he muttered as he put the car in reverse and backed up. I watched until the car was out of the camera's view. Wait until I told Hoss his brother was around. No doubt he wanted money since that was all he ever wanted, according to Hoss.

Fed up with Max and the lack of a good show to watch, I shut off the television and decided to go to the bedroom and curl up in bed. There was a television and a DVR in there. He had a large selection of movies. I'd choose one of those and watch it. Maybe it would put me to sleep, and I'd get some rest until Hoss came home.

I found what I was looking for and got into bed. I clicked the buttons, and one of my favorite old movies came on. It had John Wayne and Maureen O'Hara in it. I loved just about any movie she was in, and the two of them together were great. I liked her feistiness. She didn't take much crap.

I was maybe five minutes into it when there was a loud crash, which sounded like something being knocked over, and then the alarm system went off. My heart jumped into my throat. For a couple of moments, I didn't know what to do. Then, my brain began to work, and I recalled what Hoss had told me to do if anyone ever broke in. There was a concealed panic room built into the master walk-in closet. He'd shown me where it was and put my handprint into it. I threw back the covers and ran for the closet. I had enough sense to snag up my cell phone as I did.

My hand shook, and it took a couple of tries before the system could read my print and the hidden door opened. I rushed inside and shut the door. Lights automatically came on. It was equipped for more than one person to be able to stay there for an extended period of time. There was even a tiny bathroom. Along one wall were several screens. I ran to it and hit the main button. Again, Hoss showed it to me. The cameras around the house came on.

As I scanned to see the intruder or intruders, my cell phone rang. I jumped. *Christ, calm down, Cady*, I chided. I glanced at it, and Hoss's name was on the screen. Relief hit me. I answered it immediately.

"Cady, the security company said there's an alarm going off at the house. Did you forget the code and set it off?"

"No. I heard a crashing sound, and then it started blaring."

"Are you in the panic room?" His tone changed from somewhat amused to stressed. He really thought I'd accidentally set it off.

"I am. Are they sending someone?"

"Hold on a second, and I'll let them know to send the police. They're on the other line."

His being off the line made me more anxious. I was still busy scanning the screens. He was back quickly. "Cady, they're sending the police. I want you to stay in that room. You don't come out for anyone other than me or the cops. I'm on my way. Remember, whoever it is doesn't know about the room, and even if they did, they can't get in. You're safe. I'll be home as fast as I can. Hang tight."

"I will. Magnus, please hurry." I let him hear my fear.

"I will, baby."

Letting him hang up was tough. I kept watching the monitors. I had no idea how long it would take for the police to get there. I was about to concede it was a false alarm despite the crashing sound when I saw a shadowy figure slowly entering the kitchen. It was dark in there, so I couldn't tell who it was, but the height and build made me think it had to be a man. He had a hood pulled up over his head, further disguising him.

The way he moved made it appear that he was familiar with the house. He was going straight through the living room and down the hall to where Hoss's home office was. Fiddling with the buttons that worked the monitors, I got it to switch to that area. The intruder went inside Hoss's office and to the desk, where he began rummaging through the drawers. As he did, he clicked on a flashlight he was carrying and laid it on the desk. The beam lit up his face. My fear changed to fury as I recognized the face. It was Max, Hoss's brother. I guess he hadn't left after all.

I knew Hoss had said to wait for him and that the cops were coming, but my anger at his brother doing this overrode my common sense. I went to the cabinet against the wall. Hoss had given me a thorough orientation to this room. There were weapons. I knew how to shoot a gun thanks to Tajah's dad, who had been a cop, teaching me years before he died. I removed one of the handguns in there. I checked to be sure it was loaded and that a round was chambered. Once I had it, I went to the door and eased it open. I slipped out and made sure it was closed behind me. Then I went hunting. No way was I letting that slimy bastard steal from his brother.

I made my way to the office, where I stood outside the door. I hadn't seen if he had a gun or not on the monitor. There was a chance he did, and if I confronted him, he'd shoot me. However, I was determined not to let him steal. Holding the gun down along my leg, out of sight, I called out.

"Max, I know it's you. Come out. Why're you breaking into your brother's house?"

I was peeking through the crack where the door met the frame. I could see him, barely. He jerked, and his head snapped to look toward the doorway. He wasn't able to see me.

"You wouldn't let me in, so I came in. Turn off that damn annoying alarm. I wondered where you ran off to. Hoss owes me. I'm here to collect."

"He owes you? I don't see that ever happening. Hoss takes care of himself and others. He has no need to take anything from you."

"Well, he doesn't take care of me! He knows that with Dad and Mom dead, it's his job to help me. It's what family does. I need cash, and he has plenty of it. Look at this house, his cars, and that fancy office he has. He's rolling in it. He can spare some. I bet that's why you're with him, isn't it? You want his money," he snapped.

"No, I don't, and you're not stealing anything of his. The cops are on their way. You should leave before they get here. If they find you, they'll arrest you."

"My brother won't let that happen."

"Oh yes, he will. I know all about how your parents enabled you, and you sucked them dry. Hoss is too smart to allow you to do it to him. If your parents listened, they might still be alive. You should've been cut loose a long time ago," I instigated. What made me do it was anger over how he affected Hoss's life. He moved around the desk as if he was going to come toward the door, and I eased back. As I backed up the hallway, I kept talking.

"Hoss told me all about you. You only come around when you want money, and he never gives it to you. Trespassing on his property is one thing, but you broke into his house. The house where his girlfriend is. He's a very protective man. You don't want to be here when he arrives."

"I don't believe you're his girlfriend. My brother doesn't have serious relationships. He fucks and moves on. If you want me to go, then tell me where he keeps his emergency cash. I know he has it here. He always has some, no matter what. Get it for me, or if not that,

I want jewelry and anything else that's valuable. If you get me those, I'll leave."

I knew he was lying, but I pretended to believe him. "Alright, let me go get it. It's in the master bedroom. It'll take me a couple of minutes to get it all. There's a lot. Stay here."

I took off rushing to it. I'd come to the conclusion I should've stayed in the panic room. Hoss would lose his shit when he found me out of it. I wasn't up to testing him. My safety was one of the do-not-break rules. I heard Max coming after me. I sped up and almost fell, getting back to the bedroom and to the panic room door. I hit the palm scanner, and it let me in. I was closing it when he appeared. He saw me and ran toward me, but I got it secured in the nick of time. He pounded on it and shouted.

"Open the fuck up! I know his stuff is in there. Give it to me. I need it. You have to give it to me now!" he hollered.

The way he was acting and the escalating demands made me wonder if he was either high at the moment or if he needed a fix and didn't have the money to get it. That was why he came here. Although knowing Hoss the way he did, why would Max ever think he'd give him anything? He kept screaming and pounding. I sat on one of the cots and waited. *When would the police get here?* I fretted.

I didn't know how long it was before I heard more voices. They were male. I heard them identify themselves as cops and demanded that whoever was in the house come out with their hands up. I heard it coming over the monitor. The yelling and pounding had stopped, but that didn't mean Max was gone. I tried to see where he'd gone. Surely, he wasn't stupid enough to stick around for the cops to get here? But if he was high or desperate enough, he might.

I saw two of the cops moving through the house with their guns drawn. I continued scanning the other rooms until I saw Max crouched in a secondary bedroom. He had his gun in his hands. I didn't want the officers to get shot. Frantically looking over the buttons, I found the one that I believed would allow me to talk. I pressed it.

"He's on the second floor, in the last bedroom on the right. Be careful. He has a gun," I announced.

I saw the officers startle, but nothing like Max did. He couldn't run unless he jumped out of a second-story window, and that would most likely end in him breaking something. And the cops were coming up the stairs, so there was no way to get past them. He was frantically twisting his head left and right, looking for a way out. Not knowing what else to do, I began talking to him. I wanted him distracted and not focused on the cops.

"Max, it's over. Put down your gun and come out. If you do, no one gets hurt. If you don't and those policemen get hurt, you're going to be in a world of shit. Breaking and entering and attempted burglary is a lot less intense than attempted murder or the actual murder of an officer.

"What do you think Hoss is going to think and feel when he finds out his brother broke into his house and terrorized his girlfriend? That you demanded money and valuables? You're better off going with the cops. Maybe they'll lock you up for a long time, and it'll give you the chance to detox and then turn your shit around."

As I talked, I noted that I had his attention. He was scowling, and I saw his mouth moving even though I didn't have the sound on to hear him. The two policemen made it right outside the bedroom door. I shut up and held my breath. I sent up a prayer that neither of them got hurt. It was over in a blink. They entered the room and had him in their sights. He was disarmed, then taken to the ground and handcuffed. It was kinda anticlimactic, but at least everyone was safe.

I didn't know what to do. The officers had no idea where I was in the house. If I came out, I didn't want to be accidentally shot. I was debating talking to them over the speaker system and telling them I was coming out and not to shoot when Hoss came striding into the house. He appeared fierce. There was another person with him, who the police obviously knew. I turned on the audio to listen.

"Where's my woman?" Hoss demanded of the officers.

"Sir, we don't know. She spoke over your PA system, but we have no idea where she is," the shorter officer holding Max said.

"She must still be in the panic room. Hold him here. I'll be right back," he ordered.

I wasn't surprised when they did as he said. He wasn't a man to ignore. I shut off the monitors and went to the door. I barely opened it and stepped outside when I was scooped up in a bear hug. Hoss held me tightly to him as he kissed me. In between kisses, he kept muttering, "Thank God you're alright, Tiny."

"Magnus, I'm fine. Put me down, and let's go deal with your stupid brother. What an absolute idiot. Are you sure you're even related? Maybe he was adopted or switched at the hospital," I told him.

It did the trick. It made him chuckle. Soon, he was laughing and easing his hold. He finally sat me on my feet but kept an arm around me.

"Come on then, let's get this over with."

I went with him to the living room, where the cops were still waiting. He marched right up to Max.

"What the hell were you thinking? Wait, you weren't. Those drugs have finally eaten your brain away, Max. You came onto my property and broke into my house when my woman was here alone. How dare you?" he roared.

"Mr. Sacket, calm down. We've got him, and we assume you're pressing charges," the guy who came in with him stated. He wasn't in a uniform but had a badge pinned to his belt. I hadn't seen it on the monitor.

"You're goddamn right that I'm pressing charges. He's damn lucky he didn't harm her, or he'd be dead," Hoss snarled.

"We'll disregard that statement, guys. Get him out of here. I'll talk to the lady about what happened," the lead man said. Nodding, the two policemen led Max toward the door.

"You can't do this, Hoss! I'm your brother. Family takes care of family," Max shouted.

"You're not my family. Mine wouldn't do this. This is the final straw, Max. You're dead to me. Never contact or come near me and mine again."

Max let out a frustrated scream as they dragged him out. He was fighting to get loose. Hoss turned his attention to me. "Cady, this is Detective Saller. Detective, this is my girlfriend, Cadence Anderson. Let's go sit in the living room." On our way to the living room, Detective Saller started the conversation.

"It's nice to meet you, Ms. Anderson. I wish it were under better circumstances. I'm with the Nashville Metro Police. Iker Sullivan called to advise me that I should be here." I shook his outstretched hand. Hoss turned on the lights as we went. We settled on the couch. Saller sat in the chair across from us.

"Just start at the beginning and tell us what happened," Saller suggested.

As concisely as possible, I told them what happened from the moment Max rang the buzzer until they arrived. I felt the tension grow in Hoss. I left nothing out, including how I'd ignored his order to stay in the panic room. I did emphasize how I thought better of it after the fact and returned there to wait for the police. When I was done, I gave Hoss a nervous look.

"I'm sorry, Magnus. I should've listened. I know that it's one of the rules, but I didn't want him to steal your stuff."

"Cady, I don't give a fuck about my stuff. It can be replaced. You can't. You put yourself in danger for nothing. You and I will talk about your disobeying later. Saller, do you have any other questions for her?" He was curt and dismissive. I felt slightly sick.

"No, I think I have it all."

"Do we need to come downtown and sign anything to have him prosecuted? Or to give another statement?" Hoss asked.

"I don't think it'll be necessary. Her statement and what Sullivan will provide from the security videos make it pretty airtight. If your brother is smart, he'll plead guilty and save us all a trial. He'll be going away."

"Good, but he's never smart, so he'll probably claim he's innocent even after seeing the damn security video. If you need anything, just let us know. If you don't mind, it's late and we're tired. I know you have to be as well. We'd like to get to bed," Hoss said.

Saller rose, and after handshakes and goodbyes, Hoss escorted him to the door. I hung back in the living room. I didn't know what form my punishment would take, but I knew I was in for it. I'd violated one of his biggest rules. Something told me I wouldn't enjoy it this time.

Cady: Chapter 18

It had been a week since the break-in. Max was taken care of and was sitting in jail. He was smart enough to plead guilty. You'd think that meant Hoss and I were happy. We weren't. The reason was Hoss had gone silent on me. I thought after Detective Saller left, I'd get yelled at, and he'd punish me. Wrong. He said we needed to get some sleep and went to the bedroom. In bed, he didn't hold me or make any attempt to talk or initiate sex. I thought he'd be over it by morning, and we'd talk. He just needed to calm down. Wrong again.

The silent treatment and not touching me intimately continued. He wasn't even kissing me. I tried to get him to talk about it and to punish me, no matter how bad it was, but he would give me a disinterested look and go on with whatever he was doing.

He returned to work at Lustz Friday night, but I was left with a guard on the property. I had no idea who he was or where he came from. He just appeared and stayed out there all night. Suffice it to say the weekend passed uncomfortably. I was glad to go to work on Monday. I needed the break. However, going back to his place at the end of the workday, I discovered he was working late in his home office. He came to bed after I was asleep. This has happened every night since. He was still not speaking to me except for the barest amount needed. He was working sixteen-hour days. He ignored all attempts to discuss what happened.

Well, I'd had enough. If he thought he'd push me away and ignore me for days on end, then he was wrong. If he didn't want to be near me, and it was obvious from his actions that he didn't, then I wouldn't foist myself on him. I was in familiar territory.

We'd been driving separately to work this week. This morning, he left before I did. Again, there was no goodbye kiss. As soon as he was gone, I got to work. I packed up the stuff I'd brought to his house—it was more than I knew. I put it in my trunk and then headed to work like usual. The day crawled by despite having a busy day. I thought it would never end. When it was three o'clock, I ushered the staff out and almost ran out of the clinic. We had no more appointments.

I got in my car, started it, and began driving. Only it wasn't toward Belle Meade. I headed out of town. I went south on I-65. I knew if I went to my apartment, he'd find me like last time. He might not want me, but I could see him insisting that in order to be safe, I had to return to his place. He'd be thinking of Tajah. It wasn't happening. There were no more break-in attempts at the clinic, and Flint hadn't shown his face in weeks. This time, I'd be somewhere I couldn't be found.

I wasn't able to handle any more of this. I knew these signs. I'd been treated to them several times in the past. He no longer wanted me. I was too much hassle. The guys who didn't leave in a rage had frozen me out until I left them. I'd be given the silent treatment, and all intimacy or even affection had disappeared between us. It was a familiar scene.

I fought to hold in the tears that threatened to fall. My chest hurt. It felt like my heart was breaking. As

I continued to drive, I placed a call. I didn't want her to worry, so I had to tell her my plan. Tajah answered me quickly.

"Hey, Cady, I was just thinking about you. I need to see your face, girl. You and Hoss should come over for dinner this weekend," she chatted happily.

"Taj, I can't." I tried to keep the pain I was feeling out of my tone, but I guess I wasn't successful. I wanted to come across as unconcerned about the break-up.

"What's wrong? Are you crying?" she asked with concern. I could lie, but it was too much effort, so I told her the truth. She wouldn't buy me taking a short trip without Hoss anyway.

"I'm not crying. I can't come for dinner, and if I could, it sure wouldn't be with Hoss."

"What did he do?"

"What do you think? He's just like the others. Unable to handle me. Sure, he's not the physical type, but he's made sure I know that he's no longer interested in me or my shit behavior. Why can't I be different, Tajah? Why can't I find someone and be happy? I need to face it. I'm destined to be alone for the rest of my life. I'm done trying. No more men. Ever."

"What the hell?" she uttered.

"I called to let you know that I've got to get out of town for a few days. I didn't want you to worry. I'll be fine. Don't panic if I don't answer your calls right away. I'll have my phone off. I need peace. Clearing my head is in order. I'll call you in a couple of days."

"Cady, no, don't leave. Come here. You can stay with us," she pleaded.

"I can't. It'll put you and Mikhail in the middle, and I won't do that to the two of you. Hoss is Mikhail's friend and employee. That wouldn't be fair. I'll be okay. I'm a big girl, and I've been here before. Just give me time to get my head on straight, and I'll be back. We can do a girls' day out somewhere. Love you."

"I love you too, but I can't believe that Hoss is done with you, Cady. He's crazy for you."

"He was, but no more. He won't touch me, kiss me, or even talk. We might as well be roommates and barely friendly ones at that. It's been a week, Taj. It's time to accept the inevitable and get on with my life. It's not as if I haven't been here before. Listen, I've got to go. Talk to you later."

"Cady—" I cut her off.

I couldn't continue to belabor it. The tears had escaped and were running down my face. I swiped at them to clear my eyes so I could see the road. The last thing I needed was to have an accident because I was mooning over a man. Seeing the sign for I-840 East, I took it. I knew it would lead to I-40. It had been a while since I'd been to East Tennessee. There were countless places to stay out there, especially in the Gatlinburg area. I'd get a hotel or something for a while. Fresh air and the mountains would help. I hoped.

Hoss:

It had been a goddamn week since the whole episode with my stupid-ass brother breaking into the house and Cady having to hide out. Every time I thought of what he might've done in his doped and desperate state, I was scared all over again and wanted to put my hands on him.

When I first got the call from Iker saying the alarm was going off at the house, I assumed Cady had forgotten it was on and accidentally triggered it, then forgot the code. I'd shown it to her, but it wasn't something she was used to. I'd been drilling into her the importance of having it on anytime we were home. Since her apartment didn't have one, it wasn't ingrained into her. Belle Meade wasn't a high-crime area, but it was better to be safe than sorry.

I'd called her to give her the code and tease her before they called the police. When she said there was breaking glass and then the alarm sounded, terror filled me. Images of her hurt or, worse, dead flashed through my mind. That was when I put her on hold, even though it killed me to do it, and told Iker to call the cops and get them there ASAP.

I barely took time to call Mikhail to tell him I was leaving my post and why as I ran for my car. He said not to worry and to go make sure Cady was okay. He also said to let him know if we needed anything. I couldn't drive fast enough to get there. It was pure luck that Detective Saller and I arrived at the same time. We'd met in the past through Iker, so he was fine bringing me inside. He did settle my nerves by reporting one of the officers had called an all-clear over the radio moments ago.

Walking in to find Max in handcuffs and no sign of Cady had triggered my fear again. When the two officers said she spoke over the PA, but they had no idea where she was, I was relieved as hell that she was still in the panic room. I didn't want to let go of her when she came out. However, my relief changed to anger when I found out she'd left it despite my order. She knew when it involved her safety, she wasn't to disobey or challenge me on the matter. To know she did, pissed me off.

I admit I went into my own brat mode, which consisted of me ignoring her and avoiding a discussion. I knew I couldn't do it forever, but I wanted her to know how upset I was so she'd never do it again. However, it had been a week. It was time to talk to her and clear the air so we could get on with our lives. Tonight, when I got home, I wouldn't be locked up in my home office for hours. Cady and I would be sitting down for a deep discussion. A part of it would be talking about her punishment. I never wanted her to endanger herself again, especially all over fucking useless objects. The most valuable thing I had was her. She had to know that.

I was jarred from my thoughts by my phone ringing. I recognized the ringtone as Mikhail's. I wondered why he was calling in the middle of the day. If he wanted me to work tonight, he was out of luck. Cady and I needed to clear the air without delay. Besides,

I'd been thinking of giving up my doorman job at Lustz. I only did it to de-stress and give me something to do. With Cady in my life, I no longer needed it. I wanted to spend all my free time with her. I detested going there and leaving her at home alone. I'd give him notice, and hopefully, he'd find someone to replace me quickly.

"Hey, man, good afternoon. If you're calling to ask me to work tonight, I can't," I told him.

"Afternoon, and no, that's not why I'm calling. I called because I have a crying Tajah in my office. She's bawling one minute, and the next, she's threatening to find you and cut your balls off," he said.

"What the hell did I do?" I asked, mystified.

"She said—" he was cut off by the irate voice of Taj.

"Is that him? Are you talking to that no-good rat bastard? Let me talk to him," Tajah snarled.

"Sweetest Dove, let me take care of this. There's been a misunderstanding," he said soothingly, or at least he tried.

"You're damn right there's been a mistake! The mistake was ever introducing or allowing him near my best friend. I can't believe he had me fooled," she half-hollered.

"Mikhail, put me on speaker. I'll talk to her. I have no clue what's sent her on the warpath," I told him.

"You're on speaker, Hoss," he said loudly to be heard over Tajah, who was still ranting about me in the background.

"Tajah, stop shouting and tell me what the hell has you so upset?" I shouted. Damn, she had a mouth on her. ˙

"Oh, don't act like you don't know. Why did you

start something if you weren't man enough to stick to it? If I'd known this would be how you acted, I would've had her stay clear of you."

Taj referring to her, clued me into the fact she was referring to Cady. The only explanation was she'd told Tajah I was punishing her for her actions. Whatever she said had lit a fire in Taj. I wasn't sure why, though.

"Tajah, how I choose to deal with Cady is between us. I know you're best friends, but I wouldn't get in the middle of a disagreement between you and Mikhail, and I expect you and him to give us the same courtesy. I know Cady is upset, but this reaction from you is over the top," I chided her. If it angered Mikhail, I'd smooth it over later.

"You can go fuck yourself. A disagreement! You call what you've done a disagreement? It's a helluva lot more than that, mister. You and Mikhail may be friends, but you and I no longer are."

Her anger wasn't abating. I tried again. I hated the idea of losing her friendship, and for what? "Tajah, I don't understand why you're so mad at me. Yes, I've been punishing Cady to a degree for her coming out of the panic room when I told her to stay there, and she said she would. Do you understand, my brother could've hurt her? When he's high, there's no way to know what he'll do. She tried to protect my possessions rather than herself. I can't let that go."

"If that was all you did, then I get it. But to end your whole relationship over it is ridiculous. It tells me and her that you were never in it for the long haul. She thought she'd finally found a man who could handle her, accept her as she was, and love her. Instead, she got more of the same. She's alone and hurting because another man kicked her to the curb." She was no longer shouting. Instead, it sounded like she was half-crying.

My heart lurched. "Tajah, what're you talking about? I haven't kicked Cady anywhere. What did she tell you?" Dread began to fill me.

"She called to let me know she was leaving for a few days to clear her head. She would have her phone off and didn't want me to worry. She told me that you've been ignoring her, not even kissing her, much less anything else. She said she knows the signs. The guys who didn't get physical with her in the past would go silent and freeze her out until she left. You're doing the same, so she decided to put an end to it. She sees the writing on the wall, so to speak."

Dismay took over. I felt sick to my stomach. Bile rose up in the back of my throat. "Cady did what? Where did she go?"

"Why do you care? She's not your problem," was her response.

"Because she's my woman, and I love her. Nothing is over between us. If I have my way, it never will be. Please, Taj, tell me where she went." I was anxious because two days ago, I told Iker to pull her protection detail. Flint had remained gone, and I didn't see a need to continue to have her watched.

"You love her?"

"Damn right, I do. I'm going to marry that woman. Tell me," I demanded this time.

"I don't know. She didn't say. I'm not sure she knew. All she said was she'd call me in a few days, and we'd do a girls' day when she got back."

I was kicking myself for dismissing her protection. I had no idea where she was. And if her phone was off, how was it possible to track her? "Jesus Christ! Okay, let me think. Is there anywhere special she likes to go to be alone, to think, or just get away from it all?"

"Not really. She rarely takes time away. Cady has always focused on the clinic. I honestly can't think of a place," Taj answered.

"Goddamn!"

"Hang on, don't get all crazy. Let me see if there's something Outlaw can do to find her. He's resourceful as hell when it comes to finding people. Speaking of him, he sent over the names and locations of those guys you wanted. I'll send it over to you today. I bet he can find her. Why don't we put a pin in this and get back together later? By then, I might know something from Outlaw. Why don't you come here after work?" Mikhail suggested.

"Do it. And I'll be there soon. First, I'll check her apartment in case she changed her mind or just said that so no one would bug her there. I swear, the last thing I want is her gone, Tajah. I love her so damn much, it's crazy. Hell, I'm planning to ask her to marry me. Does that sound like someone who's fed up with her? No. She can be the biggest brat in the world, but she'll be my brat."

"Oh my God, that's so sweet. Oh shit, I'm sorry for calling you names and swearing at you." She sounded aghast now.

"Don't worry about it. Just let me know if you think of a place she might go. I need to get to her place. See you in a while."

"Sure thing. Come over whenever you want," Mikhail added. I ended the call before it could drag on any longer.

I hardly took the time to close down my computer before I was on my feet, rushing out the door. I went to Alicia Ann. "I've got to go. Cancel the rest of my appointments for today. Reschedule them for later next week. I may have to take a few more days off, but I'll let you know," I told her as I rushed by her. She was up and jogging beside me as I explained. I did it as I headed for the elevator.

"I'll get it handled. Is there anything I can do?" she asked.

"No, this is my mess to clean up. Thanks."

"You're welcome," were her last words before the elevator doors closed to take me to the garage in the basement of SacketEdge. I got into my car and peeled out of the garage and parking lot. I had to remind myself not to speed like an idiot. I'd been a big enough one of those as it was. As I headed for Cady's apartment, I called Iker. I wasn't sure why.

"Hey, miss us already?" was how he answered his phone.

"Shit, so you did pull your people," I muttered. I'd had the slightest hope that it hadn't happened yet.

"Uh, yeah, the day you asked me to. Why? Did something happen?"

"You could say that. Cady got the wrong idea about a situation, and she left. We don't know where she went. Her phone is supposedly turned off. I was hoping you hadn't done it yet and could tell me where she went."

He whistled. "Damn, it sounds like you're in the middle of a shitstorm. I'm sorry. I wish I had good news for you. What're you gonna do? Did she call Tajah?"

"She did, but only to say she was leaving and not to worry, that she'd call in a few days. It's alright. You just did as I asked."

"If you need me, just holler. Did you check her apartment?"

"I'm headed there now. Thanks. Talk to you later."

"Sure thing."

It took me another twenty minutes to make it to her place. There was no sign of her car in the parking lot, but I still got out and went to her door. I knocked. There was no answer. I called out her name. Nothing. As a last effort, I took out the key I had. She'd given it to me two weeks ago to pick something up for her, and I hadn't returned it. Walking inside, I knew immediately that she hadn't been there. It had this still, stuffy feel. I did a fast walk-thru, then locked up and got back in my car.

I sat there, trying to think of where to go next. I racked my brain, trying to remember if she'd ever talked about a place she got away to or loved. Zilch. I knew what my next move had to be. I got out my phone again and placed the call.

After three rings, it was answered. His tone was cautious. "Hello? Hoss?"

"Hello, yeah, it's Hoss. Sorry to bother you, Carver, but I need to talk to you about Cady."

"Is she alright?" he asked somewhat urgently.

"Shit, sorry, yeah, she's alright, or at least as far as I know. I hate to bother you, but I need to ask. Has she ever talked about any places she's gone or wants to go to get away and relax, maybe to think?"

There was a long silence before he answered. "Not that I can recollect. Why? What did she do?"

"Why do you automatically make it sound critical

of her?"

"Because I've discovered that when it comes to my sister, she gets into situations mainly with men. I told you before, Hoss. Cady isn't someone you can be with long-term. Don't get me wrong, I love her, and she's loving and sweet at times, but her mouth and attitude wear on people, and they can't cope. It sounds like the same thing happened with you two. She left."

"She did, but the misunderstanding between us is just that, a misunderstanding. It isn't the end of us by a long shot. Cady is mine. I'm keeping her. If you can't say nice things about her, I don't want to hear it. I've got to go. Call me if you think of anything. Bye." I hung up. I knew I was short and rude, but the way he acted and spoke of his sister set my teeth on edge. If he'd been before me, I would've throttled him. I pounded my fist off my steering wheel.

"Where are you, Cady Cat? Call us. Or better yet, come home, baby. Please, come home," I uttered to the wind as I sat there, straining to remember a place.

After sitting there for a good half hour, I gave up and decided it was time to go to Mikhail's. Maybe I'd get lucky, and when I got there, he'd have good news. The drive there was no faster. I fought to contain my impatience with drivers dawdling on the highway. It was a relief when I got to Lustz. I zipped up to the third floor. I'd texted to say I was here, and Mikhail had told me to go right up to their home.

Tajah answered the door. She stepped up and gave me a hug. "I'm sorry I was such a bitch to you. If you truly love and want to keep my bestie, then I'm sorry. If you're not, then I'll kick your ass later," she threatened, even as she hugged me. I wasn't able to hold in my chuckle. She was crazy, but I did like her. I patted her back gently.

"It's okay, I forgive you, and there won't be a reason to kick my ass later. Can I come in, or are you going to continue to maul me? Mikhail! Your woman won't let go of me," I playfully called out, so she knew there were no hard feelings. She giggled and gave me one more squeeze before she let go and walked over to Mikhail, who just joined us.

"She has a habit of doing it to people she likes. I can't seem to break her of it. Although piss her off for good, and she'll stop, and I don't know what she'll do to you then." He was grinning.

"Oh, stop. Come in, Hoss. Make yourself at home. Any news?" Tajah asked as we moved further into their apartment. I closed the door behind me.

"Nope. I called Carver and asked if he knew of somewhere. He said no."

"Crap. I thought of calling him but didn't want to hear him criticize her. He loves Cady, but he doesn't totally understand her," Taj shared.

"Well, I doubt I'm on his favorite people list. I gave him a little hell about how he talks about her, and then I hung up on him. He irritates me when he does that. What about you? Anything from Outlaw? Can he help?" I directed this to Mikhail.

"I spoke to him, and he's on it. He said as soon as he finds a sign of her, he'll call. Have faith. He's relentless when he has to find someone. Let's have a drink and sit. You look like you could use one."

"I can. Thanks." I sat and let him prepare me my favorite drink as I thought of Cady and wondered where she was. As long as she was safe, that was all that mattered, except me finding her and patching things up. God, let it be soon before I lose my mind.

As time passed, they did their best to distract me and keep my mind on other things. I appreciated it, but I knew I wasn't good company. I watched the clock, paced their home, and made deal after deal with God if he'd let us find her and bring her home. I'd beg on my knees if that were what it took to bring my Cady Cat home.

Cady: Chapter 19

I decided to stop in Murfreesboro and hit an ATM. Wiser to get money from one there and not near my destination. By now, Tajah probably had Mikhail trying to locate me. I knew enough to know phones and credit cards could be used to track people. And I knew Mikhail's Bratva family probably could help him do it. I just needed to be alone and get myself together to continue my lonely existence. Sometimes, I was so depressed I wondered why keep going. The prospect of living for fifty or more years alone was beyond bleak.

After getting my cash, I kept going east. I didn't stop until I was in Gatlinburg. Too bad it was winter, not one of the other three seasons so that I could enjoy the trees. However, my disaster of a love life didn't care what season it was. Since I didn't plan to be here a week or more, I didn't look for a cabin to rent. Instead, I found a decent hotel and booked a room. Paying cash, I hauled one of my bags from the car to my room. At least I had luggage and wouldn't have to wear the same thing for days.

I'd called Dottie early, after I left, and told her I had to cancel my appointments for tomorrow and Monday. I didn't give her an explanation other than it was an emergency. She'd been so sympathetic. I felt guilty saying it was an emergency and for inconveniencing my patients' owners. If I kept it up, I'd start to lose them. Just my luck, a man ruining my life's work. I swore it would never happen, and until Hoss, no one had ever impacted it. No matter how bad it got, I always went to work.

I sat down and sent off a quick email to Dottie. In it, I advised her I'd check in tomorrow. I wasn't up to staying online, so I shut it down after I sent it. At a loss, since I was always so busy, I tried the television. It was soon apparent there was even less on than at Hoss's. He had all the primo channels, and still, I had trouble finding something to interest me. The hotel had less.

Looking around my room, I knew I couldn't stay holed up in it, or I'd go insane. Noting places were still lit up, I decided to go for a walk and see what I could. I bundled up in a sweater and my coat. It was colder in this part of the state. I didn't have gloves or a scarf. I hadn't needed them yet in Nashville. Oh well, if I found I did, maybe I'd find a shop open and I could buy some. If not, there'd be one of the big department stores nearby.

Stepping outside, the brisk gust of wind made me shiver, but I knew after I got to walking, I'd warm up. I took off in the direction with the most stores. There were still people out and about. Even if it wasn't peak tourist season, it had visitors along with the townspeople. I set a brisk pace. I found I enjoyed window shopping. It had been a long time since I'd done it. Tajah and I did need that girls' day I spoke of.

I wandered about for an hour. As it got later, it grew colder. That decided me. I would go back to the hotel. It had a restaurant in it, so I'd grab dinner there and then go to my room for the night. Maybe I'd be able to focus on my e-reader and a book. I knew I had numerous ones on it waiting to be read.

Dinner wasn't anything spectacular, but it was good. I took my time. I didn't get up to leave until I saw a couple come in, and they sat near me. They were gazing all lovingly at each other. It hurt to watch, so I called it a night. After a hot shower, I got into bed and picked up my reader. I didn't bother to look to see if there was anything on television. I struggled for over an hour before I gave up. I kept reading the same paragraphs over and over.

The reason was that I couldn't stop thinking about Hoss or about how I'd been so sure this time I'd found a man who would love me and never push me away or leave. Why I hurt so much this time, I knew the answer. I'd never loved any of the other men in my past. Yeah, there were degrees of lust and affection, but never love. None of them hurt my heart. Hoss had broken it.

Turning off the light, I buried my face in my pillow and let the emotional storm loose. I muffled my cries and screams into my pillow. I had no idea how long it lasted before I was too exhausted to do it anymore. That's when I drifted off into a fitful sleep, filled with dreams of Hoss.

᠅ ᠅ ᠅

I woke up feeling like death warmed over. I was stiff, and my eyes were sore, scratchy, and blurry. I rushed to the bathroom and splashed water on them, hoping they'd feel better, and my vision would clear up. It helped with my sight but not the other two problems. Looking at myself in the mirror, I groaned. I didn't look much better. This wouldn't do. I refused to walk around with the appearance of a zombie.

Finding my makeup, I got to work. I had to use more than I normally did, but when I was done, I appeared alive and had color. I did enough to make my hair presentable in a bun. After getting dressed, I thought about what to do with my day. Maybe this time, I'd take my car and go exploring for the day. There was so much to see.

Not risking my phone, I used my laptop. I did a quick search of area attractions, which there was no lack of, and then I picked a couple. I noted the addresses and then got offline. I didn't check my personal or work emails. I wasn't here to worry about any of that. Instead of having breakfast in the restaurant, I stopped at a nearby coffee shop and got a large coffee and a pastry. Both were delicious.

I ended up finding a ghost-walking tour that was fun and very informative. I learned so much about the area and the Cherokee Indians who called it home, and some do to this day. From there, I decided to take the self-guided walking tour of the Great Smoky Mountains National Park. By the time I was done, I was tired and hungry.

Stopping in town, I found a small restaurant and ate a late lunch slash early dinner there. When I was finished, I wasn't ready to go back to my room, so I did an aimless drive around. It was dark by the time I went back to the hotel. It ended up being a repeat of last night. God, I had to shake this off. He was just a man. How long did it take to heal a broken heart?

Hoss:

Cady had been gone for over forty-eight hours. I was about to lose my fucking mind. I couldn't eat, sleep, or work. All I did was obsessively watch my phone, bug Mikhail, drive around Nashville, and sit outside her apartment. Tajah hadn't heard from her. I went to the clinic yesterday to talk to Dottie. It was closed. I got Dottie's number from Mikhail, who I assumed got it from Outlaw. I called her to see if she knew anything. It had been a bust.

"Hello," Dottie answered cautiously. I didn't blame her. She had no idea who was calling her.

"Hi, Dottie, it's Hoss, Cady's man. I hate to disturb you, but do you have a minute?"

"Of course, is Cady alright?"

"That's what I'm trying to find out. Have you spoken to her?"

"No, not since she messaged me early yesterday evening to close the clinic for a few days and later emailed me to see if it was done. What's going on, Hoss? She told me it was an emergency, but if that's the case, why are you calling me and asking what I know?" Suspicion was evident in her voice.

"Truthfully, I was a goddamn dick, and she got the wrong idea about it, and she took off. She told Tajah she needed a few days alone. No one knows where she is, Dottie. I'm afraid she'll get hurt. She's out there alone and upset.

I've got to find her. Is there anywhere you recall her ever saying she wanted to visit?"

I held my breath, praying she'd say yes. I deflated when she denied it. "No, not that I recall. It had to be a rather big dick moment for her to leave, Hoss. Cady doesn't let her personal life interfere with her work. If she left, I think it's best if you don't call or ask me questions. My loyalty is to her."

"Dottie, please, it's not what you think! I didn't put a hand on her, I didn't cheat on her, nor did I yell at her. I swear to God. However, I still hurt her. She misunderstood why I was giving her the silent treatment."

She groaned. "You did what? Oh, Hoss, that's one of the worst things you could've done to her if what you're saying is the truth."

"It is. Ask Tajah. Listen. I know I have no right to ask, but if you hear from her, will you let me know? And tell her I need to talk to her. Please." I wasn't too proud to beg.

"I'll think about it. I'll see what Cady has to say about what you did. I've got to go."

Knowing it was as good as I was getting, I said, "Thank you and goodbye."

That was yesterday, and still not a peep out of Cady. If I didn't hear something soon, they'd need to lock my ass up before I went on a rampage tearing up Tennessee trying to find her.

Gazing out at the darkness outside the window, I called it. I couldn't stand to be here alone a moment longer. I'd head to Mikhail and Tajah's. If they were busy, then I'd go somewhere. Taking out my phone, I sent off a brief text.

Me: Do you two have plans?

A handful of seconds later, I had his response.

Mikhail: No. Come on over. We can pace and worry together.

Me: TY. Be there ASAP.

Mikhail: Come on up.

I didn't waste time getting to the garage and into a car. I zoomed off for the Gulch area. I had to contend with traffic, but it wasn't anything like it would be this time of evening on a weekday. A sense of relief came over me when I made it there as I rode the elevator up. Someone must've seen me and called up because when I got off, Mikhail was at their apartment door, holding the door open. When I got to him, he didn't say a word. He merely pulled me close for a manly hug and then let go so I was able to enter. Tajah was waiting for me. Her hug was much different. I gave her an extra squeeze. When she was done, I let her lead me to the living room, and I sat.

"You look like you need a drink," Mikhail said as he walked to the adjoining kitchen.

"I feel like I need a whole damn bottle. If we don't find her soon, I need you to knock me out and cart my ass off to the nuthouse. I can't take this. All I do is imagine she's hurt somewhere and needs me. This relationship-and-loving-someone business isn't for the weak."

Taj gave a sniff. I saw how red her eyes were. I held out an arm. She got up and came over to sit next to me, letting me hug her while her man fixed us a drink. "Don't cry," I told her.

"I should break your bones for making her cry and having her hug you," Mikhail joked. Or I hoped it was one.

"I didn't mean to make her cry. As for the hug, she

started it."

This made both of them chuckle. He was fast. In no time, I had a drink in hand along with him. Taj had shaken her head no. The burn of my favorite whiskey as it ran down to my stomach and hit was welcome. I had to hold back from downing the whole thing and asking for another. I wasn't someone who relied on alcohol to calm me. My brother's life had made me extremely careful. I never tried illegal drugs, not even weed.

"When the hell will we hear something?" I growled.

"We know we're at a standstill until Outlaw finds something or she calls one of us. Outlaw thinks she's being careful not to use her credit cards. The phone hasn't been back on. He's working to get access to her emails to see if he can find her that way. He's got alerts or whatever they are on the internet to notify him if she pops up. His words. He'll let me know immediately," Mikhail assured us.

"I know. I'm bitching to myself more than anything. What if it's not enough?" I voiced my other fear.

"What do you mean, not enough? Not enough what?" Taj asked. She'd gotten up and went to sit on her man's lap. He was cuddling her. It made me ache to be doing the same to Cady Cat.

"I mean, when she does call or even comes back, what if apologizing and explaining why I did it isn't enough to persuade her to forgive me and let me back into her life? She could say it was all a mistake to allow me a chance, and she's not willing to give me another." As I voiced what I'd been thinking since yesterday, I almost threw up.

"Cady won't do that. She's hurt and unsure, but she loves you. If she didn't, there would be no way she would've left like this. You might have to do some penance, groveling, or make a few promises, but I don't see her ousting you from her life," Tajah reassured me.

"I pray you're right because if you're not, I don't know what I'll do. I do know one thing, though, if she does forgive me."

"What's that?" Mikhail asked.

"I'm declaring my love, putting a ring on her finger, and hurrying her ass down the aisle as fast as possible. Oh, and I'm knocking her up, too. It'll be harder for her to leave me if we're married and we have kids."

"Hoss, you can't just marry her and get her pregnant to prevent her leaving you!" Tajah gasped in outrage.

"Why not?" Mikhail and I both asked at the same time.

She huffed and rolled her eyes. "Barbarians," she muttered.

"Taj, I'm not just doing those to make her stay. I want to marry her and have a family. The sooner, the better. I'm not getting any younger. I'll be forty next year. I want those things now with her."

"Well, that's better, but still. You both sound like cavemen when you say things like that."

"Ahem, primal here. Are you that surprised?" Mikhail asked with a quirk of his eyebrow. She giggled and gave him a kiss. I loved and detested seeing them be so affectionate right now. It only illustrated how alone I was.

"Change of subject because this isn't helping

Hoss. What is the latest on your brother? Is he still in jail or what?" Mikhail asked.

"He is. Since Dad and Mom are gone, he has no one to bail him out. If he has friends, which I doubt, none of them would have the cash or collateral to do it. I made sure they slapped him with every charge they could. He's pled guilty, so just awaiting his sentencing, which should be soon, and then off to prison, he goes for a while."

"Maybe he'll end up in the same one as that guy who killed Cady's mentor," Tajah mused.

"What!?" I exclaimed.

She appeared startled. "Oh, you don't know about that? Crap, I thought she would've mentioned it by now. It's why she's so paranoid about hiding and locking up her medications. When she was interning, she worked for a vet who had been one for forty years. She learned a ton from him, but he kept his medications locked in a glass case. She tried to tell him it wasn't secure enough, but since no one had tried to steal them, he waved off her concern. One night, he worked late, and there was a burglary. The thieves didn't know Dr. Hamilton was there. They killed him and then stole the meds. It was Cady who identified one of them on the security video. He wore a mask, but she recognized a tattoo that was exposed when his sleeve pulled up. It led to them finding him and having him roll on his partner for a lighter sentence. He's serving twenty years to life, I think. The other is life without parole. They've been in there for seven years. Maybe the three of them will be in the same one."

I wondered briefly why Cady hadn't told me. Then I knew why. She didn't want me to worry even more about her working late or alone. "No, she didn't tell me, but I think I know why. Are you sure the one with the lesser sentence is still in there?"

"As far as I know. Surely, they wouldn't let a man like that out after only seven years. He killed someone."

"It's happened. Do you know the man's name? After we get Cady home, I'd like to have him checked to be sure. We assumed it was random thieves trying to get into her clinic and hitting the others, but what if it's not?"

"Oh, I didn't think of that. I'll write it down," she said. I watched her pop up off Mikhail's lap and hurry to the kitchen. She came back with a pen and notebook. As she scribbled the information down, I tried to think of something else.

"Why don't—" Mikhail began to say when he was cut off by the ringing of a phone. It wasn't mine. I glanced at them and saw Mikhail remove his from his pocket. He scanned the screen. I saw his face light up a second before he answered it. His next words energized me.

"Hey, Outlaw, it's good to hear from you. Tell us you have news for us. I have Hoss here, and he's ready to go off the deep end. Tajah isn't much better. Can I put you on speaker so they can hear?" He paused for a couple of seconds and then pressed a button. A voice I didn't know came over the phone.

"Hello Tajah and Hoss. Sorry for keeping you waiting, but your Cady is a wily one. She knew enough to make me work for it. She didn't use credit cards or her phone. I found she'd gotten money out of an ATM in Murfreesboro the day she left, but from there, she could've gone in any direction. I've been waiting, and finally, I got a hit."

The ATM was news to me. "Do you know where she is?" I asked impatiently.

"I think so. She checked into a hotel in Gatlinburg. She paid cash, so I had to wait for her name to register in their system, and those aren't automatic when a credit card isn't used. Their system just updated and pinged my account. I can't promise she's still there, but she was."

"Where?" I practically shouted.

"I just sent it to your phone," he said calmly as my phone beeped with a text message alert. I fumbled to get it out. I read it as Mikhail spoke to him. I tuned out what was being said. I couldn't believe it. A real lead. I tuned back in long enough to thank Outlaw.

"I'm sorry. Thank you, Outlaw. I owe you."

"I'm happy to help. I'll keep watch in case she's moved on, but if she wanted peace and quiet, that would be a place I'd go. Good luck, and maybe one day, I'll take you up on your offer, Hoss. 'Night, and Mikhail, we'll talk later."

"Sounds good, goodnight, Outlaw. Again, thank you," Mikhail stated as Tajah called out thank you in the background. I was on my feet, aiming for the front door.

"Do you want me to go with you?" Mikhail asked. He was on his feet with Taj tucked under his arm. I shook my head.

"No, I need to do this alone. I'll call and let you know when I find her. Don't expect us back for a day or more. I might need time to talk her into excusing my stupidity. And even if she does so right away, I think we need a couple of days of just us and away from everything."

"You got it. Call if you need us."

I shook his hand, kissed Taj on the cheek, and then raced out the door and down the long hallway to the elevator. It would take less than three hours to get there. Faster, at the rate I'd drive. *Please, don't let her not be there.*

♣ ♣ ♣

Two hours and fourteen minutes later, I was outside her door. Outlaw had not only provided the address but also her room number. I stopped at the desk and asked if she was still there. The clerk wouldn't say. I walked outside, but I watched through the window. As soon as he went into a back room, I hurried inside and down to the elevator. I did it that way because I didn't want him to call her and say I was coming. However, she could still refuse to open her door. Taking a deep breath, I knocked. I listened hard and swore I heard sounds, and then her sweet voice called out.

"Just a minute. Coming."

I waited, holding my breath. I was surprised when the door swung open, and I saw her standing there wearing a smile. It instantly disappeared when she saw me. She tried to shut the door on me, but I had brute strength and desperation on my side. I caught it and pushed inside. She backed away from me. I didn't want her to fear me, but I couldn't risk her locking me out. I shut the door before saying anything.

"Cady, you don't need to be afraid of me. I'm not here to hurt you. I just want to talk," I implored her.

"Well, I don't feel like talking to you, Hoss. You need to leave. There's no need for you to come after me. No matter what Tajah asked. Tell her I'm fine and I'll be home soon."

"I didn't come because Tajah or anyone else asked me to. I came because I needed to see you, to explain."

"What's to explain? You're done with whatever this was between us. You've discovered, like the others, that I'm too much to deal with and not worth the effort. It's alright. I'm a big girl. All you had to do was tell me. There was no need to freeze me out."

"Christ, you're not too much to deal with, and I wasn't freezing you out, not the way you think. And I sure as fuck wasn't trying to get rid of you!" I told her urgently. Hearing her say that in such a doubtless tone angered me.

She shrugged as she moved closer to the other side of the room. "Even if it wasn't, it's inevitable. We need to get this over with now before one of us gets hurt. If this doesn't show you that I'm not a good partner, the next time will. We tried. It's time to get back to our lives."

Letting out a growl, I stalked toward her. She tried to evade me, but the room was too small, plus I was too big with long arms. I caught her when she attempted to dart around me for the door. I wrapped her in my arms. She struggled and kicked to get away, but I held onto her. Even fighting me, it felt amazing to have her in my arms. I inhaled her scent. Despite how serious this was, my cock stirred. I walked to the bed and sat, holding her on my lap. She glared up at me and tried to head-butt me. I chuckled. That was my fiery Tiny.

"What's so funny, asshole?" she growled at me.

"It's how determined you are. I love it. Your fiery side is one of my favorite ones."

"I'll show you fiery. How about I take a chunk out of you and leave you unable to have sex or children as a reminder?"

"Well, I wouldn't like it, but then you wouldn't either."

"Why would I give a shit?" she spat back. She continued to fight to get loose. Her wiggling was turning me on, and my cock was growing hard. She was too upset to notice, but she would.

"Because it means no more sex and no children for you."

"It's not as if I need to worry about those."

"Oh, yes, you do. I'm not letting you walk away from me over this, Cady. It'll happen over my dead body."

"Well, I can arrange that," she snapped again.

"God, stop. You're making me so damn hard, and we can't have sex right now. We have to talk this out first." I pressed my erection harder into her bottom. She gasped and stopped wiggling. Astonishment, desire, and anger were all warring within her. I saw them all in her expressions.

"I have nothing to say," was her response after she composed herself.

"Well, I do. And since you don't, let me start. I'm sorry that I went silent on you, and you took it to mean I no longer wanted you. That was never the truth, not for a second. I always want you. I was showing you my brat side. I assumed you'd recognize it as such. I forgot you're not versed in all things brat, nor did I explain how far I'd react with the silent treatment if you pushed me too far. Having you disobey me over something so important did it."

"So this is all my fault," she said.

"No, I didn't say that. It's both of our faults. Yours

for going against a hard limit of mine. Me for not explaining what I was doing and why."

"So after I leave, you suddenly want to talk and pay attention to me. Sure," she snorted.

"No, I planned to end the silent treatment when I got home Thursday only to find my woman had run off, and no one knew where she was or when she'd be back. Do you have any idea how worried I've been? I've been going crazy trying to find you. All I did was picture you hurt or, worse, dead. Cady, what do you think would've happened if you were hurt by my brother or out here? Or killed?"

"You'd move on and find someone more suited to you," she said cavalierly.

I'd never done it to a woman, and I hadn't imagined doing it to her, but I did. I shook her. It wasn't hard, but it did what I wanted. It grabbed her attention. Through gritted teeth, I reprimanded her and let her see my true feelings.

"Don't ever fucking say that. I would never move on from losing you. Don't you get it? I know I messed up this past week, but before that, didn't I show you that I love you? I do. More than anything. I can't picture my life without you in it, Cady. I love you. I want to marry you. I want you to bear my children. I've never told a woman that. Do you hear me? I LOVE YOU!" I partially hollered. What would it take to get through to her that she was worthwhile and not too much for me, no matter how bratty she got?

She gaped at me in astonishment and said nothing. I was about to crack and get on my knees to beg her when she spoke. "I, uhm, are you sure?" Her disbelief and hesitancy gutted me.

"I've never been surer of anything. God, I know we need to talk this out, but I can't wait," I muttered.

"Wait for what?"

"To do this," I whispered a moment before I took her mouth.

I needed to feel her lips and taste her. It had been far too long without both. Staying away from her and not sharing any touches or intimacies had been horrible for me. I fought every time I was near her in that week not to give her any. Assuming she took me back, I'd have to modify how I responded to things like that. Freezing her out would send Cady into a tailspin. It was clear. She might never react any differently after her history with her parents and other men.

She was as eager as I was. Our lips pressed together repeatedly, our tongues mated, and our teeth nipped. We were both panting when we parted. I initiated breaking our kiss, although I didn't want to, so we could finish talking. I pressed my forehead to hers.

"Cadence Anderson, tell me what I have to say, do, or swear to get you to forgive me and come home with me. No matter what it is, I'll do it. Just don't tell me to leave. It'll literally kill me."

She gripped my face between her hands and lifted my head away from hers. She stared deeply into my eyes. "Do you mean it? You love me and want me to have your babies?"

"God, yes. And if you'll let me, we can start tonight on the first one. I want to see you round with my baby so damn much. The wedding doesn't have to be before the baby, but I'd prefer it."

"Wedding? You meant that, too?"

"Hell, yeah. I want it all. Do you? Do you think you

can love me? I have enough for both of us if you can't."

"Hush. I told you a while ago I was falling in love with you. That's no longer the truth." My heart seized, and then she went on. "I'm past falling, and I've fallen all the way. I love you, Magnus. And while we have things to iron out, know that I'd love to be your wife and the mother of your children. As for starting on the first one now, it'll have to wait. My birth control doesn't run out for two months."

As her words sank in, I gave a whoop of jubilation. Then I kissed her again. When I came up for air, she was panting and smiling. "The two-month thing sucks, but it'll give us more time to practice," I informed her.

She laughed as I grinned. I sobered up after that. "We need to talk out the other part. The part that made you run."

"I know. And I'm sorry I overreacted. I let my past convince me that you were done with me. The men who weren't physically abusive with me ended us the way you were acting. I thought you were doing the same. I had to leave and protect myself. It hurt too much to stay and wait for you to tell me yourself."

"I know. Tajah told me. I had no idea. I can't tell you how wretched I feel for making you think it for even a moment, let alone for days. I promise, when I get into my brat mood, I'll find a different way to express it."

"No, you shouldn't have to change. You aren't asking me to. Just promise if it's new, to clue me in on what your typical bratty behavior is. I'm used to you being the handler, not the brat."

I didn't argue, but I would work to not be silent with her. "I can do that. And you have to swear you'll talk to me and not go running off if you have concerns or questions. I can't handle not knowing where you are or having to get people to hunt you down for me."

"Hunt me? That reminds me, how did you know where to find me? I didn't use my credit card. I kept off my phone."

"I shouldn't tell you, but since you're never taking off again, I will. Mikhail got Outlaw to find you. He has other methods and only had to wait for one of them to alert him to your location. I came as soon as I got the address."

"Wow, remind me to be afraid of him. Are we good?"

"We're good for the moment. We'll talk out our feelings and stuff more later, but for now, I want to snuggle with you and spend the next day or two just you and me, no outside world. Well, as soon as one of us texts to let Tajah and Mikhail know I found you and we're together. You had them worried, too."

She sighed and nodded. I let her send the message using my phone, holding her close as she did. I knew there would be more things to do, but they could wait until we got home. Tonight, I needed to hold her, make love if she was willing, and breathe her in.

Hoss: Chapter 20

Cady and I spent Sunday and half of today in Gatlinburg and the surrounding area. After stopping on our way back for dinner, we were finally back at the house. She'd talked to Tajah briefly while we were there and apologized. They were to have a girls' day next weekend. Afterward, all four of us would get together, have dinner, and hang out.

While she was talking to Taj, I let Mikhail know on another line that I was rendering my resignation. I promised I'd give him time to find someone. I was surprised when he revealed he had already been looking and thought he had a replacement. It seemed he knew as soon as I got with Cady that my days were numbered. He assured me he wasn't mad. If it were him in my shoes, he'd do the same thing. An offer would be extended to the prime candidate, and he'd start as soon as possible if he accepted. If he said no, there was a second candidate. In the meantime, Mikhail told me my shifts were covered. He knew I wouldn't want to leave her alone.

It was nine o'clock, and we were snuggled up in bed, watching a movie together. It was almost finished. When it was, I had plans for us. There were ten minutes to go and I was counting the seconds when we had to stop due to her phone ringing. She groaned as she picked it up. She frowned and looked over at me.

"It says it's Detective Saller."

"How does your phone know that?" I couldn't see him letting his name display.

"I put his name and number in my contacts the night he gave me his card when they arrested Max."

"Well, let's see what he wants," I told her.

"Do you think your brother made bail or something?" she asked before she answered it. "Hello, Detective Saller. Good evening. What can I do for you? Is everything alright?"

She listened for a moment, then became rigid. I reached over and took the phone, pushing the speaker button as I did. "Saller, it's Hoss. What's up?"

"Oh, hello, Hoss. Sorry to call so late, but I just got a notification that someone was seen attempting to get into Dr. Anderson's clinic again. Only this time, the culprit wasn't so lucky. He was caught running from the scene by a concerned citizen. I figured she'd want to know."

As he finished, my phone began to ring. "Can you hold? I have a call coming in on my phone. Just let me see who it is."

"Sure."

Lying down hers, I picked up mine. It was Iker. I bet I know what he wanted. I answered it. "Iker, I have Detective Saller on Cady's phone. It seems someone broke in. How did he beat you to the punch?"

"Because an idiot who will no longer work for me didn't call me immediately, like instructed, if there was an alarm tripped at Cady's clinic. I'll let you talk to Saller. Call me when you're done, no matter the time. I'm sorry."

"Okay, I'll call you later."

I hung up without raking him over the coals. He sounded upset enough without me piling onto him.

"Okay, I'm back. In case you didn't hear, that was Iker. He's not happy you beat him to the punch. Someone at his company isn't going to be happy."

Saller snorted. "I have no doubt. Iker expects close to perfection. Anyway, we have the suspect in custody, and I thought not only would you need to know but that Dr. Anderson might want to come down to the station."

"I do. Thank you. Do you have any idea who he is?" Cady asked. She'd found her voice.

"We do. His name is Flint Reid. That doesn't happen to mean anything to you, does it?"

We exchanged astonished looks, which quickly morphed into angry ones. "It certainly does," I said for us.

"Oh, really, well, that makes it more interesting. You should come down then and tell us how you know him. He's not saying a word. The only way we know his name is that he had his wallet with him. Not the brightest thief."

"He's an idiot. We'll be there as fast as we can," Cady ground out between her teeth. She was up off the bed and headed for the closet.

"Saller, we'll be there soon. Thanks for calling."

"Absolutely, I'll see you there. Don't rush. He's not going anywhere."

"Goodbye."

"Bye."

When I hung up, I had to hurry to get ready and prevent Cady from leaving without me. The whole way to the police station, she fumed silently. I didn't try to talk to her. I knew an explosion was coming. I wasn't sure if it would be her or me. Getting to the station at this time of night wasn't hard. Figuring out where to go was. We finally got to the correct area, and the person at the desk told us to have a seat and he'd get Saller. Cady was too wound up to sit, so we paced together. She did hold my hand.

It was about five minutes or so before I saw Saller striding toward us. We walked over to meet him. He held out his hand. I shook it. He held it out to Cady, and she did the same. The surprise on his face told me he wasn't expecting the strength of her grip. I hid my smirk.

"Thanks for coming. If you follow me, we can talk in one of the conference rooms. Reid is still being processed, so we have time."

We let him lead us to a room where he offered coffee or water. We declined both. I was anxious to get on with it, and I knew Cady felt the same.

"Alright, before I ask questions, here is what we know. A man was out walking his dog. As he was passing the clinic, he stated he heard the alarm going off. Moments later, a man came running out. The citizen chased after him, and when the thief wouldn't stop, the citizen let his dog loose. The dog is a former police dog that he took in—a German Shepherd. The dog brought Reid down, and they held him subdued until police arrived.

"The citizen claimed he wasn't about to let sweet Cady's clinic be robbed. He would take Walker to no other vet than her."

"Wait, Walker, are you talking about Mr. Casey?" Cady asked in shock.

"Yeah."

"Oh my God, the man is seventy if a day. He could've been hurt! Walker could've been hurt. What if Reid had a gun?" she asked aghast.

"He did. Luckily, he was too rattled to use it. Or by the time he remembered and pulled it, Walker grabbed a hold of that arm and bit until he dropped the gun. When we arrived, Mr. Casey had him pinned to the ground with his foot on his chest and Walker sitting on him. He gave a very concise accounting." I heard the amusement in Saller's voice.

"He should. He's a former Army Ranger and police officer. Did he tell you that? He worked in Georgia and moved here after he retired. That's how he got Walker. They usually don't give former police dogs to just anyone. Walker's partner was killed, and there was no family to take him, and he wouldn't work with anyone else. Did Mr. Casey tell you that?" Cady asked.

"He did not, or if he did, I haven't gotten that report yet. I let the patrol officers deal with the statements while I called you. Now, you said you know Reid. How?"

"He's a former boyfriend. I broke up with over a year ago. He came back, trying to get back together, about a month and a half ago. I told him we were never getting back together," she informed him. He was jotting down notes.

"And he accepted it? Stayed away?"

"No, he did not. He came to where I work at the House of Lustz, demanding to see her. Myself, Cady's best friend, and the owner tried to tell him she wasn't there, but he didn't believe us. By pure chance, Cady showed up, and he finally left after we ran him off. He acted like they'd only taken a mutual break, although Cady reminded him they broke up," I added.

"I bet there were a few threats if he didn't," Saller said with a smirk.

"I have no idea what you mean?" I said with a bland look.

"Go on," he said, amused.

"Well, he came to my work once after that, trying to speak to me. Again, he was chased off and told to stay away."

"And that was the last time you saw him?"

"No, he broke into her apartment once, too. She came home to find him there. I showed up, but we haven't seen him in weeks. For the past several weeks, she's been staying with me at my house. I have more security."

"You didn't call the cops?"

"No. It's hard to prove harassment. As for him entering my place, it was most likely he'd get a slap on the wrist, community service, a fine, and be let go," she explained.

"What if he had come back and hurt you?"

"I had her watched whenever she was at her apartment or working after hours. If she wasn't with me, she was protected," I confessed.

"You did what?" Cady gasped.

"I protected you. There was no way I was letting him or anyone else hurt you. We had no idea who was breaking into the clinic. So I had Iker put a guard on you, although getting in your house was a slip-up. The guard was watching you at Lustz and not watching the empty house. We corrected that."

"That's been weeks, Hoss. Am I still being

watched?" She sounded upset.

"I had Iker pull them a couple of days before you went to Gatlinburg. That's why it took so long to find you. You can be mad all you want, Cady, but nothing is more important than you. You know that. I won't leave you unprotected."

I thought for sure she'd yell and throw her brattiness at me, but she didn't. After several heartbeats of silence, she nodded.

"Ahm, alright, so you had her guarded. There haven't been any attempts on the clinic in weeks. I wonder why he chose to try again now?" Saller mused.

"Maybe he somehow found out we were out of town. Or he knew the clinic wasn't being watched. Even though she's been staying with me, I still had one of Iker's people watching the clinic every night. I wanted to be sure whoever had tried to get in twice before wouldn't try again. And if they did, they'd get caught. I messed up. I thought the threat was over when there were no more attempts."

"No matter, he's been caught," Saller stated.

"If he's the burglar, what if this is just a coincidence? He was breaking in because he wanted to wait for Cady to show up tomorrow. She's always the first one in. He could've thought to lie in wait for her," I suggested.

The idea made me cold inside. I didn't go inside every time I dropped her off, though I walked her to the door. The past few times, she drove herself due to our disagreement. The things that could've happened to her made me sick to my stomach.

"Stop it. I know what you're thinking, but it didn't happen. I'm safe, and it's not your fault," she said forcefully as she squeezed my arm.

"It would've been."

"Magnus, don't torture yourself, please. Detective, is there anything else you need to ask?"

"When you and Reid were together, how was your relationship? Why would he be so insistent to get back with you? Do you think he would hurt you?"

She fidgeted. I knew she didn't want to speak in front of me. "Tell him," I insisted.

"Fine. We fought often. He'd yell and get physical with me. I finally had enough, and I broke up with him. At first, he tried a couple of times to get back together, but I refused. I thought he left town until he showed up six or seven weeks ago. And yes, he would've hurt me."

"I don't mean to make you uncomfortable, and if it's easier, I can have Mr. Sacket leave, but I need to know the specifics of what he did."

I made a protesting sound. I was relieved when she shook her head. "No, he doesn't have to leave. He knows most of it. Flint slapped me, pulled my hair, hit me, kicked me, choked me, and wouldn't let me go until I submitted to having sex with him."

She'd lied to me the first time, but deep down, I still suspected he had, but to hear it confirmed enraged me. I let out a roar and hung my head to take deep breaths, so I didn't tear up the room. Her small hand rubbed my back. I turned to her. I should be soothing her.

"Baby, I'm so fucking sorry you went through any of that, but especially the last."

"It's alright."

"No, it's not. Dr. Anderson, we can add a rape charge to his case. If any ER visits document your injuries, we can use those. It may be hard to prove, but we'll do it," Saller assured her. He was scowling. He didn't like what he heard either.

"If it gets him more time in jail, then do it. If he can't be convicted of it, I'll live with it."

I hugged her to me.

"Alright, I think for now, I have enough. We're going to question him. I usually wouldn't allow it, but do you want to watch?" he asked us.

"I do. You don't need to see the bastard, Cady."

"Magnus, I do. I need to know why he's been doing this," she insisted. I would be happier if she had no more contact with him, even through two-way glass, but if she needed this, so be it.

"Okay, when can we do this?"

"Right now. He's done being processed, and they have him in an interrogation room. I just got the text telling me. If you'll follow me."

We stood and exited the room. A short walk down the hall, and we were placed in an observation room. We wouldn't be alone, it seemed. Standing there was Iker. He gave us a sad look.

"This isn't on you, so stop," I warned him.

"It feels like it. Anyway, ready to watch Saller in action. He's damn good," Iker said with a wink.

"Damn right, I am. I'll be back," Saller said before leaving us. Moments later, he entered the room where Reid was cuffed to a table. As soon as he saw Saller, he began to protest.

"Listen, officer, there's been a mistake. I tried telling the others this, but they wouldn't listen. You seem like a smart guy, so I hope you will. I didn't do what they said I did. That old man was wrong. He and his killer dog should be in here, not me. All I was doing was walking along, enjoying the night, and minding my own business. Suddenly, I heard an alarm sound, and out of nowhere, he began yelling at me. I saw him and that dog and I got scared. I panicked and took off running. When he sicced that beast on me, I took out my gun to protect myself. I did nothing wrong. It's legal for me to carry a gun for protection. I have a permit." He babbled until he ran out of steam. When he did, he gave Saller an expectant look, like he thought he'd buy his bullshit story. The detective was sitting back in his chair in a relaxed pose.

He slowly sat forward. "Mr. Reid, do you honestly think I believe your story? Do I look that stupid? After what I heard before coming in here, there's no way you're merely an innocent, wrongfully accused person —a victim in the wrong place at the wrong time. As for Mr. Casey, he's a retired police officer. He recognized you were up to no good. That the alarm coming from that clinic was tripped by you. His dog isn't vicious because if he were, you'd be in the hospital or dead. That beast, as you call him, is a former police officer, too."

"It's a damn dog! It can't be a cop." Reid scoffed.

"Yes, he can and is. Now, would you like a moment to amend your statement? It would be better for you if you told us the truth. Maybe at your trial, the jury and judge might take it into consideration. Not that you'll get off, but your sentencing could be lighter by a year or two."

"I'm not going to jail. I didn't do it."

"See, I might be inclined to give you a tiny benefit of the doubt if I didn't know about your past relationship with the person who runs that clinic, Dr.

Cadence Anderson, and if I didn't know of your recent transgressions."

"I don't know what that crazy woman and her thug of a boyfriend have told you, but I haven't touched Cady. In fact, until he came along and brainwashed her, we were getting back together. We took a break, that's all. She asked for one, and I gave it to her. I came back as we planned to take up where we left off. While I was gone, he somehow worked his way into her life. For God's sake, he's a lowlife who works as a doorman at a sex club. Hardly the kind of man you believe. I work in sales. I have a respectable job."

Saller sat there staring at him, saying nothing. Cady snorted. "Oh, he's respectable, all right. He used to work as a used car salesman. You know, there are two types of those. The decent ones and the slimy ones. He ended up being the slimy kind after I got to know him. He'd sell his mother if it made him a buck."

I had no trouble seeing him do that, but there was something about him that told me he was worse than we knew. What, I don't know. The silence in the other room ended when Reid nervously began talking again.

"Why are you staring at me? I told you the truth. You have the wrong man. You need to let me go." he was nervously bouncing his leg, and his eyes were darting around the room. It was growing worse.

"Tell me, Reid, what are you on?" Saller asked suddenly.

"On! I-I don't know what you mean. I'm not on anything," the octave of his voice went higher.

"Want to change that story? We'll be taking your blood. When we do, I'll find out."

"Uh, okay, I might've taken just a tiny hit before I

went for a walk. I needed a pick-me-up. That's all."

"This isn't you being high. It's you needing a fix. That means it's more than a tiny hit. You're an addict. That was why you're so determined to hit that clinic. You've been so determined, in fact, that you've done it three times. Some people would learn when to give up. And I bet you're the one who's been burglarizing veterinarian clinics all over town."

"That wasn't me!"

It got kind of boring to watch Reid deny and sweat. The only thing he didn't do was ask for a lawyer, which was a good thing, according to Iker. We were carrying on a conversation with him while listening to Saller push Reid. I was about to call it for the night. It was late, and Cady was ready for bed. She was leaning tiredly against me. I was opening my mouth to suggest it when our attention was snagged.

Saller was looking at his cell phone. It appeared that he was reading something. When he got done, he glanced up at Reid. "Let's talk about the abuse you put Cadence Anderson through, including the times you forcibly made her have sex with you. You raped her. Do you have any idea how much time that's going to add to your prison sentence? You'll be lucky to ever walk as a free man. We have your fingerprint at the scene tonight. It places you there, in a place you had no reason to be. I bet once we process your DNA and prints against those found at the other robberies, we'll be able to show you were there, too. Six counts of burglary, assault and battery on multiple counts, as well as rape. I'd hate to be you."

"Whoa, wait a minute. I never raped her. If she said I did, she lied. Sure, we had rough sex occasionally, but she was my girlfriend. It's not rape if it's with your girlfriend or wife."

"When a woman says no, it means no. It doesn't matter if she's in a relationship with you or not. If she said no and you did it anyway, it's rape. We'll subpoena the hospital for any and all records of injuries she sustained when you raped, beat, and choked her. She might've been too ashamed or worried to have you arrested then, but she's not now. We're done here." Saller stood and took two steps before Reid cracked.

"Wait! Wait, what if I tell you who worked with me on these robberies and who the guy behind the entire operation was? If I do that, can I get a deal? One that I won't be sent away forever. I can't survive in prison for the rest of my life."

"It depends. If it's just thievery, then no," Saller said, but he sat back down.

"What about a drug business supplying not only Tennessee but surrounding states with sedatives, narcotics, and antibiotics?"

"I'm listening. I'd have to hear what you've got first, and then we can see if the DA is willing to cut a deal. Also, Dr. Anderson may not be willing to let your egregious behavior with her slide. I'd have to do a lot of convincing."

"Find out first, then I'll talk."

The three of us on the other side of the glass exchanged shocked looks. None of us thought it was more than petty robbery and maybe selling the meds himself. This sounded much bigger if he was telling the truth. I studied Cady as Saller got up and left. What would she want to do? And would the DA go for it?

Cady:

I was still caught in disbelief. Flint was mixed up in drugs from the sound of it, and he was willing to roll over on his boss and associates in exchange for not being charged with the beatings and the rape. All I had to do was agree, and the DA had to accept the terms. As I listened to Detective Saller explain it to me, it was clear I had to make a choice. He'd left me to think about it while he contacted the DA. I had Hoss telling me it was my decision. He'd support whatever I decided. He also said if I wanted to have them prosecute Flint, he understood. Saller did warn me before he left that the DA could choose to drop the charges for what Flint did to me in the past without my approval. It would be hard to prove it. I weighed it, and when Saller returned thirty minutes later, I had made my decision.

"Cady, do you have an answer?" I'd convinced him earlier to call me by my nickname.

"Do you?" I asked.

"I do, but I want to know what you decided first." His expression gave nothing away.

"As much as I want Flint to rot in prison, if not going after him on the other things gets even more dangerous people off the streets, then I say go for it. I won't file charges for those if he gives you enough to bring down this drug operation."

Saller nodded as Hoss hugged me tighter, and a

kiss landed on the top of my head. Iker had come back during Saller's pitch and then excused himself to let us talk in private. He said to call him if we needed him.

"Thank you, and the DA was in agreement with making the deal as long as we get what we need. He did hope you'd agree, but he was prepared to do it anyway. If we have a shot at stopping the drug trade, we think this might be it. Over the past year, it has tripled in Nashville, other towns in Tennessee, and adjacent states. It was suspected a new dealer with a new supply chain was behind it. Initially, no one put together the increase in clinics hit because they were for animals, not humans. It's late. We'll be at this for a while. Why don't the two of you go home and get some rest? I'll call you later and tell you what we find out."

As much as I wanted to see Flint's confession, I was barely keeping my eyes open, so I caved relatively easily. Hoss was a rock as he supported me both mentally and physically. At home, he helped me shower and then tucked me into bed. He curled himself around me and, in no time, had me relaxed enough to fall asleep.

A phone ringing woke me up. I was groggy and had no idea what time it was. I found Hoss sitting up in bed, working on his laptop. He was on the phone. I yawned and scooted closer. The clock on the bedside table said it was eleven. Based on the fact the sun was still out, I knew it was late morning.

"Uh hmm, alright. Yeah, I'll let her know. Thanks for calling. Keep us in the loop, and if you need anything from us, just call. Thanks. Bye." He waited a few moments, then hung up.

"Who was it?" As if I couldn't guess. Butterflies

were in my stomach.

"It was Detective Saller. He wanted us to know that Flint, despite being a total idiot, knew enough about his boss and the setup that they decided to give him the deal. He'll have to testify in order for them to do it. And he's not looking at getting five years and released in two. He'll serve a decent sentence for his involvement. Saller wanted to thank us and reassure you that our names will be kept out of it. They're gathering evidence and then will be going after all persons of interest to make their arrests. We'll have to keep an eye on the clinic until then just to be sure they don't send someone else to rob it."

I sagged in relief. "That's good news. As much as I wanted him to pay, this is better. Hopefully, I won't need to pay Iker for long to provide security at night. What does he charge anyway?" I asked as I calculated what I had in savings. If it were too much, I'd take out a loan.

"Babe, you're crazy and don't know your man. If you think for a minute, I'll let you pay for security. That's my job." He set his laptop aside.

"No, it's not. I'm not with you for your money. Besides, if you go around throwing your money away on everything and everybody, you'll ruin yourself. I don't want that."

"Cady, I don't do it on everything or everyone, but I could pay for a lot and still never come close to ruining myself. How much do you think I'm worth?"

"I don't know. Too much."

"Take a guess. You've got me curious now." He smirked as he watched me.

I gave a wild guess. "Five million."

He laughed. I mean deep, belly deep laughed

at me. I punched him in the arm, which only hurt my hand. He gathered himself and then made me hyperventilate. "Cady, I hate to tell you, but you're off by a little."

"How much then? Six?"

"No, try two hundred and growing."

I gasped and then began to pant. "Million?" I squeaked out. He nodded.

I gasped even more. His smugness changed to concern. The next thing I knew, I was on the edge of the bed with my head between my knees, and he was talking sweetly to me as he rubbed my back. It took a few minutes to get myself under control so I could sit up and speak.

"Magnus, I can't believe this. You and I can't be together. You're too wealthy. You need someone of equal status. Does Mikhail know he had a multimillionaire working as a doorman?"

"Tiny, you and I are perfect for each other no matter how much money I have. You're not getting away from me. And yes, Mikhail knows. Hell, he's not a pauper. He knows why I did it."

"Did it? Don't you mean why you do it?"

"Not anymore. I gave him my resignation. He thinks he has already found someone to take my place. No more working at Lustz for me. That doesn't mean we won't visit. Personal playtime is always available. I took the job to de-stress and to keep busy. Now that I have you, I want to spend all the time I can with you and have even better ways to de-stress." He gave me a smoldering look. I knew what he wanted and wasn't about to deny him. We could debate about Iker later. I lay back on the bed and opened my arms.

"Then why don't you show me?"
He let out a growl and muttered, "I will."

&. &. &.

It had been two weeks since Flint's arrest.
Things were proceeding rapidly with the police's case.
However, that was the last thing I wanted to think
about. It was Christmas Day. Earlier, we'd spent it with
Mikhail, Tajah, Reuben, Tamara, Gideon, and Carver. We
hosted them all at our house. Suffice it to say, other than
Reuben, Tajah, and Mikhail, who'd been here before, the
others were in awe of it.

I noted how Carver had checked out the house
and property. He didn't say anything, but I knew he was
wondering if I'd be able to hang onto Hoss. My man,
whether it was deliberate or not, did something to show
we were more solid than ever. When everyone gathered,
he'd proposed a toast, then gone down on one knee
and presented me with an engagement ring. I'd been so
stunned I was speechless, and the rest of the day was
kind of hazy in spots. Every time I looked at my ring, I'd
melt.

It took a while, but about two hours ago, we
hustled everyone out and were alone. Time to celebrate
our engagement, except my man had other ideas. Oh,
we were going to have sex, but before it happened,
he was punishing me for running away and making
him worry. He'd already done it right after we made
up for endangering myself, I thought, but that hadn't
been my full punishment. When I found out what he
was about to do, my brat reared her mouthy self, and I
compounded it. Why? Because as much as I might hate
being punished, I equally loved it. Which was how I

found myself in bed, restrained. That part wasn't what was killing me. It was the fact I was blindfolded and had a headset that didn't allow me to hear anything. I was in a dark, silent world. I didn't like it at all. Before we started, he told me if it got to be too much to use my safe word.

It felt like I'd been like this forever. He'd tease me with light and then firm touches. I had been spanked. Brought to the brink of orgasm after orgasm until I lost track of how many times it occurred. I was desperate, and two seconds away from yelling Kiwi at the top of my voice, when suddenly, the blindfold was removed, and I squinted up at him. He had candles all around the bed, which were easy on my eyes. Next, my earphones were removed, and I heard soothing music playing.

"Cady Cat, you did so well. I'm proud of you. Are you ready to be a good girl and let me make love to you?" As he asked, he stood there, a naked Adonis, stroking that huge cock of his. It was almost purple, telling me he was more than eager to be inside me. Well, I had news for him.

"I need to be untied. If my punishment is over, it's my turn to give you something for our engagement. I've been waiting all day."

He gave me a questioning look, but he did undo the restraints. I rolled over onto my stomach. As I did, I told him what I wanted next. "I need you to remove this butt plug for me."

He got on the bed to do it, although being Hoss, he teased me with strokes over my ass cheeks first. That was fine. Over the past few weeks, we'd played even more extensively with anal toys, and unknown to him, I'd worn a few during the day. It was all leading to this.

Once he removed it and set it aside, I took the object under my pillow out and held it up. It was a bottle of lube.

"What's that for? I removed your plug, babe."

"I know, but you'll need this for your cock if you want to fuck my ass."

I was gazing at him over my shoulder. He froze, and a disbelieving look overcame his face. He was quiet for several moments before he asked hoarsely. "Did you say I need lube to take your ass?"

"I did. It's time. I've been working up to this. I think on our engagement night and Christmas, no less, it's a great idea. Don't you?"

"Christ, Cady, are you sure? I don't want you to feel you have to give me this."

"I'm sure. Now, hurry up. I want to know if I can handle that monster or not. Just go slow."

I knew he'd been researching it. I saw his browser history on his computer. It told me how much he wanted it, and to be truthful, as painful as it might be, I did too. If we did this right, we both could get pleasure. I needed to give him something no one ever had. His hands shook as he took the bottle. He squeezed a generous amount on his hand. He applied it to his long length, then used the rest to slick my asshole, even though it still had lube from the plug. When he was done, he wiped his hand on the sheets.

He surprised me when, instead of getting behind me, he lay down next to me. "What're you doing?" I asked.

"I want you to get on top. If we do it this way, you control the pace, and if it's too much, you can just lift off me. But, Cady, I want you to swear to me that you won't go past your acceptable pain threshold to give me this. If it hurts too damn much, you stop." His warning was clear. He wouldn't let me go unpunished if I did.

"I promise." I moved and straddled him.

Getting into position, I lifted my hips while he held his cock erect. Taking a breath, I consciously relaxed my body and bore down. I let the head of his cock touch my opening then I lowered myself just enough to force the head inside my ass. I won't lie. It burned and hurt—more than I recalled in the past. I stopped, took a couple of breaths to gather my courage, and then pushed out and down again. He slipped further in. When he caught at the first sphincter, I knew it was too much to go slow past it and the second ring.

"It's too much. Stop," he ordered.

Before he could lift me, I rapidly sank past them. There was relief when I did. It was still painful, and it burned, but not as much. I grabbed his hands, which were gripping my hips to lift me off him.

"No, it's better. Getting past those rings is the worst. Let me."

He hesitated, but he did let go. I worked myself up and down on him. The strain on his face and the way he was moaning told me he was more than liking the sensation. "Tell me what you're feeling, Magnus. Do you like how my ass feels, or do you hate it and never want to do this again?" I teased.

"Fuck, Cady, it's incredible. If you go no further than this, it's enough. Thank you."

"Oh, no, you're getting more. I may torture you for a while to get it all, but call it punishment." I taunted. As I said it, I slid up and then came back down, taking him deeper. He groaned and closed his eyes. I worked him inside. As I got used to the stretch, the burning and pain decreased, and the pleasure started to come through. When it did, I knew I could totally do this.

Eventually, I had him all the way there. He was staring at me, and his eyes were wild. I knew what he wanted, but he was afraid. I did it for him. I raised until just the head was inside and dropped down. As I did, I clenched my ass and swiveled my hips. A tortured sound came out of him. His hands came up to tightly grip my tits.

"Mmm, that's it. Does that ass feel good? I bet you'd love to pound it, wouldn't you?"

"Don't," he snarled.

"Don't what? Ask my fiancé to fuck my ass. I want it, Magnus. I need it. Take what you want. Make us both come," I whispered.

A guttural sound tore from him. Then I found myself rolled onto my back. He'd found a way to stay inside me, and he was looming above me. I smiled so he knew it was okay. He slowly withdrew until just the head remained, and then he thrust back. It wasn't extremely hard and fast, but it made us both moan. Soon, he'd set up a pace that had us both careening toward what I knew was an explosive orgasm.

"Harder. Hurry, I've got to come," I whined brokenly.

He snapped his hips a couple more times. I detonated. As I screamed and thrashed, coming so hard my vision darkened, he roared and bucked. The warmth of his cum filled my ass. As his strokes slowed and then stopped, he regretfully pulled out, took me in his arms, and rolled me onto his chest. It was a while before he said anything.

"Cady, that was, wow. I hope it didn't hurt you too much."

"It hurt, but then it became bliss, Magnus. I have to say, that's staying in our repertoire."

He hugged me tight as he ravished my mouth. I returned the favor to his. I was beyond looking forward to my life with him.

Cady: Epilogue Three Months Later

If I hadn't seen it done, I wouldn't have believed it. Maybe it had to do with the fact Tamara had not only been planning Tajah's wedding already but also the fact she had ideas and done research in anticipation of Taj remarrying one day that it came together the way it did. It was inspiring when you added in the fact it wasn't a single wedding but rather a double wedding.

Unbeknownst to me and Tajah, Hoss and Mikhail had a brief conversation about a double one when he informed Mikhail he was going to marry me. Hoss claimed he thought it was a joke, but three days after asking me to marry him, I got a call from Tajah asking us over to talk. We were stunned when they asked if we wanted to do it. Other than Carver and a few work invites, I didn't have anyone but Tajah and Mikhail to invite.

After saying we'd be willing if they were positive they didn't want to get married alone, we'd been swept up by the tornados called Tamara and Victoria. They were forces of nature, and in no time, we not only had dresses, cakes, decor, catering, and a million other things done, but we were standing before the minister who was having us exchange our vows in tandem.

It was only right to have Tajah and Mikhail finish moments before us, and then we were pronounced husbands and wives together and allowed to kiss.

Even hours later, I was still floating in what felt like a dream world. We'd taken pictures, eaten, had cake, danced our first dance, and more. The reception was winding down, and I knew my husband was more than ready to sneak off. We were flying out early tomorrow morning for a two-week honeymoon in the Bahamas. Hoss had been there, but I'd never left the States, and I always wanted to go there for some reason. Tropical locations called to me.

Mikhail and Tajah were staying in the States. I didn't blame them. She was newly pregnant, and there was no way her man would risk her or the baby. He was concerned about whether she would require medical care. He felt she'd get the best here, at Vandy. She knew his need to protect, so she didn't push back. Since I wasn't pregnant yet, although the birth control shot wasn't renewed, we weren't sweating it. We had time, and I'd only been off it a couple of months.

I caught Hoss's gaze. He curled his finger and gestured for me to come to him. I knew what that meant. A bratty wedding night was about to start. I couldn't wait. I smiled as I hurried to him.

Hoss: Epilogue- One Month Later

We'd been back from our honeymoon two weeks. Things over the past several months have been great. My brother was serving a sentence for his crime. I hoped when he got out in a few years, he'd stay away from the drugs and make something of his life. Flint Reid's trial was coming up. His information led to the arrest of thirty others involved in the drug ring, including the boss and his top enforcers or whatever you called them. They faced long sentences. Flint's would be shorter, but if he survived to be eligible for release, he'd die in a tragic prison fight before he walked free. The Bratva would make sure of it, and if they didn't, Mikhail knew a motorcycle club that would do the deed.

Thinking of the MC and Outlaw made me smile. It took a while for me to work my way through them, but the four men who'd either physically or sexually hurt Cady when they dated had finally been dealt with. I took my time due to work constraints and wedding planning. The final one I visited last weekend after we got back from the Bahamas. He'd been one who hadn't taken no for an answer.

Mikhail had insisted he wanted to be there for those conversations, as we called them, even though he knew I was the one to mete out the justice. I spent a full day with each one of them. He egged me on with ideas. When I was done, they'd never touch another woman again in anger or worse. If I had my way, I would've maimed them for life and possibly killed them, but Cady had made me promise not to do either. She said she'd rather they lived in fear. With Mikhail's help and that of his MC and Bratva connections, we left them in total fear of it.

We were in the process of moving Cady's clinic to a new, safer location where she should be able to easily gain more patients. She was bringing on a second vet and a few more staff, which would allow her not to work so hard. We were trying to get pregnant, and she and I were streamlining our lives. We refused to be workaholics anymore. It took a lot for me to convince her to let me help her move and launch an expansion, but after a month of persuasion, aka brat and handler moments and the associated punishments, she'd given in. I was now a silent partner in her clinic. She warned me not to get used to it. I wouldn't win every battle. I knew that would be the case.

Now that those men and the rest were out of the way, it should be smooth sailing. Well, as smooth as it could be when your woman was a brat and you were a brat handler. After all, tame wasn't in our vocabulary. I'd never want to lose my Cady Cat totally, and she told me she loved her handler and his punishments. We were looking forward to what was to come and discovering if Cady Cat and Hoss's Limits could be pushed to even more delicious heights.

The End Until Book Three: Title TBD

Made in the USA
Monee, IL
21 February 2025